the
FABRIC
of
US

Kimberly Wenzler

THE FABRIC OF US

by Kimberly Wenzler

Copyright © 2018 by Kimberly Wenzler
All rights reserved.

First Edition October 2018
ISBN 978-0-9905900-6-4 (pbk)
ISBN 978-0-9905900-7-1 (epub)

Library of Congress number: 2018908603

No part of this book may be reproduced in any form or by any electronic or mechanical means, including information storage and retrieval system, without permission in writing from the author except in the case of brief quotations embodied in critical articles and reviews.

This is a work of fiction. The events and characters described herein are imaginary and not intended to refer to specific places or living persons. The opinions expressed in this manuscript are solely the opinions of the author.

Cover image © 2018 Kimberly Wenzler
Cover layout and design by *Suzanne Fyhrie Parrott*
Formatted for publication by *First Steps Publishing Services*

Seaplace Publishing
Northport, New York

BOOKS BY KIMBERLY WENZLER

Both Sides of Love

Letting Go

The Fabric of Us

Chapter 1
September 2010

Olivia Bennet strode into the hotel lounge wearing a form-fitting black wrap dress and lace-up heels with one goal in mind. She'd spent extra time on her makeup and worked to tame the dark waves that fell past her shoulders.

She was getting lucky tonight.

The room was dark and cozy. Soft piano music, filtered through hidden speakers overhead, added to the ambience. She sat at the near-empty bar, ordered a Cosmopolitan and surveyed the dozen or so patrons among the couches and chairs.

"Do you have peanuts?" she asked the bartender.

He pulled a small bowl of mixed nuts from beneath the mahogany and set it before her. Grateful to have something to quell her hunger, she washed down the nuts with the vodka and hummed along with the music, waiting.

Twenty minutes later, a man stood at the entrance in worn jeans and white shirt unbuttoned at the collarbone, accentuating his tan. *Bingo.* He raked his fingers through his hair as he scanned the room. Olivia caught his eye and then turned away.

"Is this seat taken?" he said.

She watched him in the mirror above the bottles as he slid onto the stool beside her.

"Martini. Dry. Three olives," he ordered. "I'm Grant." He held out his hand, forcing her to turn to him. He had thick, wavy hair flecked with gray. She liked the way it curled on his neck.

"Maya."

His drink arrived and he sipped, swallowing the flicker of a smile.

"So, what brings you here, Maya?"

"I'm celebrating."

"Alone?"

The corner of her mouth lifted. "I'm not alone. You?" One drink and she was already feeling tipsy, her hunger forgotten.

"I'm here on business," he said.

"What business is that?"

"I'm a financial advisor, in Manhattan."

She stared at his brown, veined arms, beneath the rolled-up sleeves. "Too bad. I prefer a man who works with his hands." She lifted the glass so the remaining drops fell into her mouth.

He chuckled, a low grumble deep in his throat and looked toward the bartender. "She'll have another." He dropped a bill on the bar and turned back to her. "So, how do I come to find a gorgeous woman sitting alone at a hotel bar on a Saturday night? I must have done something right."

"You haven't done anything yet."

He bit the inside of his cheek. "Don't tease, gorgeous. It could get you in trouble."

She crossed her legs so the slit of her dress drifted up her thigh. "I don't have time to tease."

His eyes followed the dress. "I shouldn't be talking to you. I'm a married man."

"Well then, it looks like we're both looking for a little trouble." A new drink was placed in front of her. She lifted the glass to her lips. The cool liquid went down easy. "Tell me about your wife."

He awarded her a half-smile. "She's perfect. Sexy and funny. The moment I saw her, I was undone."

"If she's so perfect, what are you doing here with me?"

He paused, and then leaned toward her so his mouth tickled her ear. "I won't do to her the things I want to do to you."

He lifted his hand and with a nod, ordered another drink.

Heat travelled up her core. "You're pretty confident in yourself."

"That dress is making promises."

She flushed and tugged the waist, adjusting the bow slightly. They watched each other, fondling their glasses.

"You have beautiful eyes."

"Because they're looking at you," he said softly.

"So, you're a corny financial advisor from Manhattan. With a perfect wife." She took a long swallow of her Cosmo, pulled her hotel key card from her purse before she stood and slid it on the bar. "Don't make me wait."

Without a word, he pulled the card toward him and watched her walk away.

She answered her hotel door five minutes later, still fully dressed. She was warm and ready before he even entered the room.

He stepped over the threshold and shut the door. "Lock it," she whispered. He reached back and secured the lock before pulling her to him. His lips were soft and she wrapped her hands around his neck. When they finally pulled apart, their heavy breaths mingled together. He brushed his thumb over her swollen lips. She closed her eyes and opened her mouth slightly.

"You're beautiful," he whispered.

"You are."

"I like what you're wearing."

She looked down at herself. "It's new."

He pulled the bow at her waist and the dress fell open. "I like it." He scooped her up and brought her to the bed. As he stepped out of his jeans, she reached for her shoes.

"Leave them on." He pulled his shirt over his head, exposing a broad chest and flat stomach.

"You have a nice body for someone who pushes a pen."

He climbed onto the bed, his arms suspending him over her.

"I want to know what your wife is missing," she said.

"Oh, I'm going to show you."

She bit her lip, barely containing a smile. "You'd better hurry. My husband will be back soon."

"Husband?"

She shrugged. "He made me wait."

He ran his fingers through her hair, fanning it on the pillow. "It's okay. I only need ten minutes."

"Ten, huh? I understand why your wife stayed home."

He lowered himself on top of her. "Baby, they'll be ten minutes you'll never forget."

Thirty-two minutes later, they lay between the sheets, catching their breath.

"When did you get the dress?" he said.

"I bought it at the Gap last week during lunch. The shoes pinch my toes though." She reached down and unlaced the heels, dropping them to the floor.

He laughed. "You look great, babe."

"Thanks." She stared at the ceiling. "Grant?"

Chris turned to her. "It popped into my head. Maya."

Olivia rolled on her side and put her arm over his chest. "You're cute. Grant," she added with a giggle.

"Are you wearing my deodorant?"

"I left mine at home," she said.

"I thought I smelled Old Spice."

He ran his fingers up and down her back. "I'm sorry I took so long getting food."

She had forgotten her request for gyro. After they'd arrived at the hotel, he went out to pick up dinner. She'd texted him forty-five minutes later, threatening to find someone else if he didn't return with food soon. It's what led them to the bar and their first foray into role-playing. "Did you find anything?"

He kissed her temple. "Of course. The first two places I went to were closed. I ended up about half an hour away in Williamstown."

Olivia lifted her head to look around the room.

"On the dresser."

She spied the take-out bag next to the TV and smiled. "You've outdone yourself." She rested her head on his soft downy chest, her fingers playing with the hair.

"Anything for my wife."

The next afternoon, they walked along the path from the hotel through the woods swinging their locked fingers. The hotel, located in the beautiful Berkshires of Massachusetts, was surrounded by lovely grounds of rich green. The warm September air soothed Olivia's skin.

"Thank you for this."

"I wanted it to be special," Chris said. "There's more."

"More? What more could there be? We've had a couple's massage already, and I'm still full of breakfast."

He led her to an open field surrounded by a border of plush trees. There, off to the side, under a sprawling weeping willow, rested a low table decorated with a floral table cloth on which sat a wicker picnic basket, candles, and a bouquet of wildflowers. Olivia put her hand over her mouth.

Chris, pleased with her reaction, smiled and brought her to the table.

"Do you like it?"

She nodded. They sat on striped cushions, and he opened the bottle of champagne. When their glasses were full, he tipped his toward hers. "To us."

The bubbles tickled the back of her throat while the birds, hidden among the trees, serenaded them.

"I've been waiting for this for a long time." He looked around, put his glass down and faced her. "To our future and doing everything we've always wanted to do."

It rained on the drive home the next morning. Light drops fell on the windshield and blurred the scenery.

"I'm surprised you wanted to leave early."

Chris shrugged. "I thought we'd get a head start and miss the Labor Day traffic."

"Well, thank you for a perfect weekend," Olivia said. They'd just reached historic Wilmington.

He reached over and took her hand. "You're welcome."

Back out the window, the revived colonials passed in a haze. She loved the rain almost as much as the bright, sunny days. There was a time for everything. The weather this morning complimented her nostalgic, somber mood. The end of the summer already — time passed so quickly. When she last traveled this road, Nick had commented on the beauty of the snow. Winter was his favorite season; the mountains offered a perfect outlet for his pent-up energy. He was an avid skier and lover of cold weather. Her eyes welled, and she kept her gaze toward the window so Chris wouldn't suspect she was thinking about anything or anyone else after the effort he put into this weekend.

Olivia pulled herself together, smiled and looked at him. "What."

She shrugged. "Nothing. Just a little tired."

"You look upset. Is anything wrong?"

She sighed and leaned her head back. "Everything is perfect. I promise."

Chris squeezed her hand and then let it go.

Her phone rang as they crossed the Tappan Zee Bridge. She looked at the incoming number, biting her lip in thought before she put it down and looked back out the window.

"Didn't want to answer?"

"It was Gavin." Her boss.

"On the holiday weekend?"

"We have a meeting tomorrow."

"I thought you were taking tomorrow off."

"It's an important meeting. He asked me to come in."

Chris opened his mouth to speak but decided against it. Olivia put her hand on his cheek. "Hey, I think this—you and me—" she pointed to him and then her "—just might work." She winked. He smiled, and they drove the rest of the way listening to the radio.

They pulled up to the house, and Olivia yawned as she made her way up the walkway. The warm air hung like a cloak after the rain. Her hair felt damp. All she wanted to do was take a hot shower, put on sweats and watch television all day. She made a mental note to call Gavin back too. When she opened the door with Chris behind her, her eyes widened, and she pasted on a smile as seemingly everyone she knew crowded in the small living room to yell, "Surprise!" Beneath the large banner reading *"Happy 50th Olivia!"* stood their children, Nick and Ella and Ella's husband Marco. Nick surprised her by coming home for the weekend. He'd only left two weeks ago for RIT. She hugged her children before losing herself among her friends and neighbors.

Dana found Olivia in the kitchen later, standing at the sink drinking a glass of water. She held a cocktail in her manicured hands, her dark blond hair framing her face.

"Were you surprised?"

Olivia swallowed and turned around. "Surprised? No. That's why I'm standing here in the house with everyone one I know, wearing my travel jeans and stained tee shirt while you mock me with that gorgeous dress." She lifted her armpit to show Dana the hole along the seam of her shirt.

Dana laughed, her deep throaty notes filling the empty kitchen.

Olivia put her glass down on the counter. "I'm sure you were instrumental in helping Chris pull this off."

"He's been planning it for weeks. And Ella helped too. No detail was overlooked." Dana frowned through the window at the crowd congregating under the small tent in the backyard. "We were hoping it wouldn't rain."

"I've learned to expect the unexpected. Speaking of, I expected you to be in Bali," Olivia said.

"I know. I got your bon voyage message Friday."

"You're not going?"

"Tomorrow."

Olivia nodded. Dana was rarely home for more than a few months at a time anymore.

"Should I be thanking you for the hotel?"

"That was all your husband's doing. He was going to surprise you with tickets to Italy, but that takes more planning, and I told him you need to be involved in it."

"And there's the small hiccup of not having a passport," Olivia added. "He's been talking about finally traveling. Doing all the things we've put off."

"You should. Nick is almost done with school. This is what you've been waiting for, right?"

Olivia sighed. "It feels like yesterday we were in college. Now my baby is starting his last year." She shook her head. Dana said nothing and handed her the half-full glass she held in her hand. Olivia took a healthy sip.

Chris poked his head in the kitchen. "Okay you two. Time to come out and play nice with the others. Cake will be served, my love." He winked and backed out of the room.

The women started to follow him outside, but Olivia put her hand on Dana's arm. "Thank you."

Dana turned and gave Olivia a quick, tight hug. "I'm just happy you're finally fifty. I didn't want to walk this road alone."

Later, after the last guest left, including Nick, who had classes the following afternoon, Chris and Olivia crawled into bed.

"Good day?"

She nodded. "I totally didn't see that coming. You went all out, babe. Thank you."

He smiled. "I couldn't let the decade start without a

celebration. It's worked for us for the past three."

Chris loved parties. He threw her one for her thirtieth. She'd never forget it. His band set up in the tiny den not long after they moved into their new home in Levittown, on Long Island. The music filled the house, spilling out into the street, along with their guests. Ella and Nick were a safe distance at her mom's. She ended up sick all night, hungover the entire first day of her thirty-first year.

She glanced at her husband. His eyes were closed, and there was contented grin on his face. Now, twenty years later, they lay in bed, in time for the news, sober and exhausted. How times had changed.

He leaned over to kiss her. "Happy birthday."

"I'm old."

"You're not old. Fifty is the new forty."

"That saying was started by fifty-year olds who were jealous of forty-year olds. Fifty is fifty, no matter how you slice it."

"Babe, you're still hot."

"Not yet, but I will be. Nice and toasty." She was in perimenopause, according to Dana, who had been through it years earlier. She'd been mentally preparing for the physical and emotional turmoil her body would go through in the next years. Olivia turned to her husband. He was still handsome. It bothered her.

"You have a bad attitude," he said through closed eyes. "Embrace your age. You're young. We have so much left to do."

"I'm more than halfway through my life."

"The best is yet to be."

"Says the man who thinks Howard Stern is a main source of entertainment."

He opened his eyes. "So angry after a weekend of making love."

Olivia rolled over and pulled the covers to her chin. "What we had was good, old-fashioned sex."

"God, I love you."

Chapter 2
1979

The memory of the very first time Olivia saw him would be forever ingrained in her mind. She'd walked into Mary Ann's on Beacon Street, on a frigid Thursday night in January. Amid a packed crowd of students crammed around the bar three deep, her date was fighting for the bartender's attention while she was pushed and shoved behind him. She decided to look for a spot where she could breathe and found one tucked in the corner, near the back exit of the building. She unwrapped her scarf, unzipped her coat and waited.

Her boyfriend had convinced her to come out tonight, prying her away from her studies. She wasn't much of a barfly, preferring house parties or small groups of friends instead. He'd insisted she come see the new, popular band and now, standing in the corner of a claustrophobic-inducing, sour-beer-mixed-with-sweat-smelling bar, she regretted her decision. She'd wait for him to get back and tell him to take her home. Or better yet, she'd say good-bye, slip out of the door behind her and let him stay. She didn't need to be chaperoned home. She wasn't even sure what she was doing with this guy in the first place. She wasn't gaga over him. But she was never gaga.

She looked around the room, scanning the faces of strangers, wondering if she'd know anyone here. Boston College was large, so she wasn't surprised to find no one familiar. She was also a bit of a hermit. Her date waited at the bar so she resigned herself to be patient and followed the attention of the crowd to the stage where the band had finally set up and the music started.

There were five members in the band. The husky, bearded singer moved around the small space, clutching the mike like a bottle. He had a nice voice, clear and deep. They played folk rock and she liked the first song right away. The drummer sat in the back, behind two guitarists who moved along with the singer. They all took a few steps toward the right side of the stage and that's when she saw him. He stood over the keyboard, a beautiful, sweaty, skinny, tee-shirt-and-jean-clad boy who leaned over the keys with closed eyes, his face emoting pure pleasure.

Olivia was transfixed. Her boyfriend returned eventually with a cup of warm beer, and she took it, barely acknowledging him.

"What did I tell you?" he yelled in her ear. "They're awesome, right?"

She nodded, shrugged out of her coat and held it over her arm. They watched and listened to the band for the rest of the night. When he asked if she wanted to go home at one point, she declined. "I'd like to wait until they're finished."

When they were, she watched the keyboard player wipe down his face with a towel and help to pack up the stage. He and the drummer shared a joke, and someone handed him a beer. When he smiled in appreciation, her entire body warmed.

She thought of him throughout the week and found herself at the bar the following Thursday, alone, watching him through the sets, lost in his music. She hoped someone would bring him a beer or speak to him or do anything that would make him smile. When the singer announced they would play another song before they took a break, she went to the bar and ordered a bottle of Budweiser. When they stopped, she went to the stage and asked one of the guitarists to please give the beer to the keyboard player. She returned to the corner where she'd originally seen him and when she turned around, he was looking at her. He held the bottle up and gave her a nod. Then he smiled. It nearly broke her heart it was so endearing. She lifted her eyebrows and nodded back. She left the bar before their last song.

Olivia managed to focus on her studies during the week, pushing off thoughts of the keyboard player in her quest to remain on the Dean's list. But on Thursdays, thoughts of him consumed her, knowing she would see him in hours. She had unknowingly fallen into a wonderful ritual that took her through the day and ended with music and a wanton ache foreign to her.

She went alone, having severed ties with what's-his-name shortly after he first brought her to the bar. On her fifth visit, she arrived early. The band hadn't set up yet so she went to the surprisingly sparse bar and waited to get the bartender's attention. Someone tapped her on the shoulder. It was the boy she'd come to watch. He smiled that glorious smile, and she blushed, as if caught doing something wrong.

"Why do you leave before our last set is over every week?"

Olivia shrugged, masking her surprise he noticed. She didn't want to tell him the reason. She was afraid if they spoke, he'd shatter the image she'd built up of him in her mind. So rarely did they match up to what she imagined or hoped, which was why, at eighteen, she'd had no lengthy relationships. And, she was too serious about school to allow a distraction to get in the way of her goal.

"Please stay tonight. I'd like to talk to you."

"What's the matter? No one else paying you any attention?" She leaned back on the bar, assuming a nonchalant pose. Her knees struggled to keep her up, but she'd be damned if he knew that.

He looked around. "I've slept with everyone here. You're the last one, it seems." He gave her a self-deprecating wink, and she flushed. They locked eyes. This one was different. She could feel it in her bones. He wouldn't disappoint her. Please God, let him not disappoint her.

"Please?" A thick lock of hair fell over his forehead. He raked it back, and she stared at the chestnut tracks left by his long fingers.

She nodded, and he smiled. Then he slid beside her and leaned over the bar. The bartender moved to him at once. She wore a midriff shirt exposing her ample breasts and flat, tan belly. "What do you need, baby?"

"Jamie, give…" He turned to Olivia. "What is your name?"

She gave him her name, and he turned back to Jamie. "Whatever Olivia wants is on me."

"Sure thing, Chris." The bartender dropped her smile and looked at Olivia.

"Budweiser, please."

Jamie nodded and walked away.

"Be careful. I'm a drinker," Olivia said to Chris.

He laughed, tilting his head back. She watched his Adam's apple bob beneath his skin and breathed.

"Somehow I think you're not. Order whatever you want. Just please stay so I can talk to you, okay?" He looked toward the stage where the rest of the band took their places. "I have to go. See you later, Olivia."

She watched both sets and had nursed three beers by the time he finished at eleven. As they packed up their instruments, the thick crowd began to clear out, leaving a manageable roar behind and a few empty tables around the perimeter of the main floor. She hung at the bar and tried not to notice the small group of girls loitering around Chris near the stage. He chatted with them easily while he performed his packing ritual. When he turned his back to them, their widened eyes and swooning eager faces amused her.

"You here for Chris?" The voice came from behind. She turned to see a tall, blonde girl next to her.

"And you are…?"

The girl offered an abbreviated smile and held out her hand. "Dana Trabone. I'm here with Trevor."

Olivia shrugged.

"The drummer."

"Ah. He's very good."

Dana took a sip of her beer. "I know."

Olivia turned back toward the stage, but Dana wanted to talk. "I've seen you here the past few weeks. Be careful. He bounces around."

Olivia took a breath before turning to Dana, trying to contain her embarrassment. *Okay, so you established your dominance here. I get it*, she thought. "Thanks for the warning."

Dana hesitated. "You're welcome. Here he comes. See ya."

Chris extracted himself from his groupies and met her at the bar. He led her to a corner table. His hair was soaked, but he didn't seem to notice. She liked the way the ends curled below his neck and clung to his forehead.

"So, Olivia." He grinned and took a long swig from his bottle.

She sat still, watching him.

"What's your last name?"

"Carson."

He pulled his top lip below his bottom teeth and squinted his eyes. "Olivia Carson. What do you do when you're not sneaking out on my sets every Thursday?"

"I'm a sophomore at BC."

"Studying?"

"Communications and journalism. You?"

"Finance. Sophomore." He smiled, and she melted just a bit.

"What are your plans?"

"I'll probably work on Wall Street. Corporate finance. Investment banking. Whatever makes me the most money."

"And your music?"

"A hobby." He put down his near-empty bottle and leaned toward her. "I don't want to talk about me. I want to talk about you." His hazel eyes held hers. "Who is Olivia Carson and why did she walk into my bar?"

The lights went up, and Olivia looked around, tired and stiff from sitting. She stretched, and Chris sat back with a grin. His hair had dried while they talked, falling now in messy clumps about his head.

"What time is it?"

He looked at the clock over the bar. "Closing time." She rolled her eyes, and he laughed. "Two."

"We've been sitting here for three hours?"

"Yes, ma'am."

"I have to go." She stood, wobbly.

"I'll drive you."

"You don't have to."

Chris stood. "Olivia, I'm going to drive you back to campus so you can tell me where your classes are so I can meet you at your buildings and talk to you more."

She leaned on the back of the chair and took in his nested brown hair, hazel eyes she'd been staring at for the past hours, his lanky body, and hesitated.

"Your friend warned me about you earlier."

He frowned. "My friend?"

"Dana, I think her name is."

"Dana's harmless."

"Is she?"

He pushed his chair in and leaned toward her. "Have I given you any indication you should be wary of me?"

They stared into each other's eyes. No. In fact, she'd never felt such a strong connection to someone as she did tonight.

"Let me take you back to campus."

She nodded. "Okay."

Chapter 3
September 2010

Olivia was on the phone with Dana while making lunch.

"Want to come to yoga with me?"

"Oh sure, let me get my mat." Olivia tossed diced onion into the searing pan, followed by chopped meat. She'd had a craving for tacos. The sizzling caused her to raise the volume on her phone.

"You know, one day I'm going to stop asking," Dana said.

"One can only hope."

"You'd love it."

"I tried it. With Ella, remember? I learned I'm not bendable."

"And yet, Chris still comes home every night."

Olivia laughed.

"Come on, it's good for your chakra."

"My chakra was thrown into shock the last time. My body hates exercise. I've grown to love my handles. And who exercises on a Saturday? Weekends are to rest."

"Stop it. No rest. I have a fund-raiser next week, and I need to fit into my dress. The store sent a size six so I had it taken in and now I can only eat air until then."

"I have to find new friends." Olivia's phone clicked, and she glanced at an incoming number she didn't recognize. She was about to ignore it when the area code registered in her mind. Rochester.

"I have to take this, Dana."

Dana paused on the line. "I gotta go to yoga anyway. *Namaste.*"

"Hello?"

"Mom, it's me," Nick said.

Olivia lowered the flame under the meat and walked to the window. "Hey, babe. We weren't expecting you to call until tomorrow. What a nice surprise."

"I'm not calling to talk, Mom. I need you to..." He cleared his throat. "I need some money."

"What happened to the money you brought up with you? You were just home two weeks ago." She leaned on the sill, looking at the large tree that covered their entire yard as she listened to the sizzling of the food. The oak held onto its green leaves, well behind the colorful foliage they passed as they followed Nick upstate to school last month to help him bring his belongings to his new apartment. Deep reds and yellows, dangling on the verge of their descent to the ground before winter.

"I need more."

"I don't understand. Can you tell me why?"

"I'd rather not."

She moved from the window back to the stove. "I'll talk to your father and call you back, okay? I'd like to speak to him first."

"Mom? I only get one call. Do you understand what I'm saying?"

"What are you talking about?" She straightened and tightened her hand on the phone. "Nick, what did you do?"

Nick sighed in her ear, a shaky, verge-of-breaking-down exhale. "I'll tell you another time. Just please send up money, or leave a credit card or something. I don't want to stay here. Please."

Olivia was back at the window. She stared at the sky, the oak and upcoming winter forgotten.

"Mom?"

"How much?"

"A thousand."

She called Chris. "Nick called from school. Or somewhere. He needs money. He's in trouble."

"What kind of trouble?"

"He didn't say." She turned off the stove.

"All right. I'm on site in Riverhead. I'll be home by four. Pack a bag. We'll go up and see what's going on."

"What will he do until then?"

"He'll stay put."

They were on the Long Island Expressway by six, in time for rush hour. Most of the traffic was heading east, away from the city, but over the past decade, traffic increased going both directions. Over-crowded. Too many cars. Massive construction. Yet, they wouldn't leave. Long Island was home and still held the allure it always did. Proximity to gorgeous beaches on both shores, the ritzy Hamptons and Montauk on the forks, to Broadway in Manhattan and everything in between. But when trying to get upstate to see your son in jail, even the slightest traffic was enough to make the most avid Long Islander crazy.

Chris tuned the radio to 1010, consistent traffic and weather. He was quiet. His jaw clenched as he maneuvered the car onto the HOV lane.

"We're too easy on him," he said.

"How?"

He shook his head. "I don't know. Easy enough that he's asking for money after what he put us through in high school."

"His scholarship is saving us a boat-load of money. And that was one incident."

They'd gone out east for an extended day, treating themselves to winery visits and a picnic with the food she'd packed from home. Nick was sleeping in from a late football game the night before and didn't want to join them. Ella was in her senior year at college. They told Nick they'd be home late, possibly staying overnight in Greenport but that they'd let him know. They ended up coming home at midnight, rested and weary from a wonderful day together, a rarity with Chris's work schedule and Nick's sports games. They pulled onto their street to find three police cars and hundreds of teenagers gathered in front of their house. A disgruntled neighbor had called the authorities when they realized there were kids overflowing through the doors with no parents home.

"Was it? You turned your head when he was stealing liquor from us. Having friends over when we went out. Girls. In his bedroom."

"It was one girl."

Chris glared at her.

"Okay, two. And they ended up dating for months. And what teenager doesn't try their parents' alcohol? It's a learning experience."

"Ella never had a house party where cops were called while her parents weren't home."

Ella. She was such a good child. Behaved without enforcement. Did what was expected. A gift for young, inexperienced parents.

"Stop comparing him to Ella. That's part of the problem. It hurts him to be held to her standards."

"So, it's my fault?"

Olivia sighed. "No more than it's mine."

Chris stared at the road ahead. Olivia looked down at her hands, at the veins pulsing just below the surface of her freckled skin. They gave away her age. Necks and hands, the ultimate truth-tellers. Fifty. When did this happen? Chris reached over and put his hand on hers. "I'm sorry. I'm upset. This is no one's fault. He's an adult. It's his own doing."

An adult. Her Nick. Her baby. Twenty-two, two years older than she was when she became a mother. Could she imagine Nick doing something so adult as being a father? She shook her head. God forbid. He'd always pushed the envelope—detentions in school for speaking back to the teacher, for cutting classes and leaving school property with shady friends. Constant parties. Too many friends. Too little self-control.

Still, he received a merit scholarship for high SAT scores. He was smart. Athletic. Bored, she was told by the guidance counselor. Send him to a school that will challenge his mind and he won't have time for the extra-curricular activities. He applied to Rochester Institute of Technology and got in. An eight-hour drive through gorgeous foliage. Eight hours to ponder what he did to land himself in the town jail.

The sign "Welcome to Henrietta, Pop. 42,368" made Olivia's stomach turn. Hours of impatience led to their arrival and now all she wanted to do was turn around and go home. At heart, Nick was good. Even with the minor issues at home, she never predicted something like this could happen.

"Can you pull over?"

"Are you kidding? We're almost there."

"Please." She felt the bile move up her throat. Chris looked at her and quickly pulled to the shoulder of the road. Olivia had barely gotten the car door open before she spewed her lunch on the street, bits of digested taco meat spraying her sneakers.

Chris stayed in the car, put the hazard lights on, and checked the rearview mirror to ensure they were safe enough to the side. "Are you okay?"

Olivia leaned over, resting her hands on her thighs and nodded. She held her hand out and he handed her a crumpled napkin from his door's side pocket. She wiped her mouth, then her sneakers, and finally got back into the car.

Chris followed the directions on the GPS, and pulled into the parking lot of the Monroe County Sheriff's Office.

"You okay?"

No. She wasn't okay. Her son was being held in a jail.

"Let's go." He was out of the car before she could get her seatbelt unclasped. Her hands shook and her throat burned as she swallowed, tasting bile mixed with peppermint Altoids, before leaving the car to follow him. He stood at the bottom of the steps to the building, turned and held his hand to her. She grasped it and clutched him.

"Be easy on him, Chris."

"I will not. I want to kill him right now."

Inside, they reached a desk manned by an officer who asked they be seated while he summoned the sheriff. They walked to the offered bench, but chose to stand after their several hours' journey. Olivia's legs were stiff, and she bent them over and over, trying to get the blood circulating and to expend some sort of energy to keep her from crying with worry.

Several minutes later, a tall gentleman who introduced himself as Sheriff Lawrence Buckley, invited them to follow him through a set of doors. Mute, they found themselves in his office. He sat down and held his hand to the chairs opposite his desk before offering them a small smile.

"I appreciate you folks coming up on short notice." He ran his thick fingers through the thread of hair left on his scalp.

Chris cleared his throat. "Sheriff, can you please tell us what our son has done to be here? He wasn't forthcoming on the phone."

The sheriff sat back and dropped his smile. "Your son, it seems, was in an altercation with another student. I don't have the details of how it started or even who the student was. What I do know is Nicholas drove his car from the scene of the fight while under the influence of alcohol."

Olivia dropped her head and Chris mumbled, "Shit" under his breath.

"And," the sheriff continued.

There was more?

"He seemed to have lost control of the car he was driving and hit a telephone pole. They took him and a passenger to the hospital. He was cleared before we brought him here. He has a few cuts and bruises, but overall, he's fine."

He's fine. Olivia shook her head in disbelief. He is so not fine.

"And his passenger?" Chris asked.

"I'm waiting for an update."

"So, what are the charges against him? What's next?" Sheriff Buckley leaned forward and rested on his elbows.

"He's a fourth-year student, I understand. First offense. His blood alcohol level rendered him slightly impaired but still within the parameters of DUI, which allows him to be released on bail but his license will be suspended for four months. However," he leaned over farther and stared into Chris's and then Olivia's eyes, "I'm not sure that charges won't be pressed against him from the student he hurt. There are none at present, but he cannot leave the county right now. Do you understand? These kids think they're in a bubble of exclusivity. That nothing can happen to them away from home, and they get careless and stupid. Though not usually so close to graduating."

They were quiet until Chris spoke. "May we see our son?"

The sheriff stood and stepped toward the door before turning to Olivia and Chris, who followed.

Olivia clutched the bottom of her jacket, thinking of Nick in an accident and being brought in on charges. He beat up another boy? This was something they heard about other people in the news. Not their own child. What was he thinking?

Back near the main entrance, Chris handed money across the main desk to another officer, and they were asked to wait until finally, Nick was escorted to them. He looked like a child as he walked to his parents. Younger than his years—his sandy hair was disheveled and his right eye was bruised, his bottom lip swollen so when he saw his mother, his half-smile was crooked. Olivia wanted to take him into her arms and rock him until the pain and regret in his eyes disappeared. But she stood next to her husband, to allow Chris first to administer their disappointment before she could dote.

Nick's eyes watered as he stood in front of his father, and Chris broke all resolution, taking Olivia's desire away and hugging their son himself.

"Sorry," Nick mumbled into Chris's shoulder. "I don't know why..." He reached his arms around his father, and Olivia saw his hands, bandaged and swollen. My God, she thought.

"Okay," Chris said, patting him on the back. "We'll talk. Let's just get out of here."

Nick stood back and then fell onto his mother.

In the car, Nick stared out of the window while Olivia and Chris sat wordlessly up front. They'd decided to go to a diner. Nick was hungry and Olivia needed coffee. A computerized voice directed Chris along the streets: *In one point three miles, turn right.* Olivia wondered how anyone found their destinations before this technological onslaught invaded their world. Did we just turn in circles until we accidentally showed up where we were supposed to be? She no longer had to figure what direction she faced. Some random satellite floating in space did that for her.

"Dad."

Chris met Nick's eyes in the rearview mirror.

"I'd like to see Missy."

"Missy?" Olivia turned around to her son.

"My friend. The one in the car with me last night."

Chris glanced at Olivia. "Where does she live?"

Nick shook his head and stared back out the window. "She's not home. She's still in the hospital."

They pulled up to Monroe Community Hospital and let Nick out to walk in while they parked the car. At the information desk, Olivia repeated Missy's last name as given by Nick.

"Melissa Dunne."

They followed the instructions to the floor and found her room. Olivia pushed the door open and stepped into the short hall that led to the opening of the room. Still hidden from

Nick and Melissa, she stopped when she heard Nick speaking, held up her hand to keep Chris, who was behind her, from interrupting. Nick was crying.

"Miss, I'm sorry. I don't know what happened." He kissed her hand, held it to his lips.

"It's okay. It's okay." Her voice was soft but in control. Nick had not spoken of Melissa to them. He spent some time in Rochester during the summer, but maintained he was visiting school friends. Olivia knew nothing about their relationship, which was typical. They knew of no girlfriend back at home until she caught one in his room one morning.

"When are they letting you out?" he asked.

"Tomorrow. My parents were here before. They're coming back again in the morning to take me home."

"Home?"

"To my apartment. I'm not leaving school," she said.

"Are you going to tell them?"

Olivia heard her take a shaky breath. "No. They'll make me leave. I don't want to. I'm not sure anyone would believe me anyway."

There was a silence and then Olivia could hear their lips touching, soft sucking noises. He was kissing this girl.

"Your lip," she whispered. "Did you break anything?"

Olivia and Chris heard nothing. Did Nick answer? Shake his head?

"They took me to the sheriff's office after I left here. My parents are outside. They had to bail me out."

"Shit. That's not good. You'll have a record. That's not good, Nick. Did they know you were drinking?"

"Yes."

"You shouldn't have done it. I told you not to. It did nothing but get you in trouble."

"No. He deserved it. He deserves more. I'd do it again, Missy. Except next time, I wouldn't drive. I wouldn't have put you in danger. I was angry. I wasn't thinking."

"This isn't over, Nick."

Olivia turned to Chris, her finger over her lips, and they backed out of the room undetected.

Back in the car, Nick directed Chris to the diner, showing more life than he had in the past hour. In the booth, Chris started with the questions.

"Walk me through what happened."

Nick sipped his coffee, winced when the hot liquid touched his bruised lip. "We decided to go to a bar in town."

"Before that," Chris interrupted. "Start with this girl. Melissa. When did you start with her?"

Nick leaned back and looked at Olivia and then down at his food. He picked up a steak fry and dipped it in ketchup.

"You owe us, Nick. Start talking. We know so little."

"We started to see each other last semester, but this summer, when I came up to stay with Jake in July, it got pretty serious. And, well, we're together. She's a senior like me. Engineering. We have a lot in common."

"Does she drink, too?"

The question surprised Nick. And Olivia. Both looked at Chris as he sat stoically watching his son, trying to understand what landed him in jail on a Saturday night in his senior year of college. Olivia put her arm on Chris's, an unspoken warning to ease up. *Not so quick*, the action said. *We'll lose him.*

"No more than anyone else here. It's college."

His parents said nothing.

"You drove drunk. Should we be worried? Should we get you help?"

"Dad, no. I did a stupid thing. I shouldn't have driven. I was angry and let my emotions get the best of me. That's all. I know better."

Olivia took her hand from her husband. "Why did you fight with another student?"

Nick exhaled. "I didn't fight him. I beat the crap out of him."

"What has gotten into you?" Chris said. "I think you should take the semester off. Come home."

Olivia looked at Chris. What was he saying? He'd lose the scholarship. They'd have to pay the full tuition this year. There was no way.

"No. I want to stay and finish the year. Please. You don't understand." He took a breath. "And I can't leave the county."

"Make me understand," Chris said. "Give me a good reason for your behavior."

Nick sighed and leaned back.

"Do you know this boy you beat up?"

Nick shook his head. "Not really."

"Then why?"

"He hurt Melissa."

Chris and Olivia glanced at each other. "What do you mean he hurt her?"

"He cornered her behind the library." Nick swiped his arm across his nose, reminiscent of when he was young. "He. Hurt. Her."

"Oh, Nick. Did she tell the authorities?" Olivia said. There was so much attention around rapes on college campuses. Olivia hardly paid attention to the talk shows that focused on the growing epidemic. The last story she remembered on the news was an Ivy League student getting away with statutory rape with minimal repercussions. Not a strong message for victims.

"No. She just told me. I had to practically pry it out of her. She saw him walk past the window of the bar last night. She pointed him out, and I lost it." He looked from one to the other. "I could have killed him and I wouldn't have cared."

"Son, you can't take the law into your hands. It's not what we're about. There are rules."

"And sometimes the rules don't solve the problem, Dad. Do you know what Missy would have to go through if she pressed charges of rape against this guy? His parents have money. More than hers. He'd hire better lawyers. She'd have to pay a lot of money just to try to prove the truth. She'd be known as the girl who was raped."

They were silent.

"She begged me not to tell anyone. She begged me. I promised."

"Will this boy press charges against you?"

"I don't know. I think he won't, knowing what we know. But I'm not sure."

"When is Melissa getting out of the hospital?" Chris asked.

Nick shook his head and for the first time in this conversation, his eyes welled. He stared at his food. Olivia and Chris waited for him to compose himself.

"If I really hurt her, I would never forgive myself." Tears fell down his cheeks. "I had no idea I couldn't handle it." He looked up to his father, pained. "I put her in the hospital, Dad." He put his face in his hands and breathed and sniffed.

Chris reached over and put his hand on Nick's head. "What did the doctors say?"

Nick separated his hands so they framed his torn face. "She cracked her femur and two ribs. She's bruised on her torso. I hit her side of the car." The tears returned, silent and heavy.

Olivia looked to Chris, who shook his head and exhaled.

"So, what do we do now? How do we know this kid isn't going to sue you?"

"We don't," Nick said. He threw his napkin on the table. "Can we leave please? I don't feel good." He pushed himself from the booth and left them.

"What should we do?" Olivia asked.

Chris pulled his wallet out and rifled through his money. "We take him to his apartment, check his fridge for food, and let him deal with what comes."

At the door of the diner, Olivia paused. "His car. What will that cost?"

Chris sighed again. "We'll check after we get him back to his place."

"I'll meet you outside. I should call work. I need to tell Gavin I won't be in tomorrow. I hope he's okay with it."

Chris pushed the door open. "Gavin will have to be okay with it. This is our son."

They drove home the next evening, after bringing Nick back to see Melissa, who appeared to look better, Nick said. After an early dinner, Nick wanted to return to his apartment to study and promised his parents he was okay. They were still waiting on the car estimate, so Nick would have to find another way to get to his classes.

They were quiet on the drive home. Chris ignored his ringing phone, and Olivia stared out of the side window. When his phone rang again half an hour later, Olivia looked at it.

"It's Trevor again," she said.

Chris nodded. "I know."

"You should answer it."

Chris exhaled and put his hand on top of the steering wheel. "He wants to get the band together. Jeremy is back in New York and reached out to him last week. He thought it would be fun."

"It would be. Why don't you do it?"

He shrugged. She put her hand on his shoulder. "Babe, it was your favorite thing. You should do it."

Chris took her hand from his shoulder and held it. "My only favorite thing I still want to do is you."

Chapter 4
1979

Chris pulled the collar of his corduroy jacket closer around his neck to ward off the chill and waited in front of the building. Class had ended, and students poured through the doors, flinching from the cold after being toasty in their lecture hall for the past hour and a half. His eyes roved the small group walking down the stairs and returned to the door. It opened again, and someone walked out.

There she was. He smiled instinctively when he saw her, and a jolt went through him. It had been two months since they met at the bar and talked until closing, and he'd been meeting her after classes every day since. Not one day went by he didn't feel that now familiar pang of want at first sight of her.

She adjusted her scarf and looked up, her eyes scanning the area until she spotted him. His heart picked up pace as she walked to him and he met her the last few steps, putting his arms around her into a hug. It was his favorite place to be, right here, wrapped around her.

"Hey," she said, pulling away to look up to him, her thick hat perched back from her face, already pink with cold.

"How was class?"

"Not bad. We have a test on Friday so he worked on review with us."

They started walking to the dining hall, arm in arm.

"Did you finally get your work done last night?" she asked, and then laughed.

Her laughter was his favorite song, music to his ears.

"I did after you let me off the phone."

She lightly punched him with her mitten. "*You* wouldn't hang up with *me*, remember?"

He squeezed her to him. "Well, if you'd just come over, I wouldn't have to call you every night."

She didn't answer. He held the building door for her and followed her into the warm lobby. The dining hall was situated in the center of campus, between both of their lecture halls for their next classes. How quickly they fell into this ritual in the weeks since they'd met. They carried their trays of food to a table near the window and sat next to each other.

"Jack asked us to play this Wednesday night instead of Thursday."

"Perfect. I'll be able to study on Thursday." She ate a French fry. He put his elbows on the table and clasped his hands looking at her.

"What? I have something on my nose?" She self-consciously rubbed her perfectly sloped nose, and he shook his head.

"When are you going to come over and spend the night?"

She paused her chewing and blushed. "We see each other every day. You stay at my room until late."

"Not the same thing. Debbie is always there."

"It's her room too."

"Exactly." He leaned over to whisper. "I promise we won't do anything you don't want to do. I'll wait however long you want. You're worth the wait. I just want to wake up with you."

She slouched and her cheeks turned scarlet. Her eyes shifted to each side and back to him.

"How do you know I'm not saving myself for marriage?"

He thought for a moment. "I have an hour tomorrow between classes. We could go to the church in town. I'll make you an honest woman."

She chuckled. "Yeah, right."

His face grew serious. "I will marry you, Olivia Carson."

Her eyes widened. "You know this after three months?"

"I knew it as soon as the lights came on at the bar."

She shook her head.

"What?"

"We hardly know each other," she said.

"Good. I want to spend the rest of my life getting to know you." He put his fingers under her chin and lifted her face up to his. "I want this face to be the very first thing I see in the morning and the very last thing I see before I close my eyes at night. Until I take my last breath." His eyes held hers and he swore he heard her intake of breath. He looked around the dining hall. "I mean as soon I get you off this campus."

She grinned. "I have three more years. You're going to have to wait, Mr. Bennet. I have plans."

"Plans?"

She nodded. "I'll get my masters and backpack through Europe before settling into a job. I've always wanted to do that."

"Can I go with you?"

"We'll see."

He reached around her waist and tickled her. She squirmed and tried to mute her shriek.

"Wherever you go, I'll go," he said.

"I want to go back to Long Island. My mom is alone there."

"Fine. What else?"

"I want to travel."

"And play music," he added.

"And save money and be established."

"Okay. Europe. Career. Music. Money, then…"

"Then…You'll probably leave me by senior year," she said.

His face dropped. "You're right. You don't know me at all."

Chris stood on the stage and played his keyboard behind Jeremy, who romped back and forth, clutching the mike. He preferred to stand when he played, so he could move with the music. He was already limited to where he could go, often lost behind Jeremy and the Bloom brothers, wailing on their guitars and running back and forth after their singer. He and Trevor, his housemate and their drummer, were backdrops for the antics before them. Still, he loved it. Loved being part of the band, loved the sound of his keyboard, the feel of the keys under his fingers.

During a guitar riff, he searched the thick crowd of the bar and saw her at her usual spot, in the corner next to Dana. She raised an eyebrow when he found her and lifted her beer bottle. A warm feeling permeated his body, beginning in his chest, spreading through him. If he jumped from the stage, he'd fly. He was Superman.

Olivia and Dana waited for them to pack up their gear when the gig ended. It was late, and the crowd had thinned considerably. She waited for him every week without complaint, watching their entire sets. Every note he played, every word he wrote, every past sweat-filled performance melded in his mind into one long preparatory prologue to the moment he laid eyes on her. He now played only for her.

Chris cut through the same group of girls that sat in front of the stage every week waiting for him. He was cordial but dismissive. Didn't want to be rude—they were still fans. There were more than a few he recognized that he'd taken home last year. He couldn't remember names, but remembered quick, sometimes satisfying sex before shuffling them home in the dark hours of the night.

His eyes were focused on his girl, the one who'd been torturing him for almost four months, who wouldn't let him take her home. He kissed her before speaking, wanting to do it for hours, and then sipped the beer on the bar.

"Hey you," she said.

He kissed her again. "Hey, beautiful."

She pushed his wet hair from his forehead and trailed her hand down to his neck.

He shivered.

"You were awesome, as usual."

"Thanks. Did you like the new one we played in the third set?"

"The slow one. The words were..." She closed her eyes. "It was my favorite."

She didn't miss a thing. He kissed her again. "I wrote that one. For you."

Her hand stopped rubbing his neck, and she stared at him. "In that case," she whispered, "take me to your place."

He felt the floor move beneath him. "Are you sure?"

She nodded.

He woke at dawn and watched her sleep. Her eyelashes fluttered with her dreams, and he chuckled softly. She lay on her side facing him, the top of her breast exposed, and he covered her with the blanket before moving closer to her and indulging himself in the memory of what just happened. He'd envisioned this moment every single day since the night she bought him a beer, so he wasn't going to let a detail go unnoticed. He had undressed her with the light on, against her modest protests, so he could commit every cell of her to memory. Her skin felt like silk, and his fingers tingled where they touched her. She was warm and open, fearless yet hesitant, and when he lay with her, he felt like he'd finally found home. Eyes still closed, she nestled into him, and he drifted back into slumber.

Chapter 5
September 2010

Chris was in the kitchen, dressed in jeans and long-sleeve tee shirt, when Olivia came downstairs. He handed her a mug, cream and one sugar, and made her scrambled eggs while she sat at the table, trying to wake up. He joined her as she ate, finishing his own coffee. "How are they?"

"Delicious, as usual." She scooped another forkful from the plate.

"I added sour cream today. I like to keep you guessing so you don't get bored with me."

"As if I could."

He stood, bent over her, and whispered, "Tomorrow, frittata."

"You're so hot."

He planted a kiss on her lips and left for work. She showered, dressed and was in her car by 8:45. On the parkway, inching in traffic, the sun poured through the windshield, warming her. Olivia smiled and relaxed a bit. With worries about Nick prevalent in her thoughts, Chris could still make her smile. She loved their morning ritual, perfected over years so it ran like a well-oiled machine. Bored? Never gonna happen. Their routine calmed her. She made a mental reminder to call Chris later to thank him, as always, for breakfast. For making her happy.

Gavin Porter greeted her with a small stack of letters that needed to be reviewed before she could put down her purse and make a pot of coffee for the office.

"Everything okay, Olivia? How is Nick?"

Gavin replaced Mr. Hughes, who had retired six months ago after a successful thirty-five-year career of mediating divorces. Olivia enjoyed working for Mr. Hughes, who was careful to keep a separate professional relationship with his staff, never getting too personal. Gavin, three years younger than Olivia, blurred the lines almost immediately between professional and personal space, wanting to get to know the staff and form a friendship of sorts. It was an adjustment for sure.

"He'll be fine. Back to classes. Thank you. I apologize for the last-minute call Sunday. We couldn't get back."

He waved, swatting her apology aside while walking away.

"Whenever you need time, you take it. As long as there's coverage."

She sat at her desk and slumped over. She was so tired today. The strain from their visit with Nick had taken a toll on her.

Kayla, the new secretary to Gavin's partner in the firm, walked toward Olivia's desk. More a girl than a woman, she was fresh out of college — a sunny blond thing with a perfect figure. Olivia had overheard Kayla tell someone on the phone that her job as a lowly assistant was just a pitstop for her. Olivia had shaken off the comment, refusing to allow the girl's "pit-stop" comment to demean her own twenty-five year career with the company.

She stopped in front of Olivia's desk just as the phone rang. Olivia smiled and put her finger up, asking the other secretary to wait as she answered the phone.

"Good morning, Gavin Porter's office," Olivia said.

"It's Marco," her son-in-law said. "Can you stop by at lunch? Ella is having a rough day and I have a meeting I can't get out of."

"What's the matter?" She looked at Kayla, who sat across from her, studying her nails.

"Just, please. Come by when you can," he said with an urgent tone. Then he lowered his voice. "Thanks Mom."

Olivia hung up, distracted by Marco's request but tried to put on a smile for the girl. "How can I help you?"

"Is everything all right?"

"It was my son-in-law. My daughter is not feeling well, and he asked me to check in on her."

Kayla sighed. "Gavin said you'd help me with the scheduling program, so I can keep up with Mr. Dougherty's meetings."

"I can help you now if you'd like."

She smiled a bright, toothy grin and stood. "That'd be great."

Olivia walked her through the steps on how to use Microsoft Outlook, but she was preoccupied. She was worried about Ella, suspecting she knew what might be wrong.

The morning dragged, and as the clock struck noon, Olivia was out the door and heading to her car. Twenty minutes later, she pulled up to her daughter's house, parked in the driveway and walked the brick path to the porch. She knocked on the door. When there was no answer, she tried the doorknob and turning it, let herself in.

Ella and Marco lived in a modest Victorian in Franklin Square, complete with gables and a porch that wrapped around one side. The small den and adjacent kitchen were empty. Olivia noticed a blanket on the couch, strewn to the side, indicating someone had been lying there. There was a coffee cup on the counter in the otherwise spotless kitchen.

"Ella? It's Mom," Olivia said as she started up the stairs that led to the bedrooms. She found her daughter in bed, hidden beneath blankets. Her body was still, and Olivia thought she might be sleeping until she heard a croak coming from the pillow.

"Mom," Ella said.

Olivia dropped her purse and went to her child's head, sitting next to her. She pushed Ella's hair from her face, exposing blotchy skin and puffy eyes.

Olivia frowned. "I take it, it didn't work?" She almost said, "Again" but the word wasn't necessary and would be hurtful.

Eight months ago, Ella had a minor breakdown when her insemination didn't take. She got her period, and Marco said she didn't leave the house for two days. Her responses to the failed attempts to get pregnant had grown incrementally worse over time.

Ella rolled onto her back and looked at her mother through red-rimmed eyes.

"We're giving up."

"Oh, Ella. You're just saying that now because you're upset. Give yourself some time and try again."

Ella shook her head, and her face contorted in pain. "I can't, Mom. It's too devastating. I'm out of saved eggs, and we spent so much money."

"Maybe next year…"

"Stop. No. I'm done." Annoyed, she turned away from Olivia and sniffed.

Olivia stood, stepped from the room and called the office, telling Kayla that she wasn't returning to work for the day due to a family situation. She'd have to apologize again to Gavin. She went back to Ella, still turned away, slipped off her cotton jacket and low heels and climbed into bed, hugging her daughter from behind. The room held a soothing lavender scent that calmed her.

After several minutes of silence, Ella spoke. "We really wanted a baby, Marco and me. I want to be a mother. I've never wanted anything so badly."

Olivia tightened her hold and said nothing. It pained her to know she couldn't help her daughter. When Ella was young, it was easy—she fell, Olivia picked her up, gave her a hug and kiss and the tears magically disappeared. It was a special power that gave her peace. Now, with Nick and his legal issues and Ella trying desperately to have a baby, she couldn't swoop in with a kiss and hug and make everything better. She felt helpless.

"I feel like I must have done something terrible in my life to deserve this. People get pregnant all the time. I'm being punished."

"You're not being punished, sweetheart. You did nothing wrong."

"Please don't tell me God has a plan. I'll lose it, I swear." She sniffed. "I don't want to hear anything."

Olivia pressed her lips together. She wasn't going to say that. She was going to suggest Ella and Marco put their tests away, pack a bag and hit an island beach for some well-deserved R&R. Her daughter looked pale. She'd been overwrought with anticipated worry for the past eighteen months when they stopped trying on their own, took tests and started on the artificial insemination path, an unfriendly, rocky road that led only a select few to success.

"Don't you have to go back to work?"

"I called in." Silence. "Would you like me to get lunch?"

Ella sniffed again. "Just please stay with me."

This, she could do. She listened to her daughter breathe, her own breath in sync.

"When I was young, I thought you and Dad were going to split up," Ella whispered.

Olivia's eyes opened wide. "Why would you think that?"

Ella paused, ignoring her question. "Then I realized you weren't fighting in your room. You were crying and Dad was consoling you. As I got older, I thought maybe you were depressed at that time. But you never seemed unhappy."

"I don't understand," Olivia said, confused.

Ella turned her head up so her mother could see her face. "I was eleven or twelve, I think. There was a period when you cried a lot. And then you stopped."

Olivia held her breath.

"You had a miscarriage after Nick." She turned to her mother. "Mom, did you want another baby? You could have only been thirty-two or thirty-three."

She had been thirty-two, Ella's age, when she lost the baby. She'd wanted more children and had no idea Ella was aware of her suffering the weeks after the miscarriage and the months following, when she got her periods. Chris was instrumental in helping her through it. He could soothe her like no one else. "Yes. I did. But then I realized I had everything I wanted, and I didn't think about it again."

Tears fell from Ella's eyes, down her temples.

"Your father helped me realize that. Ella, I understand your pain somewhat. I know it's not fair for me to say that, but I do. There's a plan for you. You just have to find it."

"I told you not to say that."

"Sorry. But I do believe it."

Ella was quiet for so long, Olivia was sure she'd fallen asleep. She realized she'd dozed off herself, lulled by the lavender, when Ella woke her.

"What?"

"I said, what did you and Dad do this weekend?"

Olivia opened her eyes, realizing she hadn't told Ella about their impromptu visit to Nick. So, she spent the next hour updating her daughter on what happened.

Chapter 6
October 2010

Olivia overslept and arrived at the office without breakfast. Chris had tried to get her to sit for a bite but she opted to grab a granola bar instead and rushed out of the house. There were so many files to complete, court dates to schedule and letters to type, she had barely time to pee, let alone have a needed snack, so when Dana called her office and suggested lunch, Olivia readily agreed.

An hour before lunch, she stood at the filing cabinet when she started to perspire and felt blood rushing to her feet. She dropped the papers she held to the floor as her knees buckled. Black formed around her eyes and she felt herself falling, when arms grabbed her from behind, supporting her.

"Okay, Olivia, I got you," Gavin said in her ear and then whispered instructions to Kayla while he led her to his office and helped her on the couch. Minutes later, he placed a cool, moist towel on her forehead. Olivia opened her eyes to find him leaning over her, concerned, holding a bottle of water.

"What happened there?" he said.

Embarrassed, Olivia tried to sit up, but Gavin gently pushed her back down and handed her the water. "No rush. Just relax."

"I'm not sure," she said, sipping the bottle and pulling the towel from her head. "I was lightheaded and then I felt woozy. I haven't eaten this morning. My blood sugar is low."

He frowned. "Has this happened before?"

"No. I'm usually better about eating." Olivia didn't want him to keep looking at her this way, like she was fragile, or worse, not reliable.

Kayla poked her head into his office and retreated quickly upon seeing them so close together. "Gavin?" she said from the other side of the door, "Someone is here to see Olivia."

"It's my friend, Dana. We're supposed to have lunch."

Gavin stood. "I should take you to the hospital."

"No!" Her response came out stronger than she'd intended. "I just need to rest. Please. Do you mind telling her I have to cancel?"

"Okay. Then I'll take you home. You don't look good." He stepped from his office and Olivia could hear him speak with Dana. What the hell just happened? She was scared but didn't want to sit in a hospital all afternoon. She sipped the water, already feeling better.

Gavin walked back in. "Dana will call you later."

She rested on his couch for an hour before finally convincing her boss that she was fine enough to drive herself home. She drank the entire bottle and ate her granola bar.

Chris arrived home from work to find Olivia in sweats, lying on the couch with a cup of tea.

"You okay?"

"Just under the weather. I left work early. I'll be fine by tomorrow." She didn't want to upset Chris by telling him what happened, nor give life to her worries.

He pulled his sweatshirt over his head. "Any word from Nick?"

She shook her head. "No news is good news. Right?"

Chris nodded. "We should take a trip."

"We just took one."

"No. A real trip. I inquired about a villa in Tuscany today. Near Siena. It looks amazing."

Olivia closed her eyes. She wanted to sleep. She was so tired.

"Babe?" he said. "Do you have any thoughts on this?"

"Don't you think we should wait to make sure nothing else happens with Nick? Why don't we go somewhere next year?"

Chris sighed. "I don't want to wait. I'm tired of waiting."

They'd talked about the freedom they'd finally enjoy once Nick was out of college, the vacations they'd take, the traveling. Chris wanted to lighten his workload and urged her to go part-time. *We finally have some money saved,* he'd said. *Let's do what we couldn't do when the kids were home.* She thought of Chris's toast in the Berkshires: "To the next phase of our lives." Was it here already?

Tuscany. It was on their bucket list—a lengthy compilation of places they wanted to see before they died. They hadn't crossed off one item in all the years they were together. Something always got in the way. And they never quite had extra money for extravagances. Instead, they vacationed upstate, camping and renting small lake cabins. She wouldn't change it for a thing. But Tuscany. Tuscany had been on the list since the beginning.

Chris kneeled by her face and kissed her forehead.

"Let's talk about it tomorrow," Olivia said. She put her hand on his cheek before pulling herself off the couch. "I'm going to bed. I'm not feeling well."

She called in sick the following day, sleeping until ten am, before finding herself in the kitchen making breakfast. She felt better, couldn't pinpoint symptoms and figured, *hoped,* it was a twenty-four-hour virus. So what if it lasted for forty-eight? Or seventy-two?

She called Ella on her lunch break at work while heating the oatmeal Chris made and saved for her earlier and was pleased to hear her daughter sounded almost back to normal.

"You sound much better today."

"I feel better. Thanks for coming over the other day. I'm sorry I was such a wreck. I feel like someone else took over my body." Olivia could hear student's muffled screams and laughter in the background. "Poor Marco. He came home that night walking on eggshells."

"How's he taking it?"

"He's upset too. He just handles it better than me. Thank God or we'd both be useless."

"You're entitled to feel sad. It's perfectly natural. I think you and Marco should take a trip and relax. Get some sun."

She could hear Ella smile on the other end of the line. "How about you take some of your own advice? You have no one home. Take advantage of this new freedom. It's just you and Dad. Go somewhere. You guys never went anywhere without us."

"We didn't?" Olivia turned off the stove and reached into the cupboard for a bowl. "Sure, we did. We just went to the Berkshires for my birthday, remember?"

"Mom, a two-day stint four hours away hardly counts as a couple's getaway."

Ella was right. All the vacations they took included the kids. And while Ella was in college, they were so busy with work, Nick and his sports, they couldn't find the time. Chris had just mentioned wanting to go to Europe. Maybe she'd tell him they'd go. What were they waiting for?

"Mom?"

"Hm?"

"I said, have you heard from Nick since you went up?"

"He called Monday. He sounds better."

"Poor Nick," Ella said. "I've been thinking about what happened. He must have been so scared. And crazed. He's not violent."

"I know." Olivia cradled the phone to her ear while she spooned the food into a bowl. "He wasn't himself. He was pretty distraught."

"How are you taking it?" Ella asked.

"I'm upset, of course. I mean, my son spent a night in jail."

"That's not what I meant, Mom. I meant how are you taking that Nick is in love?"

"He's in love?" Olivia dropped the pot and seared her finger as she tried to grab it. She swore under her breath and ran the faucet cold before putting her throbbing finger under the spray.

"What's going on over there? You okay?"

"I'm fine." Olivia let the cold water run over her pained finger. "How do you know he's in love?"

"It's so obvious. He's never given much thought to anyone but himself. He got into a fight and crashed a car over a girl. He's a goner."

Olivia shut the water and dried her hands. "He was drunk."

"He's in college."

"Ella, you never did those things."

"I never got caught. I have to go. Recess is over. Time to corral these wild little munchkins and try to get them settled down for the afternoon."

She set the table for one and ate breakfast in silence.

Chris brought home dinner and a bouquet of sunflowers after work. They dined on soup while he told her about his latest project, a multi-level, floor-to-ceiling windowed house in Quogue.

"Who's the architect?" she asked.

"Cooper."

"Tell him I said hello."

"I already did." He smiled.

She knew nearly everyone Chris worked with through the years. His loyalty drew all trades to him, and they loved to take projects he was a part of. Fred Cooper designed the first house Chris built when he finally took over John's construction company after years of being mentored.

As Chris regaled the recent issues between the architect and the homeowners, Olivia's cell phone rang. She answered. It was Gavin, calling to see how she was feeling and asking if she'd be at work tomorrow. She promised she'd be there and hung up.

They sipped their soup.

"Cutting a bit into personal time. You worked for Hughes for years, and he never called the house."

"Gavin's different. Has a different work mentality." She shrugged. "He's just worried his deposition won't get done in time. More so than he's worried about me."

"I don't know, babe. You have lunch with this guy. He calls you on the weekends and after work hours. Seems a bit much."

Olivia smiled, thankful she didn't tell him how her boss helped her when she fainted at the office. "Are you jealous?"

He looked at her over his spoon. "Every time you walk out that door."

She blew him a kiss across the table. "Don't worry. We have a new girl in the office who's half my age. She's a human Barbie with a brain. I'm invisible."

Chris threw his empty soup cup into the garbage, went to her and kissed her. "Don't kid yourself. You're hot."

"Well, you have nothing to worry about."

"Is Gavin married?"

"No."

Chris returned to his seat while she finished eating. They never left the table until both were done.

"He's four-foot-ten with ear hair," Olivia added, still talking about her boss.

Chris gave a wry grin. "You just described Hughes."

"They're all the same." Gavin was a good-looking man, but certain details weren't always necessary to share.

Chris sat quiet.

"What?" Olivia said.

"You told Gavin you'd be in work tomorrow. You told me you made a doctor appointment."

"I did. For five o'clock. I was thinking about cancelling it."

"If you're feeling better, you should."

***

She decided to keep the appointment. She was feeling better the next day but still tired. Twice, she caught silly mistakes she made right before passing paperwork onto her boss. As she left the office at four-thirty, she wondered what mistakes she didn't catch that Gavin would.

After being weighed and leaving a urine sample, Olivia sat in the exam room, clad in socks and a paper-thin robe, waiting for the doctor, trying not to dwell on her age and the reality that things were going to start to go wrong. She should have a colonoscopy. That would be next.

Dr. Byrnes entered the room and nodded to Olivia. She was a new patient. Dr. Greene, who she'd known for thirty years, retired last June. Dr. Byrnes had her file, but knew little about her. No inquiries about her family or work, just the silent examination, peppered with the occasional, "Raise your arm" and, "Just shift over here for me, Olivia," until finally, they were quiet.

"How have you been feeling?" he asked when he was almost done.

"Tired. I feel like I have the flu but I don't think I do. And I'm pre-menopausal. My period has been so unpredictable the last few months."

His brows furrowed in thought as he continued to feel around her abdomen.

"What?"

He peeled his gloves off and noted something in her chart. "Let's take some blood and make sure there's no underlying cause for why you're feeling this way. I'll write you a script for the lab."

Olivia sat up. "I'm not pre-menopausal?" she asked, but she knew deep down that menopause wasn't making her feel this way.

"It's a possibility. But I just want to make sure. Your uterus seems a little distended."

"It's just keeping in line with the rest of my body," she joked while ominous thoughts rallied through her head. This happened to Dana's parents. Her father worked his entire life and one year after he retired, his wife was stricken with dementia. They had two good years together after he stopped working before her ailment took a nosedive and he was forced to place her in assisted living. Dr. Byrnes ignored her. She missed Dr. Greene.

The following afternoon, Olivia watched the lab nurse adeptly coerce four vials of blood from her vein. She decided not to tell Chris what was going on. Better to wait, she thought. It may be nothing.

Two days later, she sat in Dr. Byrnes's office, stunned and speechless after he delivered the news.

"Can I get you water?"

Olivia shook her head. She blinked slowly as if she were in a dream where she was underwater, floating, rising to the surface, and just as she was about to crash through the glassy rim, the surface moved farther away. She stood, hearing the doctor speak to her, but she couldn't decipher what he was saying. The last thing she remembered before everything went black was, what would she tell her family?

Ella called Olivia, who had been sitting in the kitchen with a cold cup of untouched tea, staring into the yard as the early autumn sun set. She answered on the third ring.

"Mom, you sound distracted," Ella said after initial pleasantries were exchanged.

"Hmm? I do? I'm sorry. I'm a little under the weather." She wouldn't tell her daughter she just fainted again, three hours earlier after hearing life-changing news.

"I just wanted to check in and let you know I spoke to Nick yesterday and he seems fine. Moving on," Ella said.

"I'm glad. Thanks for letting me know."

Ella was silent. "Okay, Mom. I'll talk to you tomorrow. If you need anything, call me." It took several seconds before Olivia realized she was listening to the dial tone. She placed the phone down and put her head in her hands.

Suddenly exhausted, Olivia dumped her tea into the sink, dropped the mug and went upstairs. Climbing into bed, she pulled the blankets over her head and went to sleep.

Chris woke her hours later when he walked into the room to change after work. She rolled over and opened her eyes to find him watching her as he pulled his shirt over his head. He was broad from years of physical labor, and his body still looked solid and strong, though he spent much of his days directing his team of employees. Sometimes he walked in the house filthy and spent, unable to stay away from the hands-on tasks for long.

The sky was dark outside. "It's late," Olivia said.

"We stayed past sunset. Trying to take advantage of the time before the clocks are pushed back. This woman." He shook his head. "She keeps making changes. Now she wants the downstairs bedroom bigger and an extra bathroom off that room." He slipped off his jeans. "You can already park a tank in it. But no, it's still too small." He dropped his pants onto the growing pile of laundry and then threw on sweats and a clean tee shirt, unaware Olivia was still staring at him.

"Still sick?" he asked.

She shook her head.

"So, is dinner out of the question? Are you on strike?" He smiled. "I'll whip something up."

Olivia sat up and swung her legs over the bed. "How about hamburgers? I have some chopped meat."

"Sure." With Chris, it was easy. He'd eat anything.

He followed her downstairs. "I want to show you something." He went to his laptop sitting on the kitchen table and opened it. Olivia pulled chopped meat from the fridge.

"Take a look," he said to her back. She turned around and

on his screen was a picture of a stone house sitting in a gorgeous setting of a grove of olive trees and fields of wildflowers. He pressed a button and they watched a slideshow of the interior of the house: simple, airy bedrooms, an updated kitchen with stainless steel appliances, then outside again to show the gardens and swimming pool. It was breathtaking.

"This is the villa I was talking about. The one in Siena. I spoke to the owner today. He said it's taken until mid-March, but then it's available through April. Off-peak, so it's even less than I expected. It's all ours for three weeks. Truffles are waiting for us." His excitement unnerved her. That was six months away. She might not be going anywhere in six months.

Olivia turned around and began pulling the meat apart.

"We'll apply for passports this month so we don't wait until the last minute." Chris closed the laptop. "Hey. What's the matter? I thought you'd be excited. You don't want to go?"

She shrugged and started forming patties. Chris stepped toward her. "We'll be back by Nick's graduation. Hey." He put his hand on her arm. "Why aren't you speaking to me?" His voice rose in agitation, but his face fell as soon as she looked at him. "What is it?"

Olivia put the burgers down and washed her hands, giving her an extra few seconds before she'd have to tell him the news.

"You might want to sit down."

"No, I don't." He stood, confused and frightened. "What?"

"I saw Dr. Byrnes earlier in the week."

"And?"

"I'm pregnant."

Chapter 7
1979

"What are you looking at?" she said.

He gazed into the one eye she pulled open. "You."

Olivia lifted her arm over her head, bending it at the headboard and arched her back in a delicious stretch, and it was all Chris could do to keep from taking her again. God, he loved her body. He'd missed her yesterday. She'd spent all day in the library studying for her final. He didn't know what to do with himself without her. His classes were over for the semester, his finals and projects complete, and he was staying in his apartment until she was done. Last night he was restless and went to campus to wait in her dorm lounge. She finally walked into the building at midnight. He walked with her to her room, grabbed her before she could get her coat off inside, and had her in bed without a word.

He leaned over and kissed her nipple.

"Hey!" She covered herself with her hand.

"Sorry, but when you put it out there, it begs to be kissed."

"It does?" She rolled over and rested her head on her hands. They'd been spending nights at his apartment every weekend since the beginning of their junior year. Their long and painful summer apart led to an impassioned reunion in August, and they'd become inseparable. His friends made fun of him, saying they were already like an old, married couple. It was all he could do to wait for Fridays after classes to have her uninterrupted.

He hated Monday mornings, like this one, when they had to get up early and leave each other for the day. He checked the clock on her nightstand behind him.

"What?"

"We have an hour," he said.

"What do you want to do?"

"You," he said and raised his eyebrows.

"Is that all you think about?"

"I also think about my music. That's enough to make me happy."

She stared at him, pensive. She'd been acting strange since last night, and he didn't want to think of what could be wrong. Maybe she was concerned about her test. Or was she getting tired of him? They'd been together for over a year, and he still woke up with one thought in mind. Olivia.

"What?"

She shrugged and shook her head. "Do you think people can be this happy their whole lives?"

He felt as if his heart might stop. "I don't know. I'd like to think it's possible."

"My parents divorced when I was three. My dad died before I was ten, but I hardly knew him." She kept looking at him as he stared at the ceiling. "Are your parents happy?"

"Maybe. They don't argue, but they're not overly demonstrative." He rolled onto his side, and his hand held up his head so he looked over her. The soft satisfied purr she exhaled as he lightly scratched her back aroused him. Pushing back his desire to envelop her, he settled for a kiss on her shoulder. "I was thinking of our itinerary for Europe when we go."

She stared ahead and didn't answer. He kept talking, trying not to read into it. His stomach turned.

"I figured we'd start in Ireland—they have great beer. Then Paris. We'll picnic on wine, cheese and bread on the grass in front of the Eiffel Tower."

Her eyes glazed over. Was he losing her?

"Then Germany. Munich and Heidelberg. And we'll end up in Greece."

"Tuscany," she whispered.

He leaned into her. "Tuscany? Done. We'll stay in a villa."

"I watched a show where people dug for truffles."

"Truffles?"

"It's a mushroom. Like a fungus, but delectable. I saw on TV they dig for them in Italy, with dogs and it's a whole thing. I'd love to do that."

He nodded, exhaling. She showed interest. Thank God. For a moment, he thought he was in this alone. But he couldn't be. He hadn't misread the way she ran up to him on campus between classes. The smile that lit up her entire face when she saw him, the one that made him feel like a superhero. But last night, when they made love, she'd seemed far away. He'd let it go, not wanting to face it. "Fine. After Paris, we'll find fungus. I can't wait."

She nodded, but her eyes filled.

"I can't wait, Liv. To do everything with you."

She turned over, put her hand on his cheek, and the tears started down her face. Oh no.

"What? What is it?" His heart was in his throat. He was going to be sick. Was he losing her?

"I'm pregnant."

It was as if everything around him was vacuumed away, leaving him breathless and alone with these two words. He fell onto his back. "Oh."

He bit his inner cheek in thought, pulled her to him, and she buried her face in his chest. He kissed the top of her head but said nothing. He barely glanced back at the clock, but he knew she had to leave soon. Finally, she pulled herself from him, her beautiful face splotchy and red. "I have to pee."

He sat in bed, stunned yet relieved, happy she wasn't breaking up with him. But now what? He listened to the water running in the bathroom. Too soon, she stood in the doorway and watched him. She looked as scared as he felt. He went to her, taking her in his arms and she nestled against him.

"I'll look into getting an… You know. I might need some help paying for it."

He nodded, dumbfounded. Of course. It would be so easy. He had an unlimited checking account his father replenished regularly. She had nearly nothing. Problem solved.

She pulled away, and he felt cold where she'd been. "I have to go. I have my test in a half hour," she whispered, when it was clear they wouldn't be talking about this now.

They dressed in silence, put their boots on and left the dorm together, navigating the snow-laden walkway, joined with their gloved-hands. They passed the parking lot and his car.

"Where are you going? You're done."

He held her hand and looked forward. "I want to take you to class."

They walked across campus. In front of the lecture building, she turned to him. He adjusted her scarf. "I'm sorry," she said.

His face fell, and he grabbed her. "Don't be sorry. Let's talk about it later."

She nodded and stepped back. Her chin quivered. He knew how hard she'd worked this semester in her literature class. How the hell would she now focus on taking this exam?

"Go kick some Brontë ass. I'll be here when you're done," he said. She smiled for the first time since midnight, and he felt like he'd won the lottery. He wanted to be the reason to make her smile into old age. She walked into the lecture hall, her head down, shoulders hunched against the cold, and a searing pain burned his gut. What the hell did he do?

He sat in his dark kitchen, staring at the stove, listening to the ticking clock on the wall. His packed duffel bag sat at his feet like a silent, obedient dog while he played every scenario in his head over and over, trying to find the right answer. But it wouldn't come.

Trevor walked in to find him sitting alone in the dark. "Dude. What's up? I thought you were leaving today. Aren't you taking Liv home?"

Chris pulled his eyes up to look at his friend.

"Whoa. Why so glum? Do you mind?" He flicked the light on and sat at the table. "Really, what are you doing?"

Chris sighed and turned to rest his arms on the table between them. "Liv's pregnant."

Trevor's eyes widened, and he leaned back. "What the hell? Why you go and do that?"

Chris leveled him with a glare.

"Seriously. Don't you use condoms?"

"Do you?"

Trevor shook his head. "Hell, no. But Dana's on the pill. I don't have to."

"I guess I've been lucky." Chris took a deep breath and exhaled loudly. "What the hell did I do?"

They sat in silence. The clock ticked over them.

"Is she open to getting an a—"

"Yes, she said she would," Chris said.

"So? That's it then. Just let her do it and be done with it."

Chris pressed his lips together. "Whenever I think of her doing that, my stomach twists and I feel this pain deep in my gut. This is our kid. Hers and mine. I can't see her going through with it. I can't see myself letting her."

Trevor shook his head.

"I mean it," Chris said. "It would screw her up. She's not that girl. She'd regret it for the rest of our lives. And she may even resent me for it."

"This is huge. This is your life you're talking about," Trevor said.

Silence.

"After graduation, we were going to make a lot of money and buy big houses near each other. Liv and Dana were gonna hang out. We'd have dinners, take vacations together." He looked at Chris, who was still staring ahead. "Any deviation from that plan will alter your life. It'll be tough."

Silence.

"Are you listening to me?"

Chris leaned over, clasped his hands between his knees. "We don't know for sure all of that was ever going to happen. But what I do know for sure is she's pregnant. With my kid. That's the only thing I know right now. And I can still graduate. I have a year left. This shouldn't change that."

"Your parents."

Chris stared at the floor, trying to imagine what his father would say. How his mother would react. Didn't they warn him to be careful? *Keep it in your pants or protect yourself,* his father told him when he dropped him off freshman year amid the throngs of girls walking around. *Your job for the next four years is to get your degree. When you're CEO, you can screw all the girls you want.* He did neither and was just fine until he met Liv. They never warned him not to fall in love.

Trevor leaned over. "What are you going to do?"

Chris rubbed his face over and over and finally dropped his hands. "I'm going to do whatever she wants to do. I want nothing but her."

"Can you promise me one thing?"

Chris pulled his head up to face his best friend.

"Promise me you'll never quit the band."

Chris reached his hand out. Trevor took it and said, "Dude. Congratulations."

As promised, two hours later he stood outside her lecture hall, his nose and cheeks red from the cold, waiting for her. She walked to him through the small group of students. They crossed the campus to her empty suite, abandoned by her roommates who had all finished their finals on Friday and left for their Christmas break.

In the empty living room, she took off her scarf, boots and coat, and he went to the mini fridge and took out two beers.

He twisted the caps off and handed her a bottle, but she shook her head, and he put it down. Suddenly, on the dark green shaggy rug, he dropped to one knee and took her hand. Her free hand shot up to her mouth.

"What are you doing?" she said, their first words spoken since he met her after her test.

"Marry me, Olivia."

She shook her head.

He frowned. "You won't?"

"You don't have to." The thin words sifted through her fingers.

"I know that. I want to. I love you. And we're having a baby. We would have gotten married anyway. Let's just do it early."

"Maybe we're too young to do this. Should we discuss options?"

"Is there another option?"

She lowered her head.

"No," he said. "Not for me, either."

"I didn't expect this."

Chris gently tugged the hand that covered her mouth and held both in his. They had nothing between them but dreams. They were going to graduate and backpack across Europe before they found a place together and start their careers. Marriage was a distant goal, and children hadn't even factored into their conversations. But life didn't go according to plan. And he wasn't about to let her do anything that might jeopardize their future together.

"I don't know. I'm scared."

"I'm not. I've never been more sure of anything." Still on his knee, he looked at her, hoping she believed him, not sure if he believed himself. "I want to be with you always."

Chapter 8
October 2010

Olivia waited as Chris absorbed the news. She'd had a full day to digest it and still, the thought rendered her mute. All that had gone through her mind at first were worries, about her health, the baby's, how their lives would be completely turned upside down now that she and Chris were empty-nesters. Dr. Byrnes implored her to consider her past experiences when making her decision. She'd had difficult pregnancies. But thoughts of an abortion terrified her. How could she ever do that? A baby...

She suspected Chris would need some time to adjust to it too. What she didn't expect was for him to be distant. His mouth pressed in a thin line, and he'd avoided her eyes the whole meal. He barely ate his food.

"Chris, I didn't expect you to whoop and whirl me around the kitchen, but this is a little drastic, don't you think?"

"What are you talking about?"

"You seem mad."

He picked his head up and softened his jaw. "I'm just surprised. It's not what I expected."

She nodded. "I didn't expect it either." Then she smiled. "That seems to be our M.O."

They stood and cleared the table, placing their dishes into the dishwasher.

"Are you sure?" Chris said.

"Yes."

"How far?"

"Five weeks."

She went upstairs to change for bed, expecting he would be behind her as was their ritual. But when she was changed and heading back downstairs, he hadn't come up. She found him standing in the dark den. "Chris?"

"I'm going to head out for a bit."

"Where are you going?"

He didn't look at her.

"Chris?"

His eyes finally met hers, and she took a step back. He looked pained.

"I won't be late." He gave her a quick kiss on her cheek, squeezed her arm and left her in the dark.

On the couch, Olivia wrapped herself in her favorite quilt, one her mother had given her years ago. She was stunned by Chris's behavior, by his lack of expression, so unlike him, and for abandoning her when they should have been able to talk through it.

She was in bed, almost sleep when he climbed in beside her after midnight. She refused to turn around to see him, upset with his reaction at the news. They were in this together. What right did he have to be so aloof?

In the dark, he took a deep breath and exhaled. She turned to see his silhouette lit up by the moon's light. She put her hand on his chest, and he covered it with his.

"You're upset," she whispered.

He paused. "Yes." He squeezed her hand but said no more.

It took a long time for Olivia to fall asleep. As she drifted off, she knew Chris was still awake.

Olivia left work the next day to meet her daughter for lunch. She picked up a dessert at the local bakery and arrived at Ella's house at one o'clock to find her in the backyard. In jeans and flannel shirt, Ella sat at the table, head tilted up toward the sun. She was beautiful like her father. Almond-shaped hazel eyes under thick brows, creamy blemish-free skin.

The sunlight glinted off Ella's chestnut hair and Olivia felt the urge to touch it, to run her fingers through it as she used to do when she put her to bed. She wanted to turn back time, to tuck her young daughter in and tell her bedtime stories while she fell asleep.

Ella sensed her mother near and lifted her head. Shading her eyes, she smiled at Olivia and motioned her closer. "I didn't hear you."

Olivia leaned over to kiss her forehead. "It's a beautiful day. I love this idea to do lunch. Thank you for getting me out of the office."

"I figured we'd take advantage of my day off. School's closed next week for Yom Kippur too, if you want to do this again. I made chicken salad with walnuts and cranberries, the way you like it."

"Sounds perfect."

Olivia placed the Danish ring on the table and sat across from her daughter.

"Have you heard from Nick?" Ella said.

"He called this morning. He sounds okay. He's getting his car back, though what good will that do without a license?"

"Anything from the other student?"

"Not yet." Olivia held up crossed fingers.

Ella shook her head. "I still can't believe he did that. It's so not him."

"I'm just relieved it's over."

"Even with this trouble, he's still acing his classes. He was always smarter than me."

"No. He's clever. He thinks differently."

Ella looked at her mother. "He's smarter than me. He'll end up making major money and will support us somehow."

"He's smarter than all of us. He owes us." They laughed.

Chicken salad on Challah bread with arugula salad and lemonade. They ate quietly, listening to the birds sing their last mating calls of the season.

"Delicious, babe."

"Thanks."

Olivia took her last bite and wiped her lip with a napkin. "Now, are you going to tell me why I'm really here?"

Ella's abbreviated laugh ended with a stifled sob. "How do you always know?"

"It's my job. I know you better than you know yourself."

Ella nodded, took a sip of her drink and looked toward the evergreens lining the fence across the yard. "I told you we're giving up on in-vitro." She turned to her mother. "I can't get pregnant. Marco and I had a long talk. No more tests. No more taking our temperatures or forced coupling. No more shots. We're tired. We're out of money. We're done."

Olivia leaned forward. "I was hoping you'd reconsider. Don't give up. You can't give up." She choked down the irony. The predominant thought that went through her mind since finding out she was pregnant was, how could she possibly tell Ella?

"The shots aren't working, Mom. They hurt and they're expensive. No more." She shook her head as if to convince herself.

Ella suffered through puberty with her menstrual cycle. It was hardly a cycle—heavy, painful clotting one month. Nothing the next. The doctors told her she had one fallopian tube. Olivia had been enveloped in guilt until Chris set her straight. There was no way she could control how her child's insides would form. It wasn't her fault. They were told Ella could have children, but the odds were exponentially lower.

"Ella."

"It's been five years and nothing. Nothing."

"Do you need money?"

"No." Ella looked away, offended.

Olivia picked at her nails and swallowed. "I don't know what to say. If I could fix this for you, I would."

"I know, Mom. This is something not even you can fix."

She looked at her daughter, wanting her to know the elation of being told you're having a baby. Feeling it grow inside, the result of love. She felt so weighed down by guilt.

"We're going to adopt." Ella watched for her mother's reaction. "I made some initial inquiries and spoke to a nice woman at the domestic adoption agency. Marco and I filled out paperwork and submitted it. Someone will be visiting the house to start the process. I think they want to meet us to make sure we're acceptable parents."

Olivia nodded in thought. Acceptable parents. The hypocrisy fueled her anger at her daughter's situation. Shouldn't every person be interviewed before they could raise a baby? How many natural parents abused their birth children? No one interviewed them. They just had sex and the baby was theirs. It was so unfair. Olivia looked at her daughter, without pity—Ella would hate that—but with compassion.

"I really wanted my own, you know, a baby with my genes. Your nose, Dad's eye color, Marco's height and temperament. Someone who was a part of me, who came from me." She gestured to her body, her flawed, beautiful body. Then she shrugged.

"Ella, once you love a child, it becomes a part of you. Don't you understand? The eyes that look at you—blue, brown, hazel—look at you for trust and guidance and unconditional love. They'll be beautiful no matter who formed the DNA because they'll be seeing you as their mother. Love is magic."

Ella blinked back tears. "Okay. Thanks, Mom."

"Ella and I had lunch today," Olivia told Chris after dinner. They were watching television. Chris sat on the club chair across from her. She kept glancing at him, wondering why he wasn't sitting beside her as he always did.

"How is she doing?"

"They're thinking about adoption," she said.

He stiffened. "From where?"

"Does it matter?"

They watched a movie in silence.

"Did you tell her?"

"No!" Knowing he'd ask, Olivia's answer came out stronger than she'd anticipated.

"Good. She doesn't have to know."

Olivia stood, blocking the screen. "What are you talking about?"

Chris's arm rested on the back of the chair. His other against his side. She could see his hand flex and his jaw tighten. "We're not keeping it."

She felt the blood drain from her face. "Shouldn't we talk about it first?"

"There's nothing to talk about." His voice rose. "How could you possibly think we can do this? What were you thinking?"

She walked to the door of the den, turned around and whispered through gritted teeth, "You act like this is all my fault."

He stared at her, saying nothing.

Tears stung her eyes. "We've done this before. We can do it again."

"Liv, disregarding the risks, I don't want to."

His statement nearly knocked her back. She opened her mouth to speak, but nothing came out. Instead she walked upstairs, the words sitting in her mouth, "Me, neither," swallowed back down.

She heard him come to bed hours later. She'd been awake, in turmoil, trying to make sense of what was happening to them.

He lay on his side, not touching her. Didn't kiss her good night as he always did. She could count on one hand how many nights they went to bed angry. Staring into the darkness, she admitted to herself that part of her wanted to feel the flutter of new life deep inside. The rumbling movement of the belly, the tiny footprint pushing against her stomach. To be able to feel that again was a last opportunity to feel the magic of life. She thought of Ella, how she wouldn't feel those first pangs of growth and her heart ached. Did she want this baby? At her age and their stage of life? She didn't know. But Chris's adamant rejection forced her to protect it. She took a deep breath to try to calm herself. What was she going to do?

Through the window, she watched the moonlight above the trees, a gnawing worry in her gut when he moved close and wrapped his arms around her. As he kissed her behind her ear, he whispered, "Good night," and she exhaled and fell asleep.

Chapter 9
1980

The January wind howled and cold air pushed its way into the apartment behind Trevor, bringing Chris to a shiver on the den couch. Draped among the cushions, staring at the television but not seeing it, he listened to his roommate drop his heavy coat onto a chair, grab a can of soda from the fridge and walk into the den.

If it were anyone else, Chris would have taken refuge in his bedroom to avoid a conversation. But this was Trevor, his best friend, who for the first time since freshman year, he hadn't spoken to the entire month they were on break.

"When'd you get back?"

"Last night," Chris said, not looking at Trevor.

"How was your break?"

Chris shrugged. "Interesting."

Trevor sat on the couch. "Where's Olivia?"

"Her place." Chris tried not to dwell on Olivia's low mood the past few days. She'd been quiet all morning and asked Chris to take her back to her suite before lunch. They always spent Sundays together. It was four o'clock in the afternoon, and he missed her.

Trevor stared at Chris, who watched a mindless sitcom until it was over.

"So, I'm guessing you told your parents?"

Chris shut the TV. "My father threatened to cut me off if I married her."

"What do you mean cut you off? School?" Trevor said.

"Everything. Spending money, tuition, rent. All of it."

Trevor shook his head. "Wow. What are you going to do?"

Chris looked at his friend as if he asked him if he still believed in Santa Claus. "I'm going to marry her."

"What will you do for money?"

"He won't do it. He's bluffing."

"Did you tell Olivia?"

Chris bit his lip. "She was with me. At the house. He said things in front of her." The scene was still so fresh in his mind. Olivia had taken a bus to Boston the week after Christmas so they could be together when they told his parents of their plans. Then they were going to Long Island together to tell her mother. His father raged at them before they stormed out of the house. *You're going to give up your life for this...girl who let herself get in trouble? She's trapping you! Don't you see it?* Olivia had visibly shrunk next to him and at that moment, Chris hated his father. His mother stood impotently in the room, saying nothing. He hated her, too. Olivia cried all the way back to the motel and begged Chris to call his mother before they left for Long Island. He refused.

"Shit," Trevor said.

Chris pulled himself from the couch as if his parents were on his shoulders, pressing him down. "She's upset. She won't talk."

"I'll have Dana try. Maybe she'll open up. You know, girls talk to each other."

Chris nodded. "Okay." He walked to his bedroom.

"Chris?"

He paused at his bedroom door.

"I've met your dad. Not an easy guy." Trevor looked around the apartment, and Chris knew what he was thinking. Their new leather couch and the large television were purchased without thought by Chris's parents. His bank account was replenished regularly. "I think you should reconsider," Trevor said.

Chris walked into his room without answering.

He lay on his bed and stared at the ceiling, reliving the scene over again, cringing every time he played back the insults and degrading comments his father made about Olivia. They stood in the living room, as defendants before a judge, in front of the roaring fire in the fireplace he once could stand in, flanked by oversized fieldstones. Fury filled him as he remembered how Olivia tried to pull her hand from his to separate herself from him to take the onslaught alone.

He'd stormed out of the house, pulling her with him as his father's threats trailed behind, his mother's spineless, muted support of her husband weighing on him. He couldn't console her back at the motel, and at one point, she stopped speaking when he refused to call his mother, though Olivia begged. The flight back to New York was quiet, and Olivia visibly calmed down when they pulled into her driveway and saw her mother waiting at the door of her small house. Janine Carson took one look at her daughter and pulled her close. Chris could see immediately the bond between the two women, something he never shared with his own, distant parents.

They sat Janine down in the living room and delivered the same news and plans as they did at Chris's parents' house. The difference between their upbringings was evident as they sat in the old, tired room, on a couch that had seen the better part of Olivia's life, surrounded by walls that had not been updated in decades, if at all. He wanted to stand up and absorb the pictures on the walls of Olivia in different stages of her childhood, but knew he wouldn't move from her side. What had Olivia thought, he wondered, when he brought her to his home, through the wide oak door that opened into the expansive Terra cotta-tiled foyer beneath the twenty-foot ceiling, past the library and to the den, where they confronted his parents and found out just how cruel they could be? He turned his head to take in the modest space. This place was filled with little more than the furniture they sat on, but it oozed love and Chris embraced it, and Janine, immediately.

When Olivia finished talking, she took a deep breath and waited. She held Chris's hand, squeezing it, as her other hand clutched a homemade quilt that draped the couch.

Janine looked steadily at Chris. Finally, she spoke. "Well, it's certainly a most interesting introduction."

"I'm sorry we're dumping this on you this way," Chris said.

Janine moved her gaze back and forth between the young couple. "I'm guessing by my daughter's face when you got here that your parents aren't as supportive as you'd hoped."

Olivia looked at Chris and pressed her lips together, trying to keep from breaking down. She looked so despondent he promised himself at that moment he would never let her down again, would never let anyone hurt her.

"They'll come around," he said.

Janine nodded, staring at Olivia. "They want you to finish school, I imagine, get a good job."

He nodded. "Yes, ma'am."

"And yet, here you are, still wanting to get married, still wanting to have this baby."

"Mom." Olivia let Chris's hand go and reached for her mother's. "What are you thinking?"

Janine dropped her head in thought before bringing her focus back to her daughter. "I'm worried."

"Please don't."

"Mrs. Carson, I promise you I will take care of your daughter and your grandchild. All I want is to make her happy. We'll get our degrees, we'll do everything we set out to do."

"Mom, this is just a minor setback." It was a whisper.

Janine gave an abbreviated smile. "I'm not sure you know what you're getting into, but whatever you need from me..." She shrugged, and Olivia reached over to hug her as Chris exhaled in relief. They stayed with Janine for three nights and returned to school in time for the second semester to begin. Even with her mother's support and on a stomach full of thick pancakes, Olivia was reserved on the drive back. Whenever he asked if she was okay, she smiled and nodded. And then she asked him to drop her directly at her dorm, and he felt scared for the first time since he learned they were pregnant. He called his brother, Brian, with whom he had a strained relationship already and who lived with his wife in Maine, asking him to appeal to their parents for support. But Brian, six years older, agreed with their father and the conversation ended in a fiery exchange of words.

Chris ignored the knock on his door at nine o'clock the following morning. From under his pillow, he heard another set of raps on the wood, harder than before, in quicker succession.

"Go away."

Trevor leaned his mouth to the doorjamb. "It's Dana on the phone. She wants to talk to you."

Chris opened his door, wearing boxers and nothing else. His eyes burned as he reached for the phone on the table.

"Hey, Dana." His voice was raspy from no sleep. He listened to the receiver and looked at Trevor as blood drained from his face. Without a word, he gave the phone back to his housemate and closed the bedroom door.

Minutes later, he emerged dressed in jeans and sweatshirt, his hair still a mess, two-day growth on his jaw. He was heading out the door when Trevor stopped him.

"Dude! Wait!"

Chris held the door open and turned to him, desperate.

"Brush your teeth. The extra minute won't make a difference."

"Won't it?" But he ran to the bathroom anyway.

Four minutes later he was accelerating through town, dodging snow drifts and fishtailing across the road, swearing to himself, cursing his father, cursing his situation, until he finally pulled into the parking lot of Planned Parenthood. With the car barely in park, he jumped out and ran to the entrance, pulled the door open and threw himself inside.

He brought a whoosh of cold air in with him and found himself in the waiting room of the clinic. The receptionist behind the counter looked up from what she was doing and stood, perhaps afraid of the crazy man who just ran into their office. He worked to catch his breath, panting, and turned to find Olivia sitting alone among the row of plastic chairs. She gasped when she saw him.

"What are you doing?" he said.

"How did you know I was here?"

"Dana."

She shook her head and whispered something to herself.

He walked to her and pulled her to stand. "Come on. You're coming with me."

She yanked her arm back from his grip. "No. I'm not. Please go. Chris, I mean it. I'll call you later."

A nurse entered the waiting room. "Is everything all right here?"

"Yes."

"No."

They answered simultaneously. The nurse lifted her eyebrows in question. "Are you okay?" she asked Olivia.

Olivia looked at Chris and to the nurse. She nodded, and the nurse backed away and through the door, leaving them alone.

Olivia's eyes welled. "Please go."

"Why are you doing this? I thought you wanted this baby."

"I'm afraid. Your father—"

"Forget him. This is about you and me."

"No. It's about this baby. If we don't have your parents' blessing, I'm not sure I can live with myself. They're your parents, Chris. They hate me." Olivia took a breath and tried to calm herself. "I don't know if we can do this on our own. I have nothing. I'm here on a grant. My mother has nothing."

Chris pulled her down to sit and took a chair next to her. "Listen to me. I love you. We're having a baby. We'll work it out. Please don't do this to me."

"Your parents," she said.

"Fuck them."

She shook her head. "Your father will completely cut you off. He said he won't acknowledge our marriage or the baby. How can you live with that?"

Chris took a deep breath. A regret he'd always live with would be that he took her home with him to make their announcement. He should have known better. His father was inflexible, cold and driven. But he couldn't change that now. He could only change the present.

"Olivia, listen to me. If my father—or anyone—makes me choose between them and you, I choose you."

She leaned her head into his shoulder, and he put his arm around her. "I choose you," he whispered again.

She sniffed and lifted her face to his. She looked so forlorn, he hurt.

"Do you want this baby?"

She nodded.

"So do I. Can we go now?"

Chapter 10
October 2010

Olivia drove to Dana's on Saturday. The foliage was in full form as she pulled into the quarter-mile long driveway that led up to the expansive property. She had been coming here for the past seventeen years, when Dana and Trevor finally moved onto Long Island from Westchester, and she never felt less than enthralled at the enormity and elegance of the house. She and Chris couldn't believe their good fortune when their friends told them about the move. They were sick of the ninety-minute drive to Scarsdale, limiting the visits to only a handful of times each year. Now only thirty minutes and a very distinctive zip code separated her from her college friend, and they got together often.

Dana answered the thick door in her leggings and sweater, holding a beer.

"Just in time for happy hour," she said, hugging Olivia. She smelled of Angel perfume and fabric softener.

"It's two o'clock."

Dana looked at the enormous clock over her mantle from where they stood in the foyer. "Hmph. So, it is. Would you like a beer?"

Olivia shook her head and held out the pie she made earlier. "Here, as requested."

Dana lifted the still warm pecan pie to her nose and inhaled dramatically. "L-o-v-e. Thank you. Come inside. If you won't have a beer, I'll make you coffee."

"Tea, please." She followed Dana into the kitchen and sat at the end of the island while her friend filled a teapot with water. "It's so quiet in here. And so clean," Olivia said.

Dana moved to the stove. "Maria just left." All three of her children were in college. Still, she employed Maria, house-cleaner extraordinaire.

Olivia looked around the kitchen, the table for twelve that sat in the alcove surrounded by windows, the pictures along the wall depicting family vacations and stages of youth, and then back to Dana, who had finished her beer, opened another one and took out a mug.

"What a departure from the chaos of only a few years ago—who's got a lacrosse game, or a basketball game or dance, who'll be home for dinner, how many friends are they bringing…" Dana leaned on the island across from Olivia. "Who's sleeping over, whose heart is broken, and on and on."

"I miss it," Olivia said.

The tea kettle started to whine. Dana reached the stove before it went into a full-fledged howl. "Not me." She stood still and put her hand to her ear. "Can you hear it?"

Olivia straightened and listened. "I hear nothing."

"That's right. Bliss." Dana poured the water, letting the steam caress her face. As usual, she wore little makeup so nothing would melt off her skin.

The tea was made, the pie was cut, and Dana sat next to Olivia. "How's Nick?"

"I think he's okay."

Dana took a bite of pie and washed it down with a pull from her bottle. "That was fucked up."

"I know. That drive up there took years off my life. But things seemed to have settled down."

"I always thought Patrick would be the one to do something like that," Dana said. "Not Nick."

"You never know."

"True." She sipped her beer. "How was lunch with Ella the other day? What's new with the pregnancy quest?"

"They're going to adopt a baby," Olivia said.

"They're giving up?"

"Yes."

"Poor kids."

Olivia's eyes welled. "I hope this whole thing goes smoothly for her. I just want her to have what she wants."

"She will. Good things happen to good people."

Olivia spit out a harsh laugh. "Yeah, right."

"I know. I'm trying to be positive."

"She wants it so bad and she did everything right—good grades, school, marriage, good job, the whole thing. I had sex at nineteen with my boyfriend and dropped out of college."

"You have nothing to do with what your daughter's body is capable of. Stop beating yourself up. And you're a good mother, even if you were a baby when you became one." Dana frowned at her friend. "Please don't make me give you these shitty pep talks. Don't feel sorry for her. Be happy she has options. She's going to be an amazing mother. That is something you'll know you taught her. That's what is in your control."

"I'm pregnant." Olivia hadn't expected to blurt it quite so bluntly, but she couldn't hold the news any longer.

Dana froze, the forkful of pie halfway to her mouth. She put the fork gently back onto her plate and stared at Olivia.

"How can that be? Are you sure?"

Olivia flushed with anger. "Why is that the first reaction? Chris said the same thing. Yes. I am sure. I'm still ovulating. We have sex. We stopped using contraception years ago when I couldn't get pregnant again." She dropped her head and took a deep breath.

Dana sat wordless.

"I'm sorry," Olivia said, recovering. "I'm emotional and having a hard time with this myself."

Dana put her hand on Olivia's arm. "I'm just surprised."

Olivia snorted. "You think you're surprised. We tried to get pregnant for years after …" She tilted her head to Dana, who closed her eyes and nodded. "And I thought it just wasn't possible. With the problems I had with my deliveries, I decided to accept the two miracles we'd been given." Her eyes welled. "But now…I've been given another chance to have another baby." She shrugged, unable to say more.

"You want this baby?"

"I don't know. I don't have a choice."

"You always have a choice."

Olivia sat back in her chair and Dana dropped her hand. "I don't know if I can do it," Olivia said.

Dana leaned forward. "That's why a doctor does it for you."

"Please don't tell your kids. Or Trevor."

"I won't. How can you even consider having it? My God, Olivia, we did it. We're done."

"I know. A part of me wants to do it again. But the other part of me, the rational part, says I'm too old."

"And Chris?"

Olivia shook her head.

Dana nodded. "Okay, if you won't consider an abortion, would you consider giving it up to a younger couple?"

There was no way she would be able to carry this baby and give it away to a stranger. "No."

Dana stared at her half-eaten pie. "You'll be buying Depends and diapers at the same time."

"You're not helping."

"You'll be teaching her how to tie her shoes and she can get you your teeth." When her teasing was met with silence, Dana said, "Let's look at the bright side. Didn't you think for a minute something was wrong with you? It could be worse. You could be sick. Though I'm not sure that's worse than this."

Yes, Olivia thought, this was true. This pregnancy was being discussed as if it was a horrible disease they needed to deal with, when in fact, they were discussing new life. Was there anything more life-affirming than a new baby?

Dana inhaled suddenly and put her hand to her mouth. "Ella," she whispered. "Cruel irony. Poor kid." She tsked to herself, grabbed her beer, and looked at Olivia. "Would you consider giving the baby to her?"

Olivia nodded through tears. "I don't know if I'm strong enough."

Chapter 11
1980

They were married during spring break in a small church near the campus with her mother, their roommates, and the rest of the band as witnesses. Janine treated them to lunch at the college diner, an offer that stretched her already thin wallet. Chris's parents and brother followed through with their threat and refused to acknowledge their union by boycotting the wedding. Chris, fearful this would happen, had withdrawn the maximum amount from the ATM twice before finding the account was empty. He had $600 to his name.

Aside from missing his whole family, the small ceremony was lovely. Olivia wore a simple cream pants suit she borrowed from Dana's sister and carried a meager spray of roses. They decided to spend their honeymoon in Chris's apartment off campus. Four days exclusively for them while the rest of the students were home relaxing or in Daytona Beach, dancing on bars, drinking too much and switching bed partners like clothes.

When classes resumed, Olivia stayed in Chris's apartment with his roommates until they took their finals.

"Do you think we're making a mistake?" she asked him one night. He had just received a letter from his father's secretary stating that the balance of the current year's tuition would fall directly onto Chris. His father had relinquished his payments to the school, as promised. It was a ten thousand dollar debt they hadn't planned on.

He kissed the tip of her nose. "No. We're going to be a family. I can't wait. And we'll be young parents. We'll go to Europe in our thirties. We'll have our whole lives together to do what we want."

After the end of the semester, they returned to Long Island and found a basement apartment for $350 a month. Janine offered for them to stay with her, but her place was tiny and Chris declined her invitation. Despite being cut off financially from his father, Chris promised Janine and Olivia he would take care of her. Within a week of their move, he managed to get a job with a construction company and would work there while looking for a position more suitable to his strengths and wallet.

"I like it like this," Olivia said. They lay on a mattress directly on the floor of the apartment, one month in, surrounded by the slight paint odor coming off the walls. The clock struck midnight.

"Should we not look for furniture?"

She sighed. "I guess we should. Where will people sit when they come to visit?"

"Who's coming over? We live in one room."

"Maybe your mother will come around and want to meet the baby. I know mine will be here."

"They don't need to sit. If we make them too comfortable they'll never leave."

She took Chris's hand and placed it on the side of her stomach, holding it there until the baby moved. He gasped as they felt the kick clear through her skin.

"Does it hurt?"

Olivia shook her head. "It feels…weird. Like having a small alien in there."

"Do you think she'll look like you?" he whispered in the dark.

"What makes you think it's a girl?"

"I can only see a girl in my mind."

"Spooky."

He chuckled softly and pulled her to him. She fit perfectly into the curve of his body, like God made them to fit only each other, she often thought. He ran his fingers down her back, barely touching her skin, sending a volt straight to her core.

"What if something happens?" she said.

His hand paused. "What do you mean?"

"I don't know. I drank before I knew I was pregnant. What if I lose it? Or what if something's wrong?"

"Nothing's going to go wrong. You're young. You're healthy. It will be fine."

"I hope so. I just worry. I worry a lot."

"Don't."

Silence. "Are you sure you're making the right decision about school?"

He continued to lightly trace her arm, giving her goose bumps.

"I'm sure," he said. "We need money more than I need a degree right now. After the baby is born and when we're settled, I'll go back. I heard some companies pay for their employees to go to school at night. Once I get a real job, it will work out." He leaned over and kissed her. "You can go back too, once you're ready. We'll both finish. It'll be fine. This is just a little detour."

Chris's optimism lifted her spirits. She wanted to believe they could do everything they wanted. How hard could one baby be? There were two of them.

"When do you go back to the doctor?" he asked.

She put her hand on his chest, fingers through his soft hair and felt better. "Three weeks. He knows what we're having." She lifted her head to look at him but could only see his profile in the dark. "Do you want to know?"

He shook his head. "I already know. He doesn't have to tell me."

"I hope she looks like you," she said. She felt him smile.

Dear Mrs. Bennet,

I hope you and Mr. Bennet are well. I just wanted to let you know that Chris and I are living on Long Island. We found a small ~~basement~~ apartment in a town called Glen Cove. It's a pretty town in Nassau County right near the water. Chris found a job right away working for a construction company until he can find a better paying position at a corporation. He's hoping not to have to commute into Manhattan but we'll see. As for myself, I haven't yet found work but know there's a job for me right around the corner. I wouldn't be surprised if I get hired before this letter reaches you. Our main priority now is to cover the rent and make a home for the baby, due the end of July.

Chris still plays the keyboard and is looking for a new band. As disappointed as he was to leave Trevor and the others, he answered an ad for a band needing a keyboardist and is scheduled to meet with the singer next week. So, all is looking up!

I've enclosed our address and phone number with the hope that you'll visit. Or call. I've also included a photo from our wedding. It was an intimate ceremony with only a few friends. You were missed.

Please know I love your son with all that I am.

Love, Olivia

Chapter 12
October 2010

"What if something goes wrong? You're well past normal age," Chris said. He was sifting through the mail when she walked in from work. On rainy days, Chris got home from work before her. She loved rainy days.

"What's normal anymore? People are starting late."

He held up a letter with a frown. "No one who is receiving AARP mail is getting pregnant. Think about it. We'll get into movies at the senior rate and then pick up our kid from middle school."

"Sounds like a good day to me."

"We won't be able to get up and go anymore. We'll lose the freedom we've enjoyed for so long."

Freedom? They were still working full-time. "Yes, but look at what we'll have."

"Debt. Responsibility. Sleepless nights."

She thought of Nick. "We already have sleepless nights."

They made dinner side by side. Tonight, spinach salad and lightly fried haddock. The television was on over the counter. Quietly they listened to the news, another mugging in Brooklyn, another attempted rape in Queens.

"Why do we want to bring another child into this world? Look at what we're doing to each other." Chris pointed the knife he held to the screen, where the story moved to a random act of violence in East New York, to a woman pushed off a subway platform.

"*We're* not doing this. And look, two good Samaritans jumped down to save her. There is good in the world, too."

"Less of it."

"That's what the media wants you to believe. Tragedy is more popular than reporting the poverty level is lower than it's ever been across the world."

The reporter segued into another bombing in Europe. Olivia flinched.

"People think nothing of blowing themselves up just to hurt others. How can we protect our children from that?" Chris mumbled.

"Right now, I'm working to protect this child from you."

***

Olivia stopped by the mall the following day and found herself wandering into the baby section of Macy's, touching the tiny onesies, the mini hats and socks. If they went through with this, would she want to know the gender? They didn't want to know when Ella came. Nor with Nick.

They'd have to start again. Dresser, changing table, crib and bedding, diapers, bathtub, bottles. This time she'd know everything they'd need. When she was pregnant with Ella, they had no idea what they were in for or what they needed. It would be easier now, wouldn't it?

She picked up a small set of overalls with a dog-shaped pocket. Puberty. She sighed. Nick was tough, always pushing the limits, testing her. As a toddler, he was temperamental and stubborn, and she struggled with him. As he grew, so did the problems. Chris was the strong one, the enforcer. She hated to see her children upset. Did she want to go through that again? Drinking, drugs, always teaching, always worrying. But she loved her son more than she thought possible. As much as Ella. She had enough love to share.

"Do you need any help?"

Olivia looked up. She'd been petting a pink elephant while lost in her thoughts.

"I'm okay. Thank you."

The saleswoman nodded and walked away. She put the stuffed animal back and sauntered through the clothes racks, through the soft, pastel pajamas and bibs, mini sweat suits, sneakers that fit on her thumb. But a baby. A baby was fresh and new and beautiful. That would never get old. Her phone rang.

"Hello?"

"Mom? It's me." Ella. Olivia glanced around, feeling foolish. In a haze of guilt, she moved away to the neighboring electronics department.

"Hi honey. What's going on?"

"We were wondering what you and Dad are doing on Saturday. We want to have you for dinner."

"Saturday? I think we're free." And if they weren't, they'd make themselves available.

"Great. How about six? Can you bring your pecan pie?"

Olivia left the store. What was she thinking? What if Chris never came around? How would she convince a man who didn't want to be convinced? She climbed into the car and stared out the windshield. Was she being fair? To him? To herself? Her shoulders slumped. To her daughter?

She started the car. This was just what they needed, a night with their daughter and son-in-law. Ella could bring Chris out of any funk. She was the light of his life.

They served chicken Française proudly on their five-year-old china, recently unwrapped and used. Marco, as adept in the kitchen as their daughter, preened under their accolades. Olivia spoke the truth when telling him she'd not tasted a better Française in any restaurant.

Ella lifted her brows and smiled at him. "I told him the very same thing."

Marco reached for her hand and Ella took a deep breath. "Mom. Dad. We want to talk with you about our plans." Together since twenty-one, married at twenty-four, Ella had found her perfect partner in Marco.

Chris picked up the napkin from his lap and dropped it on the plate, a sign he was finished or had lost his appetite. He glanced at Olivia and leaned back in his chair.

"We spoke to our counselor." Ella looked at Marco. "A lot, and decided on a domestic adoption." Back to her parents. "We considered China or Russia, but there are babies here in the US who need parents."

Chris cleared his throat. "Okay."

The four of them sat at the table. Olivia watched Marco's thumb protectively rubbing Ella's hand, which was squeezing his.

"There are a lot of things to consider," she went on, "like non-identified or identified adoption, do we want a newborn or an older child, same race, etc."

"Non-identified?" Olivia said.

Marco spoke. "We have to decide if we agree that the baby, he or she, can find their birth parents when it's older. Sometimes they want to know who their biological parents are. The birth mother has to add that stipulation."

"How much will this cost?" Chris asked.

"We can handle it, Dad. Thank you."

Olivia touched Chris's shoulder and when he looked at her, the pain she saw left her breathless. They hadn't discussed the possibility of giving their daughter their baby. Something Ella wanted so desperately. And they were considering their options of not keeping it. This was the lowest point of her life. Chris's expression mirrored her thoughts.

"Dad? What's wrong? This is a good thing," Ella said quietly. Her eyes were full, but she smiled.

Chris cleared his throat but didn't speak. Olivia squeezed his shoulder. "Honey, we're happy for you. I think it's wonderful that you're adopting. Your baby is waiting for you," she said. Marco's smile tore at Olivia's heart. Ella sniffed and stood. "I made coffee. I'll go get the pie."

The drive home was quiet. Chris stared at the road ahead, and Olivia turned away from him, glossing over the passing houses until they were on the parkway.

"I'm worried about her," Chris finally said. "I hope this works out. I'm not sure what to think."

Olivia nodded, remembering Penny Harding, a high school friend who had gone through the whole adoption process only to learn the birth mother changed her mind at the final hour and decided to keep her baby. The Hardings ended up adopting siblings from China two years later.

Their Ella. Olivia could recall with distinct precision the moment she first saw her. She was two days old, wrapped tight in a swaddle blanket, her eyes open and staring at her mother, who was exhausted and swollen and crying. Together they grew up and through trial and error, figured out their roles.

What would it be like to do it all over again, knowing everything they knew? All the mistakes they made could be erased. It would be like having a do-over. The potty-training, the homework, school events, sports and concerts, college applications. Oh Lord, those applications were the bane of her existence for months. What would college cost in twenty years?

"Should we consider giving the baby to Ella?" Olivia said.

Chris exhaled and shook his head. "I don't want you to go through with it, Liv. And would Ella want to raise a baby as her own, knowing it's her sister or brother? I just don't know."

They got ready for bed without speaking. Olivia listened to Chris's frustrated breaths in the dark.

"What is it?" she asked.

"I hate the position we're in."

"Her situation won't change, no matter what we do. Our being pregnant isn't the reason our daughter can't have a baby."

She was met with silence.

"It's wrong," he said.

Olivia squeezed her eyes. Hugging herself in bed beside Chris, who'd long ago fallen asleep, she felt lonely. Adrift on her own, she missed his enthusiasm and optimism with a painful longing. She remembered conversations and incidents from their past with a clarity that surprised her. She should be foggy now, shouldn't she? Instead, old forgotten conversations came back to her in a flood of detail. Reliving them in her mind brought her peace.

She rolled over and tried to sleep, but dreams eluded her. She touched Chris's cheek with her palm and, eyes still closed, he instinctively pulled her toward him. With a sigh, her breath began to match his, and she finally drifted off.

Chapter 13
1980

He walked in after work, his tool belt hanging heavy and low on his hips, to find Olivia sitting at the table. The homeowners had hung four cabinets and installed a half-sized fridge in the corner of the basement and called it a kitchen. There was no oven, but they had a microwave and a small stove top. The table was the segue into their "living room" which melded into their sleeping area, hidden behind a tarp she found at her mother's. As tight as it was, Olivia felt it was cozy and a good start for them on their own.

She had laid out the place settings and a roasted chicken sat in the center of the table, creamed corn on the side.

His happy smile upon seeing her drooped when she looked up. "What is it?"

She picked at her placemat. "I'm not going to find a job with this." She pointed to the distended stripes of her shirt where it was pushed out from her round belly. "I went to eleven places today to fill out applications, and they all told me they'd call." She looked up to him, her eyes brimming. "Their faces were so clear. They're not going to deal with a pregnant girl. Who would?"

Chris put down his tool belt and knelt beside her.

"They kept asking me how old I was, as if I were some knocked-up fifteen-year-old high school student."

"Instead of a nineteen-year-old college student?" Chris said.

She rolled her eyes and sighed. "And I can't really get anywhere outside of town without a car. I've almost covered the bus route."

"Okay. So, don't look. Just focus on the baby and we'll worry about it after." He looked around their tiny apartment kitchen. "We can manage for a while on what I'm making."

She ran her fingers through his thick hair. He closed his eyes and leaned into her hand as she scratched his scalp. He looked exhausted, sunburned and dirty and he still came home with a smile, optimistic about their future. His father had completely cut him off, and Chris never once complained he'd taken on too much. She had to be strong and keep going for him. For their baby. Tomorrow, she'd get up and continue to look until she found a job. He opened his eyes and looked at her half-mast. "Don't worry, Liv. I'll bring in another hundred dollars playing with the guys at Forester's." He'd met with the band a few days ago, and Olivia thought he hadn't gotten it since they'd received no word.

She blinked. "You got it?"

He wiped the tear that escaped, running down her cheek. "We got it."

She waited up for him every Thursday night, wanting to hear about the gig, how the songs were received, the size of the crowd. Each week, they gained more notice and the bar was getting full. They talked into the early morning, still able to recover after just a few hours of sleep and make it through the day. After his music, they talked about the baby.

"I'll read to her every day," she said.

"I'll teach her to play piano."

"Where are we putting a piano?" Silence. "She'll have long fingers like you."

"And your eyelashes."

"But your eyes."

They made love carefully now, aware of another being in their midst, knowing they'd have to stop soon and dreading the thought.

Her mother threw her a small baby shower with help from Dana and her high school friends and no help from their in-laws who still refused to accept Chris's decision. Olivia called Mrs. Bennet from their apartment amid the shower gifts after her mother left. As she suspected, the phone rang into the answering machine. At the tone, she took a breath and began to talk.

"Mrs. Bennet, this is Olivia. I wanted to say hello and tell you things are good here. The baby is growing and will be here in seven weeks. I hope. Chris is working hard and seems really excited." She heard a click and paused. "Mrs. Bennet? Is that you?" For a moment, she thought her mother-in-law had picked up the phone but heard nothing and exhaled. "Okay, well, I hope to talk to you—" The machine beeped and cut her off, and she hung up the phone with regret.

Chris walked in from work to find his wife sitting in the middle of the room surrounded by baby paraphernalia and wrapping paper.

"Does one small baby need all of this stuff?" he asked, dropping his heavy belt at the door.

"How would I know? All I know is we don't have to buy any of it." She bit her inner cheek. "Look at it all."

Chris scratched his head. He leaned over and picked up a shapeless fabric. "What's this?"

"It's a sling."

"What are you supposed to do with it?"

She shrugged and started to cry.

"Hey." He climbed over the bassinet and small mound of clothes to get to her. "What's the matter?"

"I'm overwhelmed." She wiped her eyes. "What am I doing? What are we doing?"

"What are you talking about?" He sat down next to her.

"I'm going to be twenty-years-old. I'm supposed to be

starting my senior year. I don't know how to be a mother." Forlorn, she looked up at him. "What if I'm terrible?"

He smoothed her hair back, tucking a thick piece behind her ear. He looked at the delicate gold-plated hoop in her lobe and touched it. "You're going to be great, babe. You have an enormous capacity to love. This baby is lucky." He put his finger under her chin and turned her face to see him. "I'm lucky."

In bed, he rubbed her belly.

"A genie won't come out of there, you know."

"Something's going to come out of there." He smiled. "I can't wait to meet her. I'm going to sing to her." He kissed Olivia's lips, then her belly. "She's going to be us."

Olivia ran her fingers through his hair while he kissed her bump. "Not me. I'm afraid. Afraid of the whole thing."

"Don't be, please. I'll take care of us. One of my co-workers said John gives raises at the end of the year. We'll save everything we can. We'll get a little house with a swing in the back, one of those big wooden ones that hangs from an elm."

"And a playroom for her to play. And her own room."

"Our own room." He rolled toward her. "You know, for S-E-X."

She giggled. "You don't have to spell it out yet. She's not even here."

"I'm practicing."

After, they lay spooning, his skin warm on hers. "Where do you want to go tonight?" she said into the dark.

She felt his breath on her hair. "Let's go back to Paris."

"Okay." She thought a moment and began. "We're walking the cobblestone streets in Montmartre. The rain just stopped, so the air is warm and moist and my hair is frizzy." He chuckled. "Of course, I'm hungry, so I make you stop in a boulangerie, and we're leaning forward against the glass protecting the freshly baked loaves of bread, drunk on the aroma until an old woman walks out from the kitchen. Through broken French and English, we understand each other enough that she wraps a loaf in a paper bag and hands it to me. Then she puts her finger up, asking us to wait, and runs back into the kitchen. She returns holding two hot, chocolate croissants and pushes them to us, no charge, and we gratefully say, '*Merci*' over and over until we are outside."

"Why did she give us the croissants?" Chris asked.

"Because she sees how happy we are. Then we take our goodies up the road, past the children who are playing in the school courtyard."

"Where are we walking?"

She smiled against her pillow. "We're going to see the Sacré-Coeur, of course."

He groaned. "Another church."

Last night they toured Notre-Dame. Chris had started to complain until she stood in reverence in the holy house with her hand down his pants to quiet his complaints. Of course, she would never do that should they find themselves in the awesome structure, but she took imaginary freedoms during their bedroom trips.

"Chris, Europe is filled with churches. Just wait until we get to Rome."

He tightened his hold on her. "I'll just keep wearing easily accessible sweatpants," he whispered, and she giggled.

"Anyway," she went on, "we decide to sit on a wall in front of Sacré-Coeur, because it's so beautiful, and eat our warm bread and croissants."

"I'm going to be thirsty."

"I know. Therefore, we're going to walk back down into town and stop at a café where we'll share a bottle of white and a plate of fresh cheese."

He didn't respond.

"Chris?"

"Wait, I'm still enjoying the view of the church."

"I love you."

***

Olivia cradled the sleeping newborn in her arms when her mother walked into the hospital room holding a small package. Chris was napping in the upright pleather chair beside the bed. She tilted her head up to meet Janine's kiss before her mother very lightly kissed her granddaughter.

"How are you feeling?"

Olivia smiled. "Better. Sore and tired, but much better."

Janine looked at Chris passed out, his head lolling to the side.

"He's exhausted. The nurse told me he stayed up all night and wouldn't leave. They let him hold her for hours."

"He's already a good father," Janine whispered.

"The nurses told me you were here with him. You must be tired too, Mom."

"Not too tired to see this little one." She placed the gift on the bed and reached for the infant. "I brought you something."

"You've done enough already. I got most of what I needed at the shower."

Janine rocked the baby and walked to the window. "This is not something you need."

Olivia opened the box to find a small quilted blanket divided into four sections, each a different color. In each corner was a small heart sewn in.

"It's for the baby," Janine said as Olivia rubbed her hand over the different fabrics. Her hand stopped on a pale-yellow cotton square.

"I brought you home in that blanket."

Olivia looked up.

"It was a little darker than what it is now. So soft, and against your skin…" She sighed at the memory. "You slept with it your first year. And now your daughter will have a piece of it too."

Olivia stared at the small quilt as Janine went on.

"Below that is the shirt I wore when you spoke your first word." She paused when Olivia looked up at her with tears in her eyes. "The navy square is from the shirt Chris said he was wearing when you met. And the pink…"

"Is for Ella. Mom, I don't know what to say."

Janine leaned her head to the infant and inhaled deeply.

"What was my first word?" Olivia asked.

"Vodka."

They both started to laugh and woke Chris up. He rubbed his eyes and stood, embarrassed. "Hi, Janine."

Janine gave him a small wave and returned to the baby.

"I'm going to stretch my legs. I'll be right back." He kissed his wife and left the room.

The women were quiet.

"That was quite a scare you gave us," Janine said.

"I felt so good throughout the pregnancy. I don't know why that happened. I'd never heard of anyone hemorrhaging during childbirth." She pulled her thin blanket up to her engorged chest. "Not that I knew much about labor before Tuesday."

Janine sat down in the chair Chris had vacated minutes ago. She cradled the infant easily.

"How long was I out?" Olivia asked.

"Twenty-two hours. Do me a favor, don't do that to your husband again. I've never seen someone so terrified." She handed the fussing bundle back to her mother. "He was a shell of himself. He clutched that baby like she was his lifeline."

Olivia pulled her cotton gown down, exposing a breast, and worked to fit the tiny, searching mouth over her nipple. The nurses had to feed Ella formula for the first feedings while Olivia was in recovery. Her breasts were hard, painful mounds when she was finally able to sit up slightly and feed her daughter. That was three feedings ago, and she felt better with each one.

"I'm so glad you're here, Mom."

Janine smiled. "Where else would I be?"

***

Dear Mrs. Bennet,

Enclosed is a picture of your new granddaughter, Ella Grace, at two days old. I missed her first day of life as there were some minor complications during delivery and I spent a full day in recovery, sleeping. The doctors joked it would be the last time I'd sleep so soundly for the next eighteen years, but I didn't share their jubilance. While I slept, I was told Chris held Ella for hours in my room, not wanting her to be alone, while he waited for me.

I'm so happy to report that Ella is a beautiful, healthy, seven-pound, six-ounce mound of pink, doughy flesh. As you can see in the picture, Chris is beside himself with pride. I think she already looks like him. Lucky girl.

By the time you receive this letter I will have been discharged from the hospital, so I wrote our address again below in case you misplaced my earlier letters. I would love to introduce you to your granddaughter.

Love,

Olivia

Chapter 14
October 2010

Olivia stood on line at the food store after work, holding her basket, waiting for the two people in front of her. A teen was paying for his sandwich and soda while Mrs. Johnson, the widow who lived across the street, slowly placed her items on the conveyor belt.

She lifted a clear bag containing two apples, a half dozen eggs, three yogurts, and two soup cans to the rolling belt. Olivia averted her eyes and swallowed her discomfort, trying not to wonder what this woman did all day alone.

She started to put her own items on the belt as Mrs. Johnson wrote a check and handed it to the cashier. Olivia was ignoring her when she heard the older woman say something.

"Hmm?" She finally turned to acknowledge the woman, as if she hadn't realized she was there. She was such a terrible actress and filled with shame.

"I said, how are you?"

"Oh, um, I'm good. Fine." She cleared her throat. "You?"

The woman nodded with a smile and walked away.

For years, Olivia had been focused on the day-to-day worries of raising their children and paying their bills, but now she had ample time, and it took some effort not to compare herself with Mrs. Johnson, who had been married, raising her own children for many years before finding herself at a grocery store buying two apples and three yogurts.

"Hi, Mrs. Bennet." The voice brought Olivia back to the cashier, a young waif she recognized from the neighborhood.

"Hi, honey." Her term for any person whose name escaped her. She could hardly keep up with the large circle of her children's friends.

The girl rang up and bagged her food while Olivia searched her wallet for her money.

"How is Nick doing?"

Olivia pressed the cash in her hand. "He's fine." She took some solace in the fact no one on Long Island heard about his recent brush with the law. Not yet, anyway.

"Please tell him Jess said hi."

Jessica. Right!

In the dusk-covered parking lot, she saw the older woman still in the lot, gently placing her two bags in her backseat. Olivia, holding three full bags in one hand, passed the car as Mrs. Johnson turned to wheel the empty cart back under the store awning.

"I'll do it," Olivia said, taking the cart from the woman. "These bags are too heavy for me. You're doing me a favor."

Mrs. Johnson smiled at her, knowing. "Thank you."

Several spots away, Olivia put her groceries in her car and returned the cart to the store. A young mother walked past her, holding donuts with one hand and pulling a crying toddler with the other, ignoring his screaming protests as he swung about like an angry rag doll. Olivia winced. That could be her in a few years. Would she have less patience, she wondered, or more?

Mrs. Johnson was finally pulling out of her spot when Olivia got into her car. All this time to buy food. Was this her big outing of the day? As she drove by the young woman who was now trying to lift the writhing child from the ground and place him in the minivan amid kicks and head-thrashing, Olivia thought of Nick. She missed him. She worried about him.

When she got home Chris walked into the kitchen, showered from work, as she put food away.

"We should visit Nick to see how he's doing."

Chris pulled an apple from the fridge. "Why don't you just call him?"

"I want to see him. I was thinking this weekend. I can take Friday off."

"As in two days from now? I can't. I just started a project in Ridge and need to be there on Saturday." He bit into the apple. "How do you know he's free?"

"I don't," she admitted. But when she called, Nick embraced the idea of a visit, and they made a plan.

She woke on Friday morning as Chris dressed for work.

"What time are you leaving?" He said.

She rubbed the sleep from her eyes. "After breakfast."

He watched her.

"Do you want to come? You can start your project on Monday," Olivia said.

"I'll stay here." He buttoned his shirt with a frown and left the room.

Olivia felt gut-punched. She stayed in bed and listened to him downstairs. At any other time, he would have pushed his start date back a few days to see their son, or have his foreman take his place. This weekend, he wanted to be alone. She swung her legs over the side of the bed and sat up.

Chris appeared in the bedroom doorway, holding her phone. "Gavin left two messages." He tossed the phone on the bed and walked out.

She sat in her car and hour later, a bag of snacks on the passenger seat. She went to enter the address in her GPS and saw it was already programmed. Chris. She backed out of the driveway.

After a stop at the office to meet with Gavin, she made it to Nick's apartment in seven hours, just in time for dinner.

Nick led her inside and disappeared with her small duffel.

"Are you hungry?" he asked, walking back into the room.

"Always. But first, I need the bathroom." She'd stopped twice on the way and had waited the last two hours to get here.

Nick had made pasta for her, *with jarred sauce*, he said, placing two bowls on the table.

"Where are your housemates?"

"Rod's home for the weekend and Dave is at his girlfriend's."

"You're here alone?"

"I'm not alone." He smiled. "You're here."

She reached over the small table and touched his temple. He had a small scar where he was stitched after the accident. He leaned back when she touched him, as if still embarrassed by what he'd done.

"Any trouble with that boy you hurt?"

"I hurt? He did way more damage than me."

"I mean, do you see him at all around campus?"

"No. I could go all of four years and never see some of these students. It's over, Mom. Let's move on."

She nodded. "So, what would you have done this weekend if I hadn't come up?"

"Not much. I keep it low key lately. Studied, gone to a quiet bar." He shrugged, shoveling food in his mouth.

"Do you want to go out tonight? I won't hold you up." She took a forkful of penne. "Or I can go with you."

Nick laughed. "That's what I want to do, go out drinking with my mother."

"I could be your D.D."

The smile dropped from his face. "I'm good, Mom. I don't feel like going out." He stood and refilled his bowl. "I'd like you to meet Melissa."

"Who?"

"My girlfriend. Melissa. Missy." He said.

The girl in the hospital, the one he'd avenged after she was violated behind the campus library. The reason he most likely wouldn't be home until Thanksgiving.

Nick waited for her response, his face an unreadable mask.

"I'd love to meet her," she said and filled with a mixture of love and fear as her son's face emoted relief.

After calling his girlfriend, Nick washed the dishes and cleaned the kitchen while Olivia stared in surprised awe at the spectacle. The phone rang, and Nick tilted his head toward the receiver, his hands still in sudsy water. "Can you get it? It's gonna be Dad anyway."

"How do you know?"

"Because you're here and your cell phone must be in your pocketbook."

Olivia lifted the receiver and laughed when she heard her husband's voice.

"See?" Nick said.

"What's so funny?" Chris asked.

"Your son knows you well."

There was a pause. "I just wanted to make sure you made it okay."

"I'm sorry. I got so caught up by the fact Nick made dinner, I wasn't thinking straight. I should have called."

"Nick, our son, made dinner?"

She laughed again, happy she'd decided to come this weekend. She needed to know, to see, that their son was okay after the way they left him last month, even though she would much rather Chris had been here with her. "Wait for it—he's washing dishes now."

"Okay Liv, don't make any sudden movements. Carefully work your way to the door and run. Someone's taken over our boy."

She sighed, relieved to hear some semblance of normalcy in Chris's voice.

Nick turned around. "Whatever he's saying, he'll pay for when I get home."

"Tell Nick I'll see him soon," Chris said and disconnected the call.

They sat in the den on two shabby sunken couches, Olivia under a thin blanket to ward off the evening chill.

"This room reminds me of your dad's apartment in college."

Nick looked around the room. "Does it?"

Olivia nodded. Chris and Trevor's furniture had been new, as was their television. Chris's parents bought them all their furnishings, but the aura was still a college home. Even with leather couches and state of the art media (for the time), young men lived there, and it felt like a comfortable bachelor dwelling you knew they wouldn't stay in for long. She felt nostalgic for those days.

"He lived with Uncle Trevor, right?"

"And one other guy who dropped off the radar."

Nick turned the television on, more as background noise since he didn't look at the screen.

"Have you talked to Ella?"

Nick shook his head. "What's up?"

"They're going to adopt a baby."

"No shit? They can't get pregnant?"

"No."

"They should just relax. What's the big deal about having kids?"

"Your sister wants a baby more than anything."

He glanced at the TV in thought. "I'll call her," he said, more to himself. Olivia didn't reply, grateful her children got along. After she and Chris were gone, they'd only have each other. And possibly a brother or sister, she thought, who most likely wouldn't have parents for more than twenty or thirty years. A wave of remorse swept over her, but she pushed it away just as Melissa walked into the apartment.

Nick jumped up as if on fire and ran to greet her. She clasped his hand when he walked her to the room to meet Olivia. She was nothing like Olivia envisioned—a petite beauty wearing a turtleneck and baggy jeans. Her auburn hair was pulled back in a ponytail, and no makeup covered her freckles, which creased on her nose when she smiled.

Chris was watching television in the den when Olivia walked in Sunday evening. She stood at the room entrance and leaned on the frame.

"How is he?" Chris asked from his seat.

She was momentarily thrown-off having expected him to greet her at the door with one of his bear hugs. Instead, he kept his eyes to the TV, his silent anger drowning all sound.

"He's good. Happy."

Chris nodded, held the remote up and switched the channel.

"I met Melissa." She tried to draw him into conversation.

"Who?"

"Nick's girlfriend. She spent the day with us yesterday."

"This is the one…"

"Yes," she interrupted. "Her."

Chris's eyes met hers. "What is she like?"

Olivia replayed pieces of the day in her mind, noting the way Nick and Melissa looked at each other, spoke softly, touched often. There was no doubt they were intimate. He called her Missy, affectionately, almost reverently, as if he spoke her name as a prayer. Olivia had never seen her son so taken with someone. They spent a few hours at the apartment on Friday evening and Olivia tried not to notice the regretful way they said good-bye at the end of the night. Her visit had cut into their time alone together. If she weren't there, Olivia knew Melissa would have spent the night.

"She's not what I expected but then, I didn't know what Nick's type was if you'd asked me. He never dated the same kind of girl."

Chris nodded.

"We went for a walk yesterday, more like an easy hike, at a nearby nature preserve. It was pretty. Melissa was shy at first but eventually loosened up enough to talk about her family.

She has two younger brothers—her parents are married. Her mom is a stay-at-home and her father owns a bar."

"Wonderful."

Olivia frowned. "She's bright. Reserved. Sounds driven. She talked a lot about trying to get into graduate school at a prestigious university. She studies biotech engineering."

"Did you talk about what happened last month?"

"No. They avoided the subject." Both seemed to have gotten past it. She'd taken them to dinner and tried to ignore their silent looks and constant hand-holding.

"So? What's the verdict on this Melissa?"

Olivia envied them the newness of their relationship, the beginning of it all. She thought a lot about the first year she and Chris spent together, how she watched him play in his band every week, anticipating the promise of their night together, making love, getting no sleep, not caring at all.

"Liv?" Chris nudged her from her thoughts.

"She reminds me of myself."

He waited.

"In love."

He stared at her.

"I'm going up," she said.

"Night."

With a heavy heart, she went upstairs and to bed.

Chapter 15

1985

Dear Mrs. Bennet,

I can't believe how fast time is passing. Tomorrow is Ella's first day of kindergarten already! She is so excited; her Hello Kitty backpack has been packed for three weeks. We have her clothes laid out for the morning so she won't feel nervous about catching the bus. Yes, she will be taking the bus. A new experience for all of us. I think Ella is most excited about meeting other girls her age. With Chris and I both working and Ella in full time summer camp, there was little opportunity for her to meet children in the neighborhood.

Did I mention in my last letter that I work for a divorce attorney? Well, he just made partner and asked me to stay on as his personal assistant! I also got a raise—a dollar more an hour.

I wonder, do you ever want to meet your granddaughter? I know she'd love to meet her daddy's parents. Don't think it would be weird. I'll make sure it's not. Just feel free to come by at any time. We'd even come to see you, if you'd like. Ella's never been to Boston. She's never been off Long Island, in fact. We're at the same address. Same phone number.

Love,

Olivia

"What time are Trevor and Dana coming?"

Chris walked from behind the tarp blocking their bed. "Seven, I think. Have you seen my tool belt?"

Olivia pointed to the corner near the door, next to Ella's backpack. "Will you be able to see Ella onto the bus today?"

Chris lifted his belt and walked to Olivia to kiss her goodbye. "I can't. We have a job starting out east, and I want to get there before John." Olivia pulled him back to her for another kiss. He put his arms around her waist. "I'll try to be home before they come tonight. See you later."

Ella's first day of kindergarten fell on a warm, rainy day. Olivia waited with her at the bus stop, on the corner of Sycamore and Elm, huddled under a ripped umbrella. She tried not to leer too closely to the two girls waiting with their mothers a few feet away, each holding their own mini, pink matching umbrellas, jumping up and down in their name-brand water boots while Ella stood close to Olivia so not to get her sneakers, bought from the bin at McCrory's last month, wet, watching the girls, too. She looked up to Olivia.

"Want to say hello?"

Ella glanced back over to the girls and back to her mother. She shook her head.

"Don't forget Aunt Dana and Uncle Trevor are coming over later, okay?"

Ella perked up and smiled and Olivia felt grateful. Her daughter loved their college friends as much as she and Chris did. They hadn't seen each other in months. Too long.

As the bus pulled up, Olivia kissed her daughter good-bye and waved while she went up the steps and found a seat. The other women, however, had their two girls pose with their arms around each other in front of the bus and then each girl paused on the bus steps while their parents took pictures. The bus driver smiled through her impatience.

"Sorry," one of the women said.

"No worries," the bus driver responded. "How many first days of kindergarten do you get?"

Olivia looked away. They had no camera to record these events. It hadn't even occurred to her. Besides, it was a frivolity they couldn't justify. Ella wanted to play soccer so their spending money went to sign her up. Chris was adamant about not touching their savings. They were not far from reaching their goal of a down payment for a starter house.

The bus pulled away slowly, leaving the three women standing in the rain. One dabbed at her eyes. The other laughed and wiped her eyes, as well. "You're so sentimental, Claudia."

"Well, she's my last," the other woman said. "And you're doing it, too."

One turned to Olivia and turned away dismissively. For the sake of her daughter, who would have to share the bus ride with these two women's girls, Olivia cleared her throat and spoke. "I'm Olivia, by the way. My daughter is Ella. She'll be riding to school with your girls this year." Hopefully no longer than that, she thought.

"Oh! So sorry! We thought you were a babysitter. You're so young. I'm Denise. This sap is Claudia." The other woman, Claudia, offered a small smile and nod. She failed to hide her disdain of Olivia, giving her outfit a quick once-over—leggings with a tee shirt and Keds, no socks, hair in a messy ponytail. Claudia was sporting a pair of pressed khakis and polo shirt under an open tan Burberry rain jacket. Her short dark hair was pushed back off her lined face.

"Which house are you in?" Denise asked.

"We're on Sycamore." Olivia pointed to the street behind her. "We rent from the Schmidt's."

Denise and Claudia gave each other a quick glance and a raised eyebrow. "Is your daughter signed up for dance class next week?"

"Dance class?"

"Yes, all of the girls do dance. The first deposit was due already, but I can put in a word with Miss Eleanor since you're new."

First deposit? They'd have to dip into their savings. Chris would never allow it.

"I have to see if Ella wants to."

Denise smiled and waved her hand, dismissing Olivia's response. "Oh, they all want to. And if they don't, they will. Don't want to be left out."

Claudia turned to go. "See you later. The bus drops them at 3:10."

"My mother will get Ella off the bus later."

"Your mother?"

"Yes. I work, so she helps me."

The women looked at each other. "So, you won't be putting in for class parent?"

Olivia had no idea what Claudia was talking about. "I'm not sure." She glanced at her watch. Mr. Hughes hated when she was late. "I have to go. It was nice to meet you."

She walked to her apartment, feeling the judging stares at her back. She couldn't wait to move.

Olivia walked in from work at six o'clock with chicken cutlets and a small bag of potatoes. Janine unpacked the food while Olivia said hello to her daughter.

"Do you need help with dinner before I go?"

"I'm okay, Mom. Thanks. I'll just change quick and start. The cutlets were on sale so I decided to splurge. I'm getting sick of pasta."

It wasn't until after Janine left and the potatoes were on the small stove that Olivia noticed her mother cleaned the apartment before she got home. It was so like Janine to quietly help her and ease her burden. Without her mother's help, Olivia knew she wouldn't be able to afford paying a babysitter. She made a mental note to call her and thank her.

When Chris got home from work, Trevor and Dana were already in the main living space playing with Ella. Wrapping paper littered the small room. Trevor stood to shake Chris's hand and Dana blew him a kiss from the floor, not willing to interrupt the Barbie playing.

"Dude, nice tan." Trevor scrunched his nose. "Or is that dirt?"

Chris's skin was dark, his hands rough with callouses, and he often came home reeking of hard physical labor. Olivia loved the way he looked, healthy and strong, a complete departure from Trevor's pale face and soft hands. The downside was the significant difference in their paychecks. Trevor was making bucket-loads of money on Wall Street while they were living in a basement apartment.

After dinner, the four sat at the kitchen table and Ella lay on the couch watching television a few feet away, hugging the small quilt her grandmother made when she was born. "Thank you for the gifts for Ella. You're spoiling her," Olivia said.

Dana smiled. "You only turn five once. I love that little girl."

Trevor glanced toward Ella and back to the table. "I still get floored when I see you guys. It's like you're playing house and I'm way behind."

"This is a very real game," Chris said, and they all laughed. He sipped his beer and ignored the pie they'd brought.

"Well, we're jealous, which is why we wanted to come over tonight. And of course, to see our goddaughter. But we have news," Dana said. She lifted her left hand, which now wore a ring she'd been missing when they'd first arrived at the apartment. On her fourth finger sat a large, round, brilliant diamond.

Olivia's eyes flew open wide. "How have you been keeping this from us for three hours? I can't believe it!" She grabbed Dana's hand and pulled the ring closer to her eye while Dana preened.

Chris lifted his beer bottle and clinked with Trevor's. "Congratulations, man."

"How'd he do it?" Olivia asked.

Dana, obviously hoping to be asked this question, sat back and crossed her legs, looking at her ring. "He asked in Mexico. We were in Riviera Maya, lying on the beach. The waiter brought us our drinks and the ring was at the bottom of my glass. Needless to say, it didn't take me long to find it." Laughter around the table. "When I did, he knelt in the sand and proposed."

Olivia clasped her hands together and put them to her chest, her thin, gold band the only ornament on her fingers. "That's so romantic. When's the big day?"

Trevor held up his hands. "I made her promise we'd wait. I want to get out of the city and find a house." He looked at Chris. "We're thinking Westchester. I want an easy commute to the office. Sorry, bro."

Chris frowned. "The band."

Trevor shook his head. "We've already replaced Jeremy. And Derek has cancelled so many times, it was bound to happen."

Olivia watched her husband's reaction. After Trevor graduated, he brought the band to New York City. But every fourth Thursday they played in Long Beach, on Long Island, and Chris joined them.

He enjoyed a weekly gig with the new group he'd found, but playing with Trevor and the original band was the highlight of his month, pearls amid the stones of daily physical work. One of the members had to quit last year and lately they'd been subbing for Trevor on the drums, due to his longer work hours and commute from the city. But Chris was there religiously on that keyboard.

When they left, Ella was sleeping and Olivia cleaned the dessert dishes while Chris got ready for bed. Finished, she turned around and jumped back, startled to find him watching her.

"You scared me."

He said nothing, standing by the table.

"What is it?"

"You don't have a diamond ring."

She moved to her husband. "I don't need a diamond, Chris. I don't need a stone some poor abused soul had to dig up in Africa under the tyrannical thumb of some ruler just because Tiffany's decided diamonds are a show of love." She nodded her head in Ella's direction. "There's my precious stone." She kissed him. "And right here." She kissed him again.

"You seemed impressed with Dana's ring."

"I had to. That's what she expected. You must fawn over someone's new engagement ring. If you don't, it's like saying you're not happy about the news."

He shook his head, confused.

"Don't try to understand. And please don't ever compare what I want to what anyone else has."

"You didn't feel a tug of envy that they went to Mexico?"

She pressed her lips together. "Maybe a slight tug," she admitted. "But we're going to get there. Sooner than you think."

"Want to go there tonight?"

She looked at him for a full minute. "Let's go somewhere else. Let's go to New Zealand."

He hugged her tight. "I love you so much."

"I know."

Chapter 16
October 2010

Dana called Chris at work. "Olivia told me what's going on," she gushed before he could say hello.

Chris had been speaking to the general contractor on a site where they had just broken ground on a new property. He moved out of earshot when he heard what Dana said.

"Yeah? So?"

Dana sighed. "Chris? What the hell does that mean? What are you going to do?"

He heard his name called from the small tent set up near the foundation. A cluster of hard hats leaned over drawings, and voices were raised as they discussed a new setback they'd discovered.

"Dana, I can't talk now. I'll call you later."

"Where are you?"

"Port Washington."

"Great. You'll pass me on your way home. Stop over. I want to talk to you."

He hung up and walked back to the tent, sorry he'd answered the phone.

He showed up at Dana's at five-thirty, feeling worn and chilled from being outside for the past eight hours.

"I'll make coffee," she said, leading him into the kitchen where a bottle of wine and a half-filled glass sat on the island.

He sat on one of the wrought iron stools at her island and rubbed his eyes.

"You finished early," she said.

"We're losing sunlight earlier by the day."

Dana measured coffee grounds and set up her extravagant machine.

"Dinner plans tonight?"

At almost six o'clock, there was no odor of food coming from the oven, no prep on the immaculate counter. Dana started the brewing and nodded to her wine.

"You're looking at it. Want to join me?"

"No."

"We have to talk about this," she said, putting a steamy mug in front of him.

"No, we don't."

Across the island, she leaned on the counter as she reached for her wine glass. "Weren't you blown away when she told you? I almost shit my pants."

"Always a lady."

Dana ignored his comment. "Chris, how can she be pregnant?"

"I've been asking myself the same question for the past few weeks."

"She told me you're not taking it well."

"Did she?"

Dana nodded.

"Do you blame me?"

"Yes. I do."

He leaned back and crossed his arms. "Dana… Don't start."

She straightened and held onto her near empty glass. "She couldn't have cheated on you, right?"

He clenched his jaw and breathed through his nose. "Did you just ask me that?"

"I'm sorry."

Chris shook his head.

"It's just that, I met her new boss. He's young and hot and likes Olivia."

Chris rubbed his hands over his face. He pushed away thoughts of Gavin calling her in the evenings and weekends, taking her word that the guy was a workaholic. Why would Dana suggest this?

"I'm going through some stuff right now, and I don't need you making these suggestions." He breathed through his nose and glared at her.

They were quiet.

"Did you tell Trevor?"

"No. Did you?" he said.

"No."

He left the coffee untouched and stood. "I have to go home."

Dana followed him to the door. "You're going to have to tell her what you did. You should have done it years ago."

"I didn't. And I won't now. Dana, drop it."

He left her standing at the threshold as she watched him drive away.

***

Olivia pulled into her empty driveway at dusk. As she walked to the front door, she glanced over at Mrs. Johnson's house, something she'd rarely done in the years she'd been living here. How was it she knew only a handful of neighbors after more than twenty years on this block?

Three families had children the same ages as Ella and Nick, and those were the people she spent time with—summer barbecues, winter nights drinking and talking while the children amused themselves. They never socialized with other couples or families around them. The common denominator was the kids. Now two of the families had moved away, and Chris and Olivia managed to get together with the remaining couple only a handful of times each year. Busy with work, with household projects, her complacency to spend her free time with Dana.

She dropped her purse and bag in the kitchen as the phone dinged. Chris texted saying he'd be late due to a meeting. She changed into worn jeans and sweatshirt, puttered back into the kitchen and took inventory of the fridge, trying to ward off pangs of nausea. She was not in the mood to cook and took out the tray of leftover lasagna just as another text showed up on her phone. *I'll bring home dinner. Don't bother cooking.*
We have leftovers. She texted back.
I'm sick of lasagna.
She was just about to put the food back in the fridge when she hesitated. Grabbing her jacket and the tray, she walked across the street to Mrs. Johnson's house. The sky was orange and the outside air had turned chilly as soon as the sun disappeared.

The woman smiled in surprise when she opened the door to find Olivia standing on her porch holding a tray.

"I thought you might like some lasagna. I made it myself, but it's too much for me and Chris." She held out the tray until Mrs. Johnson took it.

"Would you like to come in?"

"I have to get back home. Chris is on his way from work. Thank you."

"Some other time then. Thank you, Olivia."

"If you ever need anything Mrs. Johnson, we're always home."

The older woman tilted her head. After all this time, she seemed to say, and now you're offering? But she said, "Please, call me Sophia. And stop back again."

Chris was quiet during dinner. They ate gyro sandwiches he'd brought home. It was their go-to meal, the first they shared together when they started dating in college and still their favorite.

"How was your meeting?" Olivia asked.

He chewed and swallowed before he answered. "It was a waste of time. How was your day?"

"Nick called my office."

Chris looked up in surprise, wearing the same concerned reaction she had earlier today.

"I know, I thought the same thing. He just wanted to tell us he's going to Melissa's for the weekend and won't call until Monday night."

"Who?"

"His girlfriend. Stop saying who?"

She could hear it in Nick's voice through the line, the dreamy contentment of love.

After dinner, Chris went to grab a beer from the fridge. "Liv? Where's the lasagna?"

Chapter 17
1986

They were eating breakfast when Olivia suggested she might go back to school part-time to get her degree.

"We can't afford it," Chris said.

"I can't keep typing letters for the rest of my life." Silence. "I'll take classes at night so I can still work during the day."

Chris picked at his food.

"I can make more money eventually," she added.

Her last statement cut through him. They needed more money if they were going to get out of this dank, tiny basement. "But my music," he said. "I can't quit the band. You know I can't."

Olivia put down her fork. "I quit a lot of things for us, too." She stood from the table and went into the bathroom.

He left for work without saying good-bye. They had never done that and it left him feeling unraveled. He waited at the traffic light, with all the windows down, perspiring in the heat as his old pick up grumbled and moaned in neutral. He thought about their situation, how he was failing her, failing himself. The cars passed his vision as rage and impotence rose from the base of his gut. He hit the steering wheel. "Fuck!" It felt good. He yelled it louder and hit the steering wheel again and again. The light turned green, and Chris looked to his side to see a woman and child staring at him in horror. He gunned the engine and took off.

He went through the day in a haze of frustration. He'd been working this same job for six years. He should be wearing an expensive suit, crunching numbers on Wall Street next to Trevor by now. Instead, he wore dirt encrusted carpenter pants and a tool belt. Was this what he'd end up doing as his career? The midday sun beat down on him. He sought refuge from the strong rays in his truck and ate the sandwich Olivia made for him this morning, the same sandwich she made for Ella every day, American cheese with mayo on rye, and contemplated his future. For six years, they'd lived in the basement apartment on Sycamore Drive, watching feet walk by the window, envisioning the day they would get out and move into a home. Ella was starting first grade in less than a month. Olivia'd sprung her idea on him this morning. How long had she been waiting to approach him about this? He walked in every night, barely able to stand from physical exhaustion. His music kept him going. His music and their dream of moving on. Had he not noticed she needed more? While he felt his dream of returning to school begin to fade, hers had strengthened.

With a college degree, she'd have more choices. She'd make more money. You had to spend it to make it, right?

He returned home that evening, passed a sleeping Ella, and found Olivia already in bed. He climbed onto the bed behind her. "Okay. Take classes. I'll tell the guys to find another player."

She turned to look at him. "You'd do that for me?"

He brushed her hair back from her forehead and kissed her nose. "Babe, I'd do anything for you."

The next night, he brought her a bouquet of flowers. Olivia jumped into his arms and wrapped her legs around his waist. After showering him with kisses, she told him she went to the community college on her way to work and met with the registrar. Using her seven-year-old transcript from Boston College, they figured out the classes she'd need to get her degree. Paying a late fee, she enrolled in three classes and would start after Labor Day.

***

Olivia returned home from work the last week in September to find her mother and her daughter on the floor in the center of the small apartment doing homework.

"Mama," Ella said as she jumped up from the floor. She thrust a green piece of construction paper in her hand. Olivia took the paper and admired her daughter's painting of fall, depicting red leaves falling around an orange pumpkin. Her signature was haphazardly scrawled across the bottom below two sentences of what fall meant to her.

"This is beautiful, Ella. I know just where to hang it." She walked the few steps to the kitchen and placed it in the center of the refrigerator. Her mother followed. "How was the party?" Olivia said.

"It was sweet. The teacher had the class sing songs for us." Janine's smile faltered, and Olivia realized she was frowning. "Ask her to sing them for you."

Olivia shook her head and pasted on a smile. "It's okay. I'm glad you were there, Mom. Thanks."

Chris walked in, looking tired and dirty from work, and Janine said good-bye, leaving them to themselves. Olivia made spaghetti with jarred sauce and put it on the table near the two place settings she'd set up. She crossed the adjoining room and pulled back the tarp, exposing their bed and dresser. Chris was showered and in jeans, bent over an open drawer, rifling through tee shirts. She watched him, admiring his strong back, muscular and wide from work. He sensed her and stood, holding a black tee in his hand. "You're leaving?"

She nodded. "Dinner's on the table. Ella's homework is done. I'll be home by eleven."

"See you later."

***

In bed, while Ella lay sleeping several feet away on the other side of the tarp, they whispered about their day.

"How was school?" he said.

"It's different than when we went. I'm one of the oldest in the class. It's strange. I can't fully concentrate."

He yawned and rolled toward her. "You'll get used to it. Now you're working and have Ella. When we went, it was just you and all you had to do was go to class. It's a different situation. Give it time."

Not too long ago, it seemed, they used to go to class and take naps on her single bed, watching the black and white, thirteen-inch television on her dresser. They spent weekends at his place and had no worries outside of exams and how they could spend even more time together. They talked of their future—graduate school, traveling across Europe, settling down, starting careers, getting married, buying a house. They rarely talked about children. They were so far from that responsibility. They had so much to do first. Could that have been only seven years ago? Olivia sighed. Oh, had life made other plans for them.

In the dark, she felt for his hands, rubbing the callouses on his palms. "What are you building now?" Chris's boss, John, had told Chris he appreciated his work ethic and saw how the others looked to him for guidance in such a small amount of time. So, he took him as an apprentice, and Chris had been working directly under him since. The hours were longer, but the raise in pay helped him cope.

"We took a job in Amagansett. You should see the way some of these people live. It's another world from us."

"Tell me." She nestled into his arms, and he explained all the intricate details of the homeowner's plans to build an extra wing onto their already large home, their surrounding property, in-ground pool with slide and cabana bar while she fell asleep with dreams of her own.

Chapter 18
October 2010

Olivia stopped at Ella's on her way home from work. Her daughter was wrapping the vacuum cord and left her mother in the den while she put it away.

"How does it look?" she asked Olivia when she returned.

Olivia looked around the spotless room. "It looks like no one lives here."

"Perfect."

"Ella, stop worrying. You'll do fine. They're going to love you."

Ella wasn't listening. She'd taken to straightening the book shelf and framed photos of her and Marco on their honeymoon. Olivia stepped to her daughter and put her hand on her shoulder. Ella turned, her forehead creased in worry.

"Babe. Enough. Be yourself. If the nurses would have seen the basement apartment we were bringing you home to they wouldn't have let us leave the hospital." Olivia's smile evaporated as her daughter frowned.

"It was your baby you were taking," she said. "You could have brought me to a dumpster, and they couldn't have said anything. This is someone else's baby I'm asking for. It's different."

Yes, of course. "What time are you expecting her?"

"Seven-thirty."

"Good. That leaves us two hours. Let me take you out to eat."

"I'd rather stay here. How about a sandwich?"

"Fine."

In the kitchen, Olivia let Ella fuss over the sandwiches, happy to see her not cleaning. It disturbed her to see her daughter so unhinged at the thought of the upcoming social worker's visit.

Once seated, Ella rested her elbow on the table. "Talk to me. Tell me something to get my mind off this meeting later."

Olivia thought of her obvious dilemma—*I'm pregnant while you run yourself ragged trying to impress a perfect stranger in the hope you get approved for a baby.* For a moment, she could see Chris's point of view clearly. Oh God, what were they going to do?

"Mom?"

"I met Nick's girlfriend, Melissa, when I went up to see him last week."

Ella's eyes opened wide. "Wow. What's she like?"

"She's not at all what I expected. Nothing like his past girlfriends."

"Do you like her?"

"I do. She's reserved, bright, and doesn't like to be too far away from Nick for any length of time."

Ella laughed, and Olivia smiled in relief.

"Do you remember Mrs. Johnson?"

Ella pursed her lips, confused.

"The woman diagonally across the street?" Olivia added.

"Oh, Billy's parents. I vaguely remember them. Bill was much older than me. Dreamy, but out of college by the time I was in middle school. Why?"

"I stopped by her house and brought her some food the other day."

"Why? Did someone die?"

"No. I wanted to say hi."

Ella frowned. "That's weird, Mom. We've been neighbors for so long. Why now?"

"I don't know. Maybe I have more time on my hands? I saw her at the grocery, and I've been thinking about her. It was nothing really, she invited me in but I said no."

"I'm sure she'd love the company. What about the husband?"

"He passed a few years ago, I think."

Olivia took a bite of her turkey and Swiss.

"Speaking of weird," Ella said, "is Dad okay? I called the house the other day, and he seemed short. You know, distracted."

"You called the house? He didn't tell me."

"I told him it wasn't important. He probably forgot."

Olivia kept chewing.

"Mom, is everything okay? You're not yourself either. Are you guys going through a mid-life crisis or something? Is Dad going to show up in a convertible with a twenty-year-old?"

Olivia opened her mouth to respond when the doorbell rang. The women looked at each other. Ella went pale.

"Don't even tell me this woman showed up early to surprise me. I'm going to freak out."

The social worker arrived ninety minutes before expected, and Ella pasted a plastic smile over her frantic face. Olivia placed her hand gently on her daughter's back as the corners of Ella's mouth shook through introductions. The social worker, who apologized for having the wrong time scheduled, said Olivia was welcome to stay, so she did, to support Ella until Marco came home. She wanted to shake the visitor and tell her they would be lucky to have a couple like Ella and Marco raise a baby. No need to put them through this. Instead she remained tight-lipped and cordial and left when her son-in-law walked in.

On the parkway, Olivia turned on the radio and took a deep breath. It'll be fine, she told herself. The DJ played an old Barry Manilow song that her mother used to sing to her and her eyes filled. She shut the radio, annoyed with herself. Did her other pregnancies wreak this much havoc on her emotions? Or was it her age? She worried about Ella, she worried about Nick. She missed her mother every day. She couldn't have a glass of wine. She was a mess.

She saw Sophia Johnson pulling an empty garbage can from the curb. She checked her watch. Chris wouldn't be home for another hour. Still in her work clothes, she walked across the street.

"Are you going to come in this time?" Sophia said as she placed her can next to the near empty garage.

"Sure." The woman's directness surprised her. She found it refreshing.

Sophia led Olivia into her ranch-style house through the garage and into the kitchen. The outside landscape was reminiscent of the seventies, late-blooming rhododendrons overgrown along the side of the house, an old post-and-rail fence serving little purpose short of décor, shrubs and spindly trees that needed shaping. Olivia expected a dark, paneled, mothball-odored claustrophobic space and was pleasantly surprised by the open layout and modern décor.

"Coffee? Tea?" She looked at her watch. "Wine?"

"Water, please."

"If you want coffee, say so. It's no trouble at all. I have a Keurig. I've become an instantly gratified woman." She winked before pulling mugs from her cabinet and a box of cookies from her pantry. "I have no plans this evening, so this is a treat for me."

Olivia waited for Sophia to bring two piping mugs of coffee to the table. She placed a small plate of cookies between them.

"Lorna Doones," Sophia said, taking one. "Still nothing better."

Olivia picked up a cookie and nibbled. Her mother loved Lorna Doones, too. She missed her so much, it physically hurt sometimes.

"So," Sophia started, "now we get to know each other." She smiled, and Olivia blushed.

"I'm sorry. I've lived here for twenty years and I've never been in this house. Nor have you ever been invited to mine. I'm a terrible neighbor."

Sophia laughed. "Terrible? Hardly. Busy? Certainly. When I was raising Amanda and Bill, any free time I had was spent cleaning the house or visiting with my sister. Or Nora, down the block. Our children were friends. When you moved in, my babies were in middle school already. I remember seeing you with two young children and I thought to myself, I could never go back to that again." She drank from her mug. "Now, though, I do miss those days. They were harried, but simple."

"Yes, they were. And I guess I was so busy with work and trying to raise them I never paid much attention to anything farther than my own front yard."

Sophia put her hands on the table. She wore her wedding ring. "So, better late than never, right?"

Olivia walked home an hour later, feeling like she'd made a friend.

Chapter19
1986

Olivia could barely keep her eyes open in her Communications class. The lack of sleep combined with the professor's monotone voice lulled her to a twilight doze. She'd been attending classes for three months, waiting for some sign she was doing the right thing. She started to dread going, hating to leave Ella and Chris four nights a week. Last week, Ella cried as she told her that every mom had signed up for a class party except for Olivia.

"Why can't you be a class mom?" she'd whined through tears. "You never get to see us sing or read us stories or bring in cupcakes. Allison and Meg's moms do everything."

Of course, they did. Olivia thought of the two women at the bus stop. Allison and Meg with their matching designer boots and clothes, enrolled in three dance classes each while Ella could only participate in soccer because those classes were so expensive.

"Honey, I'm doing this for us. I'm trying to work on getting a career so I can make more money and be able to buy you nice things or join a dance class."

Ella ran her arm across her eyes and climbed onto Olivia's lap. "I hate dance and I don't want things. I want you to come to my school and see me."

So, last night Olivia stayed up until two am sewing Ella's pilgrim costume while she baked cupcakes that she designed to look like pilgrim hats using marshmallows and licorice. She promised Ella she'd be at the Thanksgiving party tomorrow. She'd lose a day of pay, but the look on Ella's face, pure joy that her mother would be like Allison's and Meg's was enough to make the sacrifice worth it.

At ten forty-five, Olivia dragged herself from the one truck she and Chris shared and walked to the back of the house, to their entrance to the basement apartment. She walked in to the soft sounds of music and could make out Chris sitting at his keyboard in the dark, leaned over the keys, lost in his song. Ella slept nearby. Olivia choked back tears. This was how she often found him when she returned from her classes. Ella fell asleep to his lullabies, and he stayed at that keyboard playing for hours long after she'd dropped off.

She put down her books and purse and walked to him, hugging him from behind. He stopped and put his arms around her neck, pulling her closer. She stepped around and straddled him on the small bench.

"Hey."

"Hey, you."

They kissed, and she felt him respond immediately. She pulled back to see his silhouette in the dark. "Take me to bed."

Without a word, he lifted her and brought her behind the tarp.

Olivia walked in from work the following week to find her mother in the kitchen washing a pot. Ella was on the couch watching Arthur.

"Mom, what are you doing here?" Olivia glanced around the kitchen. "Why is Ella home?"

She wasn't due to be home for another half hour. Every Tuesday and Thursday, Olivia managed to get home in time to get Ella off the bus. These were her favorite days.

Janine shut the water and dried her hands. "The nurse called me around ten thirty. She left a message for you too, at the office. Did you get it?"

Olivia thought back to the morning. There were missed call messages on her desk after she sat in on the early meetings with Mr. Hughes. She'd answered the first few and then neglected to look at the rest after lunch. She was so tired, she just wanted to get through the day and get home.

"She said Ella seemed weepy and lethargic," Janine said. "I picked her up a little before eleven. I offered to take her to my house, but she wanted to come here. She ate a few spoons of soup. I put the rest in the fridge."

Olivia hugged her mom. "Thanks."

She walked around the couch, and Ella started to cry when she saw her mother. "I feel bad, Mama," she said, clutching her quilt. The television was on low and could barely be heard over her whimpering. Olivia sat down and brought her daughter to her lap, kissing her forehead. She felt warm but not burning.

"I gave her some Motrin," Janine said from behind. "She shouldn't be too warm now."

Ella wrapped her arms around Olivia's neck and rested her head on her shoulder. "Why didn't you come for me, Mama? I asked for you."

Olivia glanced up at her mother. *Sorry*, she mouthed to Janine.

"They always want their mother," she said, dismissing Olivia's apology. "Especially when they're sick." Olivia filled with gratitude and regret.

"Maybe we should wash the quilt?" Janine said. "She's been lying on it all afternoon."

Ella, hearing mention of her favorite blanket, pulled it close to her chest and leaned back against her mother.

"I'll wait. She sleeps with it every night."

Janine smiled. Olivia kissed the top of her daughter's head.

Did she even know what she was aiming for anymore? She was not the same girl with the same goals and drive as she was seven years ago. Her priorities had shifted. Ella yawned. She lifted her daughter and brought her to bed.

She was sitting at the table, staring out at the darkness when Chris walked in from work. His cheeks were rosy from the cold and snowflakes melted on his shoulders in the warmth of the apartment. His face held none of the humor or lightheartedness it once did. She felt as he looked. Did she look the same? Could he tell?

"Hey," he said, dropping his heavy belt and shrugging out of his coat. "Aren't you going to class?"

She nodded and stood. "Are you hungry?"

"Starved. Where's Ella?"

"Sleeping. She's not feeling well."

She uncovered a bowl of pasta from the counter and put it in the microwave. Chris sat down heavily onto his chair and put his head in his hands.

"Rough day?" she said.

He sat up when she put the hot plate in front of him. "It's better now."

Olivia sat down and listened to him talk about his day. For the past months, he increased his hours to make up for the money he lost by not playing in his band at night and to offset the cost of her classes. He looked like a fifty-year-old man tonight instead of twenty-seven. They were just about making it, like he promised they would. But he wasn't happy, and she knew it. She wasn't happy, either.

"I need to talk to you."

Chris shoveled the rigatoni into his mouth like a starving puppy. "Shoot."

"I'm going to stop school after this semester. I'm not going back for spring."

He stopped eating and looked at her. "Why the hell not? You have to finish."

She shook her head. "It's harder than I thought it would be."

Chris put his fork down and ran his hand through his hair. "We made a lot of changes to get you back. This is what you wanted."

"What I want is to alleviate some of your stress. I thought if I went back to school, I could get a better job and you wouldn't have to work so hard. But everyone's suffering." She took a breath. "I'd like to cut my hours at work so I can be with Ella more. We'll still be in better shape with me working five less hours without the tuition fee. I figured it out."

Chris sighed and stood up, bringing his plate to the sink. "I don't know. You're close. You have a year and a half and then you can do what you want."

"I can't keep up this schedule. I'm exhausted all the time. I've been snapping at Ella for no reason. I fell asleep at lunch last week, and my boss woke me up. I was so embarrassed. I either have to quit my job to do this effectively or quit school. I decided to quit school."

He watched closely, and her eyes shifted to her feet.

"Quit your job."

"What?"

"You heard me. Quit your job. We'll make do."

"Make do? We're barely making it now, Chris."

She could see it hurt him, but she spoke the truth. They had so little left over after their bills were paid, she wondered if they'd ever break out of the cycle. On top of their rent, food, gas, clothes and limited extra expenses, Chris still carried school debt left to him when his father stopped payments. She had more to say, but didn't think he could handle more right now.

He stepped away from her and turned around. "I'll make it work. I told you I'd take care of you and I will. So, quit your goddamn job and don't worry about it."

She was stunned into silence. He never spoke to her this way. "Chris, don't be angry."

"Then don't make me feel like…" He clenched his jaw and left her with the words *like less than a man* unsaid.

She washed the dishes and fought back tears. When the kitchen area was spotless and she could think of no other reason to avoid facing him, she crossed the room, pausing at Ella's bed to feel her forehead before pulling the tarp back. Chris was in bed, eyes closed.

"Don't go to sleep angry."

"If you don't quit your job tomorrow, I'll call your boss and do it for you."

She climbed onto the bed and faced his back. "Please don't."

He sat up and glared at her. "Liv."

"Chris, I'm pregnant."

His eyes opened in surprise and he fell back.

"Are you angry?"

He stared at the ceiling and let out a deep breath. "You should have told me before. I thought—"

"Don't ever think that." She cut him off. Then she laid her head on his chest and squeezed her eyes tight in relief.

"I'll talk to John and get more work. I'm sure he'll have something else for me."

"No," she said. "No more hours at work. Do one thing for me." She looked up at him. "I want you to play. You're not happy. I see it. I know you. Playing in the house for Ella isn't enough. You need more."

He took her hand and kissed it. "I need you. That's all I need."

"You need your music. And I need my husband."

They lay silent while Olivia listened to his breath. "A baby?" he whispered. "We have to get out of here."

Dear Mrs. Bennet,

I hope this letter finds you and Mr. Bennet well. It's been a year since my last letter. I have been so busy with work and Ella that I used to fall into my bed at night with not a morsel of energy left to fill you in on what's going on.

I have a few moments now, so I will.

Chris just celebrated his seven-year anniversary with his construction job. Every time he looks elsewhere for work, his boss, John, gives him more incentive to stay. He's mentoring Chris to one day take over the business entirely. The other men respond to Chris and he has a knack for the business side of the job, which should come as no surprise. Still, I find it interesting that he often prefers wearing his tool belt to lifting a pen. He walks into the apartment at night totally exhausted but content.

Ella is growing at an alarming rate. She is already reading (smart like her daddy) and excelling in second grade. She is so beautiful, I really wish you were here to see her. You'd be continuously dazzled by her charming personality. And the girl plays a good soccer game too. Ella is particularly excited lately because (and here's the underlying reason for this letter), I have just given birth to a baby boy. His birthday is June 6th, exactly two months before my 27th birthday. We are filled with a mixture of love and relief. It was a tough go for a while. I had some complications during my pregnancy and a close call during the birth, I was told. Thankfully, I was unconscious at the time. But I am happy to report mother and baby are doing well. The father, however, is still emotional and will hopefully see past the recent issues and embrace his son. We named him Nicholas.

He is the antithesis of Ella, who is fair with brown-ish-red hair like Chris. Nick, as we will call him, arrived in the world with a shock of black hair and olive skin like me. I can't stop looking at his face. But something tells me this child won't be as easy as Ella. So far, he's proving me right. They are holding me here at the hospital for another few days to ensure I am okay and then we'll be going home,

*to our new ranch house in Levittown. You'll notice our
new address on the envelope.*

*I hope you're receiving these letters and haven't moved.
Chris doesn't know I write to you. I think it would hurt
him even more to know you don't respond. I know this
must be so hard for you. As a mother, I can't fathom not
being able to speak to my child. Still, I will keep trying.*

*Well, that's all for now. As always, I hope to hear from
you,*

Olivia

***

Chris walked into the hospital room with Ella, who insisted
she bring her baby brother another stuffed animal from home.
Olivia was writing while Nick slept in the bassinet beside her.

"What are you doing?"

She looked up and pushed the papers into her drawer. Her
pale, drawn face lit up, and she reached her arms out for Ella,
who climbed onto the bed and into her mother's embrace. Chris
leaned over and kissed her before dropping onto the chair. He
studied her while she played with Ella's hair and listened to her
ramblings about school news. He felt like he'd aged a decade
this week. And Olivia, God bless her, looked a bit better today.

He made a promise to himself not to allow her to do this
again. The pregnancy was bad enough—the bleeding and
forced bed rest for the last month, the missing paychecks from
her job because she was saving the allotted pay for her maternity leave. The labor almost did him in. He stood by her head,
coaching her in her breathing and pushing when she suddenly
let out a guttural scream he'd never heard before and one he
would never forget. The doctor and nurses, seeing something
he didn't, strapped an oxygen mask over her face and ushered

him quickly out of the delivery room. He sat in the waiting room for four hours, imagining all different outcomes he'd face, things that could go wrong with the baby or with Olivia or both, wiping fearful tears from his cheeks while Janine sat silently across the room, intently focused on sewing something onto Ella's quilt, until finally, the doctor came to see him with a smile.

When he was allowed into the recovery room, he found her asleep, looking peaceful and alive, and he wept over her. Then he went in search of his baby. The tiny face peered up at him with a determined look that said, *I'm here dammit* and then broke into a fierce yawn. For the first time in years, he thought of his own father.

Watching Olivia talking and laughing with Ella, the previous days seemed light years behind him. And not once in the scenarios he imagined during those agonizing hours in the waiting room did he not take his wife home.

Chapter 20
October 2010

The phone rang and Olivia answered her bedroom extension on the second ring. It was Melissa.

"Hi, Melissa, how are you?" Olivia said, looking at Chris, who shrugged.

"Well, I'm okay. I'm calling about Nick." Her voice shook. "He's in the hospital—the same one I was in when, um, when—"

"Why is Nick in the hospital?" Olivia yelled, cutting the girl off mid-sentence. She turned to see Chris stop dressing and walk toward her.

"He, um, he had a run-in with the guy he beat up last month. He's okay, Mrs. Bennet. He's just a little banged up. He asked me to call you."

When Olivia hung up the phone, she dropped onto the bed. "I don't know if I have the constitution for this, Chris. This kid is going to kill me." She put a hand over her still flat belly and inhaled a shaky breath before telling him what Melissa said.

While Chris called into work, she called Gavin and explained she needed to take a few days off. *Take the time you need, Olivia. Let me know how he is,* he told her.

They were quiet during the ride up to Rochester. Every now and then, Olivia put her hand on her stomach and Chris turned to her. She nodded, and he looked back to the road. They still hadn't agreed on what to do. And they hadn't discussed it, as if by ignoring it, the whole situation might resolve itself. She was seven weeks along.

"Did you call Ella?" They were on the thruway, passing Albany.

Olivia nodded. "She wants us to keep her posted."

"Any more news on…?"

She shook her head. Ella had called her when the social worker left and only said she hoped it went well. That was a week ago.

"Liv, it went well. I'm sure of it."

Olivia reached her hand to hold his. He knew what she was thinking. They were so in tune. Then a thought clouded her mind. What would she ever do without this man?

He didn't react when her hand touched his, and she pulled it back, stung.

"I want you to make an appointment for a physical," she said.

"Why? Do I look unhealthy?"

"No one looks unhealthy before they drop dead. I can't see through you, Chris. But a doctor can. It's time. You're getting up there."

His shoulders tensed. "Hey, back off. You're telling me I'm old but that you're going to have a baby? Make up your mind. I can't be both."

"Yes, you can. And *we're* having this baby. Not just me."

He shook his head.

Her cell phone rang. She answered and for twenty minutes, discussed the details and answered questions for Gavin on two cases she filed the previous day. Chris stared at the road.

They pulled up to the same hospital they'd brought Nick to when he visited Melissa six weeks earlier. Filled with trepidation, she reached for Chris's hand in the parking lot. This time, he took it and they walked in together.

Nick was sleeping when they arrived in his room. Melissa sat beside him, her hand over his.

"Mr. and Mrs. Bennet," she whispered. "You're here." She stood and held her hand out to Chris. With a shaky breath, she said, "I'm Melissa." To both, "He woke up earlier and asked for you."

She stepped quietly from the room, leaving Chris and Olivia alone with Nick. His face was distorted by lumps and bruises. He had a large bandage wrapped around his chest, and she could see little else damaged.

"Other than IV, he's not attached to anything. It's a relief," Chris said behind her.

"Is it?" She sat beside her son and gently ran her hand over his forehead, the patch of skin clear of bruises, and down through his hair.

"Hey, babe," she said softly. "We're here." Chris put his hands on her shoulders for support. She heard his rattled sigh above her. They sat and watched Nick sleep. Olivia stared at his face, this beautiful face she never tired of. Even while he screamed and carried on as a toddler, she thought he was exceptional. Today, however, he didn't look like himself. He looked like a monstrous manifestation of a boy in pain.

"He has less than a year left to get through," Chris said. "Why is he making it so difficult?"

The doctor came into the room, saving Olivia from having to respond. Chris stepped back and allowed her to stand to say hello. He was young, a child himself it seemed, but shook their hands in an authoritative, confident manner.

"Let me take a quick check." He stepped toward the bed, looked at Nick and then back to Olivia and Chris. "I won't interrupt his sleep. He had a rough night last night."

"Can you tell us what happened?" Chris said.

"He was brought in yesterday evening to the ER. He'd been jumped, his girlfriend told the admitting nurse. They did a pretty good job on him. Bruised his face, left a few lacerations on his left cheek and temple, cracked three ribs, and lacerated his kidney."

Olivia's eyes opened wide, and Chris cursed under his breath. "Is that even possible?"

The doctor nodded. "Quite. He took a few kicks to his side. That is where the pain will affect him most. He's on morphine now. I'd like to keep him here a few more days." He looked from Chris to Olivia. "The police were here earlier to speak to him and the girl."

The doctor stepped toward the door.

"Thank you," Chris said and the doctor disappeared.

Alone, they sat on either side of Nick.

"This kid," Chris whispered and sighed.

"Do you remember the first time we brought him to a hospital?"

Chris nodded and stared at his son. "Like it was yesterday."

"We were so young. He was so young." She moved closer to Chris. "I was so scared."

They stood in silence. "It's not any easier now, is it?"

Chapter 21
1987

At five months old, Nick still slept in two-hour intervals, forcing Olivia to bid an unenthusiastic, bleary-eyed send-off to Ella in the mornings.

"Babies are hard," Ella said one morning over waffles. "I hear him cry every night. Why does he scream like that?"

"He cries when he's hungry or if he needs a diaper change. He can't do anything himself so he relies on us to help him." Olivia took Ella's empty plate to the sink and handed her the backpack – a sign she should move along.

"Did I do that?"

"Not nearly as much as he does. You were a different baby." And she was a different parent at twenty. Olivia had the energy to wake multiple times for Ella and still function during the day. Her twenty-eight-year-old self was finding it harder to maintain the momentum. Ella stepped outside and turned partway down the walk.

"Mama, when can I have a baby?"

"You have one now."

"No, a baby of my own. Not a brother."

"When you're an adult, after you finish college, perhaps get your doctorate and when you're ready."

"What's a doctat?"

"I'll explain another time. It was a little joke for Mommy's benefit."

"When I have my baby, I won't care if he cries."

"We'll see."

"What?"

"Nothing. Zip your coat. It's chilly. Have a good day at school."

At the end of the walkway, Ella turned back. "Will you be at my game later?"

"I'm getting my hair done for Aunt Dana's wedding, remember? It's tonight. Grandma is watching you. Jenny's mom will bring you home." Ella's new friend, Jenny, played on the same soccer team. Her mother was friendly and easy-going. She and Olivia gelled right away.

Olivia had taken the day off from work figuring she'd grab a quick nap before her hair appointment. She hadn't gotten a cut and style in ages, and Dana was treating her as a matron of honor gift.

Ella stood perplexed while Olivia strained her neck to see if the bus was coming.

"Mom? Can Gramma take care of Nick?"

"Of course, she can. She took care of me when I was a baby."

"Did you cry like him?"

"I don't know. Here comes your bus."

In the kitchen, Olivia cleaned the breakfast dishes while Nick fidgeted in his swing. Back and forth, back and forth, he moved his head as if he were uncomfortable, trying to clear himself of something. She checked behind his head and neck, saw nothing and felt down the seat behind his body but found no obstruction. "You have to let Mommy clean, okay?" Staying in his line of sight, Olivia managed to clean the kitchen in one straight exercise while monitoring his agitation. She wiped down the Formica counter, enjoying the proud feeling that filled her. Her own kitchen—normal stove and oven, full-size fridge. How could anyone complain about cleaning? She embraced it. They'd been in the new house almost a year, and she still marveled as she walked into each room. They had rooms!

She was heading to the clothes dryer, just off the kitchen, to take out clothes that had been sitting since yesterday, but it was not meant to be. She'd neglected to turn the swing around and disappeared for thirty seconds, causing an angry uproar from his perch.

Lifting the baby, she whispered, "You're a demanding little man, aren't you?" He looked at her and frowned as if knowing she were leaving him that evening.

"How about we both take a nap?" On the couch, she laid the baby on top of her, covered him with the quilt, larger now with the additional cobalt-blue squares her mother added while Olivia was in labor, and he rested his head on her chest. She touched the soft fabrics of the blanket. "You know, Grandma must have known what a strong personality you'd have. She picked the perfect color for you." Olivia chuckled to herself.

She looked around the room, their very first den, and filled with angst. So much to do and here she was, trying to take a much-needed nap so early in the morning. She smelled Nick's head, breathing in his aroma deeply before kissing him. His small body warmed hers, and he rose and fell with her breaths until finally he gave a sigh of contentment that matched her own and drifted into slumber while she envisioned Dana and Trevor's wedding later, she in her bridesmaid dress, which set her back $90.

"He feels warm. Like really warm," was how Olivia greeted Chris when he walked in from work carrying his tool belt in one hand and his rented tux in the other. Nick lay against her chest, eyes half closed, flushed.

Chris leaned over and felt the baby's forehead with his lips. "Did you give him something?"

Olivia nodded and rocked. Nick, half asleep, seemed agitated. He moved his face back and forth against her chest, groaning while trying to get comfortable. When Chris returned an hour later from checking in on Ella's game, Nick's fever spiked higher. He gently took him from Olivia's arms.

"He's wheezing, Liv."

"I'm waiting for the doctor to call me back." She watched Chris hold Nick, pacing the floor while whispering to him. The baby now lay like a rag doll, his breath a rattled exhale. The phone rang, and Olivia jumped, lifting the receiver on the first ring. She explained to the doctor Nick's quick progression from agitation earlier in the day, how the fever started and finally the heat radiating from him and the wheezing that sounded to her like thick netting blocking his air.

She hung up. "He said it sounds like croup and to drive him around in the car with the window open. The cold air should help him breathe." She took the baby from Chris and walked toward the nursery.

"You're kidding."

"I wish I was."

"What kind of quack are you using, Liv?"

She turned around, her eyes bloodshot from worry and holding back her fear. "Don't give me that crap. Don't get on me for picking the doctor. Are you going to blame me for him getting sick, too?" He'd been going to a daycare near her office since he was twelve weeks old.

She placed the baby down on the changing table and pulled back his diaper. His chest sucked in with his breath, and his skin was hot to the touch. She quickly wrapped him back into his clothes and added a heavy onesie to cover him.

Chris was at the door waiting for them. "I'm sorry. I'm worried."

Olivia ignored him, put on her coat and led the way out to the car. They did what the doctor suggested, but when they saw no improvement, they took Nick to the emergency room. The ten-minute ride lasted an eternity. Olivia closed her eyes and breathed in the cold, autumn air through the open window, holding Nick toward the breeze as the doctor ordered. She answered questions at the admitting desk while Chris walked the floor with the baby. They were ushered inside to a bed where they waited to see a doctor. Olivia sat on the bed with Nick, who lay against her, immobile. She looked at the clock.

"You have to go to the wedding."

Chris shook his head and crossed his arms. "I'm not leaving you both here."

"You have to. You're Trevor's best man. He needs you there."

"I don't want to leave you, Liv." He looked sincere, and she knew he'd stay with them and not think twice about the wedding, but Trevor and Chris were as close as brothers and this was the most important day of Trevor and Dana's life. It was bad enough she'd have to miss it, but there was no way she'd allow them both not to go.

"Chris, please. I'm in the best place for Nick right now. I'm covered. My mom's with Ella. You have the weddings rings. If you don't go, I won't forgive you."

They waited in silence until a doctor pushed past the curtain and joined them. He asked Olivia to repeat Nick's behavior throughout the day, examined the lethargic body in her arms and stepped back. "I am almost certain he has respiratory syncytial virus."

"What does that mean?"

The doctor put his penlight back in his breast pocket. "It means I'm admitting him."

He left, and Chris paled and shook his head. "I can't."

"Please go. I'll call if I need you." She felt strong, and Chris's reaction to the news that Nick would have to stay in the hospital was more than she could take.

A nurse stepped behind the curtain. She wheeled a small enclosed bed beside her. "Are you ready?" she said to Olivia.

Olivia placed the baby in the bed and looked to Chris. "Go," she mouthed silently. She turned to the nurse. "We're ready." She followed the nurse and refused to look back to her husband, who she knew stood lost in the hall.

In the small room, the pediatrician on duty walked in and

checked Nick. "His oxygen is low. I'm going to order a tent to help raise it. It will be easier than trying to keep a tube around his face."

She nodded, frightened and numb. An hour later, she watched in horror as Nick's crib was covered with a thick plastic tarp, essentially keeping her from him. "It's not for long," the doctor assured her, "and it will help tremendously."

She sat beside Nick's crib, watching him sleep, her eyes tearing whenever she focused on the IV taped and wrapped on his tiny arm as the early November sky darkened out the window. Finally, she could no longer keep her eyes open and climbed into the bed the nurses wheeled in for her, thinking she'd rest for a few minutes.

A feathery touch of her cheek jolted Olivia awake, and she opened her eyes to see Chris kneeling at her side. His tux shirt was unbuttoned with the bowtie untied and hanging around his neck.

"What time is it?"

"Nine," he whispered. He brushed her hair back from her face.

"I fell asleep early."

"You had a day, babe."

On her back, she looked at Nick as he lay sleeping.

"I've been watching him sleep for a while. He seems more comfortable already," Chris said. "But what's with the tent?"

"His oxygen is low."

Chris bit his inner cheek and stared at the baby while Olivia looked at her husband. His hair was gelled back from his face, and she thought he looked more beautiful than ever. "What are you doing here so early? Isn't the reception still going on?"

Chris pulled his eyes back to her. He sat on the bed and rested his hands on either side of her. "I made it through the ceremony and pictures and took off after my speech."

"There are three hours of partying left. You're missing the best part."

His put his palm on her cheek. "I had no one to dance with. My best part is here."

Her eyes filled, and she sat up, hugging him. "I'm scared, Chris."

"Don't be. He's a fighter. He's us."

Chris left at midnight to relieve Olivia's mother from watching Ella, and Olivia fell back to sleep.

She woke with each nurse through the rest of the night, silently watching as they checked on her son, recorded their observations, adjusted machines and his oxygen tent. He was the boy in the bubble.

Chris returned at eight the following morning to find Olivia awake and in the chair next to a sleeping Nick. He handed her a paper bag and hot coffee.

"Did you sleep?"

"Here and there," she answered through a yawn and then stood and let him envelop her in his arms. "How about you?"

"I didn't." He tightened his hold on her. "I don't sleep when you're not with me."

She pulled back. "That's a lot of pressure. I'd better not die."

"Don't you dare."

She sat back down and lifted the lid of the paper cup. "Mmm. Thanks for this. Where's Ella?"

"At Mom's." Chris moved to the other side of the crib and sat down. "How's he doing?"

She took a sip from her cup. "I don't think there's any change." She let out a shaky sigh. "It's hard not to be able to touch him."

As if sensing his parents were talking about him, Nick turned over, opened his eyes and lifted his head, his curls pressed to one side. "Baba," he said, though the sound was muted by the plastic.

"Hi, baby. Look." She pointed to the other side of his crib. "Daddy's here, too."

"Hey, Nick. How'd you sleep, big boy?" His throat caught,

and he coughed, trying to keep his emotions from getting the better of him. Nick gave a half smile before his face crumpled into a cry.

Olivia stood and put her hands over the crib while Chris stepped outside in search of a nurse.

Chris brought Ella to the hospital on the third day. Olivia met them in the lobby and swept her up in a fierce hug. In her mother's arms, Ella leaned back and put her palms on Olivia's cheeks. "Mommy," she said, smiling. At eight years old, it had been a long time since Ella called her that.

"Oh, little girl, I do miss you." She took Ella to the cafeteria and bought them both chocolate milk and cookies and seated them at one of the tables while Chris went to sit with Nick in his room three floors up.

"Did you have fun at Grandma's yesterday?"

"Can I see Nicky?"

"Not yet. He's sleeping a lot, trying to get better, so he can come home and play with you."

Ella nodded as if she completely understood what was going on. "Can I sit on your lap?" Olivia was about to say she was a little old to be held when she saw the longing in the girl's eyes. Instead, she pulled her close and held her tight. If she were twenty and wanted to sit here, Olivia wouldn't question it even then.

Later, Chris found them in the lobby. They were on the couch watching television and chatting about third grade. An hour later, Olivia stood at the entrance to the hospital watching her husband and daughter walk away, feeling a piercing, painful pang in her heart.

Trevor and Dana stopped in on their way to the airport for their honeymoon just as Chris returned from dropping Ella back at Janine's. Their bright, happy newlywed faces were a sharp contrast to Olivia's exhausted bags beneath her eyes. The same age, she felt a decade older than her friends.

"Let me see him," Dana said, carrying a furry pale blue teddy bear. Chris and Trevor waited outside the room talking.

They stood at the crib, and Dana gave Olivia a half-hug. "You look like crap. I didn't want to say it in front of Chris."

Olivia let out a tired laugh. "He's got eyes. He sees."

"Not when it comes to you."

Olivia kept her focus on Nick.

Dana leaned over the crib, finally free of the thick, plastic tarp that had been covering the baby for the past three days. She put the bear on the small table next to the bed. "He looks okay. He has some color. Chris said he looked pretty bad when you brought him in."

"We were so scared, Dana. I've never been so scared."

Dana sat down opposite her friend. "What the hell is RSV? I've never heard of it."

"It's a respiratory infection."

"When can he go home?"

"Soon, I hope."

"Has Ella been in to see him?"

Olivia shook her head. "I don't want to scare her. I keep telling her Nick will be home soon, and she's taking everything in stride. You know how self-involved eight-year-olds can be."

"I've never really grown out of that."

Olivia chuckled. "Thank you for bringing the bear. He's going to love it."

"I brought you something, too." Dana pulled a flask out of her pocketbook and raised her eyebrows.

"Are you kidding me? I can't drink here! You're crazy."

Dana glanced at the sleeping baby, twisted the top off the flask and drank. She winked at Olivia and replaced the top. "It's here for you. Just so you know."

"When we get home, I'll find an AA group for you."

Dana checked her watch. "I have to go. We have to get to Kennedy."

"Where are you two off to?" she asked Dana as they walked outside the room to find Chris and Trevor still there. Dana looked at Trevor who winked at his new wife. Their enthusiasm and excitement was palpable and couldn't be hidden beneath their concern for Nick.

"Rome."

Olivia stood motionless for an extra beat and put a smile on her face. That's right. She knew that. "Wow. That's awesome. Send us a postcard."

"Don't we always?"

As she hugged Dana good-bye, she whispered, "Leave the flask."

They watched their friends walk down the hall and get into the elevator.

Without a word, Chris and Olivia went back into Nick's room to wait.

Chapter 22
October 2010

A nurse walked in and woke Nick when she checked his IV and adjusted the tube. To Olivia, he appeared confused at first, until he saw her sitting beside him. He gave her a crooked smile and then winced.

"Yup, I just gave you more," the nurse said, as she passed his bed. "You'll be back in la la land in no time."

Nick mumbled something incomprehensible, ignored by the nurse as she left the room.

His eyes moved back and forth to Chris and Olivia.

"Is this the boy who you beat up last month? Did he do this to you?" Chris said.

Nick nodded very slowly and opened his mouth to speak. Olivia leaned forward to hear him. "He had friends."

She turned to tell Chris what he said, but it appeared Chris already knew. "I figured as much." He sighed. "Nicholas, when is this going to end?"

Nick squeezed his eyes and took a tenuous breath. "It's over. Melissa talked to the police. She told them everything." His voice was raspy and low. "She's pressing charges."

Olivia found Melissa at the end of the floor in a small, windowless waiting room. She was folded onto a chair and looked like a young girl, picking at her nails, her long hair hanging over her face. She looked up and quickly stood when she saw Olivia at the door.

"Mrs. Bennet, I'm sorry."

Olivia took Melissa's hand and placed her other one over it. Melissa looked down, and a tear fell.

"Are you okay?" Olivia asked.

The girl shrugged and pulled her face up to look at her. "This is my fault." She started to cry, and Olivia put her arms around her.

"It's not your fault. But you need to speak up for yourself. There are consequences for actions, and that boy needs to pay for what he did." She pulled back to see the girl's red, mottled face. "It's not Nick's job to punish him. He could have gotten into a lot of trouble."

"I know, believe me. I tried…" Olivia pulled her back into a hug, allowing the girl to let go. Finally, she settled into a hiccuped breath and stepped back. "My father's making me go home. At least for the rest of the semester."

Olivia sat her down and handed her a tissue from the small table in the corner. "That sounds like a good idea. You can come back in January. Or next September. Start fresh."

The girl shook her head. "I don't know if I'm coming back. And Nick…he'll be out in May." She blew her nose and groaned at the thought.

Olivia could remember all too clearly being in love in college. What would she have done if she was forced to leave Boston and Chris behind? The thought dismayed her even now. She could tell this girl she was so young and there were plenty of other men out there. But at eighteen, she had found her own love and not a day passed where she regretted it. Few did it, but she was proof it was possible to find love so young.

"Everything will work out. I promise."

When Melissa composed herself, Olivia told her Nick was awake and wanted to see her. They stayed with him for the rest of the afternoon, and at sunset, she and Chris left the two alone to check into their hotel.

Over dinner, Olivia told Chris of her conversation with Melissa. He was pleased she'd be going home, allowing Nick to fully concentrate on finishing his courses and graduating in May.

"Nick's going to be devastated when she leaves."

"It'll be good for them both. They're young. They need to focus."

"Says the former nineteen-year-old who wouldn't leave my side for one day. Don't you remember what it was like?"

"Yes, which is exactly why I'm happy she's leaving."

Olivia stared at him over his hamburger. "That hurt." She dropped her fork and threw her napkin on her plate. She'd lost her appetite.

"Liv, look at what we went through. I'm not nearly as bright as Nick is and threw away an education. My parents exiled me."

She didn't answer and wouldn't look at him.

"It hurt me that I couldn't give you more. Do you have any idea what I went through?"

She raised her eyes to him and Chris, upon seeing her face, leaned back.

"I didn't want more. It was a partnership. We went through it together. How could you not see that? How could you be so egotistical as to think you shouldered everything yourself?" She stood, mumbled "Men," and left him to pay the check. Chris walked outside moments later as she finished a call with Gavin.

At the hotel they lay in bed, both on their backs. Neither had spoken since they left the restaurant.

"Olivia, I feel the same way about you now as I did when I was nineteen."

"No, you don't."

He thought a moment. "You're right." He turned his head to her. "I thought I loved you in college," he said, "but that was only the beginning. The more I learned about you, the deeper I fell. Until recently, I knew everything and my heart was irrevocably yours. You're my air and my breath. You've always been it."

She turned to him and their eyes locked. "Until recently?"

He looked up to the ceiling. "Do you still feel the same way about me?"

"How could you possibly ask me? What have I ever done to give you any idea I don't?"

She watched him closely. He opened his mouth to speak and then closed it.

"Chris, what's the matter?" She put her hand on his chest.

He hesitated before putting his hand on hers. "Nothing. Go to sleep. It's been a day."

"Do you think he'll be okay?" she whispered into the dark.

"I do," he whispered back, and she fell into a deep sleep.

They returned to the hospital in the morning to find Nick distraught. "She's going home on Friday. They're pulling her out."

Olivia went to him and took him carefully in a hug. "I know. But it's for the best. She'll come back next semester or finish her classes somewhere else. Somewhere she won't have to worry about what happened."

He looked down at his hands. "She's the first…" He kept his gaze away from them. Olivia looked at Chris who widened his eyes and shrugged. This child rarely communicated his emotions, let alone offered a glimpse into his personal affairs. This girl was his very first love. The hardest to let go. And he was sharing it with them. Olivia kissed the top of his head.

"I promise, with everything I know, you will be okay. If she comes back, you'll continue. If she doesn't, then you'll figure it out. Trust me."

He remained quiet and dismayed. They sat with him for the entire day, until the doctor finally stopped in before dinner and told them he could be released the following day, with instructions for follow-up visits throughout the month.

"Do you want to come home?" Chris asked him when the doctor left.

"No."

Chris glanced at Olivia, who stood silently at the end of the bed. "Do you think it's safe for you to go back?"

"Melissa pressed charges. I did, too. I should have seen this coming. I was stupid to think he'd just walk away. The balls on him. After what he did to her…" The words dropped off as Nick closed his eyes and clenched his jaw. He took a deep breath and exhaled.

Olivia let out her own relieved breath. Six months. That was all he needed before getting his degree and coming home. As nervous as she was to have him so far away, she was happy he wasn't going to quit.

"Dad? I don't regret what I did. I'd do it again."

"That doesn't ease my mind, son."

They drove home two days later after settling Nick back into his apartment and making dinner for him and his two roommates, who inhaled the food amid promises of keeping Nick out of harm's way until graduation. Olivia turned to Chris, who stayed focused on the road. "It seems we're making this trip a few times too many."

Chris stared forward. "I worry about him. Making his way in the world."

She watched the lines on the road pass ceaselessly beneath them, until they were a blur moving beyond her eyes. "It's ironic. We worry so much about them, but we winged it ourselves. We were clueless about everything. About how to keep a marriage together, balance work with family. All of it. We figured it out. He will, too."

Chris looked at her. "How the hell did we do it?"

"We did it together." She laid her head back on the seat. "Chris, we're going to have to talk about this, you know. It won't just go away." Back to the pregnancy.

"I'm hoping it does."

She felt the heat rise to her face and forced herself to stay calm. "Pull over."

"What?"

"Pull over." They were on the thruway, passing fields of horses and cows. "Now!"

He gradually pulled onto the shoulder, and she bolted out of the car before he came to a complete stop. "Jesus!" he yelled, catching up to her as she stormed inland. He grabbed her arm so she faced him and was surprised by what he saw. "Hey! I should be the one who's upset!"

Tears stung her eyes. "You won't even talk about it!"

"Well, I don't like being in a position where I have no control. Do you know what you're suggesting for the rest of our lives? Has it occurred to you what's in store for us?" he yelled over the passing traffic. "We're fifty years old. You want to have another baby. What the hell does that mean for us?" He took an angered breath, and his shoulders sagged. "I can't do it again, Liv. I don't want to. I'm sorry. We had plans, I thought. Why does it upset you so much that I want only you for the years we have left? I don't get it. We've waited our lives for this."

"I've been here with you the whole time. What do you think we've been doing all these years? My God, we've been together forever. It's not going to change."

He stepped back, putting his hand on the back of his neck and shook his head. "You're wrong. Everything's changed."

He walked back to the car and sat in it, staring ahead while she stood on the grass trying to understand, oblivious to the upstate October chill and dazzling fall foliage that hadn't yet reached Long Island. When she calmed herself down and her eyes cleared, she got back in the car.

Wordlessly, he drove home.

Olivia was upstairs alone when the phone rang. She placed Chris's clean tee shirts in his drawer and went to answer. She picked up the receiver after the third ring to hear Chris and Ella already speaking. His angry, rattled tone earlier in the day was replaced by the warm, measured voice he saved for Ella. Olivia listened, loving the way he spoke to their daughter, enamored, completely in love. How could he now be so against a baby when he was so deliciously in love with their children?

"Liv, you on?" she heard him say, breaking through her thoughts.

"I'm here."

"Okay Boo Bear, talk to you soon."

"Bye, Daddy."

Olivia squeezed her eyes, missing the full support of her husband as Ella regaled her follow-up visit with the adoption representative and the next steps they'd take in the process. Olivia interjected appropriately, wondering how she was going to get through this.

In their bedroom, she undressed and climbed into bed, exhausted from the week and the ride home. She felt sad. She didn't plan for another baby at this stage of their lives, but she couldn't always control fate. She wanted to move on as well, though she found it hard to admit it to Chris because she would also be admitting to not wanting to do this over and she felt it was unfair to the baby. Their baby. Then she thought of Ella in her quest to be a mother, nature stacked against her for some unknown reason and how she would tell her daughter she was doing it again, however wrong or unfair it seemed.

She fell asleep alone in the bed. He was gone before she awoke the following morning. Did he come to bed at all? She brushed her teeth, remembering he'd kissed her lightly along her face—tiny, featherlike touches down her temple to her ear, something he did and she loved. She paused, the toothbrush in her hand. Did she imagine it?

Chris's watch lay forgotten on the sink. She grabbed it and went to put it back in his drawer when she saw a neatly folded brown paper bag lying on top of his tee shirts. She thought it odd to see it there, having just put his laundry away the previous evening. She opened it up and read what was written. She pressed the paper to her chest and closed her eyes as she remembered.

Chapter 23
1990

"Mom? Can you watch the kids for me on Thursday? I want to see Chris play."

She could hear her mother flip the pages of her calendar. How many sixty-five year olds kept a busier schedule than her mother? "It's okay. Don't cancel whatever it is you are doing. It was just a thought. I can go another time."

"No, no. I can make it. It's just another candle party at Miriam's. How many candles do I need? I just say yes to give me something to do." A widow for more than half of her life, Janine learned to fill up her time to avoid being alone. Olivia envied her. What would she do when she ended up alone? The thought upset her too much to dwell on it. Not to mention she was way too busy for the luxury of worrying.

Janine showed up on Thursday and was escorted immediately into the den by Ella, who had the whole evening planned with her grandmother. Nick was asleep in his toddler bed, and Olivia hoped he wouldn't wake up and interrupt Ella's plans.

"You look wonderful," Janine said as she passed her daughter in the hall. "You should wear that more often instead of your usual baggy jeans and sweatshirt."

"I don't wear baggy jeans to work. Just when I'm home." She checked herself one last time in the bathroom mirror by the front door and frowned. Tonight, she'd opted for a white blouse and flared pants. Turning sideways she saw the last of the baby weight she'd yet to lose. How long was it acceptable to call it baby weight, she wondered. Nick was two-and-a-half.

"Olivia, you look good," her mother said. "Bring a coat. It's still February and frigid out there. Now go." She walked inside with Ella.

The crowded bar held the odor of stale beer mixed with Paco Rabanne. The band was already playing, the crowd moving and swaying to the music as Olivia pushed her way toward the stage and stopped near a table several feet away. Her husband was leaning over the keyboard, his hair damp with perspiration. He liked to stand during much of the sets. She stared at his back, at the shirt clinging to him while he moved and rocked to the beat. This was where he was happiest. She felt good about her decision to quit school again. She looked at the drummer, half-expecting to see Trevor, though she knew he and Chris so rarely played together anymore. Trevor and Dana just had a new baby and were now settled in Westchester, too far to make these gigs. She missed seeing them at these shows. It wasn't the same. The singer in this band didn't frolic around the way the other one did. Older, maybe.

There were two men sitting at the table as she stood watching Chris. One motioned for her to sit, and she smiled gratefully, lowering herself onto the available seat. She draped her coat around the back of the chair.

"Beer?" he yelled to her, holding up his own bottle.

She shook her head and returned her attention to the band where she stayed for the rest of the set. When the lead singer announced they'd be taking a twenty-minute break, the standing crowd moved closer to the stage. Olivia stood and waited for Chris to look around and see her. She didn't tell him she was coming. She wanted to surprise him.

He took a towel from the bench next to him and wiped his face and neck as one of the guitarists leaned toward him to say something. They laughed, and Chris walked toward the ledge of the stage and squatted to talk to someone. The crowd blocked him, and Olivia took a step to her right to see who he was talking to. She flushed when she saw the target of his attention was a redhead in tight jeans and a form-fitting sweater. She couldn't be more than twenty. An age that seemed so young to Olivia now. She watched them talk and laugh. The redhead handed him a beer, which he took and drank, an act of familiarity that rattled Olivia.

"Now, do you want a beer?" She turned to see the same guy at the table holding a fresh bottle for her. "You look like you could use it."

Olivia studied them, as they talked, laughed, drank. Chris had no idea she was here. He didn't look for her. Now he sat, with his legs swinging in front of him, and the girl leaned next to him, close to his knees. Did she touch him? Someone else walked to him, and he said something, shaking his hand. *My husband has groupies.* Olivia turned to the guy holding out a beer.

"No, thank you. I gotta go." She left and drove home, trying not to overthink what she saw. Her mother was surprised when she walked into the house.

"You're home early." She stood from the couch when Olivia walked into the room.

"I have a headache."

"How'd he do?"

Olivia gave her mom a smile. "He was great. As always."

She peeked in on Nick, motionless in his crib and then Ella, sprawled on her bed, deep in sleep, and made her way to bed. When Chris came home hours later, she pretended to be asleep.

Olivia and the children were in the kitchen when Chris finally came downstairs the following morning. Nick sat in his booster chair eating cereal while Ella did homework, her waffles getting cold in front of her.

"There are my two lovely ladies," he drawled in his thick,

early-morning voice. He bent over to kiss the top of Ella's head. "Hey, little man," he whispered to Nick, gently touching his food-encrusted cheek.

Ella looked up at her father in defeat. "How are your math skills?" She sat back and waited for him to look over her work. Olivia watched her husband lean over the page and point as he explained to Ella how to figure out her answer. His hair hung over his head, hiding those hazel eyes she loved. His arms supported him over his daughter, the sinews of his lean muscles showing through his skin. Married for nine years, she felt like a newlywed every time she saw him. Still had butterflies when he walked into a room. Or when she saw him on stage, like last night. It felt like the first time she'd ever seen him and knew she wanted him. The redhead saw the same thing, Olivia knew. And it scared her.

He kissed Ella's head again and went to the coffee pot.

"How was last night?" Olivia asked as Chris poured coffee from the stove in a mug.

"It was fine. Good gig." He stirred in sugar followed by cream. "Had some extra requests and Jim let us stay on, so I'm tired today." He took a loud, slurpy sip. "Ahh. I'm going to jump in the shower."

She went to watch him the following Friday night. This time she asked Jenny's mom for the favor of babysitting to save her mother from having to give up a planned night with her girlfriends. Barbara arrived with Jenny, who was excited at the prospect of an evening together. Nick was already asleep.

"You should get someone else to watch them and we could go together," Barbara said when she showed up at eight-thirty. "I love live music."

"Next time," Olivia promised. "I just want to hear how they sound. It's been awhile." She hadn't told Barbara of her night out the week before, knowing if she did, she might tell her what she saw and by voicing her fears, would give them life.

"Ella's in the den watching TV, and Nick is asleep. I really appreciate this."

Her friend brushed off her gratitude with a wave. "I'm sure I'll be asking for a favor at some point. That's what we do for each other."

They couldn't afford to pay a babysitter yet. And she didn't want to explain to Chris where money went while she was spying on him. No, not spying. Just watching.

She arrived at the bar in the middle of their first set. They were playing at a different venue this week, another of their regular gigs. This one was on the south shore of Long Island, and farther east, so it took her a little longer to get there. She paid the cover charge and walked into a sea of fans bouncing to a new song she hadn't heard, an original. This time she went to the bar and bought a bottle of beer, sipping it as she maneuvered her way toward the stage. Her eyes were trained on him, the way he leaned over the keyboard, his hair wet with sweat, and breathed in. The stage was too crowded to approach, so she stayed along the side closer to him. Her view afforded his back, unfortunately, but she didn't want to fight to get to the other side of the room, so she stayed put.

The song ended, and the singer moved off-stage, along with the drummer and both guitar players, leaving Chris alone. He pulled the bench near his keyboard and sat down, ignoring the cheers and applause as he started to manipulate the keys with his elegant fingers. The fans seemed to know what was coming, and Olivia was surprised to see them already swaying back and forth with only the first notes.

She knew this song. He played it at home. As with the audience, she was mesmerized while he played the beautiful rendition of a love song he'd written for her. He was not a strong singer, but his voice was beautiful and soft and inflected the meaning of the words. He had them. He held the attention of every single person in the place, including hers.

Who was he playing for now?

Olivia managed to turn away from him and scanned the crowd. There she was. Right in front. The redhead who had permeated her dreams for the past week. Did she follow him to all his shows? Who was she, and what the hell was she doing with Chris? Was she doing anything? Olivia's eyes filled as much because of her emotions with the song as her sense of dread. Was she strong enough to put up with this?

He finished the song, the gentle resonance of the final notes drowned out by enthusiastic, raucous cheers. The rest of the band returned to the stage and together they played more until finally, the set was over. The singer announced a break, and the level of noise in the bar died down a blessed decibel. Olivia didn't move. She should have. She should have walked over to her husband and allowed him to be happy to see her, to hold her, and to hear her gush over his beautiful performance. But she stood where she was, out of his line of sight and watched him instead enjoy the small group of fans who surrounded him. The redhead stood by his side, possessive and glowing. Someone handed Chris a beer, and he drank it while chatting, laughing occasionally at something, and stayed with them until the second set began.

She finished her beer and waited until the band was into the second set at eleven-thirty before she went home.

She started to pull away. She didn't want to. What she wanted to do was keep him from going back to the bars, to that redhead, by wooing him with her easygoing manner and lovemaking. They were so sexually active and, Olivia thought, fulfilled. For years, she stayed up waiting for him, so they could talk about his night. They never tired. Lately, she pretended she was sleeping when he returned from his playing.

He never complained or asked why.

On those nights he reached for her, she found a reason to push him off—she heard Nick calling, she didn't feel well, too tired, hard day, until finally, he stopped trying. She existed through her days on autopilot, meeting Mr. Hughes's needs enough he didn't take any notice. And Ella was chatty and thriving, plowing through fourth grade.

Olivia's mother said something. They were at the park with the children on a Saturday morning in late April. Chris was sleeping in from another late night out.

"Things are different with you two," she said to her daughter while her eyes stayed on Ella across the sand near the slide. Nick sat near them, digging a hole with his plastic shovel.

She turned to her mother. "How so?"

Janine shrugged. "You're giving up. Don't shake your head. I can see it. And if I can see it, so can he."

Tears filled Olivia's eyes. "I can't help it. I shut down, but he doesn't ask. He doesn't care."

"That's bullshit," her mother said, surprising Olivia. "He cares. He's a man who isn't making his wife happy. Do you know how that must feel to him?" Janine sighed loudly and leaned over to rest her elbows on her knees as if she were paying closer attention to Ella, who was talking to another girl now on the swings. "You're twenty-nine years old, for Pete's sake. You're a grown woman. You'd better start communicating with that man before you lose each other. You have children. Grow up."

"But he's—"

Janine held up her hand, preventing her daughter from continuing. "I don't want to know. He is my son-in-law. I don't want to know things I shouldn't. Work it out. I promise you, regret is a sorry bedfellow. Take it from me."

She couldn't heed her mother's advice, and she also didn't voice her real worry. That she trapped him too young with the pregnancy, keeping him from a life he envisioned for himself that included more. It wasn't the attention of the redhead herself that Olivia was afraid of. It was what that another woman represented—everything Chris hadn't yet experienced, every-*one* he hadn't experienced. Had he been with enough women to know she was the one for him? A man wasn't supposed to be married and a father by nineteen. Not in the nineteen eighties. Neither was a woman. But Olivia was happy. She didn't feel like she'd missed out on anything. Her abandoned career was solidly replaced by her new job as a mother and wife. God, she felt old-fashioned. Today's women weren't supposed to be satisfied with the unambitious domestic setting as solely fulfilling. But she was. She felt fulfilled.

Her mother was wrong. It wasn't that Chris couldn't make her happy. It was she who wasn't making Chris happy. The thought nearly knocked her over.

It was a rainy night in May. She made macaroni and cheese for dinner, Nick's new favorite meal. She cleaned up the kitchen and after bathing and putting Nick in to sleep, she and Ella watched Mulan, (for the tenth time). Ella could recite almost every word while Olivia quietly absorbed it again. What was it that allowed children to re-watch something over again without getting bored? Olivia relished the quiet time with Ella and regretfully pulled back the blanket when the credits started rolling up the screen.

"Time for bed, El," she whispered to a sleepy girl. Ella nodded, eyes half-mast, and allowed Olivia to lead her to her bed down the hall. Olivia had grown to love this little house, a cozy ranch on a quiet street. The bedrooms were small, as was the kitchen, but it suited their needs and their wallets for now. Chris kept referring to this as their starter home, wanting to eventually buy something bigger, but Olivia was happy here.

She climbed into bed and looked at the clock. Ten pm. It would be several hours before Chris would be home. Friday night gigs always ran longer than weekdays. She opened her book and settled onto her pillow, listening to the patter of drops against the pane.

A shock of thunder woke her from sleep. She had drifted off with her bedside light still on and her book on her chest. She shut the book and turned off the light. The clock read 2:00 am. Olivia stared at the ceiling, trying not to worry about her husband out in this storm. When would he be home? A flash of lightning was followed by another crack outside, and Olivia jumped. Ella. She got out of bed and padded down to her daughter's bedroom, peeking in to find her sound asleep. Lucky girl. A quick glance into the baby's room showed a content, oblivious Nick also sleeping.

He walked in at four-thirty am. Olivia breathed a sigh of relief and tried to push off feelings of anger that threatened. She had been worried and couldn't fall back to sleep, imagining every horrific scenario possible, expecting the phone to ring, hearing he'd been in an accident or worse. Now that he was safe, she wondered where the hell he'd been. They stopped playing at one. Took half an hour or so to pack up the stage. This much she knew. What had he been doing for the past two hours?

She waited for him to walk into the bedroom, but he didn't. Finally, she got up and went into the dimly lit den. He was sitting on the couch, his head in his hands. He was so still she was sure he'd fallen asleep sitting up. The rain pounded outside, drowning out the sound of her footsteps. She touched him on the shoulder, and he pulled his head up to look at her. He'd been drinking. That much was clear. But there was more. He didn't look directly at her. He focused, or tried to focus, on something behind her.

"Where were you?" she asked.

He shrugged and kept staring at the spot. His jacket was still on and was dripping on the couch but she didn't care. She was seeing something about him that unnerved her, and she couldn't put her finger on it.

"Chris? What happened?"

He shrugged again and kept his gaze away from her.

"Look at me. Chris. Look. At. Me." Her voice grew stronger, though still muted by the storm, he heard her.

When he brought his eyes to hers, she covered her mouth and stepped back. He didn't need to verbalize anything. She knew. Tears fell down his cheeks, and he dropped his head back into his hands. Hot tears filled her eyes too, and anger flew from her feet up through her body until she was so filled, she went to him and pounded her fists against his arms and shoulders, her screams of "How could you? How could you?" over and over mixed with the storm outside. He took her raging blows silently until finally, depleted, she fell to the floor in a heap of angry sobs.

He didn't speak. He didn't move. He kept his head in his hands like a guilty child. She wiped her eyes and her nose and pulled herself from the floor.

"Stay out here." Her voice cracked in pain. She walked back into their bedroom and climbed into bed, pulling the blanket over her, trying to stop her shaking.

***

She woke to the aroma of bacon and eggs and lay in bed listening to the sounds of Ella and Chris talking while incoherent ramblings of Nick could be heard in the background. Their forks clanked against the plates as they ate breakfast like nothing in the world was wrong. Olivia couldn't muster the energy to move so she closed her eyes and went back to sleep.

When she woke next, the house was silent. In the bathroom, she looked in the mirror. Her eyes were swollen, and she looked like she'd been to battle and lost. The rain had stopped, but the day was still overcast and gray. She pulled a sweatshirt over her tank and went into the kitchen in search of coffee, thankful she was alone. She had no idea what to say to Chris. What would they do now? Where would they go from here?

She was surprised to see him sitting at the kitchen table waiting for her. The dishes had been washed and put away. There was no sign of the children. She stood at the entrance and said nothing.

He cleared his throat. "I called your mother. She took them for the afternoon."

Olivia walked to the coffee pot and filled her mug.

"Let's talk, Liv. Please."

She sipped the coffee and winced at the pain she felt when it slid down her throat. It was sore from yelling and crying, and fresh tears filled her eyes. She walked into the den and sat down on the couch, dry from last night. He'd stayed out of their bedroom, but there was no sign he slept here. Did he sleep?

He walked in and stood watching her. No. He looked like he'd been up all night. His eyes were red and underlined with dark circles. What must her mother have thought when she picked up Ella and Nick? Janine had suspected something was wrong. Maybe she even predicted it. Olivia took in her husband, in sweats, hair mussed, looking miserable. She knew she was partly to blame. No. No, she wasn't. There was no excuse for infidelity. Not even when your spouse keeps pushing you away. She wished she could go back to the first night she saw the band, those months ago. She would have told him what she'd seen, and he'd have put her worries to rest. Or would he have?

He knelt in front of her. "Liv, I don't have an excuse for what I did. It meant nothing. It was nothing." He ran his hands through his hair. "I'm going to have to live with it for the rest of my life. But I need to know something." His eyes watered, and he kept his focus on her. "I need you to tell me why I'm losing you. Before last night. You've been pushing me away. What have I done?" He kept his hands on his lap, and that hurt her more than his words because whenever she was this close to him, he touched her, brought her closer, as if he couldn't get close enough, as if he wanted her inside of him. Today his hands stayed still, and she heaved over in pain.

He waited for her to compose herself. "I don't know if I'm enough for you," she said finally.

He squinted in confusion. "What have I done to ever make you feel like this? Or that I want anything else? I reach for you, and you back away. You've been pushing me away for months."

She sighed. "I watched you. With the band. I saw...someone with you. You knew her. You talked to her. I watched." The words came out like shards of broken glass, piece by piece, paining her more.

His face broke. "When did you come? When? Why wouldn't you tell me?"

Ashamed, she sniffed and looked down at her hands. She'd acted like a jealous girlfriend instead of his wife. "I'm so angry at you."

He stared at her. He still didn't touch her, and she felt cold. To be so close to him and feel so far away. She understood now, what she'd been doing to him over the past months. She was a fool.

"It was the redhead," she said. It wasn't a question.

His face crumpled, and he dropped his head. "I don't know why. I don't really remember how anything started. She was there, and I was drinking..."

Olivia squeezed her eyes shut, trying to keep the image of him touching someone else out of her mind. The thought made her want to run through the streets screaming until she was so far away, she wouldn't have to think or to know.

"Liv." She opened her eyes. He reached out his hand toward her cheek.

"How would you feel if I were with someone else?"

His hand stopped before he touched her skin, and he pulled it back. His face expressed grief she hadn't seen. He shook his head. "I'd die," he said simply. "I love you more than anything." He wiped his eyes. "I don't know how to undo it."

They faced each other, and it was unbearable. They'd been together for ten years—inexplicably, undeniably together. She was his from the moment they met. Didn't know how to be anyone else.

"I want to touch you, and you won't let me. I don't know what to do. Tell me what to do," he pleaded.

She said nothing, inside of herself.

"Liv, don't send me away. Come back to me, and help me make it right."

She put her head in her hands. "I'm afraid, Chris. I was afraid of losing you, and that fear sent you to someone else."

"No. It was a stupid mistake. I'm not with anyone but you. I'll always be with you."

"That's no excuse."

He sat back on his heels. "I know. What I'm trying to say is you're the only one who has my heart, who has me." He poked his chest hard. "No one else will ever have it. No matter what happens. No matter what you decide to do. I promise you that."

He stood and walked into their bedroom. Olivia sat on the couch and replayed their conversation over in her mind. She re-enacted her visits to him in the bar, the way the other girl watched him, in lust and entranced and his nonchalant reaction to her. He was friendly. Was he anything more? Did she allow her imagination to take over? Olivia sighed. She was wrong, too. Their lines of communication broke down. They both acted immature. She was hurt before she was really hurt. It was so backward, she wanted to laugh. But all that would come out of her were muted sobs.

On the couch, she fell onto her side, not bothering to wipe the tears that seemed to form from an unending source. She felt like she could cry forever. She wanted to rewind the months and do it differently. She wanted to forgive him and continue with their lives. Could she do it? She squeezed her eyes shut and images of Chris and that girl appeared in her mind. She gasped and opened them, a fresh wave of grief washing over her. Pushing her head into a pillow, she screamed and pounded the cushion in anger.

Spent, she stared at the ceiling, thought about all they'd been through until now, the odds they faced together leaving school and the security of his family, their education. Ella and Nick and how much joy they brought. And how happy Chris made her.

Pulling herself up to sit, Olivia leaned over and hugged her empty stomach. The realization that she couldn't imagine a life without him brought her a certain sense of peace. She took a deep, cleansing breath. They were stronger than this. They had too much to lose.

The shower went on, pulling her from her thoughts. She pushed the bathroom door in and saw him under the spray, his head down in defeat. He stood for a long time until the steam prevented her from seeing him. When he finally came out, wearing a towel around his waist, she was waiting for him in the bedroom. He stopped when he saw her.

"I don't want to fight," she said.

He shook his head and took a step to her. She held up her hand to stop him. "No." He paused. "I'm going to need time, Chris. To forgive you and to try to forget the image I have in my mind."

"There's no image. There's nothing to imagine. Please don't do that to yourself. To me."

"Give me time."

"Okay," he said, and she left the room.

She went with him to the bar two weeks later to watch him play, at his insistence. Tonight, he would tell the group to find another keyboardist. Olivia's mother stayed with the children.

The redhead was there, and when Olivia walked in with Chris, she took note of them and moved to the corner of the bar. He placed Olivia at a table in the center of the room. When he sat down to do his solo in the first set, he dedicated it to her.

She was in the bathroom later when the redhead walked in. Olivia caught her eye through the mirror and held them until the girl disappeared into a stall. Olivia considered waiting for her, to lay into her for what she'd done but when she saw herself in the mirror, she saw a girl who couldn't put blame on someone else. It was Chris's own fault. She couldn't worry about every woman who came into his life. She had to believe he was with her and no one else. Tough to do now, but she hoped she'd be strong enough to hold onto forgiveness.

When she walked out of the bathroom, the redhead was still in the stall.

Olivia helped the band pack up their gear. When Chris called the singer over to speak with him, she put her hand on his arm. "Before you talk to him, let's discuss it more."

He looked confused. "It's what I want to do. Let me do this for us."

It took another two weeks before she let him back into their bed. Another week of stilted good nights. Tonight, Chris whispered *I love you*, as he did every night, and touched her cheek. They hadn't been intimate in three months. She ached for him and only now would she allow herself to really feel it.

Chris breathed deeply beside her. Olivia moved to him in the dark. He responded immediately. A sound escaped him, a mix of a moan and groan.

He took her into his arms and held her to him tightly. "Baby," he whispered. "God, I missed you."

They made love roughly, pulling at each other in an angry haze of need and regret. Chris silently accepted her cold, purely sexual connection. When she climaxed, she squeezed her eyes tight so not to see the fear and sadness in his own. After, in a sheen of sweat and tears, they lay side by side, breathing hard.

He turned to her. "I'll never hurt you again. I promise on our children. My life is nothing without you."

"I won't hurt you, either." She allowed him to hold her hand and they lay silently until she climbed on top of him. They locked eyes and made love slowly, never once breaking their gaze. When they finally fell asleep, they were a mix of limbs and torsos. And relief.

Olivia opened her eyes to find Chris watching her. Pale light sifted into the room through the blinds. "Hey," he whispered, lightly touching her nose.

"Hey yourself." She smiled, feeling satiated, warm and the

first feeling of peace in a long time. The feel of her husband close to her felt like a gift. "Where's Nick?"

"He's sleeping. I just checked on him. So is Ella. It's early yet."

"Mmm." She rolled over onto her back and tucked the sheets under her arms. He put his hand over her chest and pulled her closer to him. He kissed her cheek, then whispered, "Let's take a trip."

She put her hand on his head, lost her fingers in his thick hair. "Where do you want to go this morning?"

"No. I mean a trip. Physically go somewhere."

She pulled her hand back. "Where do you want to go?"

He shrugged. "Anywhere. Everywhere. There's so much world out there."

"Sesame Place? Disney World?"

Chris sighed. "No, I mean us. I want to take a trip with you. As adults. How many times did we stare at those postcards on the fridge and want to be in one?"

"I've always wanted to go to Italy," she said.

He smiled. "We have to find fungus."

"I'll just get a few things together. Ella will love to tour. And Nick is all over the place so it will be easy to keep up with him."

Chris frowned. "You're making fun of me."

Olivia shook her head. "I'm not. I'm being realistic. We can't take them with us. And I won't leave Nick this young."

"Your mother is more than qualified. The kids love being with her."

She looked at him and finally said, "We have no money."

Chris stared at her for a full minute. She thought he might be angry or hurt. He was trying to do something nice for them, and she had just shot him down. They had two children. They couldn't just up and go to Europe. They could barely pay their mortgage. She breathed and waited for him to say something. This was exactly what she feared and part of the reason she pushed him away, believing she'd stopped him and herself from living a fuller life. A baby changed everything. Her friends graduated college and backpacked through Europe or Australia before settling down to find jobs. She'd amassed postcards from dozens of countries that summer after their graduation while she stayed home and planned Ella's first birthday party. Her friends were seeing the world while she watched Sesame Street.

Chris climbed out of bed, and she held her breath. He wasn't even finishing their conversation. Where was he going? He walked to their closet while she enjoyed the sight of his ruffled hair and naked body as he reached up to the shelf and pulled down a paper bag. He turned it upside down, dumping a stack of clean music paper onto the rug and climbed back into bed. He reached into his nightstand and grabbed a pen.

Olivia waited silently for him to reveal what he was doing.

"Our bucket list," he said, writing on the paper bag. "As soon as they're old enough, we'll do everything we want to do that doesn't include Big Bird or Mickey Mouse. Number one, travel to Italy."

"Tuscany," she corrected, smiling. Oh, how she loved this man. She turned to her side to face him.

"Right, Tuscany." He wrote more.

"I'd love to rent a villa there. Travel to Florence, Siena, Lucca. What do you think?" she asked.

"Baby, I want to be anywhere you are." He returned to the paper. "Number two. Write music."

"Tour," she added.

He shook his head. "Only if you're with me. Otherwise, I stay here."

"Go to the Grammys."

He moved his eyes sideways to her. "Bring date."

"Do you think you'll find one?" She chuckled.

"Fine. I'll bring Ella."

They talked, laughing and wistful, until they'd created a list of things they wanted to do in their lives. Most of their goals involved travel, pictures Olivia memorized from all those postcards and travel books she read that enabled them their bedroom trips.

"We have nineteen." He turned to her, his pen at his chin in thought. "We should round it up to twenty."

"I have one. Here." She held her hand out, and he gave her the list and pen. She added number twenty and gave it back to him. He stared at it and his jaw dropped.

He looked at her as if she suggested they travel to space. "You're kidding, right?"

She looked in his eyes, and they held each other's gaze for several seconds. Then she shook her head.

1. Travel to Tuscany. Rent a villa.
2. Write music.
3. Tour with family.
4. Go to the Grammys. Bring date.
5. Walk on the Great Wall of China.
6. Eat a Vegemite sandwich in Australia.
7. Picnic in front of the Eiffel Tower.
8. Stand next to a redwood tree.
9. Look out over the Grand Canyon.
10. Cross the intersection at Abbey Road.
11. Ride a camel.
12. Swim with dolphins.
13. Ride in a hot-air balloon over the Rockies.
14. Drink milk from a fresh coconut in Hawaii.
15. Bicycle across the Golden Gate Bridge.
16. Eat sushi in Japan.
17. Soak up the sun in Santorini.
18. Eat a snake in Thailand.
19. Ski the Austrian Alps. (learn to ski)
20. Meet baby in November

"Do you think we'll complete this list?" she said.

The bag dropped to the floor, and Chris fell back on the

pillow. She rested her head on his shoulder and draped her arm across his chest. He played with her hair, distracted, and stared at the ceiling.

"I thought we were done," he said. "I thought you were taking the pill."

She squeezed her eyes. "I ran out."

He stayed quiet, and she waited for his anger. He'd begged her to go back on the pill after her labor with Nick. The doctor told him she'd been close to...she couldn't even think it. But she'd been wanting another baby. To be surrounded by a big family, to make up for what they didn't have. She was an only child and his older brother, Brian, hadn't reached out to them since they'd been married. But for her mother, they were alone.

"When?"

She grimaced. "Four months ago."

He stiffened. "Liv, this is something we need to talk about. This is not just something we jump into. You can't decide to do this by yourself."

"I know." She swiped a tear quickly away. "I didn't really think it would happen."

"You just pointed out to me we have no money. How do you think we're going to do this?"

"We'll manage," she whispered.

He was quiet for a few moments. "The risks. The doctor said… I'm afraid."

"I'll be fine. I promise."

He said nothing more. She eventually relaxed against him and knew it would be okay.

Dear Mrs. Bennet,

As always, I hope this letter finds you well.

Nicholas is two years old and a terror. But he's so cute and can be charming when he wants to be. Chris said

Nick reminds him of his dad. I thought you might want to relay that message to Mr. Bennet.

We're doing well. We hit a brief rough patch, but I think it was necessary to keep moving forward. I love your son. More than I could love anyone (except for our children). It is important that you know that. To know that what we have is very real and not the childish romance as you voiced those many years ago. We're continuing to build our life together. Our children are happy and healthy (knock wood) and we live in a modest house that suits our needs. It may not be the enormous estate that you are accustomed to but we don't need that to be happy. I'm sorry if I'm coming off a bit cavalier today. I may not even send this letter when I re-read it later. But I feel strongly that you must eventually want to meet your grandchildren and see your son. I don't even care if you lay eyes on me again. Really.

Well, I must go. I'll leave you with this final thought: I'm pregnant. That will be three grandchildren for you. Just something to think about.

Love,

Olivia

Chapter 24
November 2010

Olivia woke up on the first Saturday in November to find Chris had already left for work. Their thirty-year ritual of waking up and eating breakfast together had been abandoned for the past month, and it rocked her. She felt untethered and out of sorts. The sky was clear blue and the unseasonably warm air enticed her to put in earbuds and take a walk down her street after lunch. In a sweatshirt and jeans, she meandered, taking little notice of her surroundings. Her argument with Chris on the side of the thruway was still very fresh in her mind. She had been reminiscing the past few days, thinking back to the early years when they were both so foolish and fought over a woman Olivia could hardly remember now. Memories of that early morning they made their bucket list rushed back in a flood of mixed emotions. Where had he been keeping it? She'd been as surprised at his sentimentality as she was that twenty years passed in the blink of an eye.

They'd barely scratched the surface of that list. What the hell had they been doing all these years? She was only fifty. They had plenty more years to come, she hoped. They were financially sounder than they'd been when they dreamed up the list. Chris had been an apprentice for John and playing nights at the time. The paint was still wet on their new house when Nick was a baby. Now, Ella and Nick were adults, raised and educated (almost) and heading down their own paths. They'd never left their starter home, couldn't leave it, and instead Chris had built a second floor himself. Chris and Olivia's future was theirs for the taking.

Olivia stopped short and gasped. For a second she forgot she was pregnant. And she saw their future through Chris's eyes. Their wonderful, carefree, exciting future. Their adventure awaited them. A wave of grief washed over her. What was she doing? How irresponsible they were. How unfair to the unborn child. To Ella. To each other.

Not feeling any better, Olivia turned back toward home and stopped in front of Sophia Johnson's house. Without thought, she found herself walking to the door, her third visit in the past two weeks, in twenty years. She knocked twice and almost walked away thinking the woman wasn't home when the door opened. Sophia smiled when she saw Olivia.

"Well, hello again."

"Hi, Sophia. I was taking a walk, and I thought I'd come by to say hello and see if you want a visit."

The woman opened the door wider and peeked outside. "It's a beautiful day for a walk, isn't it? A little reprieve before the winter." She stepped back, and Olivia walked in.

"Coffee? Tea? Wine?" In tan wool pants and a lavender sweater-set, Sophia led her unexpected guest through the living room into the kitchen. "I was just relaxing before I meet the girls for dinner later." She turned to Olivia. "This is a nice surprise."

"I hope you don't mind. I've been stopping by a lot lately. Making up for lost time, I guess." She shook her head when Sophia held up a Keurig pod and a tea bag in each hand. Sophia put them down and gestured for Olivia to take a seat. She sat across from her.

"I'm not sure that's it," Sophia said.

"What do you mean?"

"I think you're feeling a connection of some sort. Or perhaps there's something you need."

"I don't think so."

Sophia shrugged lightly. "Okay."

"I turned fifty this year. Did I mention that on my last visit?"

"No. But I understand now."

"You do?" Olivia couldn't possibly understand what she could see.

"Yes. You're wondering what the rest of your life is going to look like. You told me Nick is almost out of college."

"He graduates in May."

"Honey, they always come home. Don't worry about the empty nest. It won't be empty for a while unless the economy picks up and suddenly taxes go down. Not going to happen. Especially not here."

Olivia felt her cheeks grow warm. Chris wanted to be a full-time empty-nester. With Nick away eight months out of the year, they had a taste of what their new lives would be like. Sophia was right. Nick would most likely be returning home after graduation. What would it be like with a twenty-three-year old and a newborn?

"It's not quite that simple," Olivia said.

"It never is."

"Sophia, what is it like being alone?"

The older woman rested her elbows on the table and bridged her hands together. "It takes getting used to, like everything. It's been nine years since I lost Sol. Sometimes I still wake up and expect him to be in the kitchen preparing his oatmeal. He liked steel-cut oats. They took thirty minutes to cook. He was a patient man. He would have hated the Keurig." She smiled. "We were married for forty-five years. It's a hard habit to break."

"Your children?"

"Amanda is in Connecticut with her family and Billy is in Georgia. He met his wife at school. She's from Atlanta. They follow the women, you know. I don't really mind. I'm not too keen on her anyway."

"Do you ever think you'll move closer to your children?"

The woman stood and brought out a box of Lorna Doones. "I can't resist," she said and sat back down. "I'm not ready to leave yet." Sophia paused and looked at Olivia. "Are you planning on being alone any time soon?"

Olivia shook her head. "No. I just...you know...we're getting older..."

Sophia nodded. "Yes, it's natural. One of you will go first." She leaned over and put her soft, bony fingers on Olivia's hand. "You shouldn't fret about the future. You're still quite young. I'd give anything to be fifty again." She lifted her eyebrows. "You're thinking you're old and want to be thirty. It's all relative, my dear."

Olivia's eyes welled. Yes, of course. Fifty wasn't old. She knew that. But she'd wake up tomorrow and be sixty.

"There, there. Don't cry. Look at me. I'm seventy-nine. I'm going out to dinner with my canasta group. We decided to hit that new place over on Jericho Turnpike. There's a fixed price menu for dinner before five. Includes a cocktail." She winked, and Olivia laughed as a tear slipped down her cheek.

"You have many more years to do everything. The only part of my life I gave up, other than sex, and that was more due to pragmatic reasons than desire, is travel." She bit a cookie. "That's where I'm limited. I'm too tired to care what else is out there. I sat on a camel in Egypt." She leaned close to Olivia as if to share a secret. "It's not all it's cracked up to be. The place smells."

"You've been to Egypt?"

"I've been everywhere."

"We have a bucket list."

"And? Did you tackle the list? Do you remember what's on it?"

"We wrote it down. Together, many years ago," Olivia said.

Sophia watched her closely. "There's something wrong. Tell me. I'm a good listener, and I think you need one right now. Am I right?"

Olivia nodded. "I got pregnant my junior year of college, so we got married and dropped out of school."

Sophia sat back.

"We missed out on a lot of things to raise our children." Olivia raised her hand in self-protest. "I have no regrets." She sighed. "Though I'm not sure if he does."

Sophia appeared confused. "Honey, why is this relevant?"

Olivia took a deep breath. "My husband and I got into an argument yesterday. Our first real one since…in a long time."

The older woman leaned forward and put her hands on the table. "Start from the beginning," she said.

"Okay."

Olivia told Sophia the story of the inception of the bucket list as she remembered it. When she finished, Sophia pressed her lips together as Olivia blew air threw her mouth.

"That's a wonderful story."

"Yes."

"You have three children?" She was referring to the end of the story, when Olivia told Chris she was pregnant by adding the twentieth item to their list.

Olivia shook her head.

Sophia paused. "Ah. I'm terribly sorry."

"Thank you."

They sat in silence for a full minute.

"I'm pregnant," Olivia said into the room.

"Oh my," the woman whispered. She scooted closer to Olivia and grasped her hands, and Olivia felt at once soothed and heartbroken. She missed her mother.

"Is this what you and Chris fought about?"

Olivia nodded. "I found our bucket list in his drawer this morning. He's been holding onto it all these years."

Chapter 25

1990

I wish you didn't have to go." Olivia squeezed him again, and he kissed her behind her ear.

"It's only for a few days. I'll be home Friday."

"Call me when you get there."

"Of course." Chris put his hand on her belly. "See you later, Junior."

Ella ran to the door. "Bye, Dad."

Chris grabbed his daughter and dipped her over so her head fell back. He kissed her several times on her cheek and neck, and she screamed in happy protest.

He pulled her back up. "Where are you going?" she asked, holding onto his arms.

"I'm going to Westchester to stay with Uncle Trevor. For work. Honey, let go of Daddy, okay?" When she finally let go, he turned to Olivia. "Where's Nick?"

"Inside playing blocks. Want me to get him?"

Chris shook his head and leaned in for one more kiss. They watched him walk down the driveway, get into his car and drive away. As promised, he called Olivia a few hours later. It was a quick conversation. Not much happened in the afternoon. Ella went to school and then soccer, she dropped Nick at nursery school and went to work. Now they were alone eating dinner, rigatoni with butter for Ella and Nick, sauce and meatballs for Olivia and baby.

"I'll be busy tomorrow and Wednesday in meetings, so I'll call Wednesday night," he said.

"Good luck, my love. I hope you get it." Olivia crossed her fingers as they spoke, silently praying his presentation would go well and he'd get the job on the new hotel going up in Manhattan. He was trying to segue into commercial construction and had been preoccupied the entire week before he left. Quiet, reflective, stressed. Olivia was happy he finally left so it would be behind him one way or the other. She wanted her husband back. Their conversation ended as always, with their profession of love.

She woke up at dawn on Wednesday, cramping and frightened. She lay still in bed, perspiring, and curled into a tight position trying to alleviate the sudden sharp pain piercing her abdomen. *Please,* she whispered, *please.*

She was afraid to get up to pee, fearful of what would happen, so she waited until her bladder couldn't hold any longer. Her urine was clear, and the pain subsided. She relaxed for the first time in hours.

When Chris called that night, he sounded different. Sad. "Did you lose the business?"

"No," he said. "We meet again tomorrow and if they request a final meeting Friday, I'll stay for that, but I'll let you know."

"So why do you sound down?"

"I do? I'm...I just miss you."

She decided not to tell him about the cramping from the morning, not wanting to add to his stress. And she'd felt okay throughout the day, so it was probably nothing. "I miss you, too."

"Is Ella there?"

"Of course." She laughed. "Always within earshot." Olivia put Ella on the phone and listened to a one-sided conversation between two of her favorite people in the world. The eleven-year-old talked about her day at school, minute-by-minute, she forgot nothing, before asking to talk to Aunt Dana, who wasn't home. She handed the phone to her mother and kissed the slight bulge of her belly, as probably instructed by her father, before running the ten feet back into the den.

Olivia woke up Thursday morning with a groan. This time, when she moved the blanket to the side, she lay in a small pool of blood. She called her doctor's service, already knowing it had happened. Janine came over to put Ella on the bus and to take Nick to nursery school. Olivia drove herself to Dr. Byrne's office where he confirmed she'd lost the baby.

Numb and alone, she scheduled the D and C and drove home.

***

Chris called her in the evening. "Hey." He sprawled on the couch amid scattered toys and cardboard books in the large colonial, ignoring the lowered television as Olivia told him what happened. The blood drained from his face as the despair in her small voice tore at his heart. When she stopped talking, he lay silent, his hand over his mouth.

Dana watched from the attached kitchen, a questioning look on her face. Chris stared at her, giving nothing away.

"Chris, are you there?" Liv said.

He nodded, not trusting himself to speak. He pulled his arm across his eyes.

"Chris?"

"I'm here."

"I didn't want to call earlier in case Dana answered. I'm not ready to talk to anyone." She paused, and he berated himself. "I'm sorry," Olivia said, crying.

"No, I'm sorry. I'm sorry I'm not with you."

She cried harder, and he couldn't stop the tears. His whitened knuckles tightened around the phone as he cursed himself.

"Are your meetings done?" she said.

His meetings. He listened as Dana moved around in the kitchen. Yes. They were done. "Liv, I'll be home tomorrow."

"I scheduled the D and C for late morning. My mom will take me."

Shit. "No. I'll leave right away. I'll be there. I promise."

She sniffed. "Okay." And hung up.

He held the phone to his chest and turned his head away from Dana as she walked to him.

"What is it?"

Still looking away, he said, "I have to go home."

He felt her stand beside him and stared at the couch cushion. Her nanny's voice drifted into the room from the playroom down the hall where she kept Patrick occupied while Chris monopolized the den.

"Do you need more ice?" she said.

He gritted his teeth and swallowed down his frustration before mumbling, "No."

She walked away.

Alone in the den, he pulled himself up to sit, wincing from the pain. He took the bag of ice from between his legs and held it.

He found Dana in her guest room packing his duffel. He leaned against the door with his arms crossed and watched her fold his shirts and place them carefully in the bag. "What time does Trevor get home?"

"Late." She continued packing his things, keeping her eyes averted.

"Thank you," he said.

She didn't answer.

"Dana."

"When are you leaving?"

"Soon."

Dana nodded. "Are you going to be okay?"

His breath caught, and he swallowed a sob. When she saw his face, she dropped the shirt in her hands and went to him. He held her, burying his head in her hair.

"She lost the baby," he finally said. "What did I do?"

She squeezed him tighter. It was a few minutes before they let go. She put her hands on his face. They stood so close, he could feel her breath on his mouth. His head was down, and he pulled it back.

"Dana." It was a warning.

She stared at him. Finally, she dropped her hands. "You still have to tell her. She deserves to know."

"I can't now. Not after this. If I do, I'll lose her. I can't let that happen."

She stepped away. "Maybe she'll understand if you just explain, like you told me."

He stared hard into her eyes. "Don't tell her," he whispered.

"I'm not sure it's something I can keep to myself. She's my friend."

"You're my friend, too. Please." He held his breath.

Finally, she relented and nodded. "Fine. But I don't agree with this at all."

He exhaled. "Thank you."

"Can you drive?" she said.

"Yes."

"Don't forget your follow-up appointment."

"I won't."

She put his clothes down. "You finish doing this, and I'll make you something to eat before you go."

At nine o'clock, he held his bag at the front door.

"Thank you," he said again.

She kissed him lightly on his lips and closed the door.

***

Olivia saw the headlights coming down the street and held her breath as he pulled into the driveway. She met him at the door. Ella and Nick were asleep.

He stepped just inside the threshold and grabbed her as they slid to the floor and cried. In his arms, she felt better than she had in two days and for the first time since losing the baby, she felt hopeful and safe. Chris could do that—make her world a better place just by being near her. He let her cry until she had nothing left.

She had just started her fifth month with their son. He'd already fit into their family. He had a name. Christopher.

"I hurt so much," she said into his chest. He sniffed and pulled back, putting his hand on her barren, distended stomach. His tears still flowed and his anguish somehow strengthened her.

"Not there." She lifted his hand from her stomach and placed it against her heart. "Here."

He nodded and didn't speak. When he could, all he said was, "I'm sorry," over and over.

He lead her to bed and they held each other all night, neither fully sleeping. But they'd finally stopped crying.

Ella bounded into their room in the morning, and Chris worked hard to paste on a happy face. Olivia stayed in bed, rolled over, her back chilled by the sudden loss of his body heat behind her. He whispered to Ella and they both left the room, allowing her to be alone.

She got up in time to kiss their daughter good-bye before Ella went out for the bus with Chris. Nick sat dressed in his sweat suit watching television until Janine showed up to take him to school.

"Can I spend the day with him?" Janine asked, looking at her grandson.

Olivia nodded. "Of course. I'm sure he'd love it."

Janine hugged her daughter and, holding her grandson's hand, left the house.

Chris and Olivia got dressed and went to the hospital for the procedure. When she came to hours later, Chris was sitting by the side of the bed watching her.

"Hey," he said, putting his hand on her forehead.

"Is it done?"

He nodded, somber, dry-eyed. "The doctor stopped in but you were sleeping. He'll come back. He said you might feel some discomfort."

She held out her hand. He took it and kissed her knuckles. "I love you, Liv. Don't ever forget it."

"I know. It's what keeps me going."

Chris led Olivia into the house hours later. Janine was there with the children. She stepped into her mother's embrace, and a fresh wave of tears washed over her.

"Go rest. I'll make you dinner," Janine said. "Ella and I will cook."

"Thanks, Mom."

She climbed into bed and listened to her mother and Ella in the kitchen. The gentle tone of her mother's voice teaching her daughter to make sauce and meatballs lulled her into a doze. She woke to hear Chris and Ella talk in the kitchen over dinner while Nick added his own broken interjections to the conversation. Ella was explaining to Chris how she and Grandma made meatballs. Olivia listened to her animated high-pitched voice and found some solace. She must remember not to get lost in this grief. For her children's sake.

Later, Chris crawled into bed beside her. "I told Ella you're not feeling well. We have to tell her soon."

Olivia rolled onto her back.

"Are you hungry?"

"No," she said. She stared at the ceiling.

"How do you feel?"

She looked at him and said nothing.

"Okay." He held her hand, afraid to hold anything else and hurt her.

"Did you get the business?" she said. He didn't speak for a long time. She took it as his answer. "I'm sorry babe. You'll get the next one."

Dear Mrs. Bennet,

I am writing to you today with a heavy heart. Only last month I sent you a happy announcement that we were expecting our third child, so I feel I owe you the courtesy of giving you the news.

I lost our baby.

It's been a difficult week and I finally drew up the courage to write this letter. I am devastated. And Chris, well, he's been so strong, keeping our children busy and continuing our day-to-day duties of feeding them and making sure they get to school. I don't think they know what's going on as he is a constant positive force for all of us. At one point, I thought he was relieved by what happened. Until yesterday.

I'd pulled myself up and did a load of laundry, that mindless chore even the most grieved can perform. Carrying the basket, I walked past our bedroom door, left ajar, and saw Chris inside. He sat on the bed facing the wall and stared, not moving. He made no sound. With my heart in my throat, I moved away, unseen.

My mother has been helping us. I don't know what I would do without her. And I think of Chris without you during this time and it makes me weep.

Our saving grace is our children. Ella and Nick continue to bring sunshine to even our darkest days. They keep us busy enough so we don't completely lose ourselves to wallowing.

I hope my next letter will be filled with brighter news.

And I would like to say, I'm sorry. I'm sorry for losing your grandchild, who I'm sure was as beautiful as his brother and sister.

Until next time~

Olivia

Chapter 26
November 2010

Olivia paused by her car, clutching the door handle. She stared at the building and tried to psyche herself to move. A gentle breeze blew overhead, rattling the last of the burnt orange and red leaves still holding onto the trees. A carpet of color surrounded the parking lot.

For a fleeting moment, she saw herself at nineteen in a similar predicament, standing outside a similar building, only then she charged straight inside believing she was doing the right thing until Chris found her. If Dana had kept her secret as Olivia asked her to do, she would have never had Ella. *Don't think about it.* She glanced left and right. Chris wouldn't be coming today. No one knew she was here. What would he do if he knew? With a heavy sigh, she pushed herself away from the car.

She'd found this place online: *A private group offering fully comprehensive gynecological services to women like her.* Olivia couldn't bring herself to talk to Dr. Byrne. Not yet. First, she wanted to understand her options. Inside, she crossed the waiting room and signed her name on the clipboard at the reception desk and then settled into a corner chair.

Three women were seated with her in the small room. Olivia sat across from a teen with her mother. She picked up a magazine and tried to focus her attention on an article, but she couldn't stop staring over the pages at the teen's jittery legs in ripped jeans and Ugg boots. They moved at a spastic pace as the young girl bit her nails. Her mother, drawn and pale, stared at her phone. Neither spoke. A nurse opened the door.

"Josephine?"

A woman on the other side of the room stood and followed the nurse inside, leaving Olivia and the two across from her alone. She closed her eyes and took a deep breath. When she opened them, the girl was watching her, fingers still in her mouth. She wanted to ask the near-child if she was scared or sorry or regretful, like she was. Instead, she averted her eyes, and stared at a magazine she wouldn't remember later and wondered what she was doing here. When her name was called, she walked directly to the door held open by a nurse without a glance to the others.

An hour later, Olivia drove home in a daze. The staff member she met after she filled out the medical paperwork had been kind and informative. She explained the procedure to Olivia, how the anesthetic worked and each step involved. It took anywhere from five to fifteen minutes and it was over. Olivia shook her head again as she recalled the words. "After the procedure, we'll do a post-op sonogram to ensure it's complete and then you're brought to our post-anesthesia care unit where your oxygen, pulse and blood pressure are monitored. You remain there for about forty minutes. Then you can leave. You can return to daily activities the following day, if all goes well."

An hour and it would be as if she were never pregnant. How truly disturbing.

She didn't want to go home, didn't want to see Chris, confused by his adamant opposition to her pregnancy. Didn't want him to see she was considering doing what she never thought she would do. Not after what they'd been through.

Not sure where else to go, she pulled into the parking lot of Trevor's apartment building and walked inside. He opened the door and stood staring at her.

"Liv." His smile dropped. "Are you okay?"

No.

He pulled her in and closed the door. The house was quiet. "What is it?" he whispered.

She sniffed and looked at him, shaking her head. He hugged her and said nothing while she took shaky breaths. Her head leaned on his shoulder, and his calming demeanor made her feel less shaky.

"Come in."

She followed him into the kitchen and sat down while he took a bottle of wine from the fridge.

"Just water for me," she said.

"You're kidding. You look like you could use a drink."

Her head rested against her hands as he poured himself a large glass of red and brought an ice water to the table. Next to her, he put his hand out. She took it and looked around the spacious apartment, into the attached den decorated with a thick carpet, a long leather sectional and a massive media cabinet that framed his sixty-inch television.

"I don't think I'll ever get used to you not being with Dana," she said.

Trevor said nothing. She looked at him. "Are you dating?"

He shrugged. "Yes and no."

Olivia sipped her water.

"Talk to me, Liv. What brings you here?"

"I'm in a bit of a bind, and I didn't know where else to go. I need…I need to talk to someone. If I can't talk to him, you're the next best person."

He cocked his head in confusion. "Of course, anything you need. Is it about Chris? Is he okay?"

"We haven't been seeing eye-to-eye on something, and we can't get past it. We've been arguing for weeks. I'm afraid this might really break us."

Trevor shook his head. "Impossible."

She looked at him.

"Impossible," he said again. "Nothing can break you two."

"I thought so too, but I'm not so sure. This is big. Life-changing."

Trevor put down his glass and leaned over the table, closer to her. "Listen to me. Before you go farther, let me say something. I've known Chris most of my life. He's my brother." He took a breath. "His love for you is so pure, when they write love songs, they're talking about him. And you. I've never seen anything like it. The rest of us are envious."

He sipped his wine and ran his index finger around the perimeter of the glass creating a soft, mournful moan in its wake.

"For years, I felt superior to him." He blushed and kept his eyes on the glass. "I had a great job, made a boatload of money, still do, kids, multiple acres, live-in help. I was living the dream. But when I saw Chris, whenever you guys visited, or when he and I played with the band during those years, he would show up in that beat-up truck, in the same clothes he always wore, with five dollars in his pocket. He was so friggin' happy. Never bothered to hang out after we broke down the stage. He wanted to get home to you. You were married for years already, and he still couldn't get home fast enough."

Olivia smiled.

"Look at me now. Alone in this place. He may have had nothing of what I had, but he had everything. And he knew it. He still knows it. So, when I tell you nothing will break you, I mean it. I think you know it, too."

He stopped talking and looked at Olivia, his red cheeks returning to their normal color.

"Are you finished?"

Trevor let out a short burst of laughter, cleared his throat and nodded.

"I'm pregnant."

His jaw dropped. "You're kidding."

"I'm being completely truthful."

"How?"

She leveled him with a stare. "The usual way."

"I mean, aren't you? Didn't you go through—?"

"No, I am not in menopause."

He stared at his wine. Then he stood, put it on the counter and walked to the small butler pantry he used as a bar, just off the kitchen, returning with a bottle of scotch and a glass. "You sure you don't need something stronger than that?"

She didn't answer. He poured two fingers into his glass, tipped his head back, and swallowed. He poured more and returned to the table.

"So," she said, "you're taking it as well as he is, I see."

"I'm sorry. It's just that—" He shook his head. "Are you really?"

"Stop saying that."

"It's Chris's?"

She frowned. "I'll pretend that didn't just come out of your mouth."

"Sorry. What are you going to do?"

Olivia tucked her hair behind her ear. "For years, we couldn't conceive after Nicholas. You know what we've been through. And now, I feel like this is a gift. Something I didn't know I wanted so badly. I know it's bad timing and I know we're older, but this baby is mine. I want it."

"And Chris?"

She shook her head.

"Trevor, you're his best friend. Why would he act like this? Like I'm the enemy. Like I did something wrong? Sometimes I think it pains him to be in the same room as me. We've never been like this."

Trevor drank what was left in his glass and stared at his fingers, playing along the rim. She waited, and he finally looked at her. "I don't know, Liv. I'm sorry. I don't know."

She walked into the dark house and dropped the pamphlets she'd amassed from the clinic on the counter while she went to turn on the lights. Standing in the empty kitchen, Olivia could think of nothing she wanted for dinner. It was six-thirty. Chris would be home soon and would be hungry. She didn't care. She grabbed the pamphlets, shut the lights again and went upstairs.

Chapter 27
1992

"I love Trevor but to have to drive two hours to see him on my day off is pushing it," Chris said, switching lanes on the Long Island Expressway.

Olivia looked out the window at the buildings as they reached the Queens border. Yes, it was a drive to see their friends, but they had more space for the children to play and Olivia didn't return the invitation as much as she should.

"We'll have them out next time," she said.

Ella read a book, and Nick dozed in the back seat as they merged onto the Sprain Brook Parkway forty minutes later.

"Should I wake him?"

Chris glanced in the rearview mirror at their son. "You really want him awake with twenty minutes left in this cramped truck?"

"No. But he's going to be a beast when we get there. With energy."

"He'll have Patrick." Dana and Trevor's five-year-old son.

"I hope they get along this year. I'm tired of breaking up fist fights."

They pulled into a driveway that led to an expanded colonial as Patrick ran out of the house, followed by his two-year-old sister, Sabrina. Ella leaned up toward the front seat to see them.

"I'll give you five bucks to watch them today," Chris told

Ella as the two children outside stood on the walkway waiting for the car to stop.

"Fine." Ella sighed, pushing the door open.

It took Nick a few minutes to wake up as Olivia unbuckled his booster seat. As soon as he saw Patrick, he let go of Olivia's hand and Ella led the three children to the backyard, leaving her grateful parents behind.

They let themselves into the house, crossed the Oriental rug in the foyer, down the extensive hall and into the enormous farm kitchen where they found their hosts preparing snacks over the center island. Copper pots and pans hung over the butcher-block counter where sliced apples, brie and crackers were plated next to a platter of antipasti. Dana dropped the knife on the counter and grabbed Olivia and Chris in full hugs before gushing over the pecan pie Olivia held.

"Liv, you should box this and sell it." She smiled and took the pie, placing it on the counter.

Trevor stepped to Olivia and gave her a tight hug and cheeky kiss. "Good to see you," he said and gave her an extra squeeze before moving away and pouring her a glass of wine.

Olivia took a healthy sip.

"It's been too long," Chris said, tipping his beer bottle toward Trevor's before drinking.

"Well, we won't have to wait so long anymore," Trevor said, looking at Dana, who stood with a forced smile over her cheese platter. "We're moving to Long Island."

Chris's jaw fell open.

"Please tell me you're not joking," Olivia said, putting her glass down.

"My firm opened an office in Garden City and I'm taking it over. I found a place she'll love in Muttontown." Trevor nodded toward his wife.

While Trevor spoke of their plans, Olivia wondered how they could leave this incredible house and property. Their kitchen had a double fireplace and a pizza oven. Life seemed perfect here. She moved to the large picture window by the twelve-person refurbished barn-wood kitchen table (*I paid a fortune for something that looks a hundred years old*) and found the children on the playground next to the covered built-in pool and quiet waterfall. Ella was pushing the two-year-old on the swing. Nick and Patrick pushed themselves up and down the seesaw.

Dana stepped next to Olivia, holding the cheese platter. "I have to give your daughter something for keeping them out of our hair for the afternoon."

Olivia smiled, keeping to herself Chris's promise of five dollars to Ella. "Not necessary."

"Where did the men go?" Dana asked, turning around.

"Do you have to ask?" As Olivia spoke, they heard the tinkering of a guitar coming from somewhere in the house.

"Of course," she said. "He loves that music room. I lose him for hours at a time. They must have the door open because it's sound-proof. Let's go in the sunroom."

Olivia followed Dana through the den, rich with green and burgundy plaids, leather uprights and heavy furniture and into the sunroom, a serene spot surrounded by windows overlooking the two-acre property. Here they had a better view of the children.

"You're not excited about the move?" Olivia asked. She hadn't missed Dana's hesitant smile when Trevor made the announcement earlier. While enthusiasm oozed from him as he spoke of getting new gigs for the band, the new house he found, she remained stoic and focused on her cheese plate.

Dana put the platter on the glass coffee table and settled onto the floral sofa. "I like it here. I have my friends. My other friends." She blushed and motioned for Olivia to sit with her. "I'm sorry. You know I love you and Chris. It's just...I don't know." She avoided Olivia's eyes and reached for a piece of cheese.

"Is everything okay?"

"Oh, sure," Dana said, her mouth full of food. Olivia saw her eyes fill and looked away, embarrassed for her friend. Something was not right, but Dana didn't want to talk about it.

"So, how are you? How's work?" Dana said, composing herself. "Tell me."

"Work is work. Pays the bills."

Dana nodded. "I miss getting dressed and going to the job, but then I think I'd hate to take off my sweats to do that." They laughed, and Olivia felt relieved. Maybe she'd misread Dana's reaction to the move. She was probably tired with the two little ones. Olivia could still cry at the drop of a hat if she were tired enough.

"Is this the same woman who swore up and down she'd never give up her identity as a law accountant?"

Dana didn't smile. "I do miss work sometimes. I miss the spontaneity of life more—deciding on Friday morning to go skiing and just going, eating Chinese food on the den floor, watching R-rated movies, having cereal for dinner, sleeping all day Saturday." She frowned. "We have help, and it does afford us some freedom, but we're still parents. I can't give in to whims." She sighed. "I'm always too tired to have sex."

"That'll change."

"These little monsters expect their parents to get up before ten on the weekends," Dana said.

"The nerve of them."

"I'm selfish. I miss the single, motherless me sometimes." She looked at Olivia with her hand over her heart. "I'm sorry. I'm feeling emotional lately. I love my kids most of the time. But, occasionally, I long for the past."

"I don't remember my past. I feel like I've been a mother my whole life."

"You have. You're thirty-two with a twelve-year-old. The rest of us are old." She nodded her head outside. "I don't know how you do it, work full-time, and take care of them without a nanny."

I have no choice, Olivia thought, and sipped her wine. "I swore if I had another baby I'd stay home. I didn't know how I'd do it. It was a promise I made to myself. But..." She shrugged.

Dana shifted her eyes downward again, cut another piece of cheese, and slowly put it on a cracker. She chewed methodically and sipped her seltzer while Olivia watched. She'd made Dana feel uncomfortable. Dana had called her when she lost the baby and made an awkward attempt at consoling her. The conversation had ended quickly, and Dana had sent an enormous spray of daylilies to the house. With no note attached.

"I miss the apartment in Cambridge, don't you? Watching the guys play all night, lying around in their apartment. Those were the good days," Dana said.

Olivia nodded. She missed them, too. It was a lifetime ago. A life she hardly remembered.

Chris and Trevor found their way into the sunroom just as they heard a piercing scream from outside. Dana and Olivia looked at each other.

"Was too good to be true," Dana said.

Olivia looked up to Chris.

"I'll take care of it," he said and left to pry his son off their hosts' screaming child.

Trevor seemed nonplussed. "Boys will be boys."

Olivia shook her head and hoped it wasn't Nick who instigated the brawl. Ten minutes later, Chris returned triumphant. "Just a disagreement over sharing. All good."

"In that case, let's head to the kitchen to start dinner because we have more news to share with you over dessert," Trevor said, glancing at Dana. Olivia thought she saw Dana shake her head slightly to her husband, but decided she was imagining it.

***

The high-pitched screech of an owl brought Chris out of sleep. He pried his eyelids apart to see the moonlight through the window. It was the dead of night, his favorite time, when he was exactly where he should be. Beside Olivia. He listened to her breathe, her soft whispers of dreams exhaled into the room.

He rolled over and faced her, wrapping himself around the familiar curve of her body. He breathed the scent of her skin and felt himself get hard. It didn't take much. She turned him on just by…*being*. He wanted her now, this minute. Her back flowed up and down with her breath. *Stop thinking. Go to sleep. You have a full day tomorrow, jackass.* He rolled his shoulders back as best he could lying down, stiff from hours of lifting beams and caught a crack in the ceiling, illuminated by the pale moon. He'd forgotten to fix that. Just add it to the list of chores that weren't getting done simply due to exhaustion. His mother used to hire people to fix any house issues. Overflowing toilet? Call a plumber. Cracks in old foundation? Call a mason. Just call for help and pay the bill. He turned his head away from the ceiling. He couldn't call anyone. Stretched to cover the bills after the mortgage, the kids' clothes, soccer club uniforms, sometimes he felt as if he were drowning. How had he ended up here? Physical labor, barely making ends meet, when he was on track for a finance degree just a decade ago? Life threw him a curve, both of them. She was going to be a journalist, travel the world, have a home office filled with pictures of her conquests and published articles, and yet tomorrow she'll wake up, put on her drab uniform of skirt, blouse and low heels and type letters for a guy who hardly appreciated her. She'll come home, make dinner in a kitchen that needed updating, and they'll eat at the small, cramped table next to the stove. He thought of Trevor's digs, doing what he should have done, living as he should have lived. Taking care of Olivia like she deserved to be taken care of. The thing is, he loved his work, the sense of accomplishment he felt with each new house he built. When would it become lucrative?

They drove home after hearing the news at the dinner table. Trevor and Dana were expecting their third child. Olivia congratulated them, looking genuinely happy, but not before

Chris could discern the slightest wave of shock and sadness wash over her. It was a mere breath, not noticeable to anyone who didn't know her like he did. It passed in a millisecond, but it was enough to twist his stomach in knots. The miscarriage was a memory they held onto silently. What was there to say?

They crossed the bridge in the dark, the children in a gentle rocking slumber.

"Where is Muttontown?" Olivia had asked.

Chris stared ahead. She had no idea where one of the wealthiest neighborhoods on Long Island was. Why should she? They lived in a modest ranch on a modest street with blue collar families, a world away from the likes of Trevor and Dana.

"It's about twenty minutes from us," he said. "North."

"Oh, good."

He drove a few more miles. "It was good to see them," he said.

She'd been gazing out of her window and turned to him. She shook something from her thoughts, smiled, and nodded. "Always," she said. Then she held his hand as they drove home.

He sighed in the dark. *Enough, Chris. Get over it.*

She breathed in deeply and nestled back into him, instinctively, though she was asleep. He smiled through his lids. Okay, blue collar job, small house with a mortgage they couldn't get out from under, but she was his—this perfect woman he was blessed to wake up next to every day. His hands moved over her hips and in front of her stomach. She exhaled with a purr and turned her head toward him. Another woman might get angry to be woken in the night to make love. But Olivia never made him feel unwanted. She rolled to him and grabbed him. Slowly, in a twilight stupor, they melded into each other and when they were spent, he felt her drift back into dreams while he held her, feeling every inch of her against him. Her skin was soft and where it touched along his body, sent pulses of warmth through him. He looked through the bedroom window over her head, at the haloed moon and wondered again if he should tell her what he'd done. No, he didn't have the courage to face it or to face her if she found out. She wouldn't forgive him. She wouldn't understand his reasons, and though he still didn't regret it and might never, he'd forever be sorry for not sharing with her. He kissed her neck. He couldn't lose her. He loved her more than life.

Chapter 28
November 2010

Ella wanted to talk. She and Olivia decided to brave the chilly weather and went to the park near Ella's house on Saturday afternoon. The crisp, clear air invigorated Olivia, and she felt better than she had in weeks. They sat on an empty swing set. Ella kicked at the dirt.

"What's on your mind?" Olivia asked.

Ella lifted her head from her feet and looked out across the field where a group of children played soccer. Sounds of their happy yelling drifted to them. "I've been doing a lot of research. Do you know how many children are living in foster care waiting for a family to adopt them? It's overwhelming."

"I thought you wanted a newborn."

She brought her eyes to her mother. "I thought so, too. But I've been on all those websites, and I came across a little boy in a home in Oregon. He's three and..." Her voice cracked with emotion. "I can't get him out of my mind. He's a beautiful little boy. He has some physical issues, but his eyes looked right at me. I can't explain it."

"What does Marco say?"

"He still wants to move ahead with our plan to start with a pregnant woman through the agency we met with." She slumped in her seat.

"I see. You have to agree what you both want before you go farther."

"I know." She exhaled a shaky breath.

"How long does the process take? For a child?"

"After the complete home study, the adoption process can be quick, and I can have a child within eight months or so. It's encouraged that we be foster parents first. It might reduce the time we'd have to wait." She paused. "The wait for a healthy infant is between two and seven years."

"Oh, Ella."

"I called my adoption counselor and asked about the boy. She contacted the adoption worker in Portland. His name is Joshua. They said he doesn't speak, he's withdrawn, and they think, delayed."

"What happened to him?" Olivia asked, fearful of the answer.

Ella looked her square in the eyes. "He watched his house burn down with his mother and baby sister in it. He got out somehow. There were others in the house. Two adults walked out, as well."

Olivia closed her eyes. Any problems she had were trivial in the big picture. She needed to be reminded. "He doesn't have relatives willing to take him?"

"The home administrator inferred it wasn't the best home situation. The house fire was started by a meth explosion in the kitchen." Ella stood. "Let's walk."

They meandered along a thin, cemented path that ran inside the trees, forming a natural perimeter of the park. It felt several degrees cooler in the shade. Olivia buttoned her jacket to the neck and crossed her arms in front of her. The soccer group disbanded, the children's laughter replaced by the rustling of the leaves.

"With the difficulty Marco and I are having trying to conceive, it makes me wonder why people would have to give up their child."

"There are so many reasons, Ella."

"I know, but…" They reached an opening and Ella lifted

her head up to the sky, toward the weak sun. Olivia watched her daughter's thick hair cascade against her back. She put her hand under it and felt the silky pieces fall against her palm. "What must it be like, I wonder? For me the idea is too painful to process," Ella said.

"Think of it this way," Olivia said. "If there weren't children looking for families, it wouldn't be possible for a loving couple like you and Marco to fulfill your desire to have your own."

Ella pulled her head straight.

"You asked me not to tell you things happen for a reason. But if you and Marco could get pregnant, then you wouldn't have found Joshua. His mother had him for you."

"Do you believe that?"

"I believe you're meant to be a mom. Some aren't. You have an innate sense of compassion and an inordinate capacity to love. I know this." Olivia pressed her fingers to her chest. "I know it. This is what you were meant to be."

Ella took hold of Olivia's hand. "If I have these things, Mom, it's because I'm you."

They circled back toward the cars. "Should I wait to add Joshua to the quilt?"

Ella laughed. "You and that crazy quilt."

"I have to keep it going. If I don't, Grandma will come back and haunt me."

"When do I get it?"

"You'll soon have your own."

Ella paused and smiled to herself before continuing.

They reached the small parking lot. Ella turned to her mother, looking calmer than when they met a few hours ago. "Do you think Nick will ever add to it?"

"Not yet, I hope." They laughed. "He's got plenty of time," Olivia added.

Olivia returned home late in the afternoon to find Chris unloading his truck.

"You're just getting home now?" she said.

He pushed the back of the pickup shut and nodded. "Finishing some minor work on the Southampton house."

She walked into the garage behind him, still loved the way he looked in dirty jeans. She caught his profile as he walked into the house, his easy smile replaced by a slight frown. Where did her serene, content husband go?

In the kitchen, he pulled a beer from the fridge and sat down to look over paperwork for a new job starting on Monday. She sat across from him.

"What do you need?"

"Nothing. Are you hungry?"

He shook his head but didn't return to his work. "Where'd you come from?"

"I met Ella. We chatted and then grabbed lunch near her house. She wants to see about adopting a three-year-old boy in Oregon."

"Three? She doesn't want a baby?"

"I'm not sure what they want."

Chris pressed his lips together.

"What is it?" Olivia said.

"Are they going to feel about it the same way as if they had their own?"

Olivia didn't answer.

"I mean, can they connect in the same way?"

She thought about it. "I don't think it matters where someone comes from. Love is love. Ella will love any child as her own. I know it."

Chris stared outside the window. Her cell phone pinged, the sound amplified in the silent room. Olivia ignored the phone. Chris, still looking away, spoke. "Is that your boss?"

She flinched. Gavin called regularly, clueless to the term "personal time." Olivia always answered his calls. "I don't know. I don't care."

Chris said nothing.

She pulled the phone from her purse and looked at the message. "It's Ella, thanking me." She put it back and watched her husband.

"Chris, wouldn't you love a child that wasn't yours if we were to raise it?"

He turned to her, stricken. She tilted her head in question. "How could you not?"

She followed his gaze back to the window. "I thought of my mother today," she said. "I think of her often, but especially lately, with what's going on with Ella, with me, us. I need her. I miss her, but at times like this is when it hurts more." Her eyes glistened as she spoke. "I hope I'm of some solace to Ella. That I'm helping her in some way. And what I want so much is for her to be someone's mom, so she can experience the same feelings I do when I'm with her and Nick." She took a shaky breath. "I'm wondering if we should give this baby to them."

Chris's head jolted from the window to face her.

"It would be the right thing to do," Olivia continued, "but I don't think I'd be able to let our baby go. Not even to make our other baby happy. And it makes me feel like a bad mother."

He returned to the window.

She stood and dried her eyes. "I'm going to change my clothes." She left Chris alone at the table and listened to the silence as she ascended the stairs.

Chapter 29
1993

"I don't understand, Mama. Why can't we go with you?" Ella followed Olivia from room to room, repeating the question.

"I told you, honey, your father and I want to have a few days to ourselves."

Ella leaned on her parents' bed and gently fingered the small pile of clothes Olivia laid out next to the suitcase. "Where are you going again?"

"It's called Myrtle Beach. It's in South Carolina."

Ella plopped herself onto the bed. "Do you have to take a plane?"

"No. We're going to drive."

"Why are you going?"

"Because someone your dad works with gave us his apartment for a few days for free and we've never been there."

"I want to go. I want to go on a plane. Jenny's mom goes on a plane all the time."

"Jenny's mom is different. I've been on a plane only once, and I'm almost twenty years older than you." It was the plane ride from Boston after meeting Chris's parents, a trip she'd never forget.

Her daughter frowned and crossed her arms. "Why can't you take us?"

Olivia opened her dresser and pulled out a pajama set. "I'm not going to continue having this conversation, Ella. We don't want you to miss too much school." She stopped when she saw her daughter's face. She put her pajamas down on the pile and sat beside her on the bed. "Sometimes Mom and Dad want to be alone."

"Why?"

"Well, because right now, most of what we do and talk about revolves around you and Nick, which we love to do, but we want to spend time with each other as a couple. You'll understand when you're older. I promise."

Ella didn't answer. She picked at the ironed-on decal on the front of her tee shirt.

"We'll only be gone for five days. And you'll be so busy you won't even know we're not here. Grandma has lots of plans for you, and Jenny's mom said you can have a sleepover on Saturday."

Ella rolled off the bed and headed out of the room, mumbling her acquiescence. Olivia resumed her packing amid pangs of guilt. Chris had wanted to take a trip for years, and Olivia was able to hide behind the excuse of lack of money, but this time she couldn't put him off anymore. Nick just turned six, and Ella was old enough to handle herself with minimal input from Janine. They were basically going for free, except for gas and food. And she knew how to budget food. She'd already packed cereal and eggs for breakfasts. There was no excuse why they couldn't go. Olivia was nervous. This would be her first time away from her children for more than one night.

Chris came home from work to find his wife poring over lists. He hugged her from behind and peeked over her shoulder. "What's going on?"

"No one told me how stressful it was to take a vacation."

"What are you talking about?"

She moved from his embrace and turned to face him. "This," she held up a sheet of paper, "is Nick's schedule for school—pickup and drop off, snack days and Ella's bus schedule. And this," she pulled another sheet from behind that one, "is the mother of all schedules. I listed all of the dates and times of Ella's games and practices." Another page. "This is a list of everything Nick eats and this is a list of all important phone numbers. My mom is coming over before work tomorrow to go over everything. I want to make sure she understands it all."

Chris frowned. "Babe, she raised a daughter by herself. I think she can handle two easy children for five days."

Olivia stared at him.

"Okay, one easy child."

"I just want to be sure."

***

Janine never showed up the following morning. By noon, Olivia was worried and called the house from her office only to get the answering machine. At two, Janine's friend called Olivia to tell her that her mother was in the hospital. She called Chris, crying. "My mom had a stroke."

Chris met Olivia at the hospital an hour later. They waited, shocked and overwhelmed, until they were directed to her mother's room. Beside her mother's bed, Olivia leaned over, watching her. "I don't get it. She was perfectly fine yesterday when I talked to her. She met friends for lunch. How does this happen?"

Chris put his hand on her back. His eyes were full, and he tried like hell not to cry. Over his wife's shoulder, he grimaced at the sight of his mother-in-law, a tube coming out of her mouth, dragging her lips down on one corner. Her eyes were closed, and she appeared as if she were just sleeping and not in a coma. The doctor had been kind but blunt. "We don't know how long she went before her friend found her. Long enough for us to determine there is little we can do."

"Chris?" Olivia's voice cracked.

"I'm here, babe."

"Can you make sure someone gets Ella off the bus? Ask Jenny's mom. And maybe she can pick up Nick, too."

"I'll take care of it."

He returned minutes later to find her seated next to her mother's head. He pulled the other chair in the room toward hers and held her hand. At ten o'clock, when the evening nurse suggested they go home and return in the morning, Olivia shook her head, adamant she wasn't leaving. Chris left her to get the kids who were at Dana's after she picked them up from Jenny's mom's house. Dana gave them dinner and assured Chris they were fine to sleep over, but he wanted them home with him and showed up at her house at ten-thirty to get them.

Trevor answered the door. "I'm sorry, man. How is she holding up?"

"Not good." He was exhausted from sitting in one position for the past seven hours and for trying to control himself at the thought of what it would be like with Janine no longer in their lives, how hard it was going to be on Liv.

Dana ran into the foyer. She grabbed Chris in a tight hug. "You could have left them here."

"I want them home. The next few days will be difficult, and I want to keep them on their schedules for now." He hugged her again, then shook Trevor's hand. "Thank you."

"Are you kidding? Whatever you need."

Chris carried a sleeping Nick into the car while Ella yawned in her nightgown and followed without question.

Once home, with the kids tucked into bed, Chris lay awake on his pillow. He finally drifted off as the sun rose.

***

The next days were a whir of changing nurses, daylight and darkness, barely noticed by Olivia as she remained by her mother's bedside, believing if she willed it hard enough, her mother would open her eyes and wonder why all this fuss was being made. She ignored the doctor's suggestions that she consider the next steps, reminding her that Janine would not wake up and was in fact, being kept alive by machines. Her brain activity showed no signs of life. Even if she were to wake up (highly improbable), she would not function without the ventilator, he told her.

"Just a little more time," Olivia said to Chris when he tried to talk to her about it. "You never know."

She slept in a chair the first two nights until a nurse wheeled in a bed for her to finally rest properly. The same nurse, Rose, her name was, brought Olivia a towel and coaxed her into the shower. In the bathroom, only feet from her mother, she stood beneath the shower head, her tears mingling with the spray.

Dana sat with her on the third day. Chris stayed home with Nick, who had a cold and missed school.

"How long are you going to stay here?" Dana asked.

A nurse walked in and adjusted the machine near Janine's head.

"Rose, this is my friend, Dana."

The nurse smiled. "Hi, Dana. And how are we today, Ms. Janine?"

From the corner of her eye, Olivia saw Dana flinch at the prospect this woman was speaking to her unresponsive mother.

"No change," Olivia said.

"No, can't see no change," Rose agreed.

"Did the doctor say she might wake up?" Dana asked.

Olivia shook her head.

After a few minutes, Dana spoke. "You know, Ella was making me laugh yesterday. She does a great impression of you cooking. What a sense of humor."

Olivia let out a soft grunt meant to be a laugh.

"Do you realize you move your mouth when you read a recipe? We made chicken Marsala for Chris. She was you to a tee. He loved it, by the way."

The nurse finished her task and quietly left the room.

"You should go," Olivia said when Dana had been there for three hours. "Trevor will be looking for you."

"No, he won't. He's working late again. He'll probably stay in the city."

Olivia frowned. "He works so much."

"Yes, but at least it's stressful."

There was a pause before Olivia started to giggle, which made Dana giggle and soon the two were heaving in muted hysterics. After several minutes, Olivia pulled herself together. "We shouldn't be laughing at Trevor's pain."

"You're right." Dana wiped below her eyes. "But it's funny."

"You know, the last time you sat with me in a hospital, you brought me a flask."

Dana looked at her. "I did, didn't I?"

Olivia nodded. "Nothing for me today. I'm disappointed."

"If I recall, you threatened to bring me to AA. Why would I subject myself to that again?"

Olivia smiled. It felt good to smile. "I'm happy to note your memory is still intact. The long-term effects of drinking haven't set in yet."

They sat in comfortable silence.

"What did you say your name was?"

Olivia's laugh morphed dangerously close to a sob. She swallowed it down and took a deep breath. Dana put her hand on Olivia's back. "Cry all you want."

"I don't want to."

Later, Dana stood and stretched. "Now I'd better go. My kids'll think I've abandoned them."

Olivia shot her a look, and she held her hands up in defense. "If Trevor were home, I'd stay longer. But they're sick of the nanny by now, I'm sure. Or the other way around, and she's costing me a small fortune." She hugged her friend and walked out.

The nurse walked into the room as darkness set in.

"Well, another day come 'n gone," she said.

Olivia stood and arched her back. "You've been here all day, Rose."

"So have you."

Olivia walked to the window and stared at the pink sunset. "At home, I'd feel cooped up and restless if I was stuck inside on a beautiful day. I'd bring the kids to the yard, and we'd kick a ball around or play hide-n-seek." She turned to Rose. "I taught my daughter to play hopscotch. Did you used to play?"

"I was partial to double-dutch."

Olivia returned to the window. "My mother taught me to play. We had a small uneven sidewalk in front of our house. She drew the squares in all different colored chalk and made them extra large so I'd always land in one." The sky began to take on a purple hue. "When I think about the possibility of never seeing her again, nothing else matters. I don't care if it's warm and breezy or if the sun is out. It doesn't matter. I opened my eyes five minutes ago, it seems, but eleven hours have passed. There's no time here. No sunrise, no sunset. The hospital is a vacuum." She returned to her position beside her mother. "I have to make a decision, Rose."

The nurse put her hand on Olivia's shoulder. "Honey, the decision has been made. You just have to acknowledge it." She tilted her head toward the table beside them. "You might want to put that away before someone sees it. It's frowned upon here, you know."

Olivia turned to see what she meant and nearly laughed out loud when she saw the glittered-flask sitting there. *Oh, Dana,* she thought, *you've outdone yourself.*

She turned to explain it to Rose but the nurse had left, into the warm, breezy night.

Olivia called Chris at six the following morning to tell him she was approving the next step. At noon, they both stood by Janine's bed and watched in horror as the nurse unplugged all the instruments and removed the tubes that kept her alive.

"How long?" Olivia whispered.

"It should take anywhere from a few minutes to several

hours," the doctor told them. But at 9:00 pm, Janine's heart was still beating. Olivia made Chris go home to relieve their neighbor from watching the kids.

She sat alone with her mother, used to the familiar evening sounds of the wing, the murmuring of the nurses at their station just outside, resonant sounds from the TV in the next room. What was missing was the soft beep and whir of the machines that had kept Janine's body tethered to life. Her brain had shown no signs of improvement, no signs at all, for days, but her heart still struggled to beat.

Olivia didn't hear the nurse walk in.

"You're still here," Rose said.

"I am. What's your excuse?"

Rose sat beside her. "I wanted to say good-bye before I left. Make sure you're okay."

"She's holding on. Like she doesn't want to go."

Rose stood. "Often they won't go until they know it's okay."

"She doesn't know I'm here." She turned to Rose. "Does she?"

The nurse shrugged. "You never know." She gave Olivia a hug from behind. "I wish you well, love."

Alone, Olivia stared at her mother's face, letting her eyes trail down her arm. She took her thin fingers in her hand.

"Can you feel me?" She brought her mother's hand to her lips. "I'm going to say good-bye." She stared at her mother for a long time, drinking in her face, committing every line of her skin, her eyebrows, lips, ears, to memory. "Thank you for being my mom." She wiped her eyes with one hand, still grasping Janine's with the other. "I just wish you could hear me, to know how truly wonderful you are. I wish I said it more." She squeezed her eyes to clear them, allowing the tears to fall unchecked down her cheeks. "You can go, Mom. Let go. I'll be okay because I know you won't be far."

Olivia walked into her house five days after her mother was

brought to the hospital. The dark house was silent, and she let out a long sigh of relief, exhaustion, sadness. She dropped her pocketbook and bag of dirty clothes on a chair, kicked off her shoes and pulled herself across the kitchen toward the bedrooms. Before she reached the door, she saw the lists she'd made up, schedules and instructions for how to take care of the kids, hanging on the refrigerator amid the cacophony of postcards from friends. The pages looked bent and worn.

She kissed Ella on her forehead and cheeks, breathing in her glorious smell before doing the same to Nick. She walked into her bedroom and stood at the door. Chris lifted his head in the dark. "Liv?"

She nodded. "It's over."

He jumped up and pulled her to him.

Dear Mrs. Bennet,

I'm not sure how many letters I've written to you over the years. Twenty? Thirty? With each letter, I was careful to update you about your son and grandchildren, to help you to understand what they were like and somehow have you get to know them, even if just in this worded capacity. I thought you'd want to know how they were doing. How Chris and I were doing. I slipped each letter in the slotted mailbox believing it would be the one to end the silence. But weeks would pass without a word. And I did it again months later, with the same hope, and again with the same result.

When I had Ella, my mother made a small quilt. It had four squares: one for me, for Chris, for herself and for Ella. Ella slept with that quilt every night for years. It covered her body at first, but as she grew, it became more of a security item. She held it as she dreamed. As the years went on, the quilt grew. My mother would take it from my house (often without my knowledge) and she'd add pieces of our lives to it. She added a pale blue cotton square when Ella was ten, for the boy I lost. He was a part of Chris and me and always will be. He was loved and is a part of the fabric of us. Nick's square is a bold blue cobalt, accurately depicting his fierce, wonderful personality. It shows up amid the muted, gentle colors of the others.

Why am I telling you this? (Do you even read these letters I wonder?) I am telling you because this will be my last letter to you. Yesterday I went to my mother's house and found the quilt there. I hadn't even realized it was missing and would have laughed on any other day. She took it home because she added two more squares. One for you and one for Mr. Bennet. She believed you would come back, that you would one day want to be a part of our lives. She never lost faith in you.

My mother died last week. My heart is broken. Not even Chris, the keeper of my heart and my light, can fill this void left by my mother. Part of me belonged to only her.

Now I must face every day forward without hearing her sweet voice, receiving her sound advice, basking in her unconditional love, feeling her hugs that even at thirty-three comforted me. As I write this, I am still in bed, listening to my husband make breakfast for our children and I will pull myself from under these covers, get dressed and continue to be a wife and mother to this family I adore. I'll do it. But I'll do it with a cloud of sadness in the near distance for what I lost. My mother loved not only me, but my husband and my children with every ounce of her being. And they're richer for it. Their lives will be sweeter and filled with memories of her.

Along with myself, I will console Chris. I will console him because for the past fourteen years, the only mother he had was mine. He lost his mother long ago and the pain I am feeling right now makes me grieve for him too. Now we have no one. And now, I will stop trying to get you to do something that should have been instinctual: love your son and embrace your grandchildren.

So, I will no longer send you letters. I understand now that everything I did to try to get you to come see us was for naught. What I'll never grasp is how you did it. That is one thing I'll just never understand.

~Olivia

Chapter 30
November 2010

Olivia was helping Kayla with the updated legal software they'd just installed. She was explaining the steps again when the girl sighed and dropped her hands.

"I'm not this stupid, normally," she said.

"I don't think you're stupid. It's a tough program."

"You understand it."

Olivia smiled. "I've been doing this for twenty-five years. Eventually they all resemble each other with some slight variations."

"I don't know how you stay in one place for so long. I'd go batty." Kayla dropped her voice though they were alone in the office. "I'm out of here as soon as I get a real job. I applied to Computer Associates."

"How nice for you," Olivia said.

Gavin walked in with a large coffee. Olivia stood, leaving the girl to fend for herself with the software.

"Good morning, how was your date last night?"

"Thrilling," Gavin said drily as he passed her desk to his office. "Do me a favor? If she calls today, I'm in meetings."

"Got it." Her post-date instructions for every woman he took out. The man went through women with alarming speed, often leaving broken-hearted debris in his wake, leaving her to pick up after him.

He popped his head out before he closed the door. "You free for lunch?"

"I'm not. I have plans with my girlfriend."

Gavin nodded, glanced at Kayla and shut the door.

Dana arrived at Olivia's office at noon to find her on the phone. Gavin stepped out of his office as she hung up. "Where are you off to?"

"Diner. Do you remember Dana?"

Dana held out her hand, eyeing him appreciatively.

"Of course," Gavin said, shaking it. To Olivia, "Did she call?"

"Twice."

He sighed. "Okay, I have some things for you after lunch. Just come in when you get back."

Dana watched Gavin walk back into his office.

"Hello? Dana? Ready when you are."

They went to their usual diner a few blocks from Olivia's building. Once seated, the waitress left with their orders, and Dana smiled at her friend.

"I forgot how delicious your boss is. How do you concentrate every day?"

"You think he's that good-looking?" Olivia said.

"You're blind."

"No, I see just fine."

"Well, he made sure to step out before you left."

"What does that mean?"

"It means he wanted to see where you were going, who you were going with. You know, checking on you."

"You're crazy."

"Maybe. Does he ask you to stay late at all?"

"Rarely. He'd rather work through lunch than stay late."

"Interesting."

"It's not interesting."

"Is he married?"

"Hardly. He's looking for the perfect woman, and he'll never find her. She doesn't exist."

Dana pointed to herself, and they both laughed.

"So, what's new on the baby front?"

Olivia frowned. "Nothing new. I don't want to talk about it."

"You're kidding. What else is there to talk about?"

The waitress placed their salads before them and walked away.

"Okay," Dana said, picking up her fork. "How is Nick doing?"

The doorbell rang as Olivia put away her dish from dinner. Chris was working late again tonight, trying to pin down a start date on the new job before winter set its teeth into the area and made it difficult for his team to break ground. The owner had yet another change to the plans and Chris was meeting at her house with the designer to get her approval and move forward. This left Olivia to eat dinner alone. She stood in the clean kitchen, wondering who was at her door.

She smiled when she saw Sophia standing on her small landing, a scarf wrapped around her, blue eyes twinkling over a covered Pyrex.

"I made blueberry buckle," she said when Olivia ushered her inside.

"I've never had one," Olivia said, grateful for the company. She'd been feeling lonely lately, her third night this week eating dinner alone. It felt to her that Sophia must have sensed it.

They sat at the kitchen table, drinking tea and eating warm blueberry buckle made from blueberries Sophia grew in her yard and froze at the end of last season.

"Is your husband home?"

"He's working late."

"He seems to work a lot."

"It's seasonal. He'll be around more during the winter."

Sophia looked around the kitchen. "Lovely home. Very inviting."

"Is it? Thank you."

Sophia smiled. "We forget sometimes where we are when we're so a part of it. When someone comes in my house for the first time, I see it again with new eyes. Otherwise, I walk through rooms I so painstakingly decorated, oblivious."

"I suppose." Olivia took in the small ceramic pieces she still displayed over her sink. Her children made them for her when they were young. Though she took no active notice of them day-to-day, she would catch herself on occasion picking one up and replaying the tiny fingers and small voice handing it to her so long ago.

"My life is this house," she said to Sophia. "Every pore of every wall speaks of our story. I don't know that I'll ever want to leave."

"I understand. My daughter wants me to move closer to her, but I'm attached to my home and the street." She sipped her tea. "I have some family here. My niece has a baby, and they visit often."

"She has the blue Ford I see in your driveway sometimes?"

"That's the one."

Olivia took another piece of buckle, silently thankful Ella stayed on Long Island so she didn't have the same dilemma.

"May I see the rest of your house?"

Olivia led Sophia into the small den where the older woman went immediately to the collage of pictures on the wall. "There they are," she said. "I watched your children grow up from across the street." She leaned closer to a photo. "What does your son study in school?"

"Mechanical engineering."

Sophia nodded, impressed. "Do your children know about your pregnancy?"

"No. I think Nick will take it in stride. He's too busy doing his own thing to think much of what we're doing."

"His own thing?"

"He has a girlfriend. Melissa. She was a student, but she's taking the semester off."

"Are they serious?"

"I don't know. They talk every day, and he sees her on weekends." Another thorn in their side. She and Chris were sure the romance would fizzle when they were separated. In fact, their being apart strengthened them.

"And your daughter?

"I'm not sure how she'll take it. They can't conceive." Olivia didn't mind sharing this information with the older woman. She'd been wanting to talk to her about it. To feel better about it.

"I see."

"They want to adopt a baby. Or a child. They're in the early stages."

Sophia turned to Olivia. "Good."

Olivia didn't know why this response surprised her.

"Amanda is adopted. From Sweden."

"I didn't know that," Olivia said.

"Why would you, unless you asked. She resembles me, which is why it's not obvious to outsiders." Sophia took a step to see the last of the pictures. "My parents descend from there, so I figured it was as good a place as any."

They moved into the living room.

"Was your son adopted, too?" Olivia said.

"No."

"May I ask why, then?"

"Because I wanted another child after Bill, and labor hurt like hell."

"I know what you mean. I had a close call when Nick was born. With Ella too, but it was much worse with Nick."

Sophia paused at the couch. "Are you worried about having this one?"

"I should be. But no."

The older woman brought her eyes to Olivia's and held them. "I'm going to sit a moment." She lowered herself gracefully onto the loveseat, her hand on the quilt Olivia's mother made. The one Olivia found after Janine passed.

"Tell me more about Ella's plans."

Olivia sat across from Sophia. "They originally thought they wanted to adopt a newborn. Now my daughter thinks she wants a three-year-old boy she found in Oregon. She made inquiries through her adoption rep to see if it's possible."

"How do you feel?"

"I'm not sure. A baby would certainly be easier."

"Easier is not always better."

No, Olivia thought, but it's easier.

"I forget Amanda doesn't share my blood. I love her as much as my son, who very nearly tore me in two."

"I've been trying to tell my husband the same thing."

"Your husband and yourself." Sophia held up her hand when Olivia opened her mouth to respond. "I'm not saying you don't believe it. But I know how difficult it is to see your child venture into the unknown, wherever that venture takes her."

"I just want her to be happy. To have what she deserves."

"Of course you do. You're her mother."

Chapter 31
1994

Olivia called Chris at his job site to remind him of their schedules.

"Don't forget to pick up Ella at Jenny's house and take them both to dance. I'm going to get Nick from Lucas's and bring him to a birthday party at the bowling alley. All you have to do is make sure you're home for when Jenny's mom drops Ella off at seven. Got it?"

Chris laughed into the phone. "You forgot soccer practice. I called the extra practice because of the rain on Monday. Ella can miss it, but I can't."

Olivia sighed through the line. "I did forget. Crap. Are you sure you can't miss it?"

"Babe. I'm the coach, remember?"

"Right. Okay, coach. I'll have Ella dropped at the field after dance."

"I like the way you call me coach." His voice dropped an octave. "You know what I'm thinking?"

"You want to teach me to play soccer?" Olivia grinned.

"Only if we play naked on our bed."

"We might need a ref."

"Absolutely not. No one is allowed in our bed. Don't worry, baby. I'll keep score."

"I'm hanging up now." The last thing she heard was his deep, sexy chuckle that resonated in her ear.

Her boss walked in. "What's so funny?"

Olivia blushed. "Nothing, Mr. Hughes. I put your file on your desk as you asked."

"Thank you, Olivia."

Dana arrived at Olivia's office at noon, as planned, as Mr. Hughes walked out of his office, holding a briefcase and his coat. "Olivia, I have a lunch meeting and I won't be back. Hold down the fort, will you?"

"Of course. See you tomorrow."

She and Dana watched Mr. Hughes leave.

"That's it? He works until noon? What the hell? So, you'll work alone the rest of the day?"

"It's his practice, Dana. He can do what he wants. And he's working through lunch. The partner's secretary will be back from lunch in five minutes. We can leave when she gets here."

"Chris owns his own company and he doesn't quit work at two o'clock. He works like a dog."

"So does Trevor. What's the difference?"

Dana bit her bottom lip and averted her eyes, holding back her words, but Olivia knew what she wanted to say. She'd inferred at other times that the difference between Trevor and Chris was two zeros at the end of their paychecks. Which was why Dana sat on the other side of Olivia's desk with a Prada bag on her arm and an outfit that cost as much as Olivia's entire wardrobe draped over a body that saw a tennis court three times a week. She loved Dana, but sometimes her friend could be really trying.

"Anyway," Olivia said, taking the higher road, "I'm so happy you called me for lunch. I missed you. Where's the baby?"

Dana's older children were in school, she knew, but their two-year-old son wasn't in daycare. Olivia was hoping she'd bring him.

"He's with the nanny. I'm sorry. I know you've been trying to get together. We've had some stuff going on."

"No worries. Oh, here's Linda now." Seeing the secretary walk into the office, Olivia grabbed her purse, shut her computer, and shimmied into her coat. She and Dana left with a promise to Linda she'd be back in an hour.

Seated at the diner a few blocks away, the women placed their orders. "So now that I have you here. What's new? How's the family?"

Dana coughed and took a sip of water. "I want to leave Trevor."

Olivia's eyes widened, and she inhaled sharply.

"I thought you might react this way."

"Are you joking?"

Dana shook her head.

"What happened?"

"We haven't been happy, Liv, for a long time. I know we haven't seen you guys, so this may come as a shock. I can't pretend anymore."

"But you just had another baby."

"Two years ago."

"Still. You moved here...I don't get it."

"I thought maybe with the baby and the new house, things would get better. The only thing that changed was geography. I don't want to be married to him anymore. We never have sex. I can't even blame it on the kids. We have live-in help, for God's sake. I'm not sleep-deprived."

Olivia watched her friend, speechless.

"I fell out of love," Dana said.

"How does that happen?"

"How can you ask that? You work for a divorce attorney."

"They're strangers. They're not you."

"I don't know. I didn't know it was happening until it was gone. I was so focused on other things and...we got lazy."

Olivia stared into her water, as if the answer to her confusion was floating among the ice. "I see divorce all the time, and I still can't believe it's possible to fall out of love."

"For you, it's not. For the rest of the world, absolutely. Ninety percent of my neighbors are divorced, separated, or fucking their yoga instructor behind their husbands' backs."

They sat silently.

"Gives a new meaning to Downward-Facing Dog."

"Or Forward Bend Pose," Dana added with a brief smile. "Or Upward-Facing Dog."

"There's an upward dog?"

"You'd know this if you came with me when I asked."

The waitress brought their Cobb salads, and they waited until she left.

"How does Trevor feel?"

"He's upset, but he saw it coming. I'm sure he's got a girl in the city. He's there more than he's home lately. What man can go without sex for six months and not go batty?" She picked up her fork. "He still wants to stay married, even if we live like roommates. We should stay together for the kids, he says." Dana stabbed a piece of lettuce. "I don't want to live like this anymore. I want more than mediocrity. I want passion and something new."

Olivia put her hand to her heart. "There is nothing mediocre about your life."

Dana didn't answer.

"You guys have been together forever. I thought you were so happy."

Dana's eyes welled. "We were once. But he was never the love of my life."

Chris crawled into bed that night as Olivia read a book. He moaned gratefully as he sank into his pillow.

"Ah, feels so good to lie down."

Olivia didn't answer.

"How was lunch with Dana? Did she say why she's been so hard to pin down?"

Olivia pressed her lips together and kept reading. She and

Dana had both cried as they said good-bye in the parking lot after lunch, nostalgic for the past. She'd replayed Dana's last words as she returned to her office. *I want what you have.*

"Have you talked to Trevor?" Olivia said.

"Not since we played last week. Why?"

Lunch today dampened her mood. She wasn't affected anymore by the divorces she saw at work. Without them, she'd have no job. But when their best friends for years were unhappy, it cut her to her core.

Olivia put the book on the bedside table and shimmied down to her pillow so she lay facing Chris.

"Dana wants to leave him."

Chris stared at her.

She put her hand on his cheek. "I'm sorry. I know you're so close to him."

"Does he know?" Chris asked.

"Yes."

Chris sighed and rolled onto his back. "He seemed preoccupied last week but when I asked, he said work was on his mind. I took his word. He's got a lot of stress."

Olivia didn't respond. It felt like the death of something they both loved.

"What are they going to do?" he whispered.

"I don't know. He still wants to be married. But she says there's nothing left."

Chris stared at the ceiling. She watched him until her eyes started to close. She turned and shut her light and lay back down. Chris pulled her to him and held her as they both fell asleep.

Their morning was typical—trying to make breakfast and prepare lunches while Ella shrieked from her bedroom that she couldn't find her other shoe and her hair was not lying right and had to be re-done while Nick wouldn't get up from the den floor where he was mesmerized by *Batman* until finally,

Olivia had to pull him, now shrieking too, into the kitchen and practically force him to eat his waffles. By some miracle, within twenty minutes, Ella was out the door with her lunch in hand, her backpack stuffed, two matching shoes and a symmetrical pony tail. And Nick was back inside in front of the den TV, fed, dressed and waiting for the time he had to go to the bus stop.

Chris found Olivia half-dressed for work in the laundry room, sorting through dry clothes. "What are you looking for?"

"I thought I washed my cam—Oh, here it is." She shut the dryer door, leaving the rest of the clothes inside to become wrinkled enough that she'd have to re-wash them again. She turned to Chris, pulling her camisole over her head. "Will you be home for dinner tonight?"

"I think so." He rolled his eyes up to the ceiling in thought. "Yes. I am. We rescheduled our assessment for tomorrow. Why? Who needs to go where?"

Olivia leaned up to kiss him. "No one is going anywhere tonight. I almost can't believe it myself. We may actually be able to have dinner as a family."

Chris stepped into the laundry room and closed the door behind him. He pulled Olivia close and started moving his hands up her untucked camisole.

"What are you doing? Nick's inside."

"He's watching TV. He'll never look for us."

"Yeah, right. We'll tell him Mom and Dad went out. We're just voices from behind a door."

"Like Oz."

"Like Oz." She kissed him.

"Dorothy," he whispered in her ear, "if you want to go home, you have to do what I say." He lifted her skirt, and she wriggled out of her panties.

"What are your plans for me, Oh Wizard?"

"First, lose your three friends," he said.

She laughed into his ear and felt herself warm when he touched her.

"Mom! *Mom!*" As if he possessed the power to know his parents wanted to be alone, Nick walked into the kitchen in search of his mother.

Chris dropped his arms and stepped back with a frown. "Too good to be true."

She gave him a small smile and slipped her panties on before she opened the laundry room door.

"How many years until they're out of the house?"

Nick reached her just as the telephone rang. "Many." She put her hand on her son's head and answered the phone. "Hello?"

She froze. Nick ambled back into the den. Chris turned to her from the door as Olivia listened to the caller.

"Would you like to speak to him?" Olivia looked at Chris, who cocked his head in question. Then she held out the receiver. "It's your brother."

She went to the den to make sure Nick put his sneakers on and to give Chris privacy. In their fourteen years of marriage, Brian had not called once. It always upset her that Chris and his brother were not close. She blamed his parents. She had no siblings and would have given anything for a sister. Or even a brother for that matter. Someone to share childhood memories. Her mother was the only other keeper of her life experiences. And she was no more.

Chris walked into the den.

"What did he want?" She sat on the couch as Nick tied his laces while the television screamed in the background.

"My father died."

"When?"

"Tuesday."

It was Friday. She stood and went to him, but he remained stoic. "Are you okay?" She put her hand on his cheek.

He looked at her clear-eyed. "I have to go to work. I'll see you later." He walked out of the house.

Chapter 32
November 2010

Olivia stopped at Sophia's at dusk upon her return from a walk through the neighborhood, but there was no answer at the woman's house. She left the doorstep, marveling that Sophia had a busier social life than she did.

She enjoyed her visits with her new friend. Sophia reminded Olivia of her mother, who she missed with an insatiable hunger. She needed so much to speak to her mom. What would Janine say? Would she be happy for her? Would she agree with Chris that they were too old? Could you be too old to love and raise a baby?

Perhaps.

This would be the only time in their lives they were financially secure enough to raise a child. Ironic.

She walked into the house, still wearing her earphones and found Chris in the den.

"What are you doing?"

He sat on the rug in front of the bookcase with an open photo album on his lap and three more in a pile beside him.

"I'm just looking." He turned the page, and Olivia peeked over his shoulder. She pointed to a picture. "Remember how long it took you to put that bike together?"

Chris rubbed invisible dust from the photo of Ella, six-years-old, sitting on her first two-wheeler. It was the one with the banana seat and purple ribbons hanging from the handlebars.

Her favorite color. They'd surprised her on Christmas morning, ragged from little sleep after finally tightening the last screw at 3:00 am only to be woken up at 5:45. They'd bundled up in thick layers and gone outside before breakfast while Olivia watched through the window. Father and daughter up and down the small driveway on Sycamore Drive and finally on the front grass, erect from frost, until she wobbled across the perimeter of the house on her own. They walked into the apartment triumphant and chilled.

Both stared at the picture. It told the whole story of that morning. A memory ingrained in their minds for eternity. The rest of the book brought forth more memories, a nostalgic visit into their past. It upset Olivia to look at them sometimes. She straightened and stepped back.

"Seems like yesterday we just started." *We can do it again and re-live it all*, she thought.

Chris kept his focus on the book. "No, it seems like it was so long ago."

The doorbell rang. Chris put the books back on the shelf while Olivia answered the door. A woman stood on the landing, holding a small child bundled in a coat and matching hat and mitten set.

"Olivia Bennet? I'm Natalie. Sophia's niece."

"Can I help you?"

She shifted the child to her other hip, the girl's head now nestled against the side of her mother's neck. "I hope so. My aunt fell and I think she broke her hip. I was supposed to meet her for lunch today, and when she didn't show or answer her phone, I stopped over."

"Please. Come in." Olivia stepped back to let the woman inside. "I knocked on her door an hour ago, but there was no answer. I feel terrible."

Natalie sighed. "Don't. It's not your fault. She refuses to wear the bracelet I got her."

Olivia must have appeared confused.

"The Life Alert bracelet. You know, 'Help! I've fallen and I can't get up.'"

"Oh." She thought of Sophia, with her delicate necklace, the small diamond heart at the base of her throat and her matching bracelet, tiny diamond beads circling her thin wrist. The bulky Life Alert bracelet would have looked out of place for sure.

"The ambulance just left with her. I'm waiting for my husband to get here. Then I'll go to the hospital. Anyway, Aunt Sophia asked me to tell you what's going on. She heard someone knocking earlier and thought it might be you."

Chris stepped into the foyer.

"I'm Natalie."

He gave a small wave. "Chris."

"Would you like us to watch Brielle until your husband gets here?"

Natalie shook her head. "It's okay. I don't want to put you out. I'm not sure how she'd do anyway." She nodded toward her daughter, who now turned her head from the crook of her mother's neck to peek at Olivia.

"Why don't you both come in and wait for your husband." Olivia lowered her head toward the toddler. "Would Brielle like a cookie? I have the same ones as your Aunt Sophia."

Natalie smiled and nudged her daughter. "That sounds great."

They followed Olivia into the kitchen and Chris returned to the den.

"Can I use your bathroom?" Natalie asked, seating Brielle at the table.

Brielle remained quiet as she nibbled on a Lorna Doone. Her legs barely reached the end of the kitchen chair. She frowned at the cookie.

"I know just what you'd like," Olivia said, heading for the pantry. She pulled out homemade chocolate chip cookies she was planning to send to Nick in his next care package.

"I was saving these for my son who is away at college. He

likes to eat my cookies when he's not home because they remind him of here. But I'm sure he'd like me to share with you."

Her frown disappeared, replaced by a tentative smile as the small hand reached for a cookie.

Olivia felt victorious. "You know, I'm a friend of Aunt Sophia's. She and I have lots of cookies together." It was a one-sided conversation but Olivia was enjoying herself immensely. She turned when she heard the bathroom door open and caught Chris watching them from the kitchen door.

"Would you like a cookie?" Olivia asked him.

His thoughtful expression morphed into a smile as he patted his stomach and returned to the den.

***

Chris leaned back in the club chair with the news on low volume and rested his eyes. The women talked in the kitchen and he thought of how happy his wife was with the girl. She spoke to her softly, using the same voice she'd used with their children when they were young.

He opened his eyes when he sensed he wasn't alone. The little girl stood in the room, staring at him.

"Hi. Where are Olivia and your mother?"

She twisted her body back toward the kitchen.

"Would you like to sit with me?"

She nodded her head. Chris held a hand to her, and she walked to him, her diaper rustling beneath her pink corduroy pants. He pulled her onto the chair to sit beside him. She tilted her head up to see his face. She had big brown eyes and eyelashes that seemed to go on forever. She smelled of youth and innocence and beginnings.

"So," he said, trying to figure out what to do next. "How old are you?"

The girl looked down and with one hand, pulled two fingers up on the other.

"Two?"

She looked up at him.

"Do you know how old I am?"

She stared at Chris without answering. She was cute, this one. And quiet, her silence a far cry from Ella and Nick's non-stop chatter following him around the house trying to capture his attention when he walked in from work. He preferred the chatter. Would this next baby be so solemn?

"I'm more than twenty-five times your age. That's a lot, don't you think?"

Nothing.

He looked around the room, trying to find something to talk about. He reached over to the small shelf near his chair and pulled down a miniature ceramic turkey whose head was just a little bit askew.

"My daughter, Ella, made this for me when she was just a few years older than you." The turkey fit on the palm of his hand. "She loved pink. I've never seen a pink turkey, have you?"

The toddler stared at it.

"I've never seen a real turkey, aside from the one on the dining table next to the mashed potatoes. We take this out every November and put it away after Thanksgiving. Do you want to hold it?"

Brielle opened her hand, and Chris placed the piece in her grasp. "Just don't squeeze it, okay? It's fragile, and I don't want you to cut your hand."

He put a protective arm over her and watched her inspect the little brown turkey covered with pink spots, marveling at her small fingers, her tiny fingernails. He glanced up to see Olivia watching them. They locked eyes and at that moment, he wanted to take her close and promise he would do anything to make her happy. It was all he ever wanted. As she looked at him, he couldn't possibly understand the doubt that plagued him. How did she get pregnant?

Chapter 33
November 2010

Chris was gone when Olivia awoke the following morning. She looked at the clock on the bedside table and saw she'd over-slept again. The weight of her troubles sat on her shoulders as she climbed out of bed. She was going to have to come to some sort of decision soon. Time was not on their side. In the bathroom, she stripped out of her flannel pants and tee shirt. She caught a glimpse of herself in the mirror stepping into the shower. For anyone who didn't know, which was most everyone in the world except for a select few, she looked like a woman gaining weight during menopause. Pouchy in the middle, and legs a bit larger, Olivia knew the time had almost come. The doctor at the clinic told her the earlier she had the procedure (she couldn't even say it) the easier it would go. She'd have to force Chris into a discussion about it later. If he decided to come home, that was.

The phone was ringing as she shut the water off. Dripping, she answered in her towel and smiled, hearing Ella's voice.

"I'm going to stop over after work, okay? Will Dad be home?"

"I'm not sure. He was gone when I woke up."

Ella paused. "Really? I thought you guys did that whole coffee, breakfast thing every morning. What happened? Dad going through a crisis?"

"I'm sure." Olivia said. "I'll make dinner. Are you bringing Marco?"

"No, he's working late. It will just be me. But I'll take home leftovers for him."

Of course.

***

All morning Chris thought about Brielle—the way Olivia was with her, how easy she segued back into her role as care-taker of a young child. As he sat with the little girl himself, he couldn't help but wonder what it would be like to do it all again.

At noon, he said good-bye to his foreman, took off his hard hat and ambled to his truck. He had another appointment across the island after lunch. The days were growing shorter, precious sunlight taken from the workers by minutes each evening, but Chris knew it would be another long day. On the driveway he stretched, trying to work out the kinks in his back formed by looking over the plans for the past hour. He'd been doing this for thirty years. He'd grown to love the work only after he accepted the truth that he would never realize his earlier dream of wearing a suit and finding himself in the finan-cial district crunching numbers with callous-free, soft hands, next to his best friend. But every so often in recent years, his body reminded him he was aging and couldn't do everything his youthful mind insisted he should.

He climbed into the truck. When they turned the clocks back last week, he knew it would only be a few days before he'd be home before Olivia every evening, waiting for her with a glass of wine and dinner.

The truck roared to life and he pulled away from the site.

Okay. Maybe, he thought, going back to Brielle and Olivia last night, maybe he'd try to keep an open mind. Hear her out about this new adventure they'd embark on. It would be an adventure, he knew, having raised two children. Nothing predictable. Nothing sure. He had been so cocky and confident at nineteen when they first got pregnant. Olivia was scared and he was her rock, the foundation they built from. Now, their roles were reversed.

At the traffic light before the parkway, he rested his head against the steering wheel. Labor. It was rough with Ella. But with Nick, he'd almost lost her. The doctor said she'd come close. Too close for comfort, he'd told Chris, who replayed the words over and over for months, making sure to take gentle care of Olivia as if she were a fragile flower that might wither away at any moment. He never told her exactly what the doctor said. Never admitted just how scared he was.

She wanted more. He wanted her. When she got pregnant the third time, he hated himself for allowing it. She'd lied about taking birth control. His anger steered him to do what he did, behind her back, ensuring she'd never get pregnant again, convincing himself his lie was justified.

For months, he consoled her when she got her period, always seeing the big picture, knowing what he did was for her and for him. He'd wanted a big family too, but not at the cost of her life. What would be the point? What was life without her?

The honk behind him made him lift his head. Green light. He was holding up traffic. He raised his hand in apology and accelerated.

They needed to sit down and figure out what they were going to do. He would listen, be reasonable, try to push his emotions to the wayside and work this out with her. It was what they'd always done. They would figure it out together.

Full of renewed hope, he changed course and headed toward her office. He would surprise her, maybe take her to lunch, tell her he was ready to talk. What he wanted to do but wouldn't was ask was how she managed to get pregnant when he had no more working sperm. Maybe the procedure didn't work all those years ago? But how would that explain the years of her disappointment? If he asked, he'd have to admit what he'd done, and he could never do it. He'd never risk her knowing.

His cell phone rang as he turned around on the turnpike.

"Chris? It's Dana. Do you have any time today? I need help with my water heater."

"Why don't you call a plumber?"

"Because the last time I did that, Trevor got on me for over-paying for something that could have been done myself."

"I'm not sure what time I'll be finished. Where's Trevor?"

Silence.

"Dana?"

"He's not receptive to my calls. I don't want to take another cold shower."

Chris exhaled. How did they get to this place—where they could hardly stand to talk to each other? Where were his friends from college?

"Let me see. I'll call you later."

"Thanks."

He pulled into the parking lot of Olivia's office, feeling more optimistic than he had in weeks.

***

Olivia was helping Kayla file a deposition when Gavin poked his head out of his office.

"What are you doing for lunch?" he asked Olivia.

"I don't have plans. Why?"

"Can we bring in and work through the hour? I'll let you leave at four."

"You're the boss."

He stepped back inside, and Kayla winked at Olivia. "Lucky girl," she said.

"What are you talking about?"

Kayla sighed. "What I wouldn't do to have an hour alone with him in that office."

Olivia tilted her head in surprise. "This is a professional place of employment."

The girl blushed and returned her focus to the screen.

Olivia ordered sandwiches from the corner deli, and they sat in Gavin's office, eating and discussing the details of their newest divorce case. When he finished, Gavin sat back in his chair.

"How's Nick?"

Olivia crossed her fingers and held them up. "So far so good. Other than the girl, he's back on track."

"You don't approve of his girlfriend?"

"It's not that we don't approve. It's just, trouble seems to follow these two. Maybe they're better off apart. He says he's in love. But he's young."

Gavin drummed his fingers together, much like he did when a new client came in with his story. "I loved a girl in college. I'd just started in law school in the city and met her at a club. She was the coat-check girl. Gorgeous."

"You? In love? I don't believe it."

Gavin ignored her. "We dated a few months and I brought her to meet my parents." He shook his head, remembering the day. "My father called me the next day. Told me I was wasting my time. He didn't like her. Thought she was beneath me. Those were his exact words. 'She's beneath you. Get your career going, and you'll meet the right kind of woman. Trust me,' he said." Gavin paused and stared past Olivia.

She took a bite of her sandwich and pushed thoughts of her father-in-law from her head.

"He thought I should be with another lawyer or professional."

"What did you do?" Olivia asked.

He moved to the couch where she sat. "I stayed with her a while longer, but I had this nagging feeling, my father's voice kept popping up in my thoughts, and eventually I distanced myself from her. One night, she confronted me about my behavior, and we had a blowout. We both said things, and it was over."

Olivia wrapped the remnants of her sandwich and placed it in the bag. "That was it?"

Gavin picked invisible lint from his suit. "I graduated, got my license, started at McKimmon and Sons and then came here." He looked at Olivia. "I haven't felt the same way about another woman since Alexa."

Olivia laughed. "It's not for lack of trying." She'd commanded the new skill of blocking his calls from the poor women he ditched almost weekly. She should have a therapy license.

Gavin watched her, saying nothing.

"I'm sorry," Olivia said.

"I'm forty-six, never married. Probably never will."

"In this line of business, it's hard to see the good in marriage."

"You're married."

"That's true."

"Are you happy?"

Olivia scooted a few inches from where Gavin sat. The couch was too small for them to both sit comfortably, she thought. "I am. And I got married at nineteen."

He whistled. "Ouch."

"What ever happened to Alexa?" Olivia asked, trying to move off the subject of herself.

"She's an accountant. Lives in Brooklyn with her husband and three kids."

"Were you angry with your dad?" Olivia thought of Chris's father again, the similar way he reacted upon meeting her. Only Mr. Bennet didn't wait for Olivia to leave before voicing his opinions about her. The memory still hurt.

Gavin looked surprised by her question. "No. He thought he was giving me sound advice. The only person I'm angry with is myself. But maybe it's for the best. I'm not husband material." He put his hand on Olivia's leg. "I need someone like you, Olivia. Someone who's easy-going, attractive, bright."

She flattened her skirt, pushing his hand away, and said nothing.

"Do you have a sister?" He laughed, breaking the awkward silence.

She stood and gazed down at her boss, still sitting on the couch, his arm now draped casually over the back of the cushion, his legs crossed.

"No sister. I'm the only one," she said.

"That you are."

They looked at one another.

"I'm not coming on to you, you know. I'm just paying a compliment. Don't feel uneasy. I would do nothing to risk my right hand in this office." He flipped his tie, checking for crumbs. "Besides, I have a willing participant right outside that door if I wanted to shit where I eat."

"She's not long for this office."

He dropped his tie and returned to her with a straight face. "Well, then, things are looking up."

The knock at the door surprised them both. Kayla cracked the door and whispered through the opening, as if not wanting to see inside. "Olivia, there's someone here for you."

She walked toward the door.

"Olivia?"

She turned around.

"Your son knows how he feels. Keep that in mind," Gavin said, walking to her. "And thanks for helping Kayla earlier with Dougherty's deposition. You always go above and beyond." He put his hand on her lower back as she stepped out.

Olivia stopped short when she saw Chris standing by her desk. Gavin bumped into her, he was so close.

She blushed, feeling guilty though she did nothing to warrant it. "Chris. I wasn't expecting you. What are you doing here?"

He looked at Olivia and then at Gavin.

"Oh, this is my boss. Gavin, this is my husband, Chris."

Gavin stepped to Chris and held out his hand. "Chris, it's a pleasure." Chris nodded and dropped Gavin's hand.

"I was passing by and thought I'd stop in. Did you have lunch?" Chris said to her.

She swallowed her disappointment. "I—we just had lunch. If you would have called."

"I should have. I just figured…" He looked at her, and her blush grew deeper.

"Is everything okay?" Olivia said. He rarely stopped at her office. In fact, she couldn't remember the last time he was here.

"Everything's fine. I'll see you at home."

"Are you going home now?"

Chris stopped by Kayla's desk and turned around. "I'll be late," he said and walked out.

***

He sat in the cab of his truck and stared out the windshield. For months, he'd heard about her new boss, Gavin, picturing him to be what he felt was a typical divorce lawyer—slightly sleazy, in a brown or muddy ill-fitted suit, homely. This was what he thought his wife was going to every morning when she left for work. What he wasn't expecting was the youthful, boyish-looking man, impeccably dressed and standing so close to his goddamn wife he shared her shadow.

He shook his head and let out a long breath. *Calm down, jackass. This is your wife you're talking about. She doesn't see him. She sees you.* Right? In his rearview mirror, he caught a glimpse of himself—salted hair, lines at the corners of his eyes. An old man. He started the truck and pulled out of the parking lot just as his phone dinged with a text. He pulled over, hoping it was Olivia. What would she say that would make him feel better? How would she ease his insecurity?

It wasn't Olivia. It was Dana. *Hey, Chris, don't worry about stopping by. I'll get my neighbor to help me later. Thanks anyway. xo*

Dana. Shit. He looked at the clock on the dashboard. He had an hour before he had to be at his next appointment.

On my way.

He was at Dana's house fifteen minutes later. When she opened the door, he already regretted his decision for the second time today. He should go home, climb into bed and start again tomorrow.

She wore a tennis dress that barely covered her and a wide smile. She stepped aside to let him in.

"Heading out?" he said, passing her to enter the cavernous foyer.

"We won our tournament this morning. Haven't changed."

"Where's your water heater?"

She motioned for him to follow her and stood aside while he assessed the tank and finally figured out why she wasn't getting hot water.

"Your switch was off, for some reason. Watch me. See this lever? It should be to the left. Something triggered it off. I'd still get this checked out. It could be faulty. Tell Trevor I suggested a plumber."

She mock saluted him, and he chuckled.

"Have you eaten lunch?" Dana said.

"I'll take coffee."

In the kitchen, she put a mug under one spout of the large Cecilware espresso machine that cost more than his dining room set and came with a book of instructions. She maneuvered levers and programmed the system as he watched. If he had all the money in the world, he would still want a simple coffee machine. "Where were you that you were able to come here so quickly?"

Chris rubbed his hands through his hair. "I stopped at Liv's office."

"You had lunch?"

"No."

Dana looked at him, tilted her head. "Oh."

Chris stared at the coffee machine.

"Have you guys decided what you're going to do about the baby?"

"No."

She watched him until finally he held her gaze. He wasn't happy. He was scared. Did she see it?

She moved around the island to where he sat on a stool, sat beside him and rested her head on her hand.

"It was so much easier back in the day, wasn't it?" she said.

He stared over her head. "It was never really easy for me. Or her." He blinked and looked at Dana. "But it was always great."

She reached over and fixed the collar of his shirt. "I wanted what you had."

"You had it. With Trevor." He pulled her hand away and straightened the collar himself.

She exhaled a frustrated breath. "Did we? I'm not sure. I thought we had something, but when your husband stops coming home and you find subtle differences in his behavior, you question your worth, you know?"

"Dana—"

"Did you know he was cheating on me?"

Chris shook his head. "He never told me."

"But you knew."

"No, I didn't."

She stared at him as if trying to uncover the truth.

"Well, if you knew or not, you would have kept his secret. That's what friends do, right? They keep secrets. Like the one I kept for you all these years."

Chris rubbed his eyes. What was happening? He stood to leave.

"You didn't have your coffee." They could hear the elaborate machine expelling the final drips into the mug.

"I'm going to go."

She leaned back against the counter. Her breasts fought against the material of her skimpy outfit. "Do you wonder if maybe that baby isn't yours?"

Chris bit the side of his lip and clenched his fists. If he ever wanted to hit someone, it was now.

She gave an abbreviated smile. "I thought so. That hot boss is into her."

"Dana, whatever beef you got, don't take it out on me."

She crossed her arms and her eyes filled. "I thought Trevor would never cheat on me. But I was wrong."

"What are you saying?"

"I'm just saying you never know. Look what you did to her. How do you know she didn't do something, too? No one's perfect. Not even Olivia," she added in a whisper.

He reached the door and grasped the handle. "Why, Dana?"

She remained at the entrance of the kitchen and sniffed. She turned away, and he walked out.

***

Ella walked into her parents' house at six-thirty. Olivia was already in sweatpants, stirring chili over the stove. There were grocery bags on the kitchen table that had not been put away.

Ella started to unpack the bags as if she were still living home and did it every day. Olivia loved seeing her revert so easily back to her actions. She missed being around her more.

"What's with the bags of flour?"

"I'm going to send up oatmeal raisin cookies to Nick—my last care package before Thanksgiving break. I didn't get a chance to unpack those. I wanted to get the chili on first."

"Mom, there's enough oatmeal and sugar in this bag to feed all of RIT."

Olivia shrugged and took the sugar from her daughter, putting it away in the lazy Susan. "I'll make enough for him to share with his housemates. Do you want to bake with me? It's been years since we've done that."

Ella smiled. "I can't tonight. I'm being observed tomorrow, and I want to make sure my lesson-plan is foolproof."

"Do you get nervous being watched?" Olivia went back to the stove and stirred the thickening rice.

"Not really. I know the superintendent well. She's a nice woman. And I love what I do, so I try to just focus on the kids and forget she's there. Easier said than done, but what are you going to do?"

Olivia helped Ella finish unpacking the rest of the groceries. She envied her daughter's confidence and was proud of her. Ella had known what she wanted to do from age five. She'd focused on school and graduated in the top ten percent of her university and had already gotten her masters plus thirty, almost reaching her full teaching requirements. A doctorate was within her reach. If Olivia had an iota of that drive, she'd be doing...what? What would she be doing besides eating lunch while questioning the motives of a divorce attorney? She thought of Chris, showing up at the office while she and Gavin were having lunch, after having pushed his hand from her leg. She wouldn't tell Chris what had happened, sure that if she did, Chris would confront Gavin and she'd have to leave her job. Anyway, she'd taken care of herself. Gavin was harmless.

"Mom? Hello?" Ella waved a hand in front of her mother's face. "Anyone in there?"

"Sorry." She started to set the table.

"Are you okay? You've been acting a little strange lately."

"I'm fine. I promise." She avoided Ella's gaze as she focused on setting the utensils one by one.

"Okay. Well, I wanted to wait for Dad to come home, but I can't hold it in any longer."

Olivia dropped a fork and looked up at Ella, hope in her eyes.

"It's not that."

"Oh. Okay." She sat down and faced her daughter.

"We're going to Portland next month. To meet Joshua." Olivia froze, and Ella continued. "I showed Marco all of the footage they have of this little boy, and he felt the same thing.

This little boy is calling to us. I want to meet him. I have to meet him."

Tears filled Olivia's eyes. "Oh, baby. I'm so happy."

Ella's smile was exuberant, and Olivia felt for the first time since her daughter and Marco started trying to be parents that they would have a family.

Chapter 34
1995

"Mom, when can we leave?"

"As soon as Nick gets home. Be patient. I already spoke to Jenny's mom."

Ella frowned and skulked into her room, eager to be with her best friend for the day. Every Saturday the girls spent the entire day together and often into the night, having developed a sleepover ritual that worked for both sets of parents. Ella would be spending the night at Jenny's, and her fun couldn't start early enough. Chris and Olivia would have Nick to themselves, though the eight-year-old would pine for his sister, feeling ditched and offended.

Olivia checked the clock, figuring she had half an hour before Nick was dropped off from his party at the movie theater. He went with his friend Lucas and his mother, giving Olivia an hour and a half to do her chores. She'd chaperoned last month's birthday party. She and Lucas's mother had a wonderful agreement that neither would have to endure every birthday party so long as both children were invited. Olivia lugged the full laundry basket to the washing machine off the kitchen, a chore she much preferred over the odor of over-buttered popcorn, sticky floors, and thirty screaming children talking over an animated screen. She was just pouring in the soap when the doorbell rang.

"I'll get it!" Ella yelled, sprinting for the door. Olivia started the machine and walked toward the front door.

Down the hall, she heard Ella speaking. Then she heard a woman's voice asking if her mother was at home. Olivia didn't recognize the voice.

"Mom? Someone is here for you." Ella stepped back to allow Olivia access to their visitor. She pulled the door open wider and froze.

"Hello, Olivia," the woman said.

Olivia inhaled sharply, staring at a soft, wrinkled face framed by dark brown hair cut in a neat bob. But it wasn't the face that had her transfixed. It was the woman's eyes. Chris's eyes. The very same.

"Mom?" Ella's curious voice lilted up at her reaction.

The woman was impeccable in a navy pantsuit with a cream silk blouse. In her hand was a Louis Vuitton purse. She didn't smile. She appeared…nervous. "I know I'm not expected. I'm not even sure I'm accepted." She gazed at Olivia for a moment. "I traveled five hours, hoping you'd let me in."

Olivia grabbed Ella's hand, keeping her by her side. They stepped back and allowed Mrs. Bennet to enter the house. The woman turned, taking in the surrounding space. Ella looked up at her mother in question. Finally, the woman faced them and she looked long and hard at Ella. Her expression softened.

"You are even more beautiful than I imagined," she said to the fifteen-year-old.

Olivia squeezed Ella's hand, forcing her to mumble, "Thank you."

Chris's mother looked at Olivia. "May I spend a few minutes with her?"

Olivia shook her head. "Not yet. I'd like to talk first." She was surprised at her own candor. Her words belied her underlying nerves, the same nerves that took over the last time she stood before this woman, sixteen years ago.

"Of course."

"Ella, please go to your room for a bit until I call for you."

"Am I still going to Jenny's?"

"Yes."

Ella returned to her bedroom, leaving the women standing awkwardly in the small entrance. "We can sit in the kitchen."

Mrs. Bennet sat at the kitchen table while Olivia busied herself making coffee. Her hands shook, and she knew she was blushing, angry with herself for feeling so emotional. Wasn't this what she'd always wanted? A chance to spend time with her in-laws?

When the coffee was ready, she sat down at the table and placed a plate of cookies between them.

"I'm sorry I don't have more to offer. I wasn't prepared for company."

Mrs. Bennet waved her hand as if to say don't bother. She didn't appear to enjoy desserts, having kept her thin frame from what Olivia remembered of her. Other than looking thinner, this woman hadn't changed much at all.

"You're grown up," she said to Olivia.

"And I was thinking you haven't changed."

"Oh, but I have. I'm not the same person you met years ago."

"Nor am I," Olivia said.

"I see that." She bit her inner mouth. The way her cheek went concave and her jaw pulled to the side was so familiar to Olivia, she had to hide her surprise. Chris did the same thing.

"I am happy to see you're well. This is a lovely home."

"Thank you. I'm sorry to hear about Mr. Bennet." Olivia said. "We only found out after the services and burial. We would have been there for you."

"Would you have?"

Olivia paused. "I don't know. I'd like to think we might have gone to say good-bye."

Mrs. Bennet sipped her coffee.

"How is Brian?" Olivia asked, more out of respect than interest. Chris's brother didn't exist in their lives, and they knew nothing about him.

"He's well. He and Robin and their children are still in Maine."

She left it at that, and Olivia didn't press for more information. They sipped quietly.

"Olivia, does Chris know you've been sending me letters and pictures through the years?"

"No."

The woman nodded. "I thought so. I fear he and I may not make amends, but I wanted to meet my grandchildren. I couldn't come earlier, if you can understand. I made my choice when you and Chris left the house all those years ago." She stared at the wall across the room. "It was tough for me for a while. He is my boy. My husband was proud and stubborn. But I loved him and I couldn't go against him. Not even for my son."

"I couldn't have done it."

The woman looked at her. "Don't say what you could do until you've been tested."

Olivia must have appeared doubtful. "Could you ever leave Chris?" the woman said.

"He would never make me choose."

"I thought the same once."

Olivia shook her head. "But your child. Your grandchildren."

A glimmer of a smile appeared. "I was able to watch them grow through photos and letters. I think somehow you understood I needed that. Thank you."

They sat in silence.

"Arthur never admitted to his regret. I think he was hoping Chris would be successful and prove him wrong," Mrs. Bennet said.

"You don't think he is?"

"It appears he does okay. That you both do okay."

Olivia glanced toward the kitchen door to make sure Ella

wasn't near. "We had a rough start. I thought, more than once, we wouldn't make it. Financially, I mean. We sacrificed…" She shook her head, thinking of the mattress on the floor of their basement apartment, their baby sleeping only feet away, staring at their bills, Chris's self-doubt of how he would do it carried on his shoulders day after day. "But Chris wouldn't give up. Neither would I. And now, I realize we had everything we ever needed." She stared at her mother-in-law. "Almost."

Mrs. Bennet listened without response.

"Forgive my disrespect, but we have so much more than you do. We have a loving relationship with our children."

"They're young. Wait until they make their own life decisions. See if they adhere to your advice. It's harder than you think."

Olivia stood to pour more coffee, though she had no desire for it. She couldn't sit there. They would never agree. She took a deep breath. The woman is here, trying to make amends. *Be kind, Olivia.*

"Where is Chris?"

Olivia turned. "He works Saturdays. He should be home by dark."

"It's just as well. May I spend a few minutes with the children?"

"Of course. Nick will be dropped off soon. Ella is in her room." She paused. "What should I tell them?"

Mrs. Bennet stood. "I suggest you tell them what you want them to know."

The woman walked to the kitchen entrance. She stopped at the threshold and peered into the den. Her hand went to the gold chain on her neck. "Is that the quilt you wrote about in your last letter?"

Olivia remained rooted to her spot across the room. In her last letter, she talked about her mother's quilt, about Janine's unwavering belief that Chris's parents would come around. *Oh, Mom,* Olivia thought, *I miss you.*

"Yes." It was a whisper.

Mrs. Bennet stared into the den for a breath. "Your mother sounded like she was very special."

"She was."

Without looking at Olivia, Chris's mother left the room. Olivia heard her gently knock on Ella's partially open bedroom door and walk in. She stayed in the kitchen, still in shock that the woman she'd been wanting to get to know since pregnant with Ella was in the next room. What would Chris say when he found out she was here? They didn't talk about his father, though she tried to get him to open up after his death. He remained resolute and shed no tears for the man who disowned him. Olivia would never understand. She missed her mother every single day, and Chris just let his own slip away without a thought. Or did he miss her, but keep his feelings to himself?

The doorbell rang, and Olivia met Nick with a hug, thanked Lucas's mom, and escorted him into the kitchen so he could tell her all about the party.

"My favorite part was when Buzz Lightyear started flying around and the toy soldiers climbed down the stairs. Who's that?" He pointed to Mrs. Bennet, who stood at the entrance to the kitchen with her hand over her heart, looking at Nick.

"This is Mrs… This is Adrian. She came a long way to see you."

Chris's mother stood still. "My God, he's a spitting image of him," she mumbled.

Nick, not to be deterred from his movie, kept talking about the different toys, his favorite being Woody, of course, while ignoring the strange woman standing in his house. Mrs. Bennet seemed to understand she wasn't going to get Nick's undivided attention with his mother in the room and settled for a seat at the table. She didn't take her eyes from him once until finally, he stopped talking and told his mother he had to poop and wanted to watch television.

Alone again, the women looked at each other.

"They're amazing. Nick is Christopher. I wonder if he realizes that."

"Thank you." She wanted to say "*Mom*" but knew she would never.

Mrs. Bennet looked at her watch. "I'd better go."

Olivia's jaw slackened and regret seeped into her bones. "Don't you want to wait for Chris?"

The older woman pressed her lips together. "I'm not sure it's a good idea."

"You came on a Saturday. I'm sure you were hoping to see your son."

"You mentioned in your letters that he works six days a week. I came today because I knew the children weren't in school."

"Please. For him."

"And if he doesn't want to see me?"

Olivia thought of her own mother, how she'd never have the luxury again to see her grandchildren or her daughter.

"Let him decide when he gets here."

Olivia called Jenny's mother and told her they'd be late. Then she sat down with her mother-in-law.

"After all these years, I have so much to say but nothing comes to mind."

Mrs. Bennet hesitated. "I planned this trip a dozen times over the past year. Cancelled flights and hotel reservations only to make them again a month later." She closed her eyes. "I finally decided I'd waited long enough. Too long. I needed to see my son, if only to tell him I'm sorry." She opened her eyes. "And I'm sorry to you too, Olivia. I was a better wife than I was a mother."

Olivia swallowed her surprise. The woman looked pained. What would she do if she couldn't see Ella or Nick, meet her grandchildren, support them through their lives? The thought wouldn't materialize.

"Mrs. Bennet."

"Adrian, please."

Olivia cleared her throat. "Adrian, Chris is a loving, giving husband and a nurturing, supportive father. He learned that somewhere. I think you must take some credit for the man he is."

Adrian's pronounced cheeks tinted pink. "Thank you for saying that, but I will give the credit for the man you describe to you."

When Chris walked in an hour later, he stood at the door of the den in a flannel shirt, jeans and work boots, stunned.

Sitting around the coffee table were his wife, children and his mother, a game of *Sorry!* in progress. Olivia stood immediately and went to him. He offered her an absent kiss while staring at Adrian, who was slower to pull herself up from the couch. They stood facing each other across the room. Adrian's hands shook. Olivia ushered the children from the room, announcing she was taking Ella to her friend's house for a sleepover.

Ella turned and gave her grandmother a hug and kiss before leaving.

"I may take Nick to the food store on our way back. I'll pick up dinner," Olivia said.

He pulled his gaze from his mother and looked to his wife.

"Fine," he whispered. "Don't take too long."

I love you, she mouthed to him silently. Then she smiled. He grabbed her hand as she passed him and gave it a squeeze.

Olivia drove Ella and Nick to Jenny's. In the car, Ella said, "How come we never met Dad's mom before?" Olivia had told the children who Adrian was when it was decided she would stay to wait for Chris. Both were struck silent at first, Ella staring at her new-found grandmother in curious surprise, before Nick barraged her with questions. *Where do you live? Did you know our other grandma? You know, our regular grandma?* Adrian answered with patient directness and soon they were involved in a game of *Sorry!* as they performed the awkward dance of trying to get to know each other, strangers connected by blood.

Ella warmed up to the woman quickly. Children were so forgiving, Olivia had thought. We should all behave this way.

She stared ahead. "I'll explain when you're a little older. Plus, she lives far away. It was hard for her to get here."

Ella thought a bit. "We could have gone there."

"Perhaps. But we didn't."

They pulled onto Jenny's street just as Nick dozed in the back seat, exhausted from the party and coming down from his sugar high.

"I wonder if Dad missed her," Ella said, grabbing her sleeping bag and knapsack from the car as she got out.

"I'm sure he did."

Olivia kissed her daughter and watched her run up to her friend's door.

Chapter 35
November 2010

It was not an anniversary or a birthday or any reason to celebrate. The tension between them the past month was palpable, so Olivia seemed surprised when Chris agreed to go out to eat at Aegean, their favorite restaurant, on Saturday night. He noticed she put extra effort into her appearance, wore a simple black dress, pulled slightly in the middle and a heavy wrap over her shoulders to protect from the chilly evening. She pulled her hair off her neck and wore small diamond stud earrings, a gift from Chris on their twentieth anniversary. Her first diamonds. She still didn't have a diamond ring, said she wouldn't replace her wedding ring. But she accepted the studs, and he was pleased.

They said little on the drive to dinner. He wanted to tell her she never looked more beautiful, but the image of her and Gavin leaving his office, with Gavin so close behind his wife he couldn't be sure if he had his palm on her lower back, kept replaying in his mind. He'd held his tongue when he got home later that evening, not wanting her to think he didn't trust her. He did, didn't he? Then why was he so upset?

She'd seemed embarrassed by what happened at the office, pushing her focus instead on Ella's visit and her news that Ella and Marco would be visiting the little boy they had seen on the internet. Chris had agreed it was exciting for the young couple, all the while wanting to ask what happened in that office before he showed up. Gavin couldn't look him in the eye. She'd appeared stunned, blushing as if caught at something. He couldn't shake his instinct. He couldn't stand his own thoughts. This was not him. He cursed Dana for putting the fear and doubt in his mind. Why would she do that, unless she knew something?

Henry, their waiter, escorted them to their table in the back and didn't bother with menus. He poured Chris a full glass of red and paused when Olivia held her hand up to stop him.

"Seltzer, Henry. Thank you. Two gyro platters please."

Chris took a healthy sip of his wine. "You're all dressed up. Are we celebrating something?"

Olivia shrugged and dipped a piece of pita in hummus. "Just life in general. We haven't been here in weeks, and I thought it would be nice not to cook."

Chris finished his wine.

"Babe? Slow down."

"Why? I have a designated driver, don't I?"

He was antagonizing her. He knew it. He wanted a fight. Part of him wanted to make her hurt and cry. She was putting him through hell, and she seemed not to know it or care. The travel agent had called him this afternoon. The villa he wanted in Tuscany had been rented to another couple. Did she want him to look for others? He told her to hold off on the search until further notice, suspecting he would not call her back. It pissed him off. He had envisioned romantic days and nights with his wife, walking the streets of Florence, her hand in the crook of his arm, window shopping. Making love on the grand, private patio under the stars.

He took a deep breath and waited while Henry re-filled his glass and stepped away. Chris took another big swig of wine.

"Is there anything, other than the obvious, that's bothering you?" Olivia said.

"The obvious? Isn't that enough, Liv? We can't get past this. Time is passing mercilessly while we sit like ducks awaiting our fate."

"Awaiting our fate? You act like life is over. I feel just the opposite. It could be a new beginning."

The waiter returned to place their dinners before them. Olivia nodded to Henry but said nothing. Her eyes were full.

"It's perspective. We are seeing this in two very different lights," Chris said. He drained his glass and leaned forward, pushing his food to the side. "You don't seem to understand. I will not be a part of what's going on. This is not my baby." The words were out before he could swallow them.

She was struck dumb. It took her a full minute to regain her composure. "What do you mean this is not your baby? Whose do you think it is?" She swiped an eye and wiped a tear on her napkin. "Don't make me choose, Chris. Don't be that guy who will live with regret for the rest of his life. Look what it did to your parents. They totally cut themselves off from us. Do you want to lose what we have?"

"Do you? You don't seem to care what I think or what I want. For years, I have been waiting for this." He roughly gestured to them both. Olivia glanced around, but no one seemed to pay them attention, thanks to the moderate noise level in the dining room. A toddler fussed and yelled two tables away. Chris didn't care who heard.

Olivia looked back to her husband. "What is happening to us?"

He bit his lip hard and didn't answer. They picked at their food, avoiding each other's eyes. He finished the bottle of wine and signaled for the check when it was clear neither of them had an appetite. He stood and Olivia said good-bye to Henry who brought carriers to take their food home. "No thanks, Henry," she said with a shaky voice.

Outside the restaurant, Olivia held her hand out. "Give me the keys."

Chris ignored her and walked to the car. It had started to rain.

"I won't get in that car with you," she said.

He hesitated and watched her. "Answer a question."

She waited.

"What were you and your boss doing in his office with the door closed when I showed up?"

Her eyes opened wide in surprise. "We were working."

He ran a hand through his hair and stared out at the street. "It seemed there was more than that. He couldn't look me in the eyes. Why is that, Olivia? And why did you describe him to me the way you did?"

"What are you talking about? Why are you asking these questions?" She narrowed her eyes and said, "What are you implying?"

Chris stared at her. "Whose baby is this?"

She looked as if he hit her and he instantly regretted the question.

"If you think anything was going on, shame on you. Only one of us has ever cheated in this marriage." Her voice trembled and his heart clenched in his chest. She had never made mention of that night since it happened. When she forgave him, they never spoke of it again.

"I can't believe you asked that question," she said.

With tears in his eyes, he spoke, slurring. "I can't have children anymore. I had myself..." he struggled for the word, "fixed when you were pregnant with—"

Slowly she pulled herself up to stand straight, a look of wonder on her face. "You what?"

He swayed slightly.

"Tell me you're lying. Tell me you didn't do that." Her voice rose.

He shrugged.

"I mourned for months and months while you consoled me and you deliberately lied to me the entire time?" She put her hand over her mouth and turned away from him. Her shoulders rose up and down and she gasped as if needing air. When she turned back around, tears streamed down her cheeks. Her nose ran and she carelessly wiped her wrap across her face. "How could you?"

"I had to!"

"You had to? What the hell does that mean? You *had* to make a life-changing decision by yourself?"

He stepped toward her. "Listen…"

She backed away, shaking her head. "No. This can't be happening." She heaved over clutching her stomach and let out a sob. He put his hand on her back and she shoved him away. "Don't touch me! I can't look at you."

"You have to look at me. I need to tell you why!" His voice rose to meet hers and he struggled to be heard over the rain. He was angry and afraid and drunk.

"What does it matter? It's done. You lied to me."

"Liv." It came out a wrangled whisper. He'd never seen her this angry and it gutted him. This was his lowest point.

"Don't say my name." She held out her hand. It shook so severely, all he wanted to do was hold her and explain why he'd done what he did but his words were no match against her rage and disappointment. He stepped to her.

"Give me the keys." The cold, detached tone of her voice went through him. Her hair was wet against her scalp. Mascara melted down her face which was covered with tears and mucus. He placed the keys in her hand and then grabbed her arm, trying to pull her toward him.

"No!" She fought to pull herself away and pushed him back with strength he didn't know she had. She climbed into the car and started the engine. He pounded on the door. "You can't leave! We have to finish this. Don't do this, Liv!" She jerked the car in reverse, out of the parking spot, forcing him to jump back, and sped away. He screamed her name as the rain poured down and the taillights disappeared.

On the walk home, he tried but couldn't erase her incredulous look of hurt and betrayal from his thoughts. He would never forgive himself for hurting her this way. He made it to the house an hour later, soaking wet and shivering.

Inside, he flung his sodden jacket on a chair and climbed the steps. He'd tell her everything, not sure if she would even listen to him. At their bedroom door, he gripped the handle. It was locked. There was no sound on the other side. She didn't call him in or acknowledge his presence, though he was sure she knew he was there. He leaned his head against the door.

"Olivia."

Silence.

"I don't expect you to forgive me, but you deserve to know, after all this time, why I did what I did." He took a deep breath, and the words he'd held inside for years poured forth in a stream of heartfelt confession.

"When we were expecting Christopher..." He paused. Saying his unborn baby's name still hurt. "When we were expecting, we had very different experiences. You were happy and optimistic, already in love with him. All I felt was anger and fear. Fear of going again through a labor where I almost lost you and anger that I allowed myself to fall into this situation. Do you know how hard it was to swallow the bitter taste of helplessness?" He sighed, and put his hands on either side of the door. "I tried to tell you how I felt, but you couldn't hear it. You were so happy, it became intoxicating. You wouldn't even consider what could happen. For God's sake, even the doctor suggested we stop after Nick. And we agreed we would. You agreed, Liv.

"I was so mad at you, I made the decision to see a doctor and make sure you could never get pregnant again, never face the danger of leaving me and the kids."

He tried the door handle again, growing frustrated.

"I was planning to tell you after Christopher was born, if nothing happened to you. But when you called to tell me we'd lost..." He clenched his jaw until pain radiated to his temples.

There was no sound on the other side of the door. It took him a few minutes to pull himself together and continue.

"How could I tell you what I'd done as you grieved? I was grieving, too. I loved him. Believe me. And then, there was never a right time. How do you tell the person you love more than anyone in the world that you lied? I thought we'd raise our children, retire and grow old together, and this would never come up."

The silence cut through him. Was she listening? He worked to contain the anger bubbling up from his core. How did they get here?

"Olivia!" He banged on the door. "Talk to me!" Before he could stop himself, he made a fist and punched the wall. "Dammit Olivia! Open the door! We've always talked to each other." His hand trembled and he stared at the hole in the wall, waiting for the knob to turn. When it was clear she wouldn't speak to him, he squeezed his eyes and took a step away.

"Know this, Liv. I've never, on our children, kept anything else from you. And I don't regret what I did."

Defeated, he walked away.

He went down to the main floor and stood at the bottom of the stairs, listening for movement or sound from their bedroom. When he heard nothing, he slipped on his shoes and went to the car. The heater warmed him as he idled in the driveway. He stared at his bedroom window and saw Olivia pull back the curtain. For a moment, he thought their eyes locked but he couldn't be sure through the rain. Still watching the window, he picked up his cell phone.

Chapter 36
1998

The drive to Ella's university was not nearly long enough for Olivia. They pulled up to the campus amid crowds of students and parents who were parked and unpacking, marching into dorms in some sort of controlled chaos. The day was warm and overcast and matched Olivia's mood.

"Mine is past this one on the right, Dad."

Chris followed his daughter's direction and parked along the grass behind another car. The three piled out and started to grab Ella's belongings. They had to leave Nick at home with Dana because there was no room for him in their sedan. And they agreed the day would be too long for an eleven-year-old to manage. The two had said their good-byes at home. It had been difficult at first. Nick locked himself in the bathroom as if by refusing to say good-bye, his sister wouldn't be able to leave. Finally, Ella coaxed him out of the room and promised he could visit next month and she'd write to him every week.

Ella's dorm was situated between two other dorms, a healthy walk from the lecture halls. It took them less than two hours to set up her room. Since her roommate hadn't arrived, they decided to walk around the campus, trying not to think about the moment when they'd have to say good-bye. Olivia wondered if she could try locking herself in a room, too. Sometimes Nick knew exactly what he was doing.

No one said much, each in their own thoughts. Olivia

caught Chris watching Ella closely on more than one occasion. She thought she'd be the one who would have a hard time. But Chris looked forlorn.

"Anyone want lunch?" Ella asked.

Ella's roommate was a bubbly, bouncing girl from Massachusetts who practically ran to Ella when they returned from lunch two hours later. Her parents had already left and within minutes in her company, Olivia could understand why. She'd set up her side of the room and pummeled Ella with questions about her music (Ella's CDs were piled on her desk) and details about Long Island. She was friendly but a bit exhausting, and Olivia and Chris took their leave amid the interrogation. Olivia was grateful for the girl's inane chatter. It seemed to take Ella's mind off her parents' leaving. She gave them both a tight hug, whispered I love yous, and went back to her new friend.

On the drive home that evening, Chris held Olivia's hand. "That was harder than I thought," he said. Olivia nodded, unable to speak. When she gathered herself as they drove onto the bridge, she said, "We just dropped our daughter off at college. Did you ever think you'd be saying that?"

Chris shook his head. "It came quick. The whole thing just flew by way too fast."

"I know." Olivia rested her head back against the headrest. "I'm going to miss her."

"Nick is going to miss her."

They drove on a bit. "I think he'll enjoy being an only child for a while. Ella enjoyed that privilege for almost eight years."

Chris put his hand on her thigh. "One down, one to go."

"We could have another one," she said.

He laughed. "Yeah, right. Can you imagine?"

"No." She looked out the window. Could she?

"We're only thirty-seven," he said.

"Your point?"

"When we take this same ride with Nick, we won't even be fifty. Think about it. We have the best of both worlds. We'll be totally young and free. We only had a year and a half to ourselves." He chuckled. "When Nick goes to college, I'd like to date you some more."

She went back to the window. It was what they always wanted. When Nick left in seven years, they'd be able to do everything they'd put off. Why didn't that thought give her solace?

"Do you want to stop for dinner?" he asked.

She shook her head, had no appetite, and wanted to see her son. She looked at Chris's profile and put her hand on his cheek. "When are you going to Boston?"

He sighed and lowered the radio. "I guess I'll go sometime next week." He moved into the left lane and sped up to pass a tractor trailer. "It's going to be weird being back in that house for the last time."

Chris's mother had passed away one month earlier. She knew she had cancer when she showed up at the house three years ago. Olivia wondered if her imminent mortality drove her confidence to see her son after so many years, trying to make amends before she moved on. Chris spent the last few days with her at hospice, telling her he forgave her. He felt a sense of calm when she took her last breath, more so than when he learned his father passed. They brought the children to her funeral, and Ella and Nick saw their father's childhood home for the first time. Ella had remarked at the size of the house, and Nick marveled over the landscaped yard, full in-ground pool with various rock formations and trickling waterfalls.

"This reminds me of Uncle Trevor and Aunt Dana's house," Ella said to her mother.

"You were rich, Dad?" Nick had asked Chris.

"No. My parents were."

Now he was to clean out her house, having agreed with his estranged brother, with whom he never re-formed a relationship, due to geography and a lifetime of personality conflicts, on a schedule that worked for both. Brian had already been there, and Chris predicted there wouldn't be much left to do.

His brother probably took everything he wanted and deservedly so. He led the life planned for him.

They arrived home in the dark to a package waiting on their front landing. It was addressed to Chris.

"Do you want me to get Nick?" Olivia said.

He picked up the box, looked at the return address and nodded. "Do you mind?"

"Who is it from?"

He met her eyes. "My mother."

***

Chris waited until Olivia had driven down the street before looking at the box. At the table, he replayed the conversation he'd had with his mother when she showed up unexpected that Saturday afternoon.

When he stepped into the den and saw Olivia's flushed face and his children with his mother, he thought he was dreaming. Olivia had left them alone, to talk. For the first time in a decade and a half, they looked at each other. Adrian spoke first.

"They're beautiful."

"I know."

Her fingers played with her necklace, a Christmas gift from his father when Chris was in high school. She loved it. He couldn't believe she still wore it.

Chris waited. The anger of all these years of silence, of abandoning him and his family prevented him from speaking.

"Brian called to tell you about your father."

Chris said nothing.

"I understand why I didn't hear from you." She looked down, still pulling the sapphire pendant. "I'd hoped you'd come and sit beside me at his funeral."

"I didn't find out until after. And...I was angry."

"You're still angry."

"No."

Adrian nodded. "I was angry. At him."

"You weren't angry enough to stick up for me. You just stood there and allowed him to berate the woman I loved. I'll never forgive you for that."

"I'm not asking for forgiveness. I don't deserve it. I was never strong enough. He was so stubborn. You both said things that day. When you left, I put on my coat to go after you. Your father told me if I walked out the door, he wouldn't take me back. I stood at the threshold watching the taillights of your car grow dimmer as you distanced yourself. I thought of all your father had done for you and I believed maybe he was right. Maybe you were being rash and wouldn't see it through. So, I closed myself in the house. We were upset. He felt disrespected and hurt." She paused. "I thought you'd come back."

"He cut me off."

A tear slid down her cheek. "I found out after he did it. It wasn't easy for me, Christopher. You were my child. But I loved that man. And I made a decision."

"You missed out on knowing my children."

"We both missed a lot." She dropped her hand. "You're just like him."

"No," Chris said. "If I were, I would have left Liv. I would have had a shitty life."

Chris squeezed his eyes shut and then opened them. It was a tough conversation. Gut-wrenching when Adrian told him what his father endured in his last days.

He lifted the top of the box and looked inside.

Chapter 37
November 2010

Chris walked into the pub and shook the cold rain from his jacket and hair. He grabbed a stool next to Trevor who had arrived minutes earlier and was already half into his mug of beer. The bartender glanced at Chris.

"Bourbon. Straight."

"So, this is a bourbon conversation." Trevor said.

Chris shook his hair out one last time.

"Dude, you're like a dog." Trevor wiped his face and sipped his beer.

The bartender placed a glass in front of Chris. Trevor threw a bill down and ordered one for himself. "On me tonight. You sound like you need it."

Chris lifted his glass in salute and dropped the liquid down his throat. Trevor gestured for another for his friend and sipped his beer while he waited for his next drink.

"Do you want to talk about it?"

Chris had called Trevor from his driveway and asked to meet. Trevor asked no questions, though it was approaching eleven o'clock. He simply asked when and where? He watched Chris suck down a second drink. But that didn't mean they'd discuss anything. Sometimes a drink and company did the trick.

Chris dropped his head. "How the fuck did I get here?"

Trevor turned on his stool. "You know it's your baby, right?"

He lifted his head and looked at his buddy. "Yes. But for a while I wasn't sure. Do you know how devastating that was? I wanted to kill someone."

"What changed your mind?"

Chris squeezed his eyes shut, remembering Olivia's reaction in the restaurant parking lot, the physical pain his accusation caused her, and he realized in an instant he'd always known it was his. He'd been rash and stupid to think otherwise. "I realized everything I built my life on was because of her. If I don't believe in us, what do we have?"

Trevor didn't respond.

"I never went back for my follow-up to see if the vasectomy worked. I figured it did. I mean, we didn't get pregnant all those years."

"Have you seen a doctor recently?"

"I called him to get tested and then didn't show up for the appointment."

"What now?"

Two more drinks arrived on the bar. Both grabbed their glasses and lifted in a silent toast. "She won't consider—"

"She might," Chris said.

Trevor smiled.

"What?"

"We had a similar conversation thirty-two years ago."

Chris looked at his friend.

"Dude, I didn't think you would, but you got it right the first time. Do you know how many of us didn't?" Trevor said. "You'll figure it out again."

Chris rubbed his hands over his face. "Tonight, I told Liv what I did. I don't know if she'll ever forgive me."

Trevor blew out a long breath. "Oh boy. Tomorrow, you'll go make this right with your wife. Do it for all of us who don't have what you have." Trevor gave a sideways glance to his friend and pushed his glass toward him. "But for now, go ahead. You can crash with me."

Without a word, Chris took Trevor's drink and signaled the bartender for another.

***

Clutching a cup of decaf tea, wrapped in the quilt her mother had made her for those years ago, Olivia watched the sunrise. She'd been up all night, finally leaving the bed and moving to the den where she fell into intermittent dozes on the couch, only to awaken with Chris's words repeating in her ears. He never came home last night. Trevor had texted her at two am, saying Chris was with him. She didn't respond, thankful to be alone, to figure out what to do.

As the sky lightened to a pale pink, she decided to get dressed and drove over to Dana's. She'd been thinking about her for the past hour, and needed answers. She put little thought into her appearance, and it was clear she looked haggard by Dana's reaction upon answering her door.

"Good Lord, what happened to you?" Wrapped in a silk robe, Dana's hair was piled on top of her head, her eyes bloodshot. She should talk?

"I need to talk to you," Olivia said, wrapped in a shawl over her sweats. Her hair was pulled back in a ponytail. She wore no makeup, feeling and looking exposed.

Dana pulled back the heavy door and allowed Olivia to walk in past her. She turned to wait for Dana to shut the door.

"Kitchen?"

"No," Olivia said, sick of that room.

Settled onto a leather sofa in the den, Olivia declined an offer for coffee and waited for Dana to return with a cup for herself. The room was gorgeous in deep browns, hunter green and burgundy. One wall was aligned floor to ceiling with books, adjacent to a small, but impressive bar where a glass sat with the remnants of a one-person party. Olivia lay back against a decorative pillow and focused on the thick, ornamental molding along the high ceiling. How could Dana live here by herself? The sheer size of this place demanded a crowd. The entire first floor of Olivia's house fit into this one room. Dana's children were rarely home anymore, leaving her to fill this space somehow. She thought of her tiny den she loved, the second floor Chris built that held two modest bedrooms and little else and knew, even by herself, she'd never feel alone in it.

Dana walked in with a plate of scones and a mug. She sat across from Olivia in a club chair and waited.

"You don't look good," Olivia said.

"Neither do you."

They regarded each other like strangers instead of the friends they had been for thirty years. If Olivia squinted, she could make out a young Dana who warned her off Chris the very first time they met.

"What?"

"I was just thinking of the first thing you said to me at the bar at school. Warning me about Chris."

Dana's smile was guarded. Olivia knew her friend was waiting to understand the reason behind her impromptu visit.

"Chris told me what he did."

Dana made no movement. She sat holding her mug in both hands.

"He stayed with you and Trevor when he had his vasectomy?"

"Yes."

Olivia nodded. "I thought you of all people would talk him out of it."

Dana looked long at Olivia. Was she trying to assess Olivia's anger? Pain? Olivia knew she showed both. She was angry with Dana and hurt by her lies of omission. She needed answers.

"I could never convince the man of anything," Dana said.

"What the hell does that mean?"

"Nothing." She brought the mug to her lips to cover her singed cheeks.

Olivia opened her mouth to speak but thought better of it. She stared at her lap, thoughts ricocheting in her head while she sat rigid on the couch.

"He was going to tell you, you know. Just as soon as you had the baby. But then he called you and you had lost..." Dana sighed. "I guess he couldn't. I told him he must, but he wouldn't listen to me. Made me promise not to tell you."

Olivia bit her bottom lip in thought. "I need to know something." She brought her eyes to Dana's, who waited. "I need to know why you broke a promise to me and you held one you made to my husband, knowing it would hurt me."

"You're referring to your weak attempt to have an abortion when you were nineteen?"

"Weak attempt?"

Dana rolled her eyes. "You wanted me to tell him. Don't shake your head. If you'd wanted to go through with the abortion, you wouldn't have told me where you were going."

"I asked you not to tell him what I was doing."

"You didn't mean it. And I did it for him anyway. Who cares about that now? You probably wouldn't have gone through with it. I just helped solidify yours and Chris's resolve to have Ella. You should be thanking me."

How had they not had this conversation in all the years they'd been together? This underlying truth between them.

"This is different, Dana. What would you have said if Trevor did something like that without your knowledge?"

Dana exhaled and put her mug down. "I don't care about Trevor. And I wouldn't have gotten myself pregnant behind my husband's back when I promised him we wouldn't have more children."

Olivia's head flew back as if physically hit.

"What you did was wrong," Dana said. "Shit, you almost died. And you wanted to do it again. And look at you now, at your age, wanting another baby. You're crazy. He did the right thing." She shook her head and reached for the blanket lying on the ottoman in front of her. "You're selfish, Olivia. That's why I never told you."

Tucked under the chenille, Dana stared at her, belligerent, as if she'd been waiting to have this conversation.

"He was hurting and it made me hurt too, but he was so in love with you he could only forgive you. I couldn't see it. I'd have been so pissed." Dana shrugged. "What do I know?"

A lone tear escaped Olivia's full eyes. She knew that, but to hear the truth hurt.

"I love you, but I love Chris more," Dana said. Then she said no more.

Olivia walked into her house two hours later, her eyes burning and puffy from lack of sleep and from crying on the side of the expressway after she left Dana's. She deserved to hear what she did. How long had Dana been holding it in? Years. Her frustration with Olivia and her allegiance to Chris, who she might even have been in love with, was evident in every word. As painful as it was to endure, Olivia needed to see herself in the mirror Dana held to her.

She found Chris at the kitchen table, looking as she felt, exhausted and sad. A covered box sat on his placemat. She opened her mouth to speak, but he held up his hand.

"Please. Let me explain before you say anything."

She closed her mouth and pressed her lips together. He gestured for her to sit, and she took a seat across from him.

"I know there's no chance of this being anyone else's baby. I'm sorry I doubted you. I never have before. I was upset." His voice wavered.

Her eyes switched between the box and his face. "We've always been able to work through our problems. That's what makes us so good together." He placed a hand on the cover. "I held something very important from you, and I'll be sorry for the rest of my life. But what I did, I did out of love and nothing else." He pulled the top from the box and gently placed it on the table. "You had your own secrets," he said and then pulled out a stack of envelopes. She recognized her mother-in-law's name and addresses written in her handwriting. "I'm grateful for what I did because if we tried for another baby, Ella and Nick might not have you right now. And we both know how it feels to lose our mom."

Olivia wiped her eyes with her sleeve. "I'm going to get an abortion."

He put the envelopes down and leaned back.

"I got caught up in the fantasy of doing it all again and didn't take into consideration what that really meant for us, for you and the kids. I was so excited to be pregnant after all these years that I pushed everything else aside. And the thought of giving this baby to Ella hurt more than I can handle."

Olivia's eyes flitted to the letters on the table. "We've been keeping secrets from each other for years. What kind of people do that who are in love?" She shook her head. "I'm ashamed of my behavior. I'm angry at you, at Dana, at myself. I feel like the foundation of our marriage is layered in lies and I don't know what to do."

She cried, unable to go on.

Chris moved from his chair and kneeled before her. "Don't. Don't feel that way." He pushed the loose strands of hair back from her face, placing his palms on her cheeks so she was forced to look at him.

"Babe, what we did, we did out of love."

She pulled back and he dropped his hands.

"Forgive me," he whispered. "I can't bear it if you don't."

She looked at her husband, the man she adored for three decades. She knew she'd harbor regret for what he'd done for the rest of her life. But she also knew that nothing he could do could keep her from wanting to be with him until she took her last breath.

"Can you forgive me?" she said.

"Liv," he whispered, and she leaned her forehead to his.

***

They made love as the sun rose higher into the sky. A cold, crisp day was promised. She nestled into his frame, spooning him as she always did. Wiping silent tears from her eyes, she said, "I feel like it's been a long time since we've done that."

He didn't answer.

"Do you know who's really responsible for this baby?" she said, facing away.

His body stiffened against her.

"That hot guy at the hotel bar in the Berkshires. Grant." She tried to chuckle, but a bittersweet melancholy engulfed her.

"You're killing me." He leaned forward and kissed her behind her ear, his favorite spot. "Should we tell the kids?"

They both thought about the question.

Finally, Olivia spoke. "Not yet," she said, feeling ashamed. Another secret. She lifted his hand from the fold between her stomach and the mattress and lightly ran a finger over his bruised knuckles. She'd stared at the fresh hole in the wall outside of their bedroom after Chris left last night, his frustration exposing the beam behind the sheetrock.

He hugged her tighter, as if understanding her thoughts. "Okay."

His breath grew steady, and she thought he'd fallen asleep when she asked, "Do you wonder what your legacy will be?"

His breath paused. "You mean, when I die?"

She nodded against him.

"I haven't given it much thought."

"I suppose it will be our children. They're what we'll leave behind for the world. Their children and so on." She watched clouds through the window. "Eventually, we'll just be one square in a long line of familial descendants. Unknown names on a huge family tree to some kid a hundred years from now who has to do a project for school."

"So? It won't affect you. You'll be long gone."

"Exactly," she said.

"What is it you're looking for? What are you afraid of?"

"Getting older. I don't want to. I want to be the young girl you just met. I want to have those days back. They were gold, Chris. I don't think I appreciated them. It makes me sad."

"It's not over." He hugged her tighter. "Liv, having a baby isn't going to prolong our lives or make us feel young again. Time marches on. No matter what we do."

She listened to his breath grow slower and deeper. When she was sure he'd fallen asleep, she slipped out of bed and went downstairs into the kitchen, needing to be alone for just a bit.

Left on the table were her letters to her mother-in-law. Lying on top of the pile was one she'd never seen.

Christopher —

If you're reading this letter, it means I have moved on.

In this box, among some items I thought you might want, I am returning these letters to you and know this will be the first time you'll see them. I felt it important to let you know that Olivia kept me apprised of your life through the years. Take the time to read them. They tell a true love story and are a clear indication that you have led a full life. I am pleased for you. Your children are bright and curious and beautiful. They are you. They are Olivia.

I will regret all the years I've missed getting to know them and you as a father and a husband but know that I watched you, and I am proud.

Love,

Mom

Chapter 38
November 2010

Nick called Olivia four days before Thanksgiving. "I'd like to go to Melissa's for the holiday weekend."

Olivia sat down on the couch, feeling exhausted and slightly nauseated. "You're not coming home at all?"

"Not this time, Mom. They invited me, and I really want to be with her. Would you mind?"

"Of course not." He was twenty-two years old. How could she tell him what to do at this point?

"I'll come home next week for Dad's birthday." And he was gone. Their son would probably leave Long Island after graduation and never look back. It was one of the many prices to pay as a parent, she was learning. No matter how much you love them, they find their own way. Away.

Olivia called to schedule an appointment with her doctor and when she learned he was on vacation, she felt almost relief. She needed more time to adjust to their decision. Chris pushed for her to go to the clinic she had visited, worried that the longer they waited, the more she was at risk but she wanted it done by the doctor she knew and trusted.

Beneath sweaters and long shirts, she wasn't showing yet.

She placed the phone down and stared out the window at the near empty trees. The temperature had dipped overnight. Winter was on its way. Until she had the procedure, she'd try not to dwell on the baby, on the wonderful feeling knowing a life was growing inside of her. She was terrified. Instinctively, she reached for the quilt and held it, thinking of her mother.

They had Thanksgiving dinner at Ella's with Marco's parents, who retired to North Carolina the previous year. Older than Chris and Olivia by a decade, Andrea and Fred had become avid golfers and enjoyed talking about the retirement community they lived in. Ad nauseam.

"So, Chris," Fred said, sidling up to him during cocktails and appetizers, "what are your plans in the next few years? Sticking around here paying these exorbitant taxes? Or can I entice you to come down to paradise?" He chuckled, pleased with his new life, and Chris smiled politely while Olivia watched from the couch.

"We plan to stay near the kids for a bit longer. Ella and Marco are starting a family, so we want to be around."

Fred patted Chris on the shoulder. "It's just a plane ride away. Think of it, no more cold, harsh winters."

"I think we'll be okay. These old bones haven't started complaining yet."

Fred dropped his hand. "Just wait until you're sixty-two. It gets hard to get out of bed in the morning." He glanced over to Olivia. "I envy you. If I could go back in time, I'd have started earlier, too. But we waited to have Marco." He smiled and shrugged. "Oh well. *C'est la vie* they say, right? It's all good."

Chris winked at Olivia as Fred returned to the cheese and crackers. She felt a wave of nausea sweep over her.

"Mom? Can you help me make the gravy?"

Olivia pulled herself from the couch. She took a deep breath, trying to quell her sudden sickness and gave Chris a quick peck on his cheek. "I don't mind the winters," she whispered as she went to the kitchen to help her daughter.

Over turkey, Ella and Marco talked about getting to know Joshua when they visited. Ella's face glowed as she explained how he wouldn't acknowledge them at first, and it took the two full days to get him to warm up to them. But then he even allowed them to sit with him while he played with his truck. Ella's voice cracked as she told them Joshua allowed her a brief hug when she said good-bye and promised to come back to see him.

"What's wrong with him?" Fred asked, cutting through the idealistic picture they'd created for their parents.

"How do you mean?" Ella said.

Marco cleared his throat. "He has some issues." The room fell quiet. Ella's eyes met everyone's and then turned to Marco, who continued, "He's socially and emotionally delayed. So far, the agency determined that by observing his conceptual skills—language and self-direction. But he's only three. And they believe," he took Ella's hand, "they believe that in the right environment and with the proper support, he will adjust and can--" Marco coughed, "*will* be a fully functioning adult."

Olivia poked at her Brussels sprouts. They were choosing a tough road. When she looked up, Ella was watching her. She smiled at her daughter. "I think it's wonderful you're giving a little boy a chance at a better life with a loving family."

Ella smiled.

Andrea, who had been quiet up to this point, spoke. "Marco, what changed your minds about wanting a newborn? Why put yourself in a position to struggle?"

"Because, Mom, Joshua needs a forever home. And we fell in love with him. He's been in two homes already and he's struggling. What child deserves that? A healthy newborn is more likely to find adoptive parents than this little boy. And we'll receive specific training to understand the effects of trauma and how to help children like Joshua heal."

"Do you know how many older children are waiting for someone to adopt them?" Ella added. "They age out of the system at eighteen. What must it be like not to sit at a Thanksgiving dinner like this?"

Chris squeezed Olivia's hand under the table.

"You can't save the world, you know," Fred said.

Ella straightened in her chair. "No. I know that. We want to have a family, and Joshua is ours."

Olivia brought the dishes into the kitchen while Ella scrubbed the roasting pan. She put her arm around her daughter's shoulders. "I can't wait to meet Joshua," she said.

Ella turned to her. "I hope we're doing the right thing. I hope we can take care of this boy. I'm scared." She shut off the water and stared down into the sink. "I want to do the right thing."

"You just voiced the concern of every waiting parent." Olivia leaned over to see her daughter's face. "Look at you. You're already a mom."

Olivia tossed and turned in bed but couldn't get comfortable. She blamed it on the extra slice of strawberry rhubarb she'd inhaled for dessert. She never enjoyed rhubarb in the past but couldn't eat enough of it last night. Ella said something to her at the table.

"Mom, I've never seen you eat rhubarb, and now you're having a second piece?"

Chris watched them both carefully. Andrea unknowingly saved her. "It's an old family recipe. No one can turn it down." She smiled benignly at Olivia, who agreed wholeheartedly while Ella kept a curious gaze on her.

Now, she was sorry. Sleep wasn't going to happen for her tonight. She gave up and puttered down the hall into the kitchen wrapped in her robe. Perhaps some chamomile tea would soothe her. She quickly pulled the teapot from the stove before its shrill whistle could wake Chris and poured the near-boiling water into her mug. She was carrying the tea into the den when she heard the front doorknob jiggling. Fear shot through her, and she froze in place, leaving herself an easy target for the intruder. The jiggling continued a few seconds longer before she realized someone was using a key to get in. There were only two people outside of her and Chris with a key to the house. Ella and...

Nick appeared in the doorway, and Olivia sagged in relief.

"You scared me," she whispered. "Nicholas, what is going on?"

Nick pulled the key from the lock and shut the door. He turned around and leaned against it. "Can we talk tomorrow? I'm beat."

"No." She placed her mug on a side table and stepped to her son. "You show up at four am and you expect me to wait for hours to hear why?"

Nick yawned.

"I don't care," she said. "Come." She turned from him, picked up her mug, and walked back into the kitchen. Nick followed. He sat at the table as she made him a cup of tea. Sitting across from him, Olivia sipped. He looked exhausted, but she needed to know what drove him to leave Melissa's house on Thanksgiving night and come home without warning.

He rested his elbows on either side of the tea and rubbed his eyes. "So..." he started and rubbed his eyes again.

She waited, holding her breath.

"So, Melissa's pregnant."

Olivia felt herself sway. She held onto the table and focused on Nick. "It's yours?"

Nick shook his head.

"Oh." Her hand flew up to her mouth.

"She told me after dinner as we were setting up the bed in the spare bedroom. Her parents were downstairs." He looked at his mother. "I walked out, got in my car, and kept driving. I want to sleep in my own bed. In my own room. Mom, I didn't know what to say."

"What are you feeling?"

He shrugged, and his head fell back into his hands. "This is fucked. Sorry."

Olivia brought her mug to the sink. "Go to bed. We'll talk to your father in the morning."

Nick stood and walked to the hall. At the kitchen door, he turned to his mother. "Why were you up?"

"Indigestion. I'm tired now."

"Okay. Night."

"Nick?"

"Yeah?"

Olivia stepped to her son and pulled him into her arms.

***

She waited for dawn's first light before gently rubbing Chris's shoulder. "Babe? Wake up."

He grunted and shifted so he lay on his back. "Was I snoring?"

"No. Nick is home."

His eyes opened. "What?"

"He's in his room sleeping."

Two hours later, they were in the kitchen drinking coffee, waiting for Nick to wake up. He walked in, disheveled and puffy-eyed. He paused at the door when he saw his parents. Olivia gasped, and Chris turned to her. Her hand was at her heart. For a moment, she saw Chris thirty years ago.

"Liv?"

She shook her head. Nick poured himself a cup of coffee and joined them at the table.

"Morning," he whispered, his voice still raspy from sleep.

"You look like hell," Chris said.

"Makes sense. I feel like hell."

Olivia stood and went to the fridge. "I'll make you eggs." Nick nodded.

"What are you going to do, Nick?" Chris said.

He exhaled and sat back in his chair. "I don't know."

"When are you going back up?"

Nick lifted his fork as his mother placed a piping hot plate in front of him.

"I'll probably spend the weekend here. I need to think."

"You've been driving without a license?" his father said.

"That's the least of my problems." He speared the eggs with his fork. "I'm being careful," he managed through a full mouth.

Olivia stood behind their son and put her hands on his shoulders. "Does Melissa know you're here?"

Nick finished chewing his food. "I called her last night before I went to sleep. She's upset, obviously."

"You don't think she'd do anything rash, do you?"

Chris's eyes shot up to his wife. Would Melissa do what Olivia tried to do all those years ago? She detected a glimmer of hope in her husband's eyes and turned away.

Nick paused in thought. "I don't think so. Not before she'd talk to me."

"What about the boy who's responsible?"

"He doesn't know. She'll never tell him."

They sat quietly in the kitchen while Nick finished his food. He stood. "Thanks, Mom. I'm going to take a shower. I think I'll stop at Ella's today."

***

When Nick left, Olivia went back to bed, leaving Chris alone, wishing he could rewind the clock three months, before his whole life began to unravel, before his son did a monumentally stupid thing landing himself in jail, before his daughter gave up her quest to have her own baby, before Olivia dropped the bomb that exposed secrets he thought long buried and shook the core of his whole marriage.

He walked into their bedroom and sat on the bed. "What do you think he'll do?"

She rolled over onto her back. "I think whatever he does, we should support his decision."

"I can't support him if he stays with her."

"He's your son," Olivia said. "If you allowed your father to convince you to re-think what you did, we wouldn't be here today. I would have raised Ella on my own and Nick wouldn't exist."

"It's different with him."

"How? He's in love like you were. Do you regret any of it, Chris?"

He sighed. "Of course not. You know I don't."

"Don't do what your parents did. Don't alienate him. He's a grown man. It's his life."

"He's a baby."

"So were you."

"But they're so young."

"Babe, we were younger when we fell in love."

"We were different."

"We knew less than they do now. And we were poor."

He lay beside her, propped up on his elbow and lightly rubbed her arm. He'd been thinking a lot about their life together, their trials and celebrations—their first apartment, lying on a mattress on the floor with no furniture, late dinners in their 6x8 foot kitchen under the glow of a dangling lightbulb, struggling through Ella's first years, sacrificing luxuries like savings accounts for warm coats and electricity, soccer uniforms and school pictures. It was a struggle he hadn't planned for. He worked long hours, six days a week, they both did, to build a life for themselves and their children. Through it all, they grew stronger together, found reasons to laugh and celebrate and here they were, thirty years later. Still in love.

Chris leaned over and kissed her cheek. "Life was good, wasn't it?"

"It still is."

Nick found his father in the early evening, tinkering on his keyboard in the basement.

"Writing something new?"

Chris dropped his hands and straddled the bench when he heard his son. "Nah, just playing around. I haven't written anything in a while."

Nick plopped down onto a bean bag chair, riddled with electric tape from years of use.

"All those wasted hours trying to get me to play that thing."

Chris smiled. "I don't consider them wasted. It was time well-spent with my son. And you picked it up quickly. You just had no staying power." Chris had tried on many occasions to teach Nick, and Ella too, how to play the keyboard. Nick picked up a couple of chords but lost interest quickly to baseball and then football. Ella never wanted to put down her soccer ball long enough to give it the college try. So, Chris would spend hours playing as they walked around the house above him.

"You saw Ella?"

Nick nodded. "She can't stop talking about that kid. I'm happy for her."

"Did you tell her what's going on?"

"Yes."

Chris scratched the back of his neck. "How did she take it?"

"She said if she got upset every time a woman got pregnant, she'd cry an ocean of tears. She's excited, Dad, for herself. And she's sorry for me."

"Did she tell you what you should do?"

Nick shook his head. "I didn't ask."

Chris rubbed his hands on his jeans.

"The only one I want to discuss this with is you."

Chris looked up, surprised. Nick watched him while lying back on the bean bag, arms crossed over his chest.

"When Mom got pregnant, you quit school and married her."

"Yes."

Nick tilted his head. "Your parents basically disowned you. And you did it anyway."

Chris could still envision that moment as clear as if it happened yesterday, the disappointment and frustration radiating from his father in waves as he struggled to hold onto his decision, his belief in himself that he could survive this without his parents' help and financial support. Ultimately, it was his blind love and devotion to Liv that gave him the strength to keep his resolve. A painful memory that still haunted him all these years later.

Nick waited for him to say something.

"That's right," he said simply.

Nick dropped his head back onto the beanbag chair. "I don't know what I'm doing. I'm not ready to be a father."

Chris exhaled. "So, don't be one."

"It's not that easy."

"It is that easy. It's not your baby."

He could see the words hurt Nick, but Chris felt he might be able to dissuade him from making this life-changing mistake.

"Dad, I love this girl. When I think about not being with her, I can't breathe. I can't see my future without her." His chin quivered, but he held Chris's gaze steadfast. "I don't have a choice. I just don't know if I can do it."

"Son, no one knows until it happens. I'm not sure I can explain just how hard it was for us. I'm asking you to really think this through. Maybe consider other alternatives. You can start a family later, when you're ready."

Nick put his hands over his face. "They're religious. I don't think it's an option."

"What if the father wants to become involved?"

Nick stood. "I am going to be the baby's father." He walked to the stairs. With a hand on the rail, he turned to Chris. "You may not have known what you were doing," he said, "but you and Mom made a great life for us. Don't you get it? You cracked the code. Most of my friends' parents hate each other. You're still in love. It's exactly what I want. I found it with Melissa."

Chris swung his leg over the bench so he fully faced his son.

"Please think about this. This is your life you're talking about."
They looked at each other until Olivia came down the stairs.

"Nick, Melissa is on the phone," she said.

He went upstairs, and Olivia went to her husband. Chris put his arms around her waist and tilted his head toward her face. She ran her fingers through his hair, pausing at the curl against his neck.

"He's taking on a mammoth responsibility. He doesn't have to do it."

"No, he doesn't. I wouldn't expect anything less from your son."

Chapter 39

November 2010

Olivia followed the signs down the hospital corridor until she entered the rehab unit. Holding a Tupperware container filled with turkey casserole and a piece of homemade pecan pie, she peeked inside Sophia's room and found it empty. She placed the food near the windowsill and waited, staring out the window over the parking lot.

"She's in therapy," a voice said.

Olivia spun around to find a nurse at the door. "It's just down the hall if you'd like to see."

"Am I allowed?"

"Sure. Come, I'll show you."

Olivia followed the scrubs down the hall, winding their way along the corridor.

"This is so confusing. I got lost twice trying to find the elevator to get up here," Olivia said.

"You get used to it. Here we are."

They stood at the entrance to a large room with various stations set up for physical therapy—small weights, a stationary bike, flat beds, parallel bars, all spaced out and empty but for a young man, no older than thirty, sitting at a table with a nurse on the other side. The young man wore a thick plastic helmet over his head, and he was trying to lift small marbles from a bowl and put them into one of three cups. The therapist working with him glanced up at Olivia and smiled. "Who are you here to see?"

"She's here for Sophia," the nurse said. The therapist pointed to the other side of the room, and Olivia spotted Sophia sitting on a large but low table, her feet resting on the floor.

She turned to thank the nurse and noted her name tag. "Your name is Rose."

The nurse smiled. "That's right."

Olivia hesitated, remembering the nurse who took care of her mother, and was about to speak when she decided against it. "Thank you, Rose."

"Pleasure." She slipped away as quietly as she'd arrived.

Sophia waved Olivia over. "James is trying to show me the right way to get in and out of bed," she said. James, her therapist, gave a brief wave to Olivia, who stepped to the side, out of the way.

"Let's try this one more time, Sophia, and then we'll get you back to your room. Now, you're sitting on the side like this. With your hand, reach over and grab a piece of your pants. Yes, like that. Pull the leg over onto the bed and then scoot yourself a bit to get the other leg up. Let me see you try it without my help."

Sophia took a breath and concentrated on her task. Olivia stood mutely against the wall and watched. She noticed Sophia wore no makeup and her hair was matted down in back, the gray growth evident in her part and along the sides of her face. She'd never seen her unkempt and glimpsed the woman as old for the first time.

"What do I do if I sleep in the buff?" she said to James.

"Well, then you just grab some extra skin and pull it on up." He winked at her.

The older woman laughed and bits of color returned to her cheeks. On the third try, she pulled her leg up onto the bed, and James gave her a satisfied nod.

"Well done. That's all for today." James turned to Olivia. "Let's get you to your visit."

Olivia followed them as James pushed Sophia's wheelchair into her room. He locked her wheels and went to move her footrests to get her into bed.

"I'd like to sit here a bit if I may."

"Certainly. Just ring for help when you want to get into bed. See you Thursday."

Sophia gestured for Olivia to take a seat in the available chair.

"James is the highlight of my week. You can see why," Sophia said, smiling through a yawn. "Cute as can be."

Olivia chuckled. "What else do you do in therapy?"

"Basic maneuvers. Getting into and out of a car. On and off a chair. Things that required no thought before."

Olivia leaned forward. "So, do you think you'll finally wear the bracelet your niece got you?"

Sophia scowled.

"You don't have a roommate, I see," Olivia said, moving from the subject.

"I did. She went home this morning. She got her new hip a week before me." She yawned again. "They worked me hard today."

"They want you to go home, too."

Sophia looked despondent. "My daughter is pushing me to move to her town. She found an assisted living community a few miles from her house." She frowned. "An assisted living community? I fell. It can happen to anyone."

"But it happened to her mother, and she's worried," Olivia said.

"I like where I am. I have my friends, my niece."

"You can make new friends."

Sophia looked Olivia square in the eye. "I just made a new friend."

Touched, she reached over and put her hand on Sophia's arm. "I'll always be your friend. Wherever you end up."

Sophia let out a long breath and gazed toward the window. "That wasn't here before I left."

"I brought you a little Thanksgiving meal."

The older woman grinned. "Thank you."

"You're welcome."

"How are you feeling?" Sophia said.

"I have an appointment next week with my doctor. Chris and I decided to…" Olivia stared at her lap. She couldn't say the words. They would celebrate his birthday on Saturday with the kids. She hoped she could hide her angst during dinner.

Sophia leaned a knobby hand over Olivia's. "Good girl."

Olivia looked at her in surprise. "You agree with this?"

She closed her eyes and nodded. How was Olivia the last to see what she'd been doing? There was a comforting feeling about this woman and Olivia was grateful she came into her life when she did, as if fate were somehow orchestrated to bring the people just as they were needed.

She would miss Sophia terribly.

"How are your children?"

Olivia picked at her thumbnail. "We've hit a bit of a blip with Nick."

"A blip?"

"It seems Nick's girlfriend is pregnant because of what happened to her in September."

Sophia's hand went to her neck, and Olivia noticed she wore no jewelry. "Oh, my. That's a blip I didn't see coming."

"Neither did we. I think he'll stay with her whatever she decides to do."

Sophia's expression softened. "He is in love."

"Yes."

"How wonderful."

Chapter 40
December 2010

Olivia stopped by Ella's on her way home from work. Marco answered the door with a smile. "She'll be home soon. She stopped at the store after school."

He moved aside to let her in. Olivia unwrapped her thick scarf and unbuttoned her coat before slipping her boots off and placing them at the door. "Are you still on schedule to go to Oregon?"

"Yes. We've been in contact with the mediator and his foster parents." Marco motioned for her to follow him and led her through the living room and upstairs. "Check out what we did." He opened the door next to the master bedroom and let Olivia step in before him.

She stood in the center of the former office, now decorated in blues and browns. The toddler bed against the interior wall had a thick comforter with trucks all over it. There was a toy chest in the corner with a tow truck on top and a thick shaggy rug under her feet. She turned around slowly, taking in every caring detail added for this lucky little boy.

"He loves trucks, so..." Marco gazed around the room. "We know it's premature, but..." He shrugged. "What do you think?"

Olivia hugged her son-in-law. "You're going to be a wonderful father. I'm so happy for you both."

"I'm nervous. We're nervous."

"It's perfectly normal. If you weren't, I'd be concerned."

He held up crossed fingers. "Hoping it all goes smoothly. I'm going to start dinner. Will you stay?"

"I can't tonight. I'm having dinner with Dana." She and Dana hadn't talked since their confrontation so when Dana invited Olivia to meet her, she accepted, wondering if they could move on and continue their friendship. After thirty years, she owed it to try.

They went back downstairs as Ella walked in. She wore a brown wrap dress and boots and carried bags from the department store. Olivia thought she looked beautiful.

"I didn't know you were coming!" Ella's cheeks were pink from the chill outside, or perhaps from the excitement of her upcoming plans. "I stopped at the store to pick up a few things for Joshua." She dropped her coat and purse and pulled out a small down vest and flannel-lined jeans, cuffed at the bottom. Olivia pulled her daughter in for a hug, relieved to see her so enthusiastic after the past painful few years. Yes, her rosy glow was not due to the chilly weather.

"Did you see his room?"

Olivia nodded. "It's perfect."

Ella put the vest and jeans back in the bag, hung up her coat properly and turned to her mother. "Sometimes I wake up from dreaming, wondering if he'll be happy here. It'll be an adjustment."

"Oh, Ella. It may take time, but how could a child not be happy here?" They heard a pot drop in the kitchen, followed by a muffled expletive, bringing them both to laughter. Olivia put her palms on her daughter's face. "Just be yourself. That's all you need to do. I'm so proud of you."

Ella's eyes welled. "Thanks." She started for the kitchen and turned around. "Where's Dad? Can you stay for dinner?"

"I can't. I'm meeting Dana not far from here."

"I spoke to Nick yesterday," Ella said, oblivious to the weight of her mother's dinner date. "He and Melissa are still trying to decide what to do."

Olivia's jaw dropped. "Trying to decide what?"

"Melissa is considering not keeping the baby. She doesn't want to trap Nick, but he's trying to convince her to keep it."

Poor Nick, Olivia thought, recalling her and Chris going through the same dilemma. Ella took her mother's silence for a different reason.

"I'm sure he'll tell you this when he comes down for Dad's dinner tomorrow. Think about it. You might be having two grandchildren before you're even fifty-one. Crazy, right?"

Chapter 41
December 2010

Olivia arrived first at the restaurant. Seated, she tried but couldn't focus on the menu. Friends since they were eighteen, she felt like she was waiting for a stranger. The things Dana said to her last week were so foreign she had to re-play the scene over and over.

Dana entered wearing a blush pashmina over a blouse and jeans. She spotted Olivia, ignored the maitre'd as she walked toward the table, removed her scarf and slid into the booth.

"Waiting long?"

Olivia shook her head.

A waitress appeared to take their drink orders.

"Water," Dana said. "Don't," she added when Olivia stared at her in surprise. "Just give your order."

"I'll have the same," Olivia said and the waitress left them alone.

They sat through awkward silence.

"I wasn't sure if you'd meet me," Dana said, finally.

"I didn't expect you to call."

Dana let out a breath through her nose. "Look at us, surprising each other."

Olivia didn't smile.

"I want to apologize," Dana started, "not for what I said. But because I waited so long to say it. And," she paused "my delivery could have been a bit more tactful."

At this, Olivia tried to hide a grin. They both knew tact wasn't a strong characteristic of Dana's. It was part of her allure.

"After I left your house, I talked to Chris. You were right. But it still really hurt. It will always hurt," Olivia said.

The water was placed on the table. Dana reached for the glass immediately and took a sip before responding. "I know. I can't change that."

They sat quietly, each with her own thoughts.

"What upsets me the most are the secrets we kept from each other. I thought Chris and I had an infallible relationship." Olivia shook her head.

"What makes you two so perfect? Everyone lies. Everyone cheats. You're human."

"I thought we were better than that."

Dana chuckled but there was no laughter on her face. "Better than human? You're not." She leaned forward. "What makes your marriage work is that you love each other and stay together despite the mistakes and the secrets. Being perfect is boring. What kind of life would that be?"

The waitress took their orders, neither having paid attention to the menu. "Just bring us the pasta special," Dana told her.

"The baby is Chris's," Olivia said when the waitress left them. "Though it shouldn't need to be said."

"I know."

"I'm getting an abortion next week."

Dana hesitated and then nodded, masking her reaction. "Do you want me to take you?"

For the first time since they sat down, Olivia felt a glimmer of hope that their fractured friendship could be salvaged. Thirty years is a hard habit to break.

"Chris will take me. Thanks."

"How do you feel about this?"

Olivia's eyes watered. "I feel it's not fair to the baby." She added in a whisper, "I'm scared."

Dana said nothing. She clasped her hands on the table. Olivia thought about asking her if she was in love with Chris. Looking into Dana's eyes, she decided she didn't want to know. The knowledge would only further weaken a relationship she needed.

"Whatever happens, I'll be here," Dana said.

"Ditto."

Dana reached over the table and grabbed Olivia's hands.

Chapter 42
December 2010

Olivia walked downstairs Saturday morning and looked through the front window to see a strange car in the driveway. It must be Melissa's, she thought. Olivia hadn't heard her and Nick come in last night. She passed out after her dinner with Dana, emotionally and physically exhausted but knew they were home when she passed his closed bedroom this morning.

In the quiet kitchen, she prepared her coffee and reviewed her meal for the evening. She loved this tradition they fell into so many years ago—celebrating Chris's birthday with a special dinner only a week after Thanksgiving. As she sipped her coffee by the breakfast nook, Olivia tried not to be consumed with thoughts of her appointment only a few days away. Nick and Melissa walked downstairs as she realized she had her hand on her belly.

"Good morning. What are you doing up so early?" And where did Melissa sleep? She wanted to ask, but held her tongue. They looked tired, but were already dressed in jeans and sweaters.

Nick filled the teapot for Melissa, put it on the stove and prepared a mug with chamomile tea he pulled from his pocket before pouring himself a cup of coffee. *Who are you and what did you do with my son?* Olivia thought, watching the scene. Melissa sat at the table.

"Thank you again for having me, Mrs. Bennet," she said.

She blushed, pulled her sleeves over her hands, and Olivia smiled, hiding her angst. This girl-child may be a mother very soon and couldn't speak to her without blushing. *Who does she remind me of? Oh, right. Myself at nineteen.*

"Of course."

"I slept in Ella's room. It's very comfortable."

"Thank you." Olivia glanced at Nick who raised his eyebrows and smiled.

When the tea was ready, he placed it in front of Melissa and sat down. "Where's the birthday boy?"

"He took the day off so I'm letting him sleep in. He so seldom does."

"I've heard so much about Mr. Bennet's birthday dinner, I'm looking forward to it," Melissa said.

"We're happy to have you."

Olivia sipped her coffee. Melissa's pink-tinted cheeks turned scarlet. It was all Olivia could do to keep from putting her hand on the girl's arm and telling her to take a breath and relax.

Nick stood and put his mug in the sink, and Melissa followed. "We're going to the outlets, and then I'm taking Missy to East Hampton. We'll be home in time for dinner."

Chris walked downstairs as Melissa's car pulled out of the driveway.

"Here and gone already?"

Olivia shook her head. "He's taking her shopping and sight-seeing."

Chris poured himself coffee and kissed his wife on the top of her head. "How are you feeling?"

"Peachy," she said, not feeling so at all. She stared out the window. "Melissa's so shy. She blushes whenever I look at her."

Chris let out a raspy laugh. "Who does she remind you of?"

Olivia started the lasagna in the early afternoon, methodically layered the meat and cheese over the steaming noodles until she completed two trays, getting them into the oven in time to take a shower. The sun had set, and the kids would be here in an hour.

Chris had been called to Marco and Ella's earlier to help fix their garage door. Olivia was in the shower when he popped his head in the bathroom to tell her he was home. He lingered in the doorway for an extra beat and watched her.

"What?" She wiped the steam from the clear glass shower wall.

"Nothing. Just enjoying the view."

"Go away. I need to wash things and I don't want a spectator."

He reluctantly pulled himself away, but was waiting for her when she stepped into their bedroom wrapped in a towel.

"You still here?" she said.

He walked over and stood before her with his hands at his sides.

"Where's your husband?"

She pressed her lips together, not feeling playful but he was so damn cute, she went along. "I'm not married."

"Oh, really?" He reached over and pulled the towel from her. "How convenient for me."

She stood before him naked and let him move his eyes down her body. She shivered though the room was warm.

"How did you get in?" she asked. He knelt on the floor and looked up at her face, putting his hands on her hips.

"You left your key under your welcome mat."

She chuckled and writhed under his hands.

"What's your name, beautiful?"

"Maya."

"Hi Maya. Grant."

She put her hand on his head and dug her fingers into his thick, salt and pepper hair. "Just do what you came here for and leave."

His heated gaze left her breathless. "Never."

Chris showered and found Olivia setting the table in the

dining room. He hugged her from behind, and she rested her head against his chest. "You know, the last time we did that, you got me pregnant."

He hesitated and kissed her neck.

She finished the table and swallowed down her fear.

Ella and Marco arrived before Nick and Melissa returned from their outing. Ella jumped in to help her mother finish setting the table. While folding napkins, she expressed concern that her visit to Joshua next month would go well.

"Ella, don't expect anything to ever go perfectly. Life will never work out that way. Take the highs and the lows and make the best of it. I promise you'll enjoy yourself more." Her own mother had spoken the same words to Olivia when she was young. And she tried to remind herself of the message through the years.

"You sound like Grandma."

"Do I?" Olivia put her hand on her chest. "I was just thinking of her. How uncanny."

Ella laughed and went inside to find Marco.

Nick and Melissa walked in half an hour later. Melissa handed Olivia a bottle of wine. "I haven't tasted it myself, but the man at the winery thought you might like it."

Dinner was boisterous and entertaining. Ella and Marco made fun of Nick's escapades at school, as older siblings do. They told Melissa stories of Nick in high school, trying to embarrass him. Melissa eventually relaxed, and when she let herself go and laughed, Olivia watched her son look at her with adoration in his eyes. It warmed her heart. For a moment, everything felt right. No one mentioned Melissa's pregnancy, and Olivia supposed it was because they were still weighing their options. It made for a nicer celebration without the added stress of the conversation.

While Ella explained to the younger couple about going to see Joshua before Christmas, Olivia couldn't help but marvel at the irony of sitting at the table. Two of them were pregnant, one too young, the other too old, and the one in the middle was getting a baby across the country. It was all too much for her to handle, and she felt herself getting flushed. Olivia stood to get some water while Ella continued about Joshua, admitting to her brother how excited and nervous she was.

In the kitchen alone, Olivia drank a full glass of chilled water. The wine poured for her sat untouched by her plate. Knowing she wasn't keeping the baby, she still couldn't bring herself to drink it. Chris was by her side before she realized he'd left the table. "Babe?" he whispered. She turned to him and nodded, feeling much better. She put her hand on his furrowed brow and kissed him.

Ella had insisted on making her father's birthday cake, and Olivia teared up as she watched her children and their significant others singing joyfully to her husband of thirty-two years. Chris blew out his candles, two large numbers, five and one.

"You're only fifty-one?" Melissa asked. "My mom's fifty-nine and I'm the oldest child."

Everyone laughed except for Olivia who imagined she would have been seventy-one when her baby turned nineteen. Stop thinking. She squeezed her eyes and when she opened them, Chris was watching her. *I love you,* he mouthed over the four chatting guests at the table, oblivious to their parents' silent conversation.

Marco and Ella left after dessert and gifts for Chris. Ella looked happy, and Olivia hoped she'd get through the last days before visiting Joshua without any setbacks.

They were in the kitchen cleaning the last of the dishes and wiping down counters when Nick and Melissa walked in, holding hands.

"Can we talk to you?" Nick said.

Chris and Olivia looked at each other and nodded. They all sat at the kitchen table.

Nick began. "I told Melissa that you both know what's going

on." Melissa clutched Nick's hand on the table. "We're asking for your blessing and support. We're going to have this baby." He looked at his girlfriend, who stared back at him wide-eyed and somber. "We're going to raise this baby together."

Chris said nothing.

"What do your parents say about this?" Olivia said.

"They're reluctantly supporting us," Melissa said softly.

"Will you be getting married?"

"Yes. We're not sure if we'll do it before or after the baby comes, but yes, we'll be getting married," Nick said.

Olivia glanced at Chris who seemed frozen in place.

"Dad?" Nick waited for his father to speak. Melissa looked at Chris, worried.

"Chris, say something," Olivia said. She remembered all too clearly a similar conversation they had with Chris's father. Except Chris had another year left of school and no job offer. She recalled with clarity the way Mr. Bennet screamed threats to the young couple, swearing he would never allow it, and finally, when Chris wouldn't back down, left the room in a heated rush. It was the last time they ever saw him.

Chris glanced at his wife, as if he knew what she was thinking. She nodded slightly, and he let out a breath. "So, you'll be living where?"

"In Rochester. For now. My company has an office in New York City, so I can put in for a transfer in a few years."

Chris remained silent, and Olivia waited, along with Nick and Missy, for his reaction.

He stood and held his hand out to his son. "Congratulations."

Olivia detected an underlying current of fear and regret in her husband's voice, but Nick smiled as he shook his father's hand.

Melissa stood and hugged Chris, who squeezed his eyes tight over her shoulder.

In bed, Olivia rolled next to Chris. "Thank you."

"It's history repeating itself," he whispered. "Same story."

"No. It's his own story. One he'll live himself, making the right decisions and maybe some wrong. Either way, we raised him. Now you have to let him do what he needs to do and just be there for him."

Chris put his arm around her.

"And," she continued, "I love the story of you and me. Anyone would be lucky to have all we have, all we did." She sighed. "We're still writing it."

Chapter 43
December 2010

Olivia woke up early the following morning as last night's lasagna wreaked havoc on her digestive system. Chris was still asleep. From her pillow, she lightly touched his cheek. Today was his birthday and they would spend it together. He was taking another day off and they planned to go to lunch in town.

Downstairs in her robe, she paused at the front window. The early morning light shone on the frosted grass. The trees were naked and waited for snow. She put the television on low and prepared tea to soothe her upset stomach.

"Tea?" came a voice from behind. She jumped, clutching her heart.

"Sorry."

"Nick, you scared the hell out of me."

"I thought you knew we were leaving early today. We're going into the city for breakfast and then to see the tree and ice skate. You know, the whole tourist thing. Then we'll drive her home and I'll go back to school."

"Who are you, and what have you done with my son?"

"Nice, Mom. Speaking of change, Dad's always up first. And what's with the tea?"

"I can't sleep. My stomach is upset." She pulled green tea from the cabinet.

"Good morning." Olivia looked over Nick's shoulder to find Melissa bundled up and ready to go.

"Good morning, Mrs. Bennet. Thank you for having me."

Nick kissed his mother on the cheek. "See you at Christmas."

Alone, Olivia steeped her tea bag and sat at the table, looking out the window at the bleak winter sky. They used to have to drag Nick into Manhattan as he got older, complaining he didn't need to see the "stupid" tree. *It's the same thing every year,* he used to complain. *Why do we have to go in there fighting off hordes of people for some tree?* And now, he was making a full day of everything he fought against eight years ago. Payback, Olivia thought. There you go.

She lifted the hot mug to her lips and dropped it on the table as a shooting pain tore through her. Hunched over her legs, she breathed quickly, trying to manage the pain. Tears sprang to her eyes, and she clenched her teeth to keep from screaming. *What is going on?*

It took ten minutes for her to catch her breath before she could stand upright. She took tepid steps to the bedroom, holding onto the wall.

Chris was still sleeping. She closed the door of the bathroom quietly and sat on the toilet to pee. When she stood, she held her chest and gasped. The toilet water was dark red. She sank to her knees. "Chris?" Her voice held a muted panic, and Chris heard it. "Yeah?"

"I need you." She held her hand over her mouth.

He walked into the bathroom and followed her gaze to the toilet. Her eyes were full, and she shook her head.

"Shh. Okay. Let's get you to the hospital. We'll call Dr. Byrnes. It's going to be okay." He gently lifted and guided her back into their bedroom, where he helped her to get dressed before taking her into the car.

***

The doctor on call stepped from the room, leaving Olivia and Chris alone. She'd been admitted into the hospital and brought to a room in record time. They were waiting for Dr.

Byrnes to come and perform the D and C procedure that was scheduled for tomorrow.

Olivia laid back and stared ahead at the hanging television in the corner, grateful the bed next to her was empty. "I know we weren't keeping her, but I'm so sad." A sob caught in her throat, and she covered her mouth with the back of her hand.

Chris took her hand and pressed it to his lips. He could say nothing. Instead, he put his forehead to the hand he held and took a deep breath. This baby brought the past back to him, exhumed secrets long ago buried, and forced them to be faced. She reminded him of the love he and Liv shared, the years they spent building their life together. She was a messenger, a reminder of all that they were. She was an angel.

Eventually, he felt Olivia's fingers move against his forehead. He lifted his eyes to see her, and a new wave of pain washed over him.

"I'm sorry," he said. "I'm sorry."

"Me, too."

She moved over toward the end of the bed and patted the mattress. He slipped his shoes off and climbed next to her, putting his arm around her so her head rested on his shoulder.

They held each other in the quiet room.

She sniffed. "Maybe she knew I was afraid to go through with it."

Chris pulled her tighter, his tears muddling his vision. The pain of losing something he didn't even want floored him. But the thought of Olivia not being here gutted him more. The mixture of pain and relief battled within, and he was exhausted.

"No," he said finally. "It's just something that happened."

She nodded and took a deep breath.

They had fallen asleep when Chris's cell phone dinged next to the bed. He looked at a text from his daughter. *Happy Birthday, Daddy.*

Chapter 44
December 2010

Olivia placed the steak on the table. She'd made Chris his favorite dinner, prime rib with garlic mashed potatoes and asparagus almondine, a new recipe she tried. She glanced at the clock on the wall. He'll be home in a few minutes. She'd timed dinner perfectly.

He walked in, disheveled and tired, to find her waiting for him in the kitchen. He smiled. "You're a sight for sore eyes. You look so much better today."

"I feel better." It had been four days since the miscarriage and she was finally feeling like herself again. Chris had been so attentive the past days she decided he needed to go back to work and resume normalcy. She practically forced him out of the house today. Looking at him now, she regretted it. He looked exhausted.

"It smells amazing, Liv. What did you do?"

"Well, we never got to celebrate your birthday like we usually do, so I made you a birthday dinner."

At the table, Olivia watched Chris take his first bite. His eyes closed, and he hummed appreciatively. "You've outdone yourself. This asparagus is delicious."

"Sophia told me how to make it."

"I must thank her when I see her."

"I told her we'd visit after the holiday."

When their plates were empty, Olivia took them to the

counter and instructed Chris to stay seated. She brought a single cupcake to him, lit with a candle and sang Happy Birthday. He put his arm around her waist when she reached him. He blew out the candle and looked up to her.

"Did you make a wish?"

"I did." He pulled her onto his lap. "I wished that you'd sing to me every day."

"You did not."

"You're right." He squeezed her gently, making sure not to hurt her.

"Wait here. I have something for you."

She returned to the kitchen holding a flat, wrapped box.

He pushed his cupcake aside, and pulled at the wrapping paper. The house was quiet, a melancholy hovering over them. He lifted a frame from the box and held it in front of him. She held her breath and let it out when she saw his reaction.

"Babe," he said. He looked at it longer.

She had framed the paper bag that held their bucket list, the list they wrote when they were beginning their lives together, naked in bed. She'd added one last goal at the bottom.

21. Tackle bucket list.

He pulled his gaze from the frame and looked up at her.

"Now we can do everything we've always wanted," she whispered.

Later, he walked into their bedroom as she was in the bathroom getting ready for bed. She found him sitting on the bed with the gift re-wrapped, placed on her pillow. Confused, she glanced from Chris to the gift and back to him. He nodded his head toward her, telling her to open it.

She pulled out the same frame.

"It was almost perfect. Now it's perfect," he said.

She held it in her hands and felt a rush of emotion rise within her. He crossed out every goal and listed one item.

#1. Grow old with the love of my life.

"I don't care if we see the world. I don't care if we never leave this house. I've been thinking a lot these past months, of all that we did to get us here and I realized that every memory I have is with you. Dinners, diaper changes, soccer games and graduations. Those were the times that brought me joy. The small moments we share make up the fabric of us. It's not where I go but who's beside me. The meals we make together, the movies we watch, talking, making love. Those are the moments I cherish. Everything else is gravy." He pulled her to him. "You're all I've ever needed." He nodded toward the frame. "You're my adventure and my song. My legacy, Liv, is love. It's that simple. It doesn't get better than this."

Chapter 45
June 2011

"Are you okay?"

Chris glanced from the road to see his wife staring out of her window, her hands clasped in her lap. She turned to him with a smile. "I'm good."

They sped up the thruway, covering a now familiar road, only this time, they weren't racing to bail their son from jail or to visit him in the hospital. Graduation was last month, a festive celebration of pride and accomplishment.

Olivia reached out to take Chris's hand from his lap. She clasped her fingers through his, a feeling he still loved after all these years. Then she returned her gaze out her window while he thought about the past year they'd been through, watching Ella learn how to mother a now four-year-old she just met, marveling at how she and Joshua gelled, as if they were made for each other.

Olivia's gentle coaxing won Joshua over so that with each visit, he ran to his grandmother with unabashed glee, leaving Chris overwhelmed with a sense of peace seeing his wife's face, her pure joy and love for this little boy. Ella called her mother constantly, asking questions, seeking advice, voicing concerns about what she was doing. And Chris listened to Olivia's calm voice offering instructions or just an ear.

The loss still showed on her face when they were alone. She couldn't hide herself from him. It wasn't possible. He understood her like they were one. They had decided not to the tell the kids what happened, wanting them to have their own joys without worrying about their parents. The sadness gradually lessoned with time, and he knew they'd be okay. They didn't talk about the future the way they used to, when they had all the time in the world. Or the places they wanted to go. He didn't care where they went or what they did, just so long as she traveled the road by his side.

"How do you think you'll feel seeing her?" Olivia asked, cutting through his reverie.

"I don't know. I'm ambivalent."

Olivia sighed and looked forward. "Babe, he has a good job. They got a place of their own already. And the company is putting him through grad school. I don't know that he would have done better if he'd come home right after graduation. Trust him."

Chris bit his inner lip, fighting his feelings against the logic of the situation. Of course, he understood the kid. He was in love.

"It's just everything happened so quickly for him. And it's not even his."

She smiled and chuckled, confusing him.

"What's so funny?"

"He didn't get her pregnant. He was careful. Not like some people I know." She winked, and he rolled his eyes.

"Make one mistake," he said, "and I'll never live it down."

Olivia dropped her smile. "Nothing we ever did was a mistake. Nothing."

"You're right." He lifted her hand and kissed it.

"And," she continued, "do you think of Joshua as not belonging to Ella? Knowing them both now, I can't conceive of either of them ever being with anyone else. A baby needs love and guidance and nurturing. Anyone can climb on top of a girl and get her pregnant. But it will take our son, *your* son, to be that little girl's father. I can think of no better person for her."

He felt Olivia's eyes on him as he drove.

"I love you more than I can love anything in the world, but sometimes you make me want to shake some sense and reason into you," she said.

Chris focused on the lane before him. "And I love nothing more than you."

They pulled into the hospital parking lot and walked to the main entrance. "I'm nervous," he said.

Olivia paused. "Wow. I can't believe you just said that."

He pulled her forward, surprised himself at his momentary lack of self-censure.

They stepped from the elevator onto the maternity ward and saw Nick at the door, speaking with a nurse. When he turned and saw his parents, his face displayed shock and joy and pride. Chris stared at his son like it was the first time he'd ever seen him. Who was this man walking toward them now?

Olivia grabbed him into a tight squeeze. "Congratulations!" She pulled back to see his face, and his eyes shone.

"Thanks, Mom. Wait until you see her. She's all Melissa. She's amazing."

He turned to his father, a thin protective shield over him, one that was missing a breath ago. "Dad." He nodded to Chris.

"Nick. How are you holding up?"

"I'm well. Tired, of course. But happy." He turned to Olivia. "I don't think I've ever been this happy. I want ten more."

Chris watched his wife, waiting for the painful flinch, but there was nothing but pure pleasure on her face.

"Where is she?"

Nick pulled her forward. "In here. Come."

They entered the room to find Melissa in bed, her parents on one side of her. Introductions were made, and Melissa's parents decided to give Nick's family some time with the new mother and the baby. They left the room in search of the cafeteria.

Olivia leaned down and kissed Melissa's cheek. The girl was

beaming, her hair piled on top of her head. "Congratulations, sweetheart."

"Thanks, Mrs. Bennet."

"Please, call me Olivia."

Melissa smiled and blushed.

Olivia and Chris looked over the bassinet. "Oh, she's simply splendid," Olivia said.

Nick bent and lifted the swaddled baby and handed her to Olivia. Chris watched over his wife's shoulder, speechless. She was so small and, he had to admit, truly beautiful. Olivia turned to her husband. "Hold her," she whispered. She didn't wait for his response, but handed the bundle to him, and he sat down beside Melissa's bed.

Olivia reached into a bag she'd put on the floor and placed a wrapped box on Melissa's lap. "It's sort of tradition," Olivia said by way of explaining the gift.

Melissa opened the box and lifted a soft quilt made of twelve squares, each a separate fabric and color. Melissa held it to her chest as she listened to Olivia explain who each square represented, beginning with her and Nick in the center, their new daughter and extending out to include Melissa's parents and siblings who were now part of Nick's family and including Ella's new addition.

"My mother made me a quilt when I had Ella. We had four squares—a very little family. That quilt is now large enough to cover my bed. Ella has one as well." She smiled. "My hope for you is that yours continually grows."

Olivia spoke with Melissa and Nick, discussed the labor and delivery and specifics Chris managed to tune out. He couldn't stop staring at this little wonder. He felt as if only yesterday, he held Ella in his arms, a twenty-year-old jumble of nerves and excitement with a helpless soul completely reliant on him to guide her through life. And he did it. They both did. His father refused to accept her and, as a result, missed out on the most special people he knew. Chris reluctantly lifted his head to see the three of them in conversation. How could he not accept this baby? How could he do to Nick the unthinkable?

He couldn't. Olivia, as if attuned to his thoughts, pulled away from them to look at her husband. With a knowing nod and smile, she relaxed.

"What's her name?" Olivia asked. "You wouldn't tell us over the phone."

"We wanted to tell you in person," Melissa said. Nick quietly moved to her side and took her hand. "Her name is Nicole." She looked at Chris. "After her father."

Acknowledgements

My deepest gratitude goes to the following people:

My first reader always, my mom, Rose Baylis, who read every draft (there are too many to count), and who has the patience of a saint.

James Granauro, awesome uncle and musician, who taught me the difference between a gig and a session.

Sue Guacci, Monica Carlsen and Katie Mittelman, for a lifetime of friendship, cheerleading and huge shoulders.

Carol Grimaldi, Valerie Dietrich, Mary Jo Haggerty, Lynn Meyer, Janice McQuaid, Nora Katz, Elaine Trumbull and Caryl Daly for early reads, input, support and friendship.

Linda and Cathy Michaels, for spending hours discussing Olivia and Chris and their story. It was exactly what I needed.

Leslie Zindulka, for answering my random, out-of-the-blue questions about adoption, without hesitation. I'm sure there are mistakes and they're mine.

Booked For Drinks: Sue Moran, Mara Kelly, Liz Tompkins, Deb Luoni, Kerri Messina, Eva Rizzi, and Patti Maletta, a deeply connected group of women with endless entertaining stories of their own, who have pulled through for me yet again.

Author Suzanne McKenna Link, I'm so happy we met. Thank you for your invaluable input.

Author CJ Pastore, who so clearly embodies the truth that authors do support each other. I look forward to meeting you.

Judy Roth, my editor, for your gentle guidance.

Editor, friend and author, Gina Ardito, for making yourself available to answer my questions at any time and helping me bring this story to the next level- I can't thank you enough.

Suzanne Parrott of *First Steps Publishing*, my sounding board, ego-booster, critique partner, amazing graphic designer and friend. Thank you for continuously guiding me through this challenging endeavor.

Much of my inspiration for *The Fabric of Us* stems from the bittersweet truth that time moves on relentlessly. Babies become young men in the blink of an eye and there is little to do but watch in awe and adoration. So, I'm doing just that. Zach and Alex, I am so proud to be your mom.

Steve, my partner in life, for maintaining a sense of humor. Please don't ever stop, even when I'm at my most cranky.

And thank you, dear reader. There are countless books you could have picked up and here you are, holding mine. I'm grateful and hope to see you again.

Kimberly

About the Author

Kimberly Wenzler, author of *Both Sides of Love* and *Letting Go,* was born and raised on Long Island, New York. On her website, she uses humor to share her personal views of life, writing and reading. She's currently working on her next novel.

www.kimberlywenzler.com

www.facebook.com/kimberlywenzler

Made in the USA
Las Vegas, NV
08 September 2022

54916816R00184